Sleep of the Innocents

Carole Fragoza Fernández

Arte Publico Press
Houston
Texas
1991

This volume is made possible through a grant from the National Endowment for the Arts, a federal agency.

Arte Publico Press
University of Houston
Houston, Texas 7204-2090

Cover by Mark Piñón
Original painting by Nivia González:
"Orchids in the Night Window," Copyright © 1989

Fernández, Carole Fragoza, 1941–
    Sleep of the Innocents / Carole Fragoza Fernández.
        p.   cm.
    ISBN 1-55885-025-2
    I. Title.
PS3556.E7242S57 1991
813'.54—dc20   90-38831
                                                    CIP

The paper used in this publication meets the minimum requirements of the American National Standard for Permanence of Paper for Printed Library Materials Z39.48-1984. ∞

For My Daughters:

Marlena, Cristina and Jessica

Sleep of the Innocents

Prologue

From inside their adobe huts, the people of Soledad watched the late afternoon sun sink slowly into the sea.

"Look," said a villager to his wife. "See how red its face is? Tomorrow will be just like today."

The woman shuffled to the entrance of their hut.

"Another day without rain," she said.

"Pilar, what shall we do if the rains never come?"

"Hush, Felipe, don't say such things! You will frighten the child!"

"Don't worry, she's sleeping."

"I wish I could sleep in this heat."

"It's the sleep of the innocents."

Felipe draped his arm over her shoulder. "Remember when we used to sleep like that?"

"No," she said and took out her fan from her apron pocket. "I would give anything for one night of blessed sleep."

"We're getting old, Pilar," he sighed. "Everything bothers us, the cold, the heat, the dampness, the dust ... We've buried four children. All we have left is Providencia to remember us when we too are buried in the field. Too soon, Pilar, we'll both sleep and feel nothing for eternity. Beware of what you wish; you might be granted it."

"Oh, why do I bother talking to you! You always say such terrible things!"

"Pilar, don't be like that. It's the truth, you know, only the truth."

"I won't listen to you!"

Pilar looked up at the sky, crossed herself quickly, and pushed his arm away from her.

"You shouldn't say such things!" she added and stepped outside the hut.

With her fan, she shaded her eyes from the afternoon sun. It was so hot! Pilar rushed into the shade of the mango tree. It was no better outside. Many of her neighbors also left their huts, searching for some cool breeze to dry sweat-drenched clothes. A few came to their doors still yawning from their siestas; others poked their heads outside and withdrew after a few seconds. Obviously they preferred the dark, cooler interior of the huts.

Standing in the shade of the mango tree, the woman frowned. It was quiet. No dog barked; birds did not twitter in the trees, and even the parrots were silent. She crossed herself again; it was too quiet, like death.

"I am a foolish old woman," she muttered, then looked around to see if anyone had heard her.

Pilar picked up the bucket to fetch water from the well in the village square. Normally it was a task Providencia did, but Pilar loved to spoil her granddaughter, and so let her sleep. Walking down the path to the well, dry leaves crackled beneath her feet; it was the only sound. Even the other women and girls, who joined her with their buckets, walked in silence.

"The heat has sapped our strength," she thought. "It must rain soon!"

"Buenas tardes, Doña Pilar." The young woman spoke in whispers as if they were in church.

"Buenas tardes, Amparo," she replied and then frowned with disapproval. "You are too close to your time to haul water. Where is your husband? He should fetch the water, not you."

Amparo sighed and rubbed her swollen belly, but did not answer. Doña Pilar understood; fetching water was woman's work, but she disapproved just the same.

When they arrived at the well, Pilar and Amparo found the women of the village standing around it in silence. Some of the older women wept.

"What has happened?" Pilar asked.

"The well is dry," someone replied.

"The well has never gone dry. Are you sure?"

"See for yourself, Doña Pilar, there's no water! What'll we do?"

"We'll walk to the river. What else can we do?" Pilar turned away from the dry well and headed for the river. Amparo followed her.

"No, Amparo," she said. "It isn't safe for you to climb down the riverbank. Go to my house and wake Providencia; she will fetch for you."

"You are so kind, Doña Pilar, so good, like my own mother," Amparo whispered. "Thank you," she added, and kissed the older woman's hand.

Pilar pulled her hand away and patted the young woman on the head.

"Give me your bucket, Amparo. Fetch Providencia and go home. We don't want the baby to come before Padre Clemente has returned for the Christening. Go. Do as I say."

Pilar led the silent women down the long, steep path to the river. When they arrived, she looked down at the riverbed and understood why the well had gone dry, and why the strange silence permeated the village.

"I never would've believed it possible!" she whispered as she crossed herself.

The river no longer flowed. Side by side, birds and small animals drank from huge puddles, remnants of the river that had roared through the forest on its course to the sea. When the other women saw the dying river, they fell to their knees and beat their chests with their fists.

"What will happen to us? What can we do?"

"Share the water with the animals, and pray for rain," replied Pilar, her voice heavy with resignation. "It is all we can do."

Later that evening the village people met in the square. It was too hot to sleep and there were decisions to be made. The river would not provide them with water for much longer.

"We shall send a message to San Bernardo and ask for help."

"What can they do?"

"Send us water in trucks. That can be done."

"Without a road? Trucks need roads."

"They can bring it to the foot of the mountain, we can haul it the rest of the way—if the livestock is still alive."

"Do you really think they'll bother with us?"

"They cannot let us die!"

It was true the people agreed, the government could not just let them die. Two young men were chosen to leave the next morning for the week-long walk to the district capital.

Two weeks went by and the young men did not return. The puddles in the river shrank rapidly and the people were frightened. Once again the people met in the plaza.

"We have two choices," Don Benito said to the others. "Either
we leave here and search for water, or we call Doña Consuelo to
help us."

"I prefer to walk to the southern mountains and search for water
than call that witch!" someone cried out. Many agreed.

"You are young," Don Benito argued, "you would probably
make it to the mountains, to where the snow melts into lakes, but
many of us cannot. We are too old for such a journey."

"The young children wouldn't make it either, don't forget them!"

"And how about Amparo? She is too heavy with child to go."
"What will happen to those who stay?"

"Yes, what about us?"

"We can bring water back to you."

"How much water can you bring? How much?"

"Whatever we bring will be more than you have."

"We've waited two full weeks, how many more days can we
wait? How much longer before the last puddles in the river dry
up?"

Amparo's husband stood; his muscles gleamed in the torch
light.

"I, for one, will not have that witch set foot in this village again.
Padre Clemente will be angry and refuse to baptize my child."

"Padre Clemente is a good man. He would not refuse the child a
baptism," Doña Pilar said, and her husband glared at her. Women
should not interrupt when men speak.

"But, Doña Pilar, Padre Clemente will be angry."

"Yes, Céspedes, that is true. He will be angry."

"But Padre Clemente is in the capital where there is water. He
does not suffer like we do," some of the women pointed out. They
insisted that the village send for Doña Consuelo.

"It would be a sin!" argued others.

"We must do all that we can," reasoned Don Benito. "To allow
ourselves to die is also a sin in the eyes of God!"

"Amen!" murmured the people of Soledad.

And it was decided. In the morning they would send for Doña
Consuelo. Late into the night the people talked and made plans. If
Doña Consuelo failed, then they would send the young and strong
to the southern mountains in search of water. Many young women
insisted that they would not leave parents or young babies behind,
but finally a simple argument convinced them: by leaving the village, the supply of water would last longer. Some were consoled by

this reasoning, but they cried through the night just the same. Others spent the night in prayer that Doña Consuelo would come, and that she would succeed where their unworthy prayers had failed.

There was no doubt in Pilar's mind that Doña Consuelo would come—although Padre Clemente had driven her from the village ten years before. He had told the people that there was no room in a God-fearing village for practitioners of magic.

Many of the villagers feared that bitterness over her past treatment would prevent Doña Consuelo from answering their plea. A few hoped she would not come. For them, the wrath of the priest was more dangerous than the difficult journey to the southern mountains.

Pilar insisted that Doña Consuelo would come. The rainmaker of Soledad was a blood relative to almost everyone in the village; such a tie was too strong to ignore.

Living in a tiny shack not far from the village, Doña Consuelo was seen occasionally in the forest gathering herbs, feathers or mushrooms. From time to time, a young girl might visit the crone for a love potion, or something to ensure the flow of her monthly cycle, but mostly Doña Consuelo lived undisturbed, ignored by the villagers.

The rainmaker of Soledad was already old when Pilar, as a young girl, had witnessed many of the marvelous things that Doña Consuelo did. Pilar also remembered hearing the witch brag that she had never failed in any of her tasks. Throughout the scattered villages of the mountains, everyone knew of the rainmaker of Soledad, and many sent for her in times of drought or epidemic. Once she even traveled to a big city to tend to the sick daughter of a rich man. When she returned to Soledad, the rainmaker wore a silver Miraculous Medal around her neck. The medal, which was rumoured to have been blessed by the Holy Father himself, was given to her, she said, for saving the rich man's daughter.

People said the rainmaker of Soledad was a holy woman with special powers, although some called her a witch. Her medicines and tonics had kept the villagers healthy long before the doctors came from the capital with their nurses and injections. But the doctors taught the people that herbal medicines and tonics were not modern, and fewer and fewer people sought out the wisdom of Doña Consuelo. Later, the priest turned against her, too, and she was cast out of the village like a leper in the times of the Bible. It was a shameful time. Yet in spite of all that had gone before, Pilar knew that Doña Consuelo would come. The rainmaker had come

when Pilar's boys had died, and she had come to try to save her
daughter when Providencia was born. Although she arrived too
late to save the mother, it was Doña Consuelo's expertise that had
saved the infant.

The next morning Pilar watched the sun rise. The sky was
clear with no hint of rain and, although it was barely past dawn, it
was already hot. Doña Pilar fanned herself as she watched broad,
misty columns rise from the jungle floor, disappearing through the
canopy of thinning leaves.

"The sun sucks the earth dry!" she thought. As proof there
was the red clay riverbed, now baked and cracked, holding only a
few shallow puddles. They had little time left; Doña Consuelo was
their only hope. Only the rainmaker of Soledad had the power to
make it rain.

Suddenly, she heard the church bell clang. The sound sliced
through the stillness of the morning and brought the village to life.
It could mean only one thing: Doña Consuelo had come!

Preparations for the ritual were made; a small altar was erected
in the village square. The villagers gathered. Heads bowed and
hands folded piously, they watched as the ancient, arthritic woman
crept with measured steps toward the altar. Even those who had
argued against sending for her, crowded into the square and pushed
for space.

The prayers began. Doña Consuelo shaped her shrunken lips
around warbling sounds that floated with the mist toward the
cloudless sky. The villagers chorused the prayers louder and louder
until they shook with exertion and sweat poured down their faces.

The sacrifice was made ready; their best chickens, squawking
and struggling, were brought to the rainmaker. With expert hand,
she silenced their screeching and sprinkled their blood onto the
ground.

"If we are worthy," she cried, "we shall see a sign!"

The villagers squinted to scan the sky.

"A sign will appear," thought Pilar, "Consuelo has never failed."

The villagers moaned with anticipation when they felt the cool
wind rise to fan their faces and rustle the dry leaves that rolled in
the dust.

"There is your sign!" Doña Consuelo shouted and she thrust
her arms skyward. "Wind, dark, pregnant clouds carrying rain
and thunder. On your knees, all of you, give thanks. We have
been delivered!"

Even as the villagers fell to their knees, however, the violent storm flashed by them, carried by the wind far to the south of the village. Few rain drops spilled from the clouds to dampen the dust at their feet; in horror, the people watched the storm perch on the tip of the tallest southern mountain.

With no time to waste now, the young and the strong prepared for the journey to the south. They left wrapped in feelings of rage, disappointment and anguish, to follow the path of the storm's wind. Doña Consuelo and her magic were trampled in the rush. Stunned by her failure, the old woman wandered aimlessly through the village until Pilar took her into her hut.

Day after day, the villagers watched in dismay as their crops withered in the field and the barnyard animals began to die. On the fifth day—late in the afternoon—the villagers heard a terrifying roar. From her bed in a corner of the hut, the child, Providencia, cried out, "Grandmother, I hear Death's roar coming to take us!"

"No, my love," Pilar said, "it is not Death!"

"Then why do you cry, Grandmother?"

"Tears of joy, Providencia, it is the river! It returns!"

Those of the people able to walk, staggered to the river's edge to watch the water's churning in its course once again. They cheered, danced and prayed. In the midst of their celebration, Pilar noticed tears trickling down the deep channels in the rainmaker's face.

" Vieja , if those are tears of joy, why do you beat your chest? Don't you see? The river moves again! It brings us life!"

"Not to me," Doña Consuelo cried, "not to me!" She screamed and tore at her clothes, and hurled something to the ground.

"But you didn't fail after all! The rain fell in the mountains, yet it found its way to us. Although others doubted you, I always believed."

"Silence, Pilar! I am not worthy of your faith!" Doña Consuelo wrapped her black shawl around her thin shoulders.

"Consuelo, please do not say such things!"

"I am not worthy, not worthy, don't you understand?"

The old rainmaker shook her leathery, brown fist at the bright, expressionless sky, and shouted, "I, too, did not believe!"

Without saying another word, she turned her back on the roar of the river and headed into the forest.

Pilar watched the old woman leave. "You should not say such things," she whispered.

"Grandmother, come here!"

Providencia and the other children laughed and splashed each other at the edge of the river.

Pilar waved at her granddaughter and started to join her. Feeling a sudden chill, however, she pulled her shawl around her. It grew colder and she shivered. Where did the cold come from? Pilar looked about her. A bright, silver disk glowed at her feet; Doña Pilar picked it up. It was the rainmaker's own Miraculous Medal. She turned in time to see a glimpse of Doña Consuelo as the rainmaker vanished into the forest.

"Doña Consuelo!" she shouted. "Consuelo, come back. Your medal!"

The rainmaker did not return, and although many went to her hut in the forest, they did not find her there. In just one growing season, the forest covered the narrow paths that led to the hut. In time, the roof of the rainmaker's hut caved in and the walls fell down; thick vines covered the floor, their roots digging deep into the rotting wood, and tiny lizards lived, bred and died beneath the leaves. In the village of Soledad, the old died and the young forgot; it was not long before no one knew where the rainmaker's hut had stood. Soon, even her name was forgotten and people began to doubt that she had ever lived.

Through the years, each time that Doña Pilar touched the Miraculous Medal, she felt cold, even if the sun were bright and her forehead drenched in sweat. It was a bad sign. Before she died, she gave the medal to her cousin, who felt the cold not at all.

One

Rosario scattered crushed bits of dry oregano into the pot and stirred the simmering broth with a large, wooden spoon. Every few minutes she glanced out at the road that curved by the house. Aníbal was late again; these days he was often late. After replacing the lid on the kettle, she added small pieces of charcoal to the fire, and reached for the small, iron pot to prepare rice. So far everything had gone well—better than she had expected. Even at the river, fish jumped out of the water as if begging to be taken; their large silver bodies reflected the sun, flashing like lightning against a dark sky. She chuckled remembering the struggle with the enormous fish that now simmered in the pot; twice it nearly got away. Twice she had slipped and fallen on moss wet with dew, but she held on, and pulled until the fish slapped its silvery body against the mud at her feet.

An unexpected shift in wind direction rattled pots and pans hung on the wall near the stove. Charcoal glowed too brightly, thin jets of flame arched upward and died; the coals would burn out before the newer pieces ignited. Rosario rushed to crank shut the metal slats of the jalousie windows, but as each window closed, the room grew dimmer. Because the windows near the worktable were farthest away from the stove, she opened them instead. Wind rattled the metal slats, and the fabric for her next project shimmied to the floor.

"Ave María purísima! Why me?" After shutting those windows too, Rosario picked up the white linen, brushed it with the tips of her fingers and held it up unfolded at arm's length to make sure it was unsoiled. It was too dim to see clearly, and she opened the door which faced away from the direction of the wind; sunlight flickered through trembling mango leaves.

A white rectangle slid across the floor; it was the letter she had received the day before and hidden beneath the linen for safekeeping. Although she was alone, Rosario looked over her shoulder before getting the letter and tucking it quickly into her pocket. She went back to the stove to finish cooking, but every time she moved, she heard the letter rustle. Finally she took it out again and unfolded it carefully, smoothing its creases with her fingers.

Rosario could recite the letter by heart. It was from Señora Miranda, the old school teacher who had left Soledad ten months before. The teacher wrote to answer the question that Rosario had whispered into her ear when she kissed her goodbye.

Señora Miranda had smiled and nodded her head. "I'll write," she said, dabbing at the corners of her eyes with a frilly handkerchief.

Now after all these months, the letter arrived. The teacher wrote that, with Aníbal's permission, the principal had decided to accept Rosario as a student at the district high school in Santa Elena.

Santa Elena, the largest town in the area, stretched from the base of the mountain to the ocean. But more importantly, the high school was close enough that she could make the trip on the bus every morning and be home by afternoon.

She looked at the wall opposite the door; it would be a perfect spot to hang her high school diploma. Just thinking about it made her stomach churn; no one else in her family had gone past the sixth grade. Suddenly remembering all the neighbors' comments, she folded the letter and shoved it into her pocket once again. Maybe they were right and it was all foolishness.

"Pride is a sin!" they said. Rosario shook her head and stirred the rice. Aníbal loved fish stew with rice.

"It will be a fine meal," she said when she heard a noise at the door and thought her husband had returned.

She called out, but there was no answer. She heard something scurry into the house and felt it rub its soft fur against her bare leg.

"Mishu!" she said. "You frightened me!"

Mishu stopped in front of the stove, meowed loudly and pointed his piebald nose upward towards the kettle. Even in the dim light his whiskers gleamed as they twitched.

Recognizing the urgent sound of the cat's two-note cry, Rosario laughed.

"So, you think it's lunchtime for you? You lazy cat! Why don't you go out and hunt? There's plenty of mice running around here. You haven't been doing your job, you know."

The cat stood its ground, tail whipping from side to side in a wide arc.

Rosario laughed again. "I've spoiled you, Mishu! What a bad boy you are."

Mishu took a few steps and meowed loudly, a sound different from the first, harsh and strident.

"Now you no longer beg! I don't know why I allow you in the house."

Purring loudly, Mishu rubbed against Rosario's leg. He looked up at her, tilted his head side to side, his wide copper eyes gleaming in the semi-darkness.

"Oh, all right! You win, pretty Mishu. Here I saved some raw fish."

Kneeling on the hard floor, Rosario offered Mishu scraps of fish. The cat purred loudly as he ate and did not object when Rosario stroked his fur.

"Rosario! What is that animal doing in here? How can you bear to have it inside the house?"

"Oh! I didn't hear you come in, Abuela." Rosario jumped to her feet and wiped her hands on her apron.

"I thought you were going to get rid of that cat."

"Mishu catches mice and keeps me company when Aníbal is away."

"Get yourself a baby instead; it'll keep you busy enough, and then you won't need that thing for company. Get out of here! Come on scat, scat!"

Doña Providencia poked at the cat with her foot. He spat at her, fangs exposed, claws unsheathed. Startled, the old woman backed away and sat on the chair farthest from it.

The sun was directly overhead, and with windows closed against the wind gusts, the room grew hotter. The old woman could not make herself comfortable, despite her fluttering a large cardboard fan against her breasts. Doña Providencia removed her shawl and wiped the sweat from her face with the white linen handkerchief she kept tucked in her skirt pocket.

Rosario watched her out of the corner of her eye as she cleared the table and set the dishes. She set a place for her grandmother too, knowing it would please her.

The old woman smiled, her lips stretching over nearly toothless gums. "I can't stay, Rosario, I have my own meal waiting, and your grandfather will complain if I'm late."

"You're sitting here anyway, and while you sit you can have a little something to eat."

The aroma from the cooking pot drew her grandmother to the stove. She raised the pot's cover and poked her nose into the escaping vapors.

"Ah, fresh fish, it smells so good, Rosario! You're a lucky girl to have such a fine provider. Angela's husband sleeps all morning and for lunch they eat only plantains and tubors. You would never find him getting up early to walk to the river to fish. If Angela wants fish, she has to fish for herself."

Rosario smiled, and remained silent.

"And he is handsome, too! Who would've thought that a skinny, little thing like you could make such a good catch?"

"Yes, he is handsome, Abuela, like a god!"

Rosario's voice rose barely above a whisper. "Sometimes I think he is a god!" She looked at the floor so that her grandmother would not see her blush.

"Ave María, Rosario! You shouldn't say such things! If Padre Fonseca hears you, he will think you blaspheme. Priests don't understand what it's like when young blood runs hot, and when the touch of his body in your bed is all you can think of."

"It's you who shouldn't say such things," Rosario said.

"Bah! Do you think I've been old my whole life? Don't you think I remember what it was like?"

Doña Providencia closed her eyes and rocked back and forth in her chair. Rosario looked up; her grandmother shivered as if with fever.

"Abuela?" Rosario stroked her grandmother's forehead.

The old woman sighed and shook her head. "Don't worry, it's nothing, just the memories of an old woman." She took Rosario's hand in her own. "Soon your belly will be hard and round with a baby! That, too, is God's way, even if priests don't understand it."

Doña Providencia reached out, patted Rosario's flat abdomen, and frowned. "Only don't wait too long! I'm growing old, and I want to see my great-grandson before I die."

"Abuela, please, you'll live for a long, long time."

"Let's pray it's so."

"Here, Abuela, sit down and eat something while it's hot."

"But Aníbal isn't here yet, and you're not eating."

Rosario frowned and picked at the lint of her apron. "He said he would be home early today, but when he hunts, Aníbal loses track of time."

"They always lose track of time! We sit home and worry. That's the way it has always been. Where's he hunting? And what?"

The old woman sat, picked up the spoon and stirred the stew in her bowl.

Rosario lowered her voice and looked around the small house.

"No one in the village is supposed to know, but I can tell you. Don Rafael has been having trouble since last Sunday."

"Oh?" The old woman put down her spoon.

"A mountain lion is killing the new calves. Already three have been lost! Since there's no better tracker and hunter in Soledad, who better than Aníbal to hunt it down?"

"Who else indeed! Three since last Sunday, you say? Must be a mountain lion with a big appetite!"

She picked up her spoon and scooped up some fish stew, puckering her lips to blow on it.

Rosario laughed. "Yes, or a busy mama feeding her cubs."

"Of course! Now I remember. Ten years ago that's exactly what happened. Let's hope the cubs don't develop a taste for human meat." Doña Providencia shivered, put down her spoon and pulled her shawl tightly around her shoulders.

"That's why no one in the village is supposed to know. Don Rafael doesn't want people to panic." Rosario reached out across the table and squeezed her grandmother's hand. "Besides, Aníbal figures the lair to be on the other side of the river because that's where the calves were killed. He's sure we're safe on this side."

"I certainly hope so!" Doña Providencia wheezed and smoothed her shawl.

"Finish your stew, Abuela."

"Make sure Don Rafael pays your husband well, the old miser, make sure that he pays! How much did he offer?"

"I don't know," Rosario picked at the lint of her apron again. "Aníbal didn't tell me, and I don't dare ask; he keeps such things to himself. He says that it's a man's business to worry about money."

Doña Providencia smacked her lips loudly. "All men are the same. I thought I had taught you better, child. You must learn to take charge. How else will things get done?"

Rosario jumped to her feet, startling the cat that slept under her chair. "How can you say that? Aníbal takes care of me. You said so yourself. He is a good provider and I lack nothing."

The old woman looked around the tiny, adobe house and snorted. The living room, dining room and kitchen were one large

room. To the left of the kitchen, separated from the rest of the
house by a flowered drape hanging in the doorway, was a small
bedroom. However, the house did have an inside stove, and there
was a water pump and a sink so that Rosario did not have to go
out to the creek. The outhouse was downwind, nine meters to the
back.

"You live like Indians!" Doña Providencia wrinkled her nose
and laughed again. "You must be in love!"

Rosario avoided her grandmother's eyes and did not answer.
Their silence hung heavy in the heat of the room, disturbed only
by the sound of Doña Providencia's spoon scraping the sides of
the bowl.

"Angela tells me that you've received another letter from that
teacher. Don't tell me that she's still asking you to go to school?"

"Yes, she is." Rosario looked out the door toward the road to
avoid Doña Providencia's gaze.

"What a waste of time! Doesn't she realize that you're a married woman now? What use have you for books and schoolrooms?
Really, Rosario, you're going to get Aníbal angry if you ask him to
let you go."

Rosario bit her lower lip.

Pulling out the handkerchief again, Doña Providencia wiped
away the perspiration gathered in the folds of skin beneath her
chin. She took off the shawl. "Talking about the lioness gave me
the chills! Tell me, have you heard anything about your mother-
in-law?"

"No, nothing. Aníbal told me he would visit her first thing this
morning. I hope nothing is wrong. That could be why he's so late."

"Bah! You worry too much. If it were bad news, you would've
heard by now. He's just forgotten what time it is. Have you managed to convince her to move into the village?"

"No, not yet."

Doña Providencia frowned. "Strange woman. I'll never understand why she insists on staying up there when she could be
comfortable in the village."

Rosario shrugged her thin shoulders. "Aníbal says she prefers
the solitude of the hills. Why is that so strange?"

"Not strange if you're an Indian. Sometimes I think there must
be some Indian hidden away in your husband's family, although
his mother denied it before the wedding."

"Oh, Abuela, I've told you a hundred times before that I
wouldn't care if—"

"Well, the thought of my blood mixing with that of an Indian's makes me uneasy. Don't forget we can trace our family back to Spain."

"Yes, you've told me many times. How could I forget? Anyhow such things don't matter, Abuela ... "

"Well, it's important to me, and to everybody else around here. Anyone can tell you that it's not normal to want to be alone so much of the time. I've said it many times before; she is a strange and difficult woman, and she has always been like that. Even as a child she was wilful; I don't know how she ever found a man to put up with her. Sometimes such things run in the blood, you know. So watch your husband; and if he begins to act strange like his mother, tell me right away."

"There's nothing wrong with Aníbal; he's perfect!"

Doña Providencia stood and smiled as she pulled her shawl over her head to protect her from the sun. She smoothed her gray hair into its coarse folds, closed her eyes and trembled slightly.

"Yes," she said as she rubbed the sides of her arms, "he makes you shiver just by looking at you. I know."

A deep rose color softened the sharp planes of Rosario's face.

"But he isn't perfect, child. Now you listen to your grand-mother and do as she says."

"Abuela! I thought you liked Aníbal!"

"I do. I really do. After all, he is a good man: he goes to church even if irregularly, he provides for his wife and he looks after his mother, but if he were perfect, he would be a saint in heaven and no good in your bed. Now stop giving me such angry looks; I think I hear your husband's Jeep."

Rosario put down the empty plate she was clearing and looked out the open door. "Yes, it's Aníbal!"

"Good. Too bad I can't visit any longer. I have my own hus-band to care for and it is a long walk home. I don't mind telling you that it's going to seem even longer with the thought of a prowling lion nearby."

"Oh, Abuelita, Aníbal will drive you home."

Doña Providencia put up her hand and waved it in the still air. "No, I wouldn't think of imposing. Besides, there's something else I want your husband to do."

"What's that?"

"Have Aníbal come to our house with you this evening; your grandfather would like to see you both. All morning he nagged me to walk over here and ask you to come until I had to put down my work."

Doña Providencia waved her crooked finger in front of her granddaughter's nose and sighed. "You haven't visited all week. Even if your grandfather's health were good, he is too old to ride his horse, and he has always been too poor to buy a car. You are a married woman now, and I don't want to rebuke you, but you must take care of your other responsibilities."

Rosario squeezed Doña Providencia's shoulder. "We'll come this evening."

"You're a good girl, Rosario, now come give me a kiss. And you, too, Aníbal," she added as the tall, young man approached. Dutifully they both pecked her on the cheek and asked for her blessing before she left.

With their arms around each other, they watched Doña Providencia cross the field behind their home. The old woman moved slowly along the footpath, which was scarcely visible in the tall grass. When she reached the outskirts of the village and the cluster of houses and stores that huddled around the square, Aníbal and Rosario turned to enter their house.

"I should have given her a ride home. She shouldn't be out walking in the heat of the day. She looks so fragile." He cupped Rosario's face in his hand. "I hate to think that someday you'll look like that, too."

"Had she wanted the ride, she would've asked for it. My grandmother is not shy." Rosario ran her fingertips along the muscles of her husband's arm. "And neither am I."

Rosario moved closer to her husband and rested her head on his chest. Mingled with the scent of his perspiration was the sharp, musty smell of the forest.

Aníbal sighed, shifted his weight and pulled away. He stood in the opening of the door and stared at the blue haze draping the distant mountains.

"What's wrong, Aníbal?"

Aníbal avoided looking at her. "Nothing is wrong. Really, Rosario, it's just that I'm tired, that's all."

"Well, come in, have your lunch and rest—"

"No!"

Wide-eyed Rosario jumped away from him; he had never shouted at her before.

"I'm sorry," he said as he threw his arm over her shoulder and pulled her close. "What I mean is that I don't have time for lunch

today or a siesta either. This time a prize calf was killed, and Don
Rafael is furious. There must be more than one lioness, I'm sure
of it."

Rosario caressed his forehead where an old scar ran into his
dark hair, and sighed with pleasure when Aníbal took the tip of her
long braid and brushed her cheeks with it. Her hair was dark, too,
and it shone like the surface of the river under a bright, full moon.
But her eyes were even darker, no light escaped them, endless night,
no stars.

"Look, Rosarito, I've got to go."

She thought of the letter in her pocket. "Will you be home
tonight?"

"I'm not sure, but that's not important. Now listen to me," he
said taking hold of her tiny shoulders in his large, work-roughened
hands. "I want you to go to my mother's house for me."

"You didn't go this morning?"

"Yes, I did, but she was sleeping and I didn't want to disturb
her. So I closed the door again and left. I think she must be ill,
Rosario. There was no cooking fire and the house needs cleaning."

"Poor Doña Corozal! I'll take care of her, Aníbal, don't worry."

"Thanks, Rosario, I knew I could count on you." He kissed her
lightly on the cheek. "Tell her I was too busy to make another visit
today, but when the hunt is finished I'll go. Make her understand,
Rosario."

"You're the one who must talk to her, Aníbal. She must move
into the village. We just can't care for her if she doesn't. You're
the only one she'll listen to."

"Mama is stubborn, Rosario. How can I make her leave her
home? She loves it there on the mountain. Life in the village
suffocates her."

"That may be so, but she is too old now to live alone. Promise
me, Aníbal. Promise that you'll talk to her today or at the latest
tomorrow morning."

Aníbal sighed and pushed her away. "I'll talk to her, Rosario,
when the hunt is over."

Before Rosario could reply, Aníbal kissed her again, jumped
into the Jeep and sped away. She watched his progress down the
road until his car disappeared around the first turn.

Growling noises in her stomach and the delicious aroma of stew
reminded her that she was hungry. Suddenly she smiled and rushed
back inside. If Doña Corozal was not cooking for herself, maybe
she would appreciate some of her daughter-in-law's stew. It only

took a few minutes to pack the food, to pull on her walking boots
and extinguish the cooking fire.

The climb to Doña Corozal's house was difficult, and the pack
she carried grew heavier with each step. Where the path was wider
and level, Rosario could see fresh tire tracks made by the Jeep that
morning. She also noted that the Jeep had skidded in the mud at
least four times. Rain the night before not only made the road
dangerous, it had also coaxed every biting insect on the mountain
into action. Perhaps, too, the smell of the food that she carried
drew them to her. Small flies and gnats dove at her face where it
was uncovered by the shawl. Rosario knew better than to try to
shoo them away when it was more important to keep her balance
walking through mud. Once she had made her way out of the
gully, however, the breezes cooled her and pushed aside the clouds
of insects that followed.

After another half hour, she could see the roof of Doña Corozal's
house through the trees. As always when she made the climb, Rosario stopped and turned to view the valley below. It was only
because of that view that she understood her mother-in-law's re-
luctance to move into the village. The straps of the pack dug into
her shoulders; she took it off and stretched her arms. She felt so
free, so light, as if the wind would lift her from the ground.

From the hilltop, she could see the entire village of Soledad in
the valley, the river to the north, and the many shades of green that
made up the fields, each shade of color representing the leaves of a
different vegetable. Beyond, in the lowlands, Santa Elena reached
to the sea.

The shadow of an eagle passed over the fields. Imagine, she
thought, seeing this every day. For a few moments, she pretended
to be the large, gray eagle itself and she spread her arms out to her
sides. Her shawl flapping sharply in the breeze, Rosario stood on
her toes; if she could fly like the eagle, she would know everything.

Once, Aníbal had taken her to the top of the mountain itself,
where the air was always cold and the wind, fierce. For the first
time in her life, she saw the sea from that peak where the light was
so intense that she had to squint in order to protect her eyes. And
she had never stopped wondering why the light was so bright that it
burned? Not even her tears relieved the pain. At first she thought
it was because they were up so high, so much closer to the sun. Yet
it was cold. If they were close to the sun, wouldn't it be hot? These
were questions that she had wanted to ask Aníbal, but never did.
Instead, with the wind tugging at her braid and at her clothes, she

had asked Aníbal to point out the sea. Although Aníbal told her which shade of bright blue was the sky and which the sea, Rosario was unable to separate the two. Aníbal kept pointing out sea and sky until he grew tired.

"How do you know?" she whispered as if in church. She cupped her hands around her eyes and searched for the line separating sea from sky. Ships that floated on the surface of the water might be flying through the air.

"What do you mean, how do I know? I just know!" Aníbal had laughed at her when she protested. Rosario hated it when he when he did that, and she stopped asking him questions.

Now months later, standing on the hillside overlooking her mother-in-law's house, she was still unable to see the bands of blue that marked the meeting of sea and sky. Suddenly, out of the corner of her eye, Rosario spotted a large bird circling overhead. The eagle's shadow stretched and contracted, sliding from village to field to mountaintop. Rosario watched. Nobody would laugh at an eagle, she thought. From its perch among the clouds, it looked down and knew which was the sea and where the forest was, and the mountains, and each hill in the mountains, and each tree. The eagle probably even watched her and knew how ignorant she was. She thought of the letter hidden in her pocket.

Suddenly, the giant gray bird aimed itself at the earth; Rosario held her breath. Seconds later the eagle was once again in the sky. In its claws, it carried its prey; she could see its small body, limp in the eagle's grasp.

When Rosario reached the house, she was tired and she looked forward to a long, cold drink of water from the well. She took off the pack that she carried and leaned it against the stone side of the well. Wiping the sweat from her brow and upper lip, Rosario heard the echo of the school bells calling the children back to their books after siesta. By this time her grandmother would be busy with her weaving. And across the river, Aníbal was probably finishing the trap for the mountain lion. She stood on the hilltop, watching the play of the clouds' shadows on the village below, and suddenly she felt idle. The school bells pealed loudly. Even children had their responsibilities to fulfill; Rosario picked up her pack. Holding her breath, she listened to familiar sounds: the birds twittering in the brush, the rustling of banana tree leaves shaken by a sudden rough wind, the soft slithering sound marking the unseen passage of a chameleon.

Rosario shook her head; Aníbal had sent her to do a job. She had no time for foolish and idle thoughts, and yet she found it difficult to move. The sun's heat burned through her clothes, but there was no warmth in its touch. Rosario held onto her shawl tightly as the wind grew stronger, the long, silky fringe tangled in the wind. Suddenly, Rosario felt cold, and she shivered.

When she pushed open the front door, an overpowering stench rushed out. Rosario stopped in the doorway, covered her nose and mouth with her hands, and peered into the dim room. All the windows were closed; only the shaft of light coming in from the open doorway lit the room. Going against her instinct to run away, Rosario put down the pack she carried and entered the house. The muscles in her abdomen contracted sharply, and without warning Rosario felt lightheaded and weak. In the heat of mid-day and trapped inside the closed house, the stench was even more intense. Her body trembled, and her stomach cramps intensified; if she were going to stay inside, she would have to open the windows. Rosario concentrated on the circular movement of her hand as she cranked all the windows open. She inched silently toward the bedroom, pushed aside the curtain and entered. She covered her mouth and nose with her shawl.

The iron bed, draped by mosquito netting hung from the ceiling, dominated the room; it left little space for the chifforobe on the far wall. Rosario held onto the side of the old wardrobe; its surface felt damp and sticky. She stared at the bed in horror.

"No, dear God, it can't be!" she shouted out loud, but the sounds of her words were absorbed by the loud rustling of the trees outside.

Rosario moved slowly toward the bed; she had to see what was hidden beneath the sheet. Trembling, she pushed back the mosquito netting and shook her mother-in-law's shoulder. The woman's body rolled over and Rosario saw her face.

Doña Corozal must have been dead at least three days. The body was bloated and, where the insect and animal scavengers had eaten, the bone shone brightly even in the dim light of the room. Suppressing her screams with her hands, Rosario fell back against the wall. She crossed herself over and over again.

Even with her eyes closed, Rosario could still see the dead woman's face. She rubbed her eyes, but could not erase the image engraved on the back of her eyelids. Before running out of the room, Rosario took off her shawl and threw it over her mother-in-law's face.

Outside the wind grew colder; Rosario shivered, yet perspiration ran down her body. The bucket she had drawn earlier was still more than half full; Rosario washed her hands and face with the icy well water. Her hands grew numb as she washed, but she could not escape the heat she felt simmering inside her, nor could she wash away the smell that clung to her skin, her clothes and her hair.

In the distance, the village glowed in the afternoon sun. Rosario could see a truck driving through the plantain field, clouds of dust billowing up and spreading far and thin on the currents of the wind as the vehicle moved through. On the other side of the village, goats and calves were being herded into overcrowded corrals in an attempt to keep them safe from the prowling lion.

Somewhere Aníbal hunted and when the people in the village saw the carcass, they would praise her husband's skill and bravery. They would slap him on the back, shake his hand, offer him drinks, just like the last time, and stare at his blood-stained shirt in awe.

Rosario shook her head. There was no doubt Aníbal had been there that morning; she could see smears of his muddy footprints on the steps of the house. He knew what awaited her inside his mother's house, and yet had said nothing. Rosario shook her head again. Wiping her face with the hem of her skirt, she started her walk back; there were things to be done.

He was home when she returned.

"The hunt is finished!" he shouted when he saw her. "Two huge lionesses! The drought to the north must have forced them down to look for food. Don Rafael is ecstatic; he promised to be most generous. The lion skins will bring a good price, and the cubs will be sold! We'll go to see the capital—"

"The capital!"

"Yes! And we'll buy you a new dress, two new dresses, and one for my mother!"

"But Aníbal—"

"Maybe even a new dress for your grandmother, too! But no more black dresses; red, we'll buy her red!"

Aníbal pranced around the room until it proved to be too small to contain him, and he danced outside the door into the front patio.

Over and over Rosario tried to speak, but he would not listen. Finally she took hold of his arm and shouted. "Aníbal, we have to talk about your mother!"

"Is she feeling better? Was she angry because I wasn't there?"

"Aníbal, please, stop talking. I have to tell you what happened!"

"Tell me later, I have work to finish before it gets dark, and preparations to make for our trip to the capital. Did you ever think you would get to see the capital? There's so much to do and so little time."

"But, Aníbal, please ... "

"Please? Please, what?" He laughed, but it was a strained, ugly laugh, and when he grabbed her arm and shook her, she felt afraid of him for the first time.

"Aníbal, you're hurting me!"

"You women are all alike," he said. "All you want to do is talk. Meanwhile, I must go to work to provide for you, and I have no time for your talk."

"But your mother—"

"For God's sake, Rosario, tell me later! Don't you understand? Can't you understand anything? I don't want to hear it now!" He let go of her arm and pushed her away from him.

"Aníbal!" she screamed, but he put his hands up to his ears and ran from her towards the village.

The late afternoon sun lit up the dark curls in his hair as he ran. Rosario started to run after him. Suddenly, the shadow of the eagle crossed his path, and she looked up into the sky. Wings outstretched capturing the wind, it seemed to hang motionless. Rosario understood. It waited for its prey to make the slightest move. Instinctively, she stepped back into the doorway. The eagle passed overhead, its exaggerated shadow sliding over the landscape.

She watched her husband cross the field; his image grew smaller and smaller and then disappeared.

Two

In the richer parts of the capital city, buildings were made of cement, which withstood the dual attack of humidity and termites, but it also absorbed the sun's heat, releasing it at night so that there was no time when it was cool. People of means stayed indoors during the heat of the day. Cooled by air-conditioners, they waited for late afternoon when the sun's cooler light ripened heavy clouds into soft orange and pink streaks that moved crab-wise across the horizon. Outside people pushed through the heat to go to work, staggered against the humidity to get to market and pushed aside the dust. There was always dust.

It was always twilight in the casino, where the temperature and the lights were low, just enough light to feed the prisms of diamond rings, tie tacks and crystal chandeliers. The brilliance of the crystal was heightened by the lights of the multicolored slot machines along the perimeter of the casino. In an alcove of their own, other slots formed a maze, where light and color flashed in a steady, mechanical rhythm, and players were drawn inside. Styrofoam cups, overflowing with coins, were carried into the maze by the gamesters who fed their contents to the machines. Over, and over again, the slot machines swallowed the coins as men and women obeyed the insistent ching, ching, ching of soft bells to open their wallets wider. In the main salon there were two roulette tables, two craps tables, and twenty blackjack tables. Chemin-de-fer was played in a mirrored room guarded by a huge man wearing a tuxedo, a blue ruffled shirt, and a bored expression.

It was still early; only a few players occupied the heavily padded chairs of the blackjack table. These were the players who preferred an empty table and a dealer's undivided attention. Most of them played quietly, with intense concentration and with none of the

flash and glitter of the evening crowds. Good players came week
after week to challenge the odds. Among themselves, dealers wagered on which player would outlast the other, or how long it would
take to wipe out a particular patron. Most players could only hold
on for a few days, better gamblers lasted for a few weeks, and the
memorable ones for three or four months.

Before the new pit boss, the unoccupied dealers would crowd
around an interesting game to cheer and encourage the patron.
Afterwards they would console the loser, or encourage a winner to
return with his winnings to try again—to give the loser a chance
to get even. Now when a dealer wasn't playing, he stacked and
counted chips, or shuffled the cards, and sometimes aimlessly filled
and refilled the shoes with cards. They did not even smile or talk
to each other across the space between tables as they waited for
customers to come and put their money down.

Just that afternoon, casino employees received another memo
reminding them of the consequences of engaging in "unprofes-
sional behavior." As usual, copies of the memo were crumpled
and stepped upon as dealers, croupiers and pit men reported to
work, but no one went against the pit boss. Especially not Zayas,
he knew what it was like outside. No matter how cool the temperature of the gaming room, Zayas could always feel the heavy
humidity and the heat on his face. It was like a cloth stuck to
his skin, covering his mouth and nose so that at times, he thought
it would suffocate him. On his days off, he would shower two,
sometimes three times a day, and still he couldn't get free of the
feeling that something clung to his flesh. Someday, he vowed, he
would breathe only air that had been cooled and cleaned like that
of the casino. If it had not been against the law, Zayas would have
worked seven days a week. The other dealers called him money
hungry and laughed at him when he begged for overtime, but the
truth was he no longer felt comfortable outside.

It was late in the evening when the blond sat down, threw three,
one-hundred dollar bills across the table and smiled. Zayas had
never seen anyone so beautiful, not even in the casino where beautiful women were plentiful. Trying not to stare at her, he counted
her chips and slid them across the table. She curled her long fingernails around the chips and smiled at him again. At that moment,
Zayas decided that she was too beautiful to be someone ordinary.
Ordinary women did not capture dim light like the crystals of a
chandelier.

Two men at the table interrupted their conversation to stare at the newcomer. Zayas thought that they were rude to stare, and he pretended not to look at her as he counted the chips of two other women who, with annoyed expressions, had suddenly and inexplicably decided that they no longer wished to play at his table.

"Why don't you girls stay awhile? You might pick up some pointers." One man laughed as the women took their money and headed for another table.

The man's companion also said something as the women retreated, but Zayas did not hear it. Suddenly everyone at his table laughed, and pretending that he understood the joke, Zayas laughed too. It was important to keep the tourists happy. Happy tourists gave big tips. Zayas was still laughing when he looked around the casino. The boss glared at him. Zayas swallowed hard and took hold of the cards; they filled the palm of his hand in just the right places. By flexing his fingers, and twisting his wrists, he made the cards whoosh and sigh.

"Hey, look at him!" one player said as he pointed at Zayas. "Look at the fancy shuffling."

"Just hope he's not too 'fancy,' if you get my meaning?" his companion whispered.

"Oh, no! These people are careful when it comes to that kind of thing. They catch one of these guys messing around with a customer's hand, or dipping, and it's all over for them. Casinos have to be strict or they'll lose their business."

"Yeah, I guess you're right. And if they lose the tourist, they might as well kiss it good-bye. No country can live just on bananas!"

"Not unless they're all monkeys!"

The two men laughed, and settled back to enjoy their game.

"You know, Harry, some of them do look like monkeys, little brown monkeys!"

"Yeah! But some of the women ... Look at that one! Oh, yum!"

"Forget it, Dave, that's expensive goods, too rich."

"All I need is a few lucky hands."

"That and a Swiss bank account."

"Shut up and play, you can lend me some ... "

"Fat chance!"

"Some friend you are. Anyhow, I think I'll stick to someone more my type."

"Like her?" Harry motioned with a nod of his head in the direction of the blond seated at the other end of the table.

"You've got it!"

"You should be so lucky to get it."

"Yeah!" The two men laughed loudly and slapped each other on the back.

Zayas had not heard or understood all the conversation, but he had heard what they said about the "little brown monkeys" and he did not like it one bit. The dealer clenched his jaw. There were many things he would have liked to say to those men, but it would have angered them, and angry customers meant a raging pit boss. No, Zayas decided, it was not worth angering Sanchez. He would take care of it in his own way. The young dealer smiled and cut the cards. With dramatic, deliberate movements, he put them into the shoe and dealt the hand.

Eight minutes, he thought as the game began, I'll give them both eight minutes before I take them, and they'll never know what happened!

He smiled again as he rapped his knuckles at the two cards that lay face up on the table in front of Harry. They added to fifteen. His own cards, one face up and the other face down, added up to twenty.

"Hit me!" Harry said, and groaned when the card turned out to be a ten. Zayas scooped up six, ten-dollar chips and turned his attention to Harry's friend, Dave. His cards added up to seventeen. Seeing that the dealer's visible card was a king, Dave decided to stand.

I've got you both, Zayas thought.

Zayas concentrated on the game, despite the two men distracting him with their schoolboy behavior, giggling and staring at the women in the casino—especially the blond.

They don't know how to hold their liquor, he thought. And they don't know how to behave around women. Zayas stood taller and smoothed his moustache with his fingers when he realized that she was looking at him. He smiled back at her, and suddenly it was an effort to concentrate on the cards. Grazing her bare shoulders, her blond hair reflected the casino's dim light and shimmied when she moved her head. He watched it fall into her eyes, and when she tossed it back from her face, he remembered all the American shampoo commercials he had seen on television.

Suddenly, he had the uncomfortable feeling that he was being watched, and when he turned his head, he saw Sánchez, the pit boss, staring at him. With his hand, Sánchez made the abrupt, choppy sign that adults use to warn children of an impending spanking. Zayas dropped his eyes; he could feel his cheeks flush, and he wondered if anyone noticed. That night, he knew the receipts of the fifth table would be studied carefully for losses during the tenth set. It was no secret that Sánchez neither liked nor trusted Zayas. None of the glowing recommendations the younger man had brought with him from dealers school impressed the pit boss. Zayas graduated at the top of his class, his teachers boasting that within a year he would become the best dealer in the country. It had been eight months since Zayas arrived to work in the casino, and Sánchez remained unimpressed.

It was common knowledge that when the pit boss got on a dealer's back, the unfortunate dealer was out on the street— usually within a week—and he stayed on the street. Other casinos would not take him, and where else could a dealer work, if not in a casino? Zayas smoothed his mustache; he had lasted all this time, but he had to be careful.

Zayas knew he was good, and he counted on it. Already he had come far from the village at the edge of the sugar plantation, and he could hit it big, with luck—really big. All he had to do was to mind his own business and deal the cards.

"Insurance," he called out as he dealt. His top card was an ace. The blond paid, the men did not. With a flourish, he turned the bottom card over. It was a ten.

In just a few weeks, the diamond ring and the cuff links he wore would become his, and he would not have to put them in the hotel safe after his shift. Although his dormitory room was comfortable, he made plans to get an apartment of his own, with a telephone and a television set. Best of all, he would live there alone with no roommate to read his mail or borrow his clothes. He was going to make it; already his hands were as soft as a woman's, and his skin was losing the ruddy coloring that characterized field hands. Although he had not worked with a machete for eighteen months, he kept one under his bed. His roommates thought he kept it there for protection during the night; that was far from true. The youngest dealer in the casino kept it there so that he would never forget what waited for him on the outside.

Outside. Remembering the touch of the tarantula that had crawled up inside his trouser leg the last time he worked the sugar harvest, Zayas shivered.

Never again, he vowed, never!

"¡Zayas!"

"¡Sí, Jefe!"

"¿Qué te pasa, hombre?"

"Nada, Jefe. ¡Nada!"

That was the third time he had caught the pit boss's eye. Three times too many. Zayas swallowed hard and smoothed his moustache. If he wasn't careful, the odds would turn against him.

Waiting for a player to cut the cards, Zayas watched the pit boss talk to a customer. There was nothing special about Sánchez, he was just an ordinary pit boss who put in much time and sweat for the casino.

"I've paid my dues," Sánchez once said at a staff meeting. "Everything I got, I got the hard way by working for it. Nobody gave me anything because I had a cute smile!" Sánchez had looked hard at Zayas and it was clear the pit boss hated him.

Throughout the night, Zayas noticed that Sánchez kept watching him, but instead of making him nervous, it inspired the young dealer to perform flawlessly. Zayas was charming, he lit each player's cigarette, he paid compliments to the ladies, and told the men how he envied their luck, or playing ability. He told jokes, and most importantly, he won for the house.

During that time, the stunning blond sampled most of the tables, but always returned to Zayas. He had seen her leave the casino with a group of seven or eight people, and he was surprised to see her when she returned alone. She took her place among the four players left at his table.

"Welcome back, señora," he said as he took her money (hundred-dollar bills as before) and counted out her chips. "I missed you!"

"And I missed you," she said. "It seems that Lady Luck is no where to be found except right here at your table."

"You stay with Zayas," he said. "Zayas will show you the best time."

"I never intend to leave," she replied as she took out a cigarette from her silver purse.

Zayas pulled out his lighter and held it in front of her. Holding the long cigarette tightly between her lips, she looked at him through the wispy ends of blond hair that fell across her face, her hand rested lightly on his as she inhaled to light the cigarette. When the tip of the cigarette glowed deep red, Zayas returned the lighter to his pocket. His hands shook.

Some day, he thought, I'll have women like this one.

During his break, the pit boss took him aside. "I've been watching you," Sánchez said.

"I know."

"If you know, then why are you making a fool of yourself over that woman?"

"I don't know what you're talking about."

"You know exactly what I mean. If you continue to drool over her, you'll have to wear a bib to protect the table from your saliva!" Sánchez laughed at his joke. "What's the matter with you? You miss the sugar fields so much? You prefer swinging the machete to dealing cards? Keep away from the customers. If she complains, you'll be out on the street!"

"Sánchez, I'm not doing anything ... "

"Look, kid, forget about everything else that has happened between us for now and take my advice. Keep away from the female customers, especially that one. She's looking for her own customers, men with lots of money. A woman like that isn't like the country girls you knew."

"What would you know about country girls?"

Sánchez waved aside the question with a gesture of impatience. "Anyhow," he said, "I've lived long enough in the capital to know women like that blond. She's trouble; I can feel it."

"Why should you care?"

Sánchez shrugged his shoulders. "I don't want anyone to say that I fell down on the job—not warning a greenhorn like you. You do what you want, but if you're smart, you'll keep away from her."

"You didn't think I could interest a classy lady like that one, did you?"

"If she knew you had no money, she would spit in your face. You really think she's interested in you? Maybe I should tell her how you haven't finished paying off your flashy ring!" Sánchez laughed.

Every muscle in the dealer's body was tense as he watched the pit boss walk away, but he neither said nor did anything; his self-control was perfect. The pit boss was jealous because the woman had not been attracted to him, Zayas thought, and that thought comforted him.

Someday he would have many women like the blond begging for him to notice them. People would call him Señor Zayas, or Don Jose, and he would be important. All it took was money.

When Zayas got back to his table, the blond was still there. It pleased him to see her there. The way she looked at him and brushed her fingers against his wrist proved to Zayas that she really did like him. His small, dark eyes glittered as brightly as his diamonds, and he stood tall behind his table. A woman like that could have anyone, but she liked him!

One by one, the other players left the table, and for the remaining two hours before closing, Zayas and the blond played alone. They talked as they played, and for the first time since he had started to work the casino, Zayas relaxed. He pretended that the two of them had spent an evening together, that they were now in some cozy place, alone. When it got to be thirty minutes to closing time, the blond asked him to cash in her chips.

"So sorry to see you go," Zayas said. "Will I see you tomorrow night?"

"No, I'm leaving in the afternoon. My vacation is over."

"You will be missed, señora!"

"How sweet of you to say so!"

"Maybe you'll come back, and we can get acquainted better next time. I would like that."

"I would like that, too," she whispered. "We can, however, get better acquainted before I leave. The number of my room is forty-six ten. You come later. Understand?" Her voice dropped to a whisper and Zayas had to lean close to hear her. He felt her breath on his skin as her words curled into his ear. He swallowed hard.

"Señora?" Zayas had not expected her to take his flirtatious comment seriously, and he couldn't believe what he had heard.

She smiled at him as she scooped up the dollars that lay on the table in front of her and shoved them into her purse. "See you later, okay?"

Zayas nodded his head. He watched her leave the casino, and he noticed that every man watched her, even Sánchez. Their eyes met. Sánchez's face twisted into a strange smile as he took a wooden pointer and did an excellent imitation of a field hand cutting cane. Zayas bit his lip, and turned away.

To keep his mind off Sánchez and his pantomime, Zayas imagined how surprised his friends would be when he told them about the blond. He knew that his best friend, Antonio, would pat him on the back and say, "I knew you were going places, Pepito! You're going to have money in your pockets and women at your feet!" It was what Antonio always said when something good happened to either one of them.

And Zayas always replied, "I'd rather have them in my bed!" Even as he thought about it, Zayas smiled.

She was waiting for him in room forty-six ten just as she said she would. Wearing a towel wrapped around her, she opened the door

and showed him in. Her hair was damp, drops of water glittered
in the low light of the room, clinging to the fine, golden hairs on
her arm. Zayas reached out for her.

"Wait a minute, fella. Business before pleasure!"

"I don't understand what you mean?"

"What's to understand? I mean, I think you're cute and all, but
business is business and I gotta pay my account in the morning. I
get one big bill, you know, a hundred dollars. Two fifty if you want
to spend the night."

"I don't have any money!"

"You've got to be kidding! You came here without money?"

"I don't have any money."

"Look, I thought you understood. You seemed to, oh damn it!
Why are you wasting my time? Now I'll have to go out again!"

"You asked me here—"

"I didn't think you were fool enough to come without money.
Get out!" She held the door open for him, and when he did not
move, she shoved him toward the open door.

Even when the door slammed in his face, Zayas still did not
believe it had happened. He blinked his eyes at the gold numbers
on the door. Forty-six ten. He could hear his heart pounding, but
he could not breathe fast enough. There was pain in his chest and
even more pain in his gut. The only way to escape the pain was
to scream. Zayas could feel the scream building up inside him.
It gathered speed; its momentum was unstoppable. He aimed the
scream at the door with the shiny numbers, and he pounded on it
with his fists. Two men jumped out of the elevator and ran to him.

"Hombre, ¿estás loco? ¿Qué es lo que pasa aquí?" One of the
two hotel security men took hold of Zayas and shook him.

Although he held his body rigid, he did not resist. "Nada.
Nothing is wrong!" he replied through his clenched teeth.

"Look, I don't want to get you in trouble. Why don't you leave
and go back where you belong?"

He looked at them. They must think I'm crazy, he thought.
For a few seconds he considered explaining to them what had happened. But how could he tell them, or anyone?

"Come on, Zayas, be a good boy and go home!"

Zayas turned and ran down the hall. His rage boiling inside
him, he took the stairs and ran back to the room he shared with
three hotel employees.

The room was dark; he could hear the others breathing softly. In
the darkness he reached under his bed for his machete; his fingers

curled around its cool, metal handle that fit into his hand perfectly. Zayas ran into the hallway with the large, heavy knife in his grasp and held it up to the blue-white light of the bare bulb.

It had been months since he had touched it, but it might have been only that morning. As if he had never put the machete away, its weight felt right at home in his hand. It was still a part of him. Swinging it side to side, he heard the familiar whistle of the blade cutting through the air. Carefully, he tested its edge; he had spent hours honing it. With this machete he had cut sugar cane in the fields and had trimmed the undergrowth around his mother's house. Since the time he was a boy, for ten and twelve hours a day, he had swung this blade to clear the land. It was how he had earned his living, and that was all that waited for him outside.

Outside! He thought he could feel the heat and the humidity press in on him, and in his nostrils the heavy, black smoke of the burning fields smothered him again. Fields were burned to cleanse them of dangerous snakes and insects, but they always crawled, slithered or flew back into the blackened fields when they cooled.

But not me, Zayas swore as he swung the blade through the air once more. He could see the light bulb's reflection in the metal. I will never see those fields again.

Suppressing his anger, Zayas went back into the room, wrapped the machete with a towel and sat down on the edge of the bed. Holding the blade on his lap, he sat very still and listened to the sounds outside.

Three

Doña Gertrudis had been up since before dawn. She dressed, made coffee, screamed at the servants who had arrived late, and created, as well as directed, the confusion whirling through her house. By noon, the preparations were completed, and Doña Gertrudis sat on the front veranda, dressed in her finest dress and wearing her best jewelry, awaiting the arrival of her son. On her lap lay the hand-painted fan he had sent her from a trip to Spain, and in her hand she held a tiny cup of fresh brewed coffee.

It had been five years since his last visit. Although she had written to Francisco many times since his departure, asking, then demanding that he come home, he always wrote back with some excuse. Just when she thought that she would have to leave Soledad, make the trip to the United States and bring him home forcibly, if necessary, his letter arrived. She tore apart the envelope and struggled to read his angular, uneven handwriting, almost impossible to decipher even with her glasses. When she came to the part that said he would come next month and stay indefinitely, she stopped and crossed herself.

"Thanks be to God!" Her eyes continued to trace each loop of the letters in the word "indefinitely" and she heard its sound echo in her head.

"At last!" Doña Gertrudis said aloud, although there was no one in the room. "At last!" She folded the letter carefully and slipped it into her lingerie drawer where the snoops in her household would not find it.

Doña Gertrudis knew that her son's absence from the village was a favorite topic of gossip. Not that anyone ever made a direct comment to her, but when they thought she was not listening, the people of Soledad whispered that he had deserted his family for a better life in the United States. Doña Gertrudis had been forced to endure the whispers and the pitying stares, but now she smiled waiting on the veranda. There was no doubt in her mind that her ordeal was over. At last she would be able to walk through the village with her head held high.

The first thing that she would do after his arrival would be to take an evening stroll through the plaza with her handsome, well-educated son. She would take his strong arm and pretend not to hear the envious murmurings of her neighbors as they passed. She would not even acknowledge admiring stares. Smacking her full lips in anticipation, Doña Gertrudis planned what she would say to Francisco when he arrived, so he would understand that it was time for him to settle down in the village and take care of his mother like a proper son.

Francisco had merely been a boy when he had left Soledad, and now he would return as a man, ready to take over the plantation that had been in his father's family for four generations. The management of the lands had been her burden since the premature death of her husband. She managed the plantation well, and at the end of each year, when all the accounts had been settled, a generous sum was set aside for deposit into her savings account. Every year Doña Gertrudis made the trip to the capital, to the large marble building with the fierce, marble lion guarding its door. Without fail, the astonishment expressed by the bank personnel at her large deposit filled her with pride. But she was tired. The constant trips to the country to survey the fields made her weary; it was time to step aside.

Lost in her thoughts, Doña Gertrudis did not notice the car when it first pulled up in front of her house. Near-sighted, but too vain to wear her eyeglasses, Doña Gertrudis squinted into the sunlight. She did not know the woman with the bright, red hair who got out of the car and walked up the stairs to the veranda. The woman carried a large bag slung over her left shoulder and helped a child climb the large wooden steps. Doña Gertrudis demanded to know who the intruder was.

Before the woman could speak, a man answered, "Mama, don't you recognize me? It's Francisco!"

Doña Gertrudis had been so involved in trying to identify the woman, she had failed to see him. With a cry of surprise and delight she jumped from her rocking chair, unaware that she had spilled the coffee and dropped her precious fan. She threw her arms wide open in welcome and nearly knocked the woman and the child off balance. After five long years, she held her son in her arms again.

She looked him over with the same meticulous care that she gave to the purchase of fine laces for her dresses. Francisco was everything that a mother could want: handsome, tall and strong. He was strong enough, no doubt, to maintain the discipline necessary for running the large plantation, and strong enough to silence the terrible gossips that had mortified Doña Gertrudis for so long. She had not held him in her arms long enough when he pushed himself away.

"Mamá," he said, "I want you to meet my wife."

All the joy vanished from her face. "What are you saying? This is not possible!"

"Yes, Mamá, it is true; she is my wife. And the child is my daughter, your first grandchild!"

"You never wrote to tell me any of this."

"Mamá, you know what a terrible letter-writer I am. Besides, I was hoping to surprise you."

"Well, you succeeded in doing that, and knowing that I hate surprises."

"Mamá, don't be angry. Come, meet her, I'm sure you'll like Jenny."

Doña Gertrudis peered at the woman and sniffed nervously. Jenny. The name was suitable for a housemaid, not for the wife of her son!

"But, Francisco, she isn't one of us," she said. "Can she understand our language?"

"She is learning."

"How about our ways, what are her manners like? Where does she come from, who are her people, her family?"

"You'll know everything soon, Mamá, come and meet her first."

"I don't like any of this. You should have written and consulted with your mother, like a proper son. But no, you hid it from me like something shameful! What will people say when this gets out?"

The woman spoke, but Doña Gertrudis didn't understand a word of what she said. Francisco answered his wife with a few short words and a wave of his hand.

Doña Gertrudis was outraged; she had been shut out of their conversation. "What does the woman say, Francisco!"

"She asks if you are upset, Mamá."

"Well, tell her, yes, I am upset. How could you do this to me? I had so many hopes and plans for you, my son."

"Mamá, please, don't make a scene. Look, all the neighbors are watching us."

Doña Gertrudis looked around at the surrounding houses. It was true; the neighbors stared at them with interest. She lowered her voice and spoke in a deep growl. "Very well, Francisco, we'll speak about this later."

Aware that she was the center of attention for the entire neighborhood, Doña Gertrudis pulled her mouth into a smile, walked over to the waiting woman who was her son's wife, and pecked her lightly on the cheek.

"And your granddaughter's name is Sally," her son said. He pushed the little girl toward his mother. "She was three years old last month."

"Sally? What kind of name is that?"

"It is a nickname for Sara. We named her after your mother."

"Oh, I see," Doña Gertrudis said and patted the child's head. "Come, let's go inside."

Seething with anger, she turned and walked to the parlor. Her son followed and then returned immediately. He had forgotten his wife and daughter on the veranda. He apologized to Jennifer.

"Frank," she said, "your mother is really upset. You should have written."

"Don't give me a hard time, too."

"Give you a hard time, what about me? What about Sally? We don't understand a word of what's happening and then you leave us standing out here. I feel like unwanted luggage."

"Don't say that. Give my mother some time and she'll come around. And how can she not love Sally, her own flesh and blood? In a few days everything will be straightened out. Now come inside and meet the rest of the family."

"If their reception is going to be like your mother's, I don't want to meet them."

"Jenny, please, it will be all right. I promise."

Even as they spoke, the servants and the neighbors whispered among themselves.

"She isn't one of us."

"He married an outsider!"

"Without his mother's knowledge! What a disgrace!"

"She doesn't look like one of us; she doesn't speak our language. Poor Doña Gertrudis, stuck with an outsider for a daughter-in-law."

"That one will never take care of Doña Gertrudis in her old-age like a dutiful daughter-in-law."

"Of course not, she isn't one of us!"

"Poor Doña Gertrudis, I almost feel sorry for her!"

During the days that followed, Doña Gertrudis studied her new daughter-in-law carefully. The young woman, Jenny, appeared to be an attentive wife and a good mother. She was a beautiful woman—if you ignored the color of her hair—and she had a soft, melodious voice that was pleasant to listen to, even if Doña Gertrudis couldn't understand a word that she said. But the way that Jenny walked annoyed her; there was no humility in that walk, and her habit of looking a person in the eyes when she talked, upset her. Furthermore, her son's wife would interrupt a conversation often to demand that Francisco translate what was being said, the woman just did not know her place.

Every time Doña Gertrudis went outside the house, she was met by the pitying stares of her friends and neighbors. And she knew that the moment she walked by them, the murmuring of their gossip would drown out the morning songbirds or the evening's crickets.

To avoid the people of the village, Doña Gertrudis began to stay inside, wondering how long she could endure the ordeal of Francisco's visit. She could not ask them to leave. What would people say? Everyone knew about the saint's day celebration; Francisco was expected to be there. She could not cancel everything: Rosario was working on the tablecloth, the goats for slaughter had been separated from the flock and invitations had been sent. In the privacy of her room, Doña Gertrudis wrung her hands and paced the floor.

Her son was charming and attentive, as always, but his wife was always there, following his every move with her eyes. The child, on the other hand, was a delight. Although Sally had inherited her mother's shocking red hair and pale green eyes, there was no doubt that she was her father's child. She had the same high cheek bones, the identical nose and the same long, tapered fingers. Doña Gertrudis sighed.

The child was indeed her own flesh and blood, but the day that Doña Gertrudis took the child with her to the market in the square, people stared at them, made pointed remarks about the girl's hair color, and whispered. It seemed to Doña Gertrudis that there was no place she could go to escape the whispers. When she tried to discuss the problem with her son, he refused to listen and told her that she was being foolish.

Foolish! Couldn't he hear it? Even when it was not spoken out loud, she could hear the whispers, and she cringed when she saw the looks of pity aimed at her.

"Doña Gertrudis has lost her son."

"Who will take care of her in her old age?"

"She should never have sent him away to study. I warned her; we all did."

"Doña Gertrudis thought that she was better than us because she had the money to send him to the United States to study, and now look what has happened."

"That's just what happens when one dares to commit the sin of pride. I don't feel sorry for her at all!"

By the end of the second week, Doña Gertrudis decided that she would make peace with her daughter-in-law for the sake of her son. From that moment on, the villagers would be given no reason to gossip about her family. The whispers would be silenced once and for all when she took the young woman to Mass with her that Sunday. Once her mind was made up, she marched into the walled patio where Jenny played with little Sally. Involuntarily, her lips puckered up in displeasure, but she forced herself to smile at her daughter-in-law, who crawled about the patio tiles with her daughter on her back.

"Jan-e-fer!" Doña Gertrudis sang out the young woman's name.

"Please, Mother, call me Jenny."

The older woman stretched her lips to prevent them from drooping and ignored what her daughter-in-law had said. Through halting language and gestures, she thought she had made it clear to Jenny that they would be attending Mass on Sunday, but the girl did not seem to understand. Jenny kept shaking her head.

Doña Gertrudis called her son to interpret.

"I'm sorry, Mamá, but Jenny will not go to church with you!"

Doña Gertrudis gasped. "And why not? It's expected."

"She's not of our faith, Mamá," he murmured softly.

At last she knew the truth; everything was clear. That moment she felt old, older than the mountains surrounding the village, older than the church in the square, older than the land that sustained them. The room blurred in front of her eyes, and she heard the words "not of our faith" echo in her brain over and over again until her head hurt and she cried out: "But you married her?"

"Yes."

"Was it in the Church?"

"No, Mamá, it was a civil wedding."

Doña Gertrudis felt her legs grow weak. "But then you are not married!"

"We are legally married, Mamá."

"No, not in the eyes of the Church, not in the eyes of God and not in the eyes of your people, your family. This is a grave sin, Francisco!"

She whispered so that the servants would not hear. It was a scandal sure to spread through the village, and she would have to endure more stares and more whispers. Was there no end to her suffering?

"Mamá, Jenny is my wife and Sally is our child, your granddaughter, your flesh and blood. You cannot deny her."

"Has the child been christened?"

"No, she will be raised in the faith of her mother."

Doña Gertrudis controlled the feeling of nausea that threatened to strike. There was no time for sickness; they had to act quickly. She looked into the solemn face of her handsome son who had caused her so much grief, and felt her love for him still strong.

"Listen to me, Francisco, perhaps you don't care if your immortal soul is in danger, but you surely can't condemn the child to suffer for your sins. We'll go to the capital in the morning. There we'll find a priest to marry you and baptize the child. Then we'll come home and no one will know. We'll be able to hold our heads up high just as before."

"No, Mamá, that's not possible," he whispered, "I'm sorry, but Jenny believes strongly in her faith, and I've agreed to raise Sally in that religion."

Doña Gertrudis looked at her son in horror. Had she lost him forever?

"Mamá, does it matter so much? I am still your son and I love you. My daughter, your granddaughter, is still your own flesh and blood, and she will still play with you, and sing you songs and kiss ..."

"What will the neighbors say?" she whispered.

"Does it matter what the neighbors say?"

"It matters to me."

Francisco opened his mouth and closed it without speaking. He swallowed hard each time his mother repeated the phrase, "It matters to me!"

Finally, he could remain quiet no longer. "Mamá, look at me. I love you. Jenny and I love you. We really want to stay here with you."

"No, no!"

Francisco took his mother by her shoulders and looked down into her eyes. "Mamá, please! You can't imagine what I've learned at the university! This old plantation will yield three, no, four times what it does. And we'll get more land and ... "

Doña Gertrudis no longer heard her son. She listened to a vague rustle of whispers carried by the gentle breeze. The messages in the whispers were indistinct, but somehow she knew that if she were to listen closely, it would all become clear.

"Mamá, look at me! We're a family! What can be more important than that."

Francisco cupped his mother's face in his hands and tried to force her to look at him, but she shook off his hands and moved away. She followed the faint whispering sounds to the other end of the patio and concentrated on them.

"Mother, please!"

Doña Gertrudis pressed the palms of her hands over the cracks in the garden wall. It was no use, the sounds grew louder. With the side of her knee, she covered one large crack, with her shoulder another, and she poked her fingers into every jagged opening she saw.

"Mother!"

Doña Gertrudis pushed him away; her hand left a bloody stain on his shirt. She did not see the tiny streams of blood pouring from her hand, nor did she feel any pain. How could she concentrate on listening if he insisted on interrupting her? She pressed against the cement wall.

"You've hurt yourself!" Jenny ran to take her mother-in-law's hand.

Doña Gertrudis pulled away from Jenny's touch. She knew it! Already they whispered about her and her problems. How could she face all the smug faces and all the knowing stares of the people in the village? It was too much.

"It is too much to bear!" she shouted.

"Mamá, please listen to me!"

"It is too much, I say!" Doña Gertrudis shouted to drown out the rustling whispers.

"Mother," Francisco's voice was low. "Do you want us to leave? Do you really want to be alone?"

Doña Gertrudis held out her hands and studied her fingers.

"Mamá, answer me! If we leave, we won't come back!"

There was a sound to the left of her; she cocked her head and followed it to the patio wall.

"I give up! Look, Mamá, if you want to talk to us, we'll be inside, packing." When she did not answer, Francisco and his family left the patio.

Alone, Doña Gertrudis looked around to see if she could discern the source of the whispers, but they seemed to be everywhere, and they grew stronger and more distinct each minute. She ran to each of the three walls of the patio and listened. If she could only tell from where they came! Suddenly, they grew louder; they were getting closer. Doña Gertrudis backed away from the vine-covered walls. The whispers grew unbearably loud. She ran inside and startled the servants by closing the windows and the doors in the middle of the day. If she worked fast enough, she might keep the whispers outside.

Four

Rosario's worktable stood by the window where the light was bright. If her eyes grew tired, she rested them by looking out at mountains draped in violets and grays, greens and whites, always the same, yet ever changing. When her muscles ached from the strain of sitting at the worktable, she walked outside and stood on the small veranda. Each time that she went outside, Rosario felt like a queen surveying her realm, and she knew her subjects well. The slow, arrogant flight of an eagle searching for prey drew her attention first and she often wondered why God had denied her wings. When there were no eagles to watch, her tired eyes were renewed by the colors that changed with the seasons or with the direction of the wind. There were the pinks, reds, yellows and whites of flowers that bloomed for a day, then faded, and the greens and blues of the parrots that hid in the trees, but were betrayed by their screeching and sloppy habit of dropping chewed bits of leaves everywhere. At night even her dreams took on the colors of the mountains, vivid and misty colors, both accented by the sharp, black edge of the unfinished highway.

It was called the Vía Panorámica; it rose from the beaches of the Caribbean coast and headed into the interior. It cut through many valleys and twisted around several smaller mountains until it reached El Gato Mountain, and there, like a ribbon sharply trimmed, the road ended before entering the great forest.

Five years before, citing insufficient funds, the government halted work on the Vía Panorámica designed to connect towns and villages on both sides of the central mountain chain. The village's only claim to fame was that road, known as the road to Soledad, the road to nowhere. At first, the people of the village smiled whenever they heard the road's nickname.

"At least," they said to outsiders, "at least now you'll know where nowhere is, and how to get there!" But the novelty and the cheerfulness faded, replaced by a slight shake of the head or blank stare.

After a few months, grass started sprouting in the road's tiny cracks, roots burrowed beneath its asphalt and vines stretched across it. At first, the men of Soledad took turns working on the road. They had believed they could stop the forest's advance toward its sharply defined black, asphalt edge, but with little free time and no money, they abandoned the work.

It was almost noon. Rosario put down her embroidery hoop and stretched her arms above her head; it felt good to wiggle her numb fingers. Leaning back in her chair, she looked out the window toward the highway. It was then she saw the stranger as he stepped out of the forest's shadows. Scissors and embroidery floss fell from her lap when she jumped from her chair to peer through the jalousie window at the edge of the road, but she could not see clearly. With her skirt sticking to the backs of her thighs, she ran to the veranda where the view was unobstructed. Had she imagined it? Rosario looked again.

She saw nothing unusual. Drought had dried the fields into yellow-orange. Leaves curled into brown fists, fell and rolled on the ground. When the wind blew, they shuffled across the baked earth like large beetles. Drained of moisture, the air was clear; the outline of the mountains was sharp against the sky, and the soft, misty colors were gone. Brown tree trunks and branches once screened by leaves were exposed and their shadows wove a giant web on the dusty ground. A gust of wind slapped her face with tiny particles of grit. Rosario moved out of the wind and stood in the shade of the mango; its leaves were also stiffening and ready to fall.

Just when we need their shade, she thought, their leaves fall.

The tree branches swayed in the wind, and Rosario remembered that she had not watered the tree in a few days. Her care was the only reason that the mango still had leaves, but the water she drew from the well was not enough.

Cupping her hands above her eyes, she squinted against the bright light. There! Near the sharp bend in the road, a shadow moved. Rosario felt her stomach churn. Who or what had emerged from the forest and traveled in the heat of midday? And at such speed!

The stranger was long and thin. He looked like the stick figures, black crayon on yellow paper, that she used to draw as a child. A stick figure come to life. Magic! Remembering childhood stories, Rosario crossed herself, stepped back into the doorway and locked the door.

Her heart beat rapidly; it was difficult to breathe. Beads of sweat rolled down her face, and her hand trembled when she reached for the crucifix hung on a nail near her worktable. Taking a deep breath, Rosario held the cross tightly and, with her eyes closed, she listened to the wind shake the trees clean. After a few minutes, when she was calmer, Rosario looked through the window again. No sign of the stranger. She shook her head; Aníbal would laugh if he knew. Why would anyone cross the forest? She must have seen Aníbal himself, or a man from the village. No, even at that distance she would have recognized anyone from Soledad.

Holding the crucifix against her breasts, Rosario opened the door slowly and inched her way onto the veranda. Something moved; a flash of color, a twig snapped. He was there! No man could have moved so quickly on foot. Yet there he was, the top of his hat level with the veranda. Before she could get back into the safety of the house, the stranger turned and looked at her through the rails. She felt paralyzed and knew that only a practitioner of magic could hold her immobile with his gaze. What kind of magic was this? Would he walk up the five steps to where she stood, or would he just float up to her? She heard the church bells; it was noon. She crossed herself.

"Holy Mother protect me!" she said loud enough for the man to hear.

The stranger's only movement, however, was to remove his hat. He pulled out a crumpled handkerchief to wipe his forehead, and she giggled. Spirits, evil or otherwise, did not sweat. This was only a man. With her hands on her hips, she stared at him.

The stranger's angular cheekbones pushed up and out against deeply tanned skin that appeared to have been pulled tight across his face, as tight as the fabric in her embroidery hoop. His nose, which always seemed to point the way, was fringed by a black moustache. He was dressed entirely in black, from his broad-brimmed hat and long-sleeved shirt, to his pants and dust-covered boots. Looking like the shadow of some other man cast against the yellow grass, he stared back at her without speaking.

Suddenly the breeze got stronger, again dust blew in her eyes, and she had to hold down her skirt.

The stranger wiped dry the brim of his hat and ran his fingers through his dark, straight hair. Rosario had never seen fingers like that; his knuckles looked like lumpy beads knotted on a string. His shirt was wet and clung to his body in deep folds; a pair of black leather gloves were tucked into his belt. Boots, similar to the ones Aníbal wore when he hunted in the forest, reached up to just below his knee. He looked familiar, as if she should know him. A friend of Aníbal's, perhaps, or a distant relative coming for a visit? She almost smiled in welcome.

"Maybe he's thirsty?" she thought, but no look of friendly recognition lit up the darkness in his eyes. Rosario backed away from the veranda railing and decided to let him continue his journey undisturbed. She would not get him a drink of water or call him to the shade of the mango on the veranda. The wind grew stronger; it was best to go inside. Just as she was about to enter the house, however, the sound of his voice stopped her.

"I've come a long way, señorita; a cool drink of water would be appreciated."

It was a voice that demanded attention; it crackled in the dry air, drowning out the hum of wind whistling through dying tree branches. She stared; a thin, reedy voice was the type of sound she would have expected to hear coming from him. Instead, the sound of his voice filled the space between them, and she felt certain he had touched her. Rosario shivered. The tiny hairs down the length of her arm stood erect, and she curled her fingers into the folds of her skirt.

The stranger hung his hat on a dry stem of the bougainvillaea, opened the top buttons of his shirt and rubbed the side of his neck with his fingers. Embedded in bluish-white flesh rarely exposed to the sun, Rosario saw a long scar that ran from the side of his neck under his ear to his throat, ending just above the collarbone; a wound like that should have been fatal. He noticed that she stared. His long, crooked fingers pulled his collar up.

"What's the matter, doñita? Cat got your tongue? You afraid of strangers?"

"Strangers are rare," she spoke softly as if in the confessional.

He brushed the dust from his shirt sleeve. "And strangers are distrusted, isn't that so?"

Rosario looked down at the tips of her shoes. "Yes."

"Speak up, doñita, I can barely hear you!"

Rosario looked up; he was a man accustomed to being obeyed. His stance—his thumbs stuck behind the large, silver buckle of his belt, his legs straight, his shoulders back, the way he held his

head—made her feel like a small child about to be punished. And
although she stood on the veranda which was level with his chest,
she would have sworn that he towered over her. He retrieved his
hat from the branch and used it to stab at the air. Everything about
him added an exclamation mark to his words.

"Are you just going to stare at me?"

He yanked at a low-growing branch from the mango; it snapped
easily in his fingers, and he pulled the few green leaves from the
stem.

Rosario squared her shoulders. That was her tree!

"I don't fear you, señor, I'm safe on this veranda and you're
down there."

"Cautious and clever, an excellent combination." He laughed
and shook his head. "Cautious and clever!"

He fanned himself with his hat as he walked the perimeter of the
small patio in front of the house. Rosario didn't like the attitude
of his walk; it suggested familiarity.

"It's a well kept farm, small, but adequate." The man looked
up at her and smiled; his teeth were even and white. "And are you
the farmer's daughter?"

"I am the farmer's wife." Rosario tossed back her head; the
heavy braid bounced against her shoulder like a pat on the back.

"Oh, I see, the mistress of the land." Holding his hat over his
heart, the stranger bowed.

Rosario stiffened with anger. There was no humility in that
bow; he mocked her.

"But tell me, señora, where is the water?"

"There is a stream past that tree to your right. The water is cool
and clear. You will like it." She spoke through clenched teeth.

"In this drought you still have a stream? You must pray a great
deal."

"Don't you, señor?"

The stranger laughed. "I'm also hungry."

"You'll find what you need in Soledad."

Pivoting on his heel, the stranger looked at the ring of mountains surrounding the village. "Soledad," he murmured, "what an
appropriate name!"

"We like it."

"I can see that strangers are received with much hospitality
here." He did not try to hide his sarcasm.

"I reserve hospitality for strangers when my husband is at
home."

"Of course, señora, forgive me. Perhaps I'll meet your lucky husband tonight, or maybe tomorrow." The man smoothed his hair again and put on his hat.

Rosario frowned. "You're planning to stay in Soledad?"

"You sound surprised? There must be someone willing to take me in. I don't take up too much room and, as you can see, I don't eat much. Do you know of anyone?"

"No!"

"Oh?" He seemed amused by her answer. The stranger took his work gloves from his belt and pulled them over his swollen knuckles. Covered by the black leather, his hands looked like claws; the sight of them made Rosario feel queasy.

When he turned to look at the ring of mountains, Rosario noticed that he fingered the leather strap holding the machete scabbard.

"Is there much undergrowth in the way."

"No, the way is clear."

He looked at her and smiled. "Good. Both my arm and the machete are tired. We shall meet again, señora. Jorge Vicente López Chal at your service." He smiled and extended his hand; Rosario took a few steps back.

The smile never left his face even when it was obvious that she would not accept his hand. He put his hat on his head.

"Hasta luego, señora!"

Rosario remained silent.

The stranger turned and headed for the stream, his legs opening and closing with precision. She watched him move over the terrain as effortlessly as the eagle flew.

Rosario went inside, bolted the door and watched the stranger through the window until he disappeared. Her hands still trembled when she replaced the crucifix on the wall. She picked up the embroidery needle to resume her work and dropped it. No matter how she tried, she was unable to concentrate on the rosebuds she embroidered. Twice she got up from the table to check the door, and when Aníbal came home late that afternoon, he found the door still locked.

It was difficult to slide the bolt open; Aníbal kept pounding on the door. She had intended to open the door before he got home; the last thing she wanted to do was upset him. When at last she managed to unlock it, the door flew open and Aníbal stumbled into the house. His breathing was heavy from the effort of trying to break down the solid door.

"Thank God you're all right," he said, "I thought something terrible had happened to you. You never lock that door!" His tall and muscular body filled the frame of the door. Normally, he took off his hat and his boots before he came inside, this time he did not.

Rosario looked up at him and tried to smile. "Aníbal, you're home early! I—"

"Something is wrong! I knew it!"

"Everything is fine, now that you're here. Please, Aníbal, calm down!"

Ever since his mother's death, Aníbal had changed. He was easily agitated. Often, when she spoke to him, he did not hear, and his eyes stared past her as if there was something only he could see. He spoke slowly—the sound of each word clear and crisp—but his jaw moved from side to side, as if there were other words filling his mouth that he would not speak. Little lines had appeared on his forehead between his eyebrows and around his eyes. Day after day those lines etched deeper into his skin until the day would arrive, Rosario supposed, she would awaken one morning and not recognize the man sleeping at her side.

"I come home to find the door to my house bolted and my wife inside, like a frightened child, yet you tell me not to get excited? Rosario, what's the matter? Why was the door bolted?" He looked past her, searching the room.

Rosario sighed. Aníbal had that strange look in his eyes again. The month before last, when Rosario had confided her fears to her grandmother, Doña Providencia had advised her to be patient.

"He is grieving for his mother, Rosario. Her death has affected his mind." The old woman had raised her crooked finger and tapped the side of her head. "But don't worry, it will pass in time, you'll see."

"But it's been almost a year!"

Doña Providencia shrugged her shoulders. "Only ten months, child. Women must learn to be patient!"

Everyone knew there was a problem with Aníbal. Even the priest patted her on the shoulder when she left church on Sunday and told her that her reward would be waiting for her in heaven. All the way home Rosario wondered why rewards were always so out of reach.

Sometimes she thought she did not deserve a reward because she lacked patience and because she did not know what to do. Even now, as Aníbal demanded to know why the door was bolted, she could not find the right words.

"Don't just stand there with your mouth hanging open. Answer me, Rosario!"

"It's just my own foolishness, Aníbal. A stranger came by this morning. I got worried and bolted the door."

Aníbal's face drained of color; he took Rosario by the shoulders and shook her.

"Tell me the truth, Rosario, did he touch you? Did he hurt you?"

"No, he did not hurt me. It's just that he startled me. I was resting my eyes for a minute and when I looked up, I saw a shadow come out of the forest. I thought it was an evil spirit. It was not a spirit, just a man looking for water. That's all there is to tell, I swear!"

Aníbal took off his hat and with a twist of his wrist, threw it across the worktable. Taking her chair, he sat down, elbows resting on his knees, hands clasped, head bowed.

Rosario knelt in front of him, the splinters of the unpainted floor caught in the weave of her skirt. She reached over, took his hands and stroked them.

"It's all right, Aníbal, don't worry."

"And he did not touch you?"

"No, Aníbal. He only asked for water, so I sent him to the stream."

"You did well. You never know with strangers." Aníbal caressed the side of her cheek and the tip of her ear. "I don't know what I would do if something happened to you, Rosario!"

His hair had fallen into his eyes, and she pushed it back with her fingertips.

The wind outside changed direction; it was cold, and seemed to sizzle as it slid past the open slats of the jalousie into the warmer air of the room. Rosario felt the tiny hairs along her arms stir; she rubbed her arm and felt little bumps, some caused by insect bites, others by the sudden shift in the wind.

"Aníbal?"

He did not answer her.

She hated his silences.

Rosario got up to close the window, then walked over to the table, picked up her embroidery hoop and put the thimble on her finger. Pretending to work, she listened to the rhythm of his breathing and watched him through the strands of hair that fell over her face. The places where he had touched her tingled; it was always

that way when he touched her. If only he would smile and take
the embroidery from her hands. If only he would take her in his
arms and kiss her in the hollow of her throat, and caress the nipples of her breasts that were hard with anticipation. But he looked
solemn, not the least bit ready to love her in the cool stillness of
the late afternoon.

But even when he was so solemn, even when he said things that
she could not understand, she loved to look at him. He was the
tallest man in the village. His hair was not black like most of the
other men, but a warm brown that glowed in sunlight like red hot
coals in the dark of the night. Hard work had twisted the bodies
of others in the village; they walked with their heads bowed, their
shoulders curved, drooping downward. But not Aníbal. His shoulders were broad, his body was straight, and up until ten months
ago, he walked with his head held high. Proud and strong.

The stillness in the room grew. Rosario picked up a thread that
lay on the table and twisted it between her fingers. It was the same
color of his hair, and she focused on the glint and shimmer of the
thread, and remembered the only words of comfort that the priest
had offered.

"This will pass, Rosario."

Rosario breathed deeply and stretched her arms above her head.
Yes, it would pass, but when? When?

Sunset. Gray shadows spread and darkened; she watched the
colors on the table pale, grow ashen and fade into the darkness.
Rosario got up to light the lamp.

"Yes!" Aníbal's voice slashed through the silence.

Rosario frowned; she had not asked a question.

"Now tell me everything again, Rosario. Where did the man
come from? What did he say and where did he go? It's important
that you don't forget anything."

Surprised, Rosario looked at him; his sudden mood changes
unnerved her. His voice sounded so strong, his eyes glowed, alert.
Her uneasiness vanished, and she smiled; this was Aníbal, the way
she remembered.

"But I told you everything before."

"That was before. Now tell me again. Tell me in detail."

"Well, for a moment, when I first saw him, I thought he came
from out of the forest, but that is just impossible. Even the government gave up on trying to cut through that wood."

"The government, bah! What do they know?" Aníbal hit his
left fist with his right hand. The sound his fist made tore through

the stillness of the room; Rosario flinched.

"Do you know what those men are like, those who decide things? Skinny, bald, pale men who have only seen jungles in Tarzan movies," he added. "A real man with a machete could cut his way through ... "

Aníbal jumped to his feet. In just five paces he crossed the length of the room to reach the machete where he had dropped it when he entered the room. He took it in his hand and tested its edge with his thumb. "With this, Rosario, I could cross to the Pacific!"

Rosario smiled; she had no doubt that he could.

"But why would he come to Soledad? And through the forest, Aníbal? It doesn't make sense."

Rosario finished lighting the lamp and sat down. The breeze coming into the house through the half-open window had created a tangled ball of the embroidery floss on the table; patiently, she picked open the knots.

"He must have come up on the road," she said, "found that it ended at the edge of nowhere and turned back."

"Yes, it could have happened like that, but if he did come through the forest, it only means trouble for us."

"Why?"

"Because respectable people would use the road. That's why."

Aníbal looked around the room, saw the open door and locked it. "Rosario, this is important. Are you sure he was alone?"

"I think I would've seen a companion."

"But you can't be sure?"

She shook her head.

"So you saw no one?"

"How many times do I have to tell you? No!"

"Lower your voice! You said he talked to you? Well? What did he say?"

"But I've already told you everything. Twice!"

"Tell me again!"

"He only wanted a drink of water."

Aníbal reached over, took Rosario's braid in his hand and stroked it. "That was all?"

"Yes."

"Did he say anything else?"

"No! Yes! He said that he did not think the people around here were friendly toward strangers."

"Why did he say that?"

Rosario shrugged her shoulders. "I don't know."

"Did you see what direction he took?"

"He said he was going to the village to look for a place to stay."

"Come on, tell me the rest of it in the Jeep." He released her braid and snatched his hat from the table.

"But there is no more to tell. Where are we going?"

"To the village. Let's see if the man is there, or if anyone else saw him. The stranger might be dangerous, and if he is, we should warn the people. You have to tell everyone what you told me."

"But, Aníbal, strangers have come to Soledad before, and we never called them dangerous."

"These are different times now. I've heard stories that I can't believe are true. We have to be careful."

"But I feel foolish."

Aníbal stopped at the door, his hand on the latch.

"Out in the forest when I hunt, do you think I care about looking foolish when I look over my shoulder? Come on, Rosario!"

Rosario took a few steps, looked back at the worktable and stopped. "I can't go anywhere, Aníbal, I have to finish this tablecloth for Doña Gertrudis."

"Woman! For heaven's sake don't be ridiculous! I'm talking about danger to the village, and you worry about a tablecloth?"

"She pays me well for my work, and you know it! It's what paid for—"

"I don't want to hear about it now. Get ready!"

"But she promised me a bonus when I said I'd have it ready for her saint's day party; I gave my word."

"Women's nonsense!" Aníbal yanked open the door. "Men talk about important things; women talk about tablecloths. What the hell do I care about saint's day parties? Listen to me, Rosario, what's important is that you can't stay here. Now he knows you're here and alone during the day. Think! What if the man comes back?"

The night wind grew strong and colder. She remembered the stranger's hands sheathed in black leather, and how swiftly he moved, his footsteps masked by the sounds of falling leaves. Without further argument, Rosario cranked the jalousie shut, picked up her things and ran down the stairs.

Aníbal was already turning the Jeep to face the road when she reached him. Suddenly, above the unmuffled roar of the engine, they heard their names being called.

"Aníbal, Rosario, wait! Wait for me!" The headlights of the Jeep shone on the boy who ran toward them.

"Enrique! What are you doing up here? Is there anything wrong with my grandparents?"

Enrique stepped out of the glare of the headlights. "No, nothing like that, Rosario. Wait; let me get my breath. ¡Ave María! That was some climb!"

"Enrique, for heaven's sake, what is it?"

"My father sent me to get you, Aníbal, because there's a stranger in town, and he's talking to all the people in the plaza."

"Well, what's the stranger talking about?" Aníbal asked.

"He talks a lot about guns and revolutions. It's the most exciting thing to happen here! My father says you should come right away!"

"Is the stranger tall and thin?" Rosario asked. The boy raised his arms above his head, stretching them to their limit. "You should see him!"

"Get in, Enrique, I'm going to see this stranger for myself. And hold on!"

The boy jumped into the Jeep.

Dust hung over the road like a semi-sheer fabric folded into heavy pleats. Rosario covered her nose and mouth with her shawl.

"Just our luck! The wind is blowing the wrong way!"

"And I can't see!"

"Use the brights."

"That makes it worse, Rosario. Just keep quiet so that I can concentrate on driving."

Rosario sank low in her seat and shook her head.

"Andate! Andate!" Enrique shouted. "Go faster, Aníbal!" The boy held onto the Jeep like the rider of an unbroken horse.

Aníbal stomped on the brake pedal; the boy lurched forward, his head almost striking the dashboard.

"Be quiet! Do you want me to throw you over the side?" Aníbal shoved Enrique back into his seat.

"Aníbal!" Rosario shook her head.

"I've never had much patience with children."

"Yes, I know. At least Enrique will behave now."

Without saying a word, Enrique folded his hands in his lap and nodded his head.

Rosario smiled; the boy's loud sigh and bowed head did not fool her.

"Enrique's father is too easy with him, Aníbal, but he isn't a bad boy."

Whatever it was that Aníbal replied was lost in the roar of sudden acceleration; Rosario held on. When Aníbal drove like that, it was the only thing to do.

Aníbal slowed down after swinging past the last curve in the road, the Jeep's brakes screeching like a parrot hidden in a tree. Rosario sat up in her seat and looked down into the plaza. As usual, people had gathered there to gossip, and to flirt, or to watch those who did. Near the fountain, Sánchez and Rodrigo played their guitars while Bartalomé accompanied them on the flute. That evening the trio was trying something new that Rodrigo had heard on the radio. Clapping their hands and tapping their feet, an appreciative crowd surrounded the musicians whose audience was not limited to those in the plaza. Doors open to the cool night breeze also captured the music and the laughter, so that the sounds reached into the houses surrounding the plaza. As soon as Aníbal's Jeep entered the village square, a group of young boys appeared and ran alongside.

"Enrique, come on! Get down from there! You'll miss everything!"

The boy looked at Aníbal, then at his friends, and without waiting for Aníbal to stop the vehicle, jumped. Rosario watched the five boys scurry behind a house only to reappear chasing a tan dog with a black ear.

"Those boys are always up to mischief," she said.

Aníbal scratched the side of his unshaven cheek and looked around the plaza. "What do you think Enrique was talking about? I don't see anything so important that anyone should send for me." He parked the Jeep.

"Well, you know how Enrique's father exaggerates. If we listened to everything he says, we would always be running from one emergency to another." Rosario shook the dust from her shawl.

Aníbal sighed deeply, sank into his seat and rolled his head against the back. "I haven't even eaten, and I'm hungry! And my clothes smell. When I get my hands on that boy ... "

"Forget it, Aníbal, now that we're here, let's enjoy the music. Grandmother will have something for us to eat, and you can wash up there."

"Might as well." Aníbal stretched his arms and yawned loudly. "Come on, get down."

Just as Aníbal started to swing his legs over the side of the Jeep, a man rushed at him from out of the shadow.

"Aníbal! It's about time you got here, hombre! I've been waiting for you!"

Startled, Aníbal pulled back, shouted and swung his fist. The man ducked to avoid the blow.

"Hey! It's me. Eugenio! What's the matter with you, compadre? Don't you recognize me?"

"¡Eugenio, por Dios! Someday you're going to get hurt scaring a man like that!"

"Come on, Aníbal, nothing scares you!"

Rosario waved her fist at Eugenio. "Well, you scared me, Eugenio! Why do you do such things? Jumping out of the shadows ... "

"You were born scared, Rosario!"

Eugenio laughed when she pretended to hit him.

"Come on, Aníbal," he said, "don't just sit there. Protect me. Hombre, no one sees you any more! Cómo estás?"

"Always the same troublemaker," Aníbal embraced his friend. "It has been a long time," he agreed.

"Come on, Rosario, stop frowning and give me a kiss. Now that you're a married woman, do you plan to forget old friends? Aníbal won't mind just one kiss; he knows you're like my little sister."

Eugenio jumped into the Jeep, gave Rosario a loud, sloppy kiss and jumped back out.

"Now, enough of kissing and hugging. Your husband and I have a lot of lost time to make up. So goodbye, little sister, we'll see you later."

"No! What do you mean goodbye? We only came because Enrique said that his father ... "

Eugenio stretched out his arms and traced circles in the darkness as if conducting the music. "I know all about that. Don't blame Enrique's father for dragging you out of the house; I did it. I sent the boy up there."

Rosario pulled at her shawl. "But why did Enrique say that his father—"

"Would you and your husband come if I sent for you? Me? The black sheep? The bad influence?" Eugenio threw back his head and laughed. "Oh, no! You kept me waiting the past two times that you were supposed to come. This time I was taking no chances. It's time for Aníbal to start enjoying life again, Rosario!"

"Yes, but—"

"Just because the man is married doesn't mean that he's dead!"

"Eugenio! What a terrible thing to say!" Rosario stood in the Jeep, holding onto the windshield with one hand.

"Oh, oh!" Eugenio laughed and pretended to hide behind Aníbal's broad back. "By now you probably know how violent she gets when she's angry, Aníbal! I have a few scars to show you that she gave me when we were kids!"

"Eugenio, that's a lie!"

"You see! Aníbal, you married one of the furies."

"And you are a drunken, lazy—"

"Ah, little sister, it's good to hear your voice again. Music, music to my ears!"

"Eugenio, go away!"

"Sure, Rosarito, that's what I planned anyhow. Come on, Aníbal, we're wasting time."

"But I can't leave Rosario."

"Sure you can. All you have to do is follow me and don't look back. It's the easiest thing in the world to do!"

"But—"

"Don't worry, compadre! She'll visit with her dear, old grandmother, and she'll kiss her grandfather even though she won't kiss me!" Eugenio puckered his lips and blew loud kisses into the air.

Rosario relaxed her grip on the windshield and laughed. "Eugenio, you are always the clown!"

Eugenio ignored her.

"Then Rosario will have dinner with the old people, and later gossip with the neighbors. You don't have to worry about her. She'll have a wonderful time, and so shall we!"

"Eugenio, we'd better leave while she's smiling."

"Good, then it's settled. We'll see you later, Rosario."

"Wait! Aníbal, what about the stranger?"

Eugenio slapped Aníbal on the back. "Aha! So you met him already?"

"No, I did not. Rosario is the one who saw the him."

"Well he's no stranger anymore, Rosario. His name is Jorge Vicente and what a man he is! Wait till you meet him, Aníbal!"

"Aníbal! Eugenio! Wait. Enrique said that the stranger was talking about guns and revolutions. I didn't like the sound of it."

"For heaven's sake, Rosario, who listens to things like that? Enrique was probably making it up to see the funny expression on your face. Anyhow, that's serious business, and I'm not in the mood for anything serious. Come on, Aníbal, Jorge Vicente has been buying drinks for everyone this evening. By now all the men in town are at the cantina, and we have to hurry before he runs out of cash! Why are you wasting time listening to your wife?"

"Eugenio!"

"Don't get mad again, little Rosarito! Your husband is safe with me."

"Not even the saints in heaven are safe with you!"

Eugenio groaned. "Who would think that her little, round mouth hides such a sharp tongue! You hurt my feelings, Rosarito. Aníbal, remember how she used to chase me with rocks?"

Aníbal laughed. "How could I ever forget?"

"It's a good thing that her aim was so bad!"

"If I had a few rocks in my hands now, Eugenio, you wouldn't be laughing so hard!"

"Oh! Oh! She's getting violent again; time to run, Aníbal. Come on, let's go!"

"Go to your grandparent's house, Rosario, and I'll meet you there later." Because Eugenio was pulling him away, Aníbal's lips missed her cheek by inches and the sound of his kiss went unmuffled.

Rosario hit the side of the Jeep with the palm of her hand. That man was always dragging Aníbal somewhere, and when they came back they were usually too drunk to stand. Maybe one of these days Eugenio would marry Carmencita and settle down. She frowned and smiled and frowned again; Eugenio always had that effect on her.

As she watched them walk to the cantina, Eugenio's short legs barely able to keep up with Aníbal's longer ones, Rosario grinned. It had been a long time since she had seen that ridiculous, mock-innocent expression on her husband's face. For the first time, she felt sure that her grandmother and the priest had been right. The bad dreams, the black moods, the long silences would soon disappear. Aníbal would be himself again, and her patience would be rewarded at last. Aníbal looked so happy that she really meant it when she called out to him, "Have a good time!"

From the Jeep, Rosario could see her grandparents when they appeared on the other side of the plaza. She waved but, preoccupied with maneuvering the old wheelchair towards the musicians, Doña Providencia did not see her. Rosario climbed down from the Jeep and ran toward them.

"So," Don Gustavo said after she had kissed him and asked for his blessing, "you don't come to visit your poor old grandfather, but you come to stroll the plaza!"

"That's not true, Grandfather, I came just to see you. Besides, I visited just four days ago!"

"Four days! Four days might as well be four years. Come now, give me another kiss, and maybe I'll give you my blessing."

"Old man! Don't say such things, not even in jest! Don't listen to him, Rosario. Of course he'll give his blessing. Now come give me a kiss and I'll give enough blessings for the two of us."

"It was only a joke, you foolish, old woman. After all these years don't you still know what a joke is?"

"Bah! All you do is flap your toothless gums, up and down and side to side. I don't know why I listen!"

"Because I am your husband, woman, and you must."

"Harumph! It would be best if I were deaf! Rosario, where's Aníbal?"

"He went with Eugenio, Abuela."

"To the cantina?"

"Yes."

"Of course, I should have known that. Eugenio was paid this afternoon. It's a good thing his mother had so many children so that she won't have to depend on that one in her old age."

Doña Providencia shook her head, her long, heavy earrings swinging in a wide arc. "And I don't know what Carmencita does for money. Ah well, it's none of my business. You know how I hate to gossip. She took hold of the wheelchair and pushed a little harder than she had to.

"I do, Abuela, but they sent for Aníbal and I thought there was something wrong, especially after I saw the stranger come out of the forest. I never suspected it was one of Eugenio's tricks to get Aníbal to the cantina."

"You really saw him?"

"Him? Do you mean the stranger?"

Doña Providencia nodded.

"Yes, I saw him when he came out of the forest."

"Out of the forest? But you must be mistaken. Nobody travels through the forest."

"No, Abuela, I saw him ... "

"You made a mistake, child, that's all. Everyone's talking about him, you know."

Their conversation was drowned out by the laughter and shouting that came from the direction of the cantina.

"Provi," Don Gustavo shouted, "stop talking and take me there; Aníbal will bring me back. I don't want to miss anything! There hasn't been this much excitement in Soledad for a long time."

"I wonder what's going on in the cantina?"

"Rosario! How can you be so innocent? They're drinking anything that can be poured from a bottle. That's what's happening inside the cantina."

"What a bad mouth you have, Providencia! The men are discussing politics with Jorge Vicente."

"Sure! Some discussions! Words washed down with liquor."

Rosario ignored her grandmother's comment. "Just who is Jorge Vicente? Do you know anything about him? What's he doing in Soledad?"

"He's a third cousin on his mother's side to Justo Díaz," Doña Providencia said. "And he came to visit his cousin."

"That's ridiculous! Justo Díaz died over three years ago!"

"Jorge Vicente did not know that!" Doña Providencia stopped to adjust her shawl as they approached the cantina. "You should have seen the look on his face when he was told the news. The poor man. He staggered against the church wall and clutched his heart! Now that's what I call real suffering! We all felt so sorry for him that everyone offered him a place to stay."

"And he's staying?"

"Why do you sound surprised? After all, the poor man just arrived. You can't expect him to just turn around and leave, do you?"

"There isn't much here to attract a man like that."

"A man like what, Rosario? What do you know about men, anyhow?

"Then, you tell me why he should remain in Soledad?"

"Rosario, some day you'll stop asking so many questions; it's not normal!"

At the entrance to the cantina, Doña Providencia stopped pushing the wheelchair.

"Shall I take you inside, Gustavo?"

"I can handle it myself, Provi. Go home and tend to Rosario!"

Doña Providencia laughed. "Come on, Rosario. We know when we're not wanted. Anyway, I'm tired of standing here. Have you eaten?"

"I'm not hungry, Abuela."

"No wonder you're so skinny! What are we going to do with you? Soon you'll be nothing but skin and bones. Come on. I'll make us some coffee, and maybe some of Pepita's sweets will tempt you."

"Shouldn't we stay a while?" Rosario stretched her neck past the entrance to see who was inside.

Doña Providencia held her back with a hand on her shoulder. "You haven't heard a thing I've said. Come on. The men don't want us around, you know that. They say we spoil their fun. But when they crawl into our beds, and wrap their legs around us, they don't complain about our being there!"

Rosario grinned and pretended to cringe.   "Abuela! You shouldn't say such things!"

"And why not? It's the truth!"

"How come you can tell the truth when you want, and I never can?"

"An old woman can afford to tell the truth."

"And how old do I have to get?"

Doña Providencia opened her mouth wide, threw back her head and laughed until several of the men in the cantina came out to see what had happened. When the old woman saw them, she laughed even harder. Rosario took her by the arm and led her to her house.

Other women also went to Doña Providencia's house that evening, drawn by the aroma of freshly ground coffee and the sounds of lively, feminine conversation. The night breezes that usually cooled them failed to appear, and the women sat outside. Moving their fans up and down and side to side, they not only tried to dry the beads of sweat on their faces, but they chased away the humming mosquitoes. They talked about babies, and cooking and weaving, and the sweetness of the corn brought up from the city market.

As the night wore on, one by one they left until Doña Providencia and Rosario were alone. So as not to disturb those who had already retired, they spoke in whispers. The chirps of the crickets grew louder.

Rosario's large, brown eyes reflected the full face of the moon. "Abuela, you were right. Earlier this evening Aníbal was like before."

"Of course I was right, child. When you are my age, you'll know these things, too. Now listen to me, gain some weight and stop wearing your hair in that braid; you look like a little girl. How do you expect your husband to give you a baby when you look like that? Look at Carmencita, already she has had two babies sucking at her breasts, and you're the same age!"

"Abuela, Eugenio and Carmencita are not married in the eyes of God!"

"A slight oversight, that's all."

It was late when Aníbal and Don Gustavo entered the patio. For a long time, Doña Providencia had struggled to keep awake, and when she saw them, she did not rebuke them for staying out late. She got up from the rocking chair, yawned, rubbed her eyes and stretched her arms.

"All right, children, we're going to sleep now. Aníbal, drive home carefully. Good night."

Don Gustavo objected; he held onto Rosario's hand.

"Speak for yourself, Providencia, I'm not tired, and I want to talk."

"Tomorrow, old man. You need your sleep."

"No, now. It's important!"

"Sleep is important."

"Aníbal, don't listen to her. We have to talk, now that we're alone. That man is—"

"Don't get excited, Gustavo, it's not good for you. How many times have I told you that?" With one hand on her hip, Doña Providencia waved her finger in front of her husband's nose.

Don Gustavo pushed it away and spit into the darkness of the patio.

"That's a disgusting habit, Gustavo! Goodnight, children, come by tomorrow, or this old man will explode!" Doña Providencia pushed the wheelchair into the house, ignoring her husband's loud objections.

Through the closed door, Aníbal and Rosario heard Doña Providencia's voice.

"You'll wake the neighbors! For God's sake shut up and go to sleep! And stop calling me an old woman!"

Able to see each other only by the headlights of the Jeep, Rosario and Aníbal looked at each other and laughed.

Aníbal rarely talked when he drove; that night, however, he spoke without stopping. Even the roar of the Jeep's unmuffled engine seemed to die down when he spoke.

"For the first time in my life, Rosario, I've met and spoken to a great man! Jorge Vicente López Chal. Remember that name, Rosario! Someday it will be on everyone's lips."

Rosario was too startled to respond; all she could do was to listen as her husband searched for words to explain the new ideas he carried home.

"All my life I thought I was free, Rosario! Now after talking with Jorge Vicente I can see that I was a fool! It's clear that things are going to have to change. We can't wait any longer; we'll have to change them ourselves, and only then will the future be different."

"What things? What are you talking about?"

"Don't talk, just listen!"

She listened to the excitement in his voice. As far as she could tell, Aníbal was sober. Rosario sighed. There was always something to worry about.

It was only a short ride to their house, but the temperature drop was noticeable. Rosario shivered, "It's always so much cooler here."

Aníbal ignored her interruption. He parked the Jeep and led the way up the stairs to the veranda.

"This time it's going to be our's! And when we have a child, it will never know a time like this."

"A time like what? The drought is no one's doing, just God's."

"Rosario, you're such a child! You don't know. You don't understand."

Aníbal's voice cracked, he coughed and tried to clear his throat. Rosario pushed open the door to the house and rushed to light the lantern.

"Are you all right?"

"It's nothing, don't worry!" He coughed again and tried to catch his breath.

Rosario went to the water jug; she dipped the long ladle into the water, poured a drink and held it out to him. His hands shook when he took the cup and held it to his lips.

"Don't talk, any more," she said, "rest. You haven't been well."

"Don't say that; because it's not true. Anyhow, I'm well enough now. Meeting this man was what I needed. Oh, Rosario! Why does everything have to be explained to you? Come on sit down! Try to understand, will you?"

Stiffling a yawn, she sat down at the table and folded her hands. The cat jumped on her lap and stretched out on his side, his paws extending past her knees. Mishu purred loudly as she stroked his fur.

"Rosario! Get rid of that cat! How can you pay attention with it on your lap making all those noises?"

Rosario pushed the cat from her lap, and leaned back in the chair. Through half open eyelids, she watched Aníbal pace the room.

Since childhood, she had watched Aníbal. Whenever he came by, toys and dolls were forgotten. The way that he held his head, his walk, the way that a particular lock of hair fell into his eyes, the sound of his voice, the words that he used, the sharp scent of his skin when he stood close to her—all this she knew as well as she knew the grain of the linen she embroidered.

Yet, he seemed different somehow. The expression on his face was one she had never seen; it changed his features subtly, and he looked like someone else. Like a relative of Aníbal's, maybe, but not Aníbal himself. Even the way that he spoke was changing right before her eyes. Only magic could change a man like that! Magic! She remembered the stranger, and suddenly she felt the need to cross herself.

The moon crossed the sky and set, but there were so many stars that the sky would never be dark. Her eyes closed in spite of her efforts to stay awake. The drone of his voice merged with the buzz of mosquitoes circling. Something moved among the fine hairs of her arm. Through eyelids barely open she saw a mosquito preparing to pierce her skin. Slap! She felt moisture on her arm, a small red stain, and she rubbed it with her fingertip.

The night breeze appeared out of the darkness and grew stronger and colder with each passing minute; it nuzzled against her face and bare arms. Yawning, she closed her eyes and rubbed her cheek against her shoulder. She stood, swayed unsteadily on her feet and, nearly tripping over Aníbal's boots, made her way to the bed. Aníbal never stopped talking. Rosario pulled off her skirt and blouse, crawled into the bed and arranged the mosquito netting around her. Individual sounds merged; she fell asleep.

Five

From the first, experienced hotel employees knew that something serious had happened. Carrying expensive briefcases, the auditors arrived by cab and limousine, singly and in pairs. They might have been mistaken for tourists or delegates to a businessman's convention, but there was a sameness about them: the dark suits, the attaché cases with initials engraved in shiny metal, white shirts, bright ties held in place with gold clips, and an identical expression of determination in their eyes. It was obvious that these men had come not to relax, but to work. Alerted, the grapevine moved into action.

Workers huddled in the hallways, ducked into empty rooms, and gathered in the employee lounge to pass along the latest observation. The new, younger workers quickly picked up the thread of the rumor and wove it into a tapestry of impending doom. Although the auditors had sequestered themselves in the executive offices permitting little contact with the employees, it was not long before the word spread: the object of their investigation was the casino.

The casino! Of course! The restaurant workers, the housekeepers, the gardeners and the clerks heaved a sigh of relief and resumed their duties energetically, casting sympathetic glances in the direction of anyone connected with the casino. They passed along the latest rumor with enthusiasm, but their own vigil relaxed. After two days, the dishwashers and busboys formed a pool, betting on the day and time that the axe would fall. When pointed fingers and sharp stares turned in the direction of Sánchez, the pit boss, the betting got even heavier; he had never been popular among them.

Speculation grew even more intense when the girls who worked in the casino office were sent home, leaving behind only one secretary and the head bookkeeper.

"¿Qué es lo que pasa?" the casino employees asked as each white-faced woman passed through the lounge on the way to the elevator.

Not one of them spoke; they stared straight ahead and shook off the hand of anyone trying to hold them. Suddenly Clotilde, the receptionist, coughed, arched her right eyebrow—as only she could do—and nodded in the direction of an auditor entering the lounge; everyone dispersed.

That evening, the dealers were called to a meeting; not one of them slouched in his seat, no one crossed his legs, nor lit a cigarette. It was a short meeting. There would be just a few minor changes in procedure, but aside from that, it was to be business as usual. The dealers relaxed; the changes had little to do with them, and the new rules were tolerable.

That night when they reported for work, however, Sánchez would not be there. Although they understood that his absence was one of the "minor changes," none of the dealers liked it, but no one dared say anything, not even in whispers to each other. The new pit boss was to be one of the auditors, an outsider. Juárez had been passed over on the promotion. In a way, all of them had been bumped.

There were few smiles in the casino for the next few weeks; dealers concentrated on their jobs, and only the bold ones looked in the direction of the new pit boss. Many of the players were the auditors themselves. "Time to relax!" they said aloud, patting each other on the back. The dealers and the croupiers tending their wheels knew better. The auditors studied them closely, too closely; this was the final exam for the casino employees.

Zayas played well even that first night; he charmed all who sat at his table, and his tips were larger than usual. Night after night Zayas won for the house; he collected more in tips than any other dealer. The new pit boss was lavish with his approval, and from the first week, Zayas found a thicker pay envelope. In the privacy of an empty stall in the men's room, he counted its contents, and was satisfied. The auditors had kept their word; it had been the most profitable deal that he had ever made. Working his way up would have taken him five years to earn so much, yet all he had to do was to write a letter and point an accusing finger at Sánchez. Everybody suspected that the pit boss stole from the casino; he lived too well with his wife, his mistress and his fancy car. A favorite pastime of the dealers was to try and discover the pit boss's method, but only

Zayas figured out how it was done. Zayas chuckled and recounted the crisp bills in his hands; it was the largest amount he had ever held in his hands at one time, and it was his. Admiring the color and the engraving on the money, his hands shook.

He would keep his eyes on Juárez. Someday the auditors would go home and Juárez was next in line for promotion. Juárez would be difficult—a religious man, a faithful husband, but a jealous one. Zayas scratched his moustache; maybe he could work something out.

*   *   *

When Rosario woke up, Aníbal was gone. It was late. Although still sleepy, she jumped from the bed, upsetting the cat hidden under the covers. Rosario frowned; Aníbal had not awakened her to prepare his breakfast. Stretching her arms above her head, she arched her back and yawned. The yawn evolved into a sigh, and she fell back into the bed. With her eyes closed, she imagined Aníbal near her, breathing softly against her cheek, and caressing her body from the point of her chin to down between her legs.

"Oh!," she moaned, rolled over and buried her face in his pillow; faint traces of his scent were there. Suddenly, she heard a loud crash; her eyes flew open. In one swift movement she leapt from the bed, grabbed her shawl and ran towards the sound.

Mishu had knocked down and broken a ceramic bowl. Without flinching at her sudden appearance, he looked up at her and meowed loudly.

Rosario rushed at the animal, ready to strike him. "You terrible cat! Bad cat! Look at what you've done!"

The bowl had been a gift from her mother-in-law, and although it was ugly, it was one of the few things Rosario and Aníbal valued most. She bent down to pick up the four jagged pieces and tried to fit them back together. They matched perfectly; perhaps the bowl could be repaired and Aníbal would never notice. Panchín was good at that kind of work; she would see what he could do to fix it.

The cat's meows grew stronger.

"Be quiet! All you think of is food and it's too early to eat."

The cat continued to fill the small house with his cries, each sound louder and more demanding than the last.

"Stop it, Mishu!" she said, grabbing the cat by the back of the neck and carrying him to the door. "You bad cat! Come on, get out, get out! If you're that hungry, go hunt for something."

The cat landed on his feet with a soft plop.

Rosario slammed the door shut, went to the worktable and found an empty basket in which she put the broken pieces of the bowl. She covered the basket with a cloth and hid it beneath the worktable. Still thinking about the broken bowl, she splashed water on her face, dressed and got to work.

Day after day she followed the same routine: the housework, preparing Aníbal's meals, the watering of the plants to lessen the effects of the drought, and the work on the linen cloth. In the evening, when the only light came from the kerosene lamp, she swept the floors, washed the day's dishes, and took care of anything else she did not have time to do during the day. Sometimes, even at night by the flickering light of the kerosene lamp, she pierced the fabric with tiny, even stitches, one after another, covering the white linen with color. As the work advanced, she even lost track of the days, ignored the housework, and forgot to water the mango that finally shed the last of its leaves. The pieces of the bowl hidden under the table were forgotten.

It was the biggest tablecloth that Rosario had ever worked on; it would cover a table where twenty people could sit down to eat. The pattern was intricate; one large bouquet of flowers filled each corner, a flowering vine ran along the edges, and in the center a bouquet of pink roses and white and yellow orchids. The embroidered cloth grew in weight and she could no longer hold it comfortably on her lap. It radiated heat; often, sweat ran down her breasts and between her thighs.

When Rosario had not gone into the village in over a week, her grandmother came to see what was the matter. She brought with her a large container of rich, vegetable soup. She also brought hours of gossip, some of which was fifty years old, but which she told and retold with the same gusto as the first time. That noon, however, Doña Providencia had something new to talk about.

"He is so tall, but much too thin, thoroughly courteous, however, charming, and helpful. He is a real gentleman, so refined ... "

Rosario shook her head, "But, Abuela, you don't know this man!"

"That's not true, Rosario, I spoke with him just this morning again. And he carried my packages from the market. Yes, yes, so refined ... "

Rosario put down her work, stood and shook threads from her skirt. "How do you know? Who is he? Where did he come from, Abuela?"

"Always with your questions! I don't know; he did not say, and I don't want to pry. How can I offend him by asking? But believe me, you don't have to know where he came from to see the gentleman that he is. If you don't believe me, ask your husband. From what I understand, Aníbal has become his closest friend."

"Aníbal?" Rosario felt the little hairs on her arm stand erect. "I knew that the stranger impressed him, but I did not realize they had become friends. Are you sure?"

"If that's what I said, then I'm sure."

"But when does Aníbal have time? He's been busy working the high range, and hasn't even come home the past two days!"

Doña Providencia grunted, and pressed her lips into a thin line. "That's not a question you should ask of me, child. A wife should know what her husband does."

Rosario sighed.

"Find out what he's been doing, Rosario."

"Yes, I'll ask the trees and the cows and the goats."

"Sometimes I don't understand you! Sometimes I don't like the things you say!"

Rosario lowered her head. "I'm sorry."

"And well you should be. Anyhow, what was I saying?"

"About the stranger."

"Oh, yes. Well, Rosario, you shouldn't call him that, it's disrespectful. In any case, he isn't a stranger anymore. Everybody in the village likes Jorge Vicente, except for my own husband. Can you imagine!"

"No, I can't! Abuelo has always liked everybody, and everybody likes him." Rosario cleared a space on the table to set the dishes and their cups. "What has happened between Jorge Vicente and Grandfather?"

"Nothing! I swear it! But Gustavo says that Jorge Vicente talks too much, and that talking is a big waste of time. Of course! That old windbag hates it when he finds anyone who can out-talk him."

"Oh, Abuela, that's not true."

"The only point on which your grandfather and I agree is that the men in the village should be irrigating instead of spending so much time in the cantina, drinking and talking. Hard work puts food on a table, not speeches. But when I said that to Jorge Vicente, he pointed out that there is more to life than just working the soil! And that's also true, you know, so true. The man is so profound!"

Doña Providencia took the food out and the house swelled with the aroma of oregano and garlic.

"Mmmm," she said, "doesn't it smell good!"

Rosario agreed.

They sat down at the table and ate in silence for a few minutes. The old woman chuckled and shook her head as she ate; Rosario watched her and smiled. It would take a lot more than midday hunger to silence Doña Providencia.

"Poor Gustavo, too old to change his ways. Jorge Vicente says that soon there will be a new order of things, and that we'll all have to change or perish! Now what do you think about that?"

Rosario shrugged her shoulders, sat back in her chair and pushed away her plate. "I don't like talk about perishing. Look at the fields! Everything is dying; that's enough perishing for me. And it's too sad to talk about."

"But he says that things change, child. It's nature's way."

"Why should anything ever change? Why should we allow it?"

"And if it's the will of God?"

Rosario shrugged her shoulders. "I don't know; I'm not smart enough to know such things. But tell me, Abuela, what are we going to change? Did Jorge Vicente explain that as well?"

Doña Providencia swallowed her food.

"Why don't you go ask him yourself? I can't explain it the way that Jorge Vicente does. Why aren't you eating?"

Rosario waved a fly away from her dish. "All I hear from you is that Jorge Vicente says this and Jorge Vicente says that. I'm tired of hearing his name. How can you pay so much attention to this stranger?"

"He's not a stranger anymore. He's one of us!"

"Oh really? Since when?"

"If you don't believe your own grandmother, ask anyone in the village."

"I don't understand this. I'll have to go talk to Grandfather."

"You can't listen to foolish old men."

Rosario waved her finger in front of her grandmother's face. "You've always told me to listen to him before."

"But not this time. Not after what he said."

Doña Providencia waved both her hands in front of her face as if to erase a terrible memory about to resurface.

"What did he say, Abuela?"

"I'm almost ashamed to tell you."

"No, you're not. You're going to tell me anyhow, you know."

Doña Providencia raised her eyebrows and puckered her lips.

"Well, I guess you'll hear about it from one of the neighbors. It's been the talk of the town! Gustavo shouted it for all to hear!"

"What? Tell me!"

"He says that he farts on Jorge Vicente and his ideas!"

The stern look on Doña Providencia's face took on a strange slant. Rosario knew that her grandmother suppressed laughter.

"Aha!" Rosario clapped her hands and jumped up and down in her chair. "Grandfather said that?"

"He said it right to his face this morning!"

"No!"

"Yes, he did! He did! And do you know what Jorge Vicente said?"

"I don't care what that man said," Rosario replied wiping her eyes with the corner of her apron. "Grandfather is right."

"Rosario! That's unfair!"

"I don't care. Jorge Vicente frightened me the day he came out of the forest. I don't think he's a good man."

"You are such a child! Are you going to hate him forever just because he frightened you once. I'm sure he did not mean it; he was probably confused, lost."

"I don't think so. I got a bad feeling when I saw him. I agree with Grandfather."

"You're just as stubborn as that old man!"

"Of course, I take after him."

"God forbid!" The old woman crossed her brown, wrinkled hands over her breasts, rolled her eyes and winked at the cloudless sky.

Rosario laughed. "Abuela, do you really understand what's going on? It seems as if all of a sudden things are happening so fast!"

"Of course I understand! What a thing to ask; I'm not a stupid woman, Rosario. Jorge Vicente says that all the people should own all the land, not like here, where Doña Gertrudis, Don Rafael and Don Benito own the best land, and have the finest houses and fine clothes and horses ... "

"But who would do all the work then?"

Rosario stood and looked out the window toward the forest.

"The people."

"What people?"

"Don't be dense, Rosario. You and me, Aníbal and your grand-father. That's who."

She turned around to face her grandmother, and on her lips were faint traces of a smile.

"And you call me a child! Do you really think the people would work if they owned everything? I know that I wouldn't. How would we eat if no one grew corn?"

"Well, yes, that's true. Rich people don't work; we all know that. After all, you don't see Doña Gertrudis doing her own embroidery."

"Thank goodness she doesn't, otherwise, I wouldn't get paid for doing it for her."

"That's not the way that Jorge Vicente explains it."

"There you go again! Really, I don't care about anything that he says."

There was such a sharp quality to her voice that her grandmother looked up at her in surprise.

Long after Doña Providencia left, Rosario thought about owning a fine house like Doña Gertrudis, with a huge table and a heavily embroidered linen cloth. As she worked, Rosario pretended that the tablecloth she embroidered was for herself.

*   *   *

Months passed and the seasons changed. Zayas also changed; he became more serious. His jokes were limited to the entertainment of the players at his table. He grew thinner, and his friends wondered if he was sick.

"You're working too much!" they complained, but Zayas just shook his head and changed the conversation.

Everyone also commented on how Zayas no longer went out with his roommates on his day off. They thought that he had a special girl hidden somewhere.

"Who is she, hombre? She must be something special!"

The more he denied the existence of this girl, the more the others pressed him for her name. Finally, one day Zayas confirmed their suspicions. He even gave them details of a love affair forbidden by the girl's family. He swore them to secrecy. His friends sighed; Zayas was in love. They patted him on the back and went out on the town without him.

Alone in the room, he stretched out on his bed and patted the lumpy mattress. He should have told them that story before, he thought. Now they would leave him alone and maybe even stop asking him for money. At last he would be able to leave the room they shared without their nagging him to tag along. It took so much time to watch Juárez and his household, but it was paying off. The man's wife had a lover; he was sure of it, but he needed time to prove it. Zayas would do anything so that his friends would leave him alone; he needed to get things ready for the day that Juárez was made manager of the casino. On that day, the new manager would receive a little packet with pictures of his wife and her lover. Well, maybe not the same day. Maybe Zayas would wait a week or two. He was a patient man and in no hurry.

Everything was going well; the new pit boss liked him, and Zayas knew that it was only a matter of time before he was promoted. Often he went into the casino before it opened to stand by the pit boss's desk. The last time he was there, Zayas ran his fingers over its perfect mahogany finish. His fingers curled over the unnicked edge; he felt his heart beat faster, and he held onto the side of the desk tightly.

His savings grew fast, faster than even Zayas hoped. There was almost enough money now to start living right, an apartment of his own, with elegant furniture and beautiful women in his bed. But he had to be careful. Already some of the other dealers looked at him strangely; Zayas would not make the same mistakes that Sánchez had made.

Zayas shook his head; no, he would not be stupid, but it was best to forget Sánchez. That was the past, and there was so much that was new and exciting to think about.

The week before he had run across an old friend of his mother's who worked in one of the most desirable buildings in the city. It had been a long time since he had seen him, not since the time that the spider had bitten him. Zayas shuddered; he did not want to remember that. The only thing that was important was that his mother's friend was going to be useful. He had promised to let Zayas know when the first vacancy in the building took place. Zayas had told him the apartment would be for one of the casino bosses, and he imagined how surprised the old man would be when Zayas took it for himself. Jumping from the bed, he grabbed his pay check and left; Zayas had a lot to do.

*   *   *

Bad news travelled fast in Soledad. Almost as soon as the first well went dry, everyone knew about it. When Aníbal came home with the news, he looked worried.

"We'll have to share with Gómez and his family. Everyone's agreed."

"Well, of course, Aníbal; that's only right."

"And you'll have to be more careful, Rosario."

"But I've been careful."

"Be even more careful."

"Will our well run dry too?"

He looked past her and shook his head. "I'm not sure."

"If it does go dry, what'll we do?"

Aníbal stood, knocking over the chair and pounded the table top with his fist.

"Why do you bother me with so many questions?"

He turned to run out the door, but Rosario blocked him.

"Aníbal, stop! Where are you going? Answer me! What'll we do?"

He pushed her aside, grabbed his hat from the peg by the door and was down the stairs when he stopped abruptly.

"Pray, Rosario. Maybe God will listen to you."

Day after day she stared at the sky as if her gaze could pierce its blue shell, releasing the water hidden within. The sky stared back, as bright and clear as ever.

Rosario used the well only for drinking and cooking, putting off washing clothes until Aníbal complained that his shirts were stiff with sweat.

"How shall I wash them with no water?"

"Stop that damned embroidery and walk to the creek, or to the river like the other women!"

Rosario jumped to her feet, her fingers curled into fists, but when she saw the expression in his eyes, she remained silent.

The creek was not far from the house; any other time it would have been a pleasant walk, but the bright sun, the dust and the high temperatures had kept Rosario inside for days. When the heat of the day passed, she packed a small basket with the clothes to wash.

From the window near the worktable, she had watched the landscape wilt, turn yellow and stiffen. Walking to the creek that afternoon, she realized that the dying was almost complete. The air was so dry that it robbed moisture from her lips, and she licked them until they tingled as if she had burned them with a hot spoon. The breeze could no longer whistle through hollow grass stalks; they had crumbled to the ground, and the dust would bury them.

When she saw the creek, Rosario put down her basket, crossed herself and wondered whether the river too had stopped its flow.

The only water that resisted the powdery advance of the dust, was teeming with thread-like worms, and was, therefore, unusable. She knelt to pray, but listened instead to the faint sighs of the breeze rubbing against the branches of leafless trees. Rosario picked up a thick grass stalk that had been hurled against her skirt by the wind, and she rubbed it between her fingers; it crumbled into flakes that drifted to wherever the breeze carried then. Now she knew that it would not be long before even the deepest well ran dry. There was nothing left to do, but pick up the small laundry basket and walk home.

Even though she wore her hat to protect her from the sun, its light was so strong that her eyes teared; waves of dust rose and settled into the weave of her skirt. Suddenly Rosario saw a large shadow on the ground ahead; she dropped the basket. Squinting and holding her hands up to shade her eyes, she looked up.

Except for the one large cloud, the sky was as clear as it had been for the past eight months. Yet the sight of that one cloud made her feel like dancing; it was the first one to cast its shade on the ground in a long time.

"Please, God," she whispered, "let it rain."

Bending to pick up the basket of clothes, she noticed that particles of dust rolled on the ground in ever widening circles, instead of the listless, haphazard drifting that had become its normal course. The circles opened and stretched into long lines, swept eastward as if by a giant broom. The wind was growing stronger and changing its direction! She ran home.

"Aníbal, come out. Look!"

"What is it, Rosario, what's wrong?"

"Nothing's wrong. Look, a huge cloud. What do you think? Does it mean rain?"

"No, the wind is wrong. You know that."

"But it's changing now."

Aníbal looked at her in surprise.

"How do you know?"

She shrugged her shoulders. "You're not the only one who knows things, Aníbal!"

Aníbal looked up at the sky and shook his head.

"You know what they say when the afternoon sun is bright red on the horizon—a clear, hot day tomorrow."

"Well, this time they're wrong, Aníbal. Look at the the way the dust is moving on the ground. The wind is changing, isn't it?"

Aníbal threw back his head and laughed.

"Don't frown like that, Rosario, and don't be angry with me. I hate it when you turn your face away."

He jumped over the veranda rail and landed by her side. Rosario took a few steps back.

"Well look," she said. "Another cloud. What else could it mean, if not rain? Maybe we should pray."

"Why is it that you always feel the need to pray?"

Aníbal moved closer to her and before she could step out of his reach again, he grabbed her long braid and pulled it gently toward him.

She slapped his hand away.

"Stop making fun of me, Aníbal!"

"I'm not making fun, and I don't want to look at clouds or pray." He stood close to her and kissed the top of her head then turned her to face him.

"But, Aníbal—"

"Not now." Cupping her face in his hands he kissed the tip of her nose.

Rosario shivered.

"Is it the wind that makes you tremble, or is it because I'm holding you so close?"

He kissed her eyelids, first one, then the other.

"Unbraid your hair, Rosario," he whispered, each word a kiss on the outer edge of her ear.

The sounds of day grew quiet as the sun set, and in the stillness surrounding them she heard her heartbeat grow louder until it was the only sound she heard. Rosario reached for the ribbons in her braid.

"Here, let me help you. You're trembling like a virgin on her wedding night."

"Every time you touch me, it's like our wedding night.

Rosario stopped struggling with the ribbons and pressed her hands over his heart; she smiled. His heart beat even stronger and more rapidly then her own. She unbuttoned his shirt, and when his open shirt fluttered in the breeze, she slipped her hands inside where the skin around his waist was warm and moist. Pressing her cheek against his chest, Rosario traced the curve of his back with the tips of her fingers. There were faint traces of perspiration mingled with the smell of the leather strap he wore when working the field, and Rosario breathed deeply; she liked the scent that was uniquely his. Rosario reached up to his neck and kissed him just below his ear; she felt his arms tighten around her.

"You're always so sensitive there," she said.

"Sometimes I think that you're a witch, Rosario. You know so much."

"I learn quickly."

"Come on," he said taking her by the hand. "Let's go inside."

"No. Why go inside? It's lovely out here this evening. And I can make love to my husband on the veranda of our home, if I want to."

The wind tugged at her unbraided hair. Aníbal looked around as if he expected to find someone watching.

"Rosario, don't say such things, it's not right for a man's wife to say such things."

"But, Aníbal—"

"Come on, let's go inside, and don't talk, and don't argue with me. Not now."

The setting sun lit up his eyes and the spirals of the curls on his forehead with touches of red-gold. She smoothed away the frown lines on his forehead and those alongside his mouth.

"I'd never argue with you, Aníbal."

Rosario followed Aníbal inside. Streams of red-gold light stretched across their bed. Aníbal started to close the metal jalousies.

"No, Aníbal, please leave them open."

"For heaven's sake, Rosario! Sometimes I don't understand you."

Rosario started to tell him that the light was magic; she bowed her head instead.

"Praying again, Rosario?"

"No, not praying, waiting."

The sun's golden streams grew thinner and paler as he closed the windows, and only when they disappeared, did he go to her.

During the night the wind stopped abruptly and the air grew heavy. Rosario tossed and turned, and when she cried out, her eyes flew open. In her dream, she had just died; Rosario pressed her fingernails into her arm and felt the pain. The dream was over. Thank God! Her body was covered with sweat; she kicked off the heavy cover. Aníbal moaned and rolled to the far end of the bed. Rosario knew that she would waken him if she did not lie still; she closed her eyes and tried to go back to sleep, but the room was as dark and as still as the void in her dream. Pushing aside the mosquito netting, Rosario slid out of bed. Her nightgown hung on a peg near the bed; she ran her fingers along the wall until she found it and she put it on.

The house was too dark, too closed up. Like a tomb, she thought remembering the dream, and Rosario crossed herself. She walked to the other side of the house, cringing each time a floor board creaked; Aníbal hated it when she got up in the middle of the night to sit on the veranda. She pulled back the latch, and opening the door just enough to let her pass, she went outside. It seemed even darker on the veranda; Rosario looked up at the sky expecting to see it bright with stars. There were none, no stars, no wind, no mosquitoes humming.

Maybe I really died, she thought, and this is what it's like. Oh, God! Let this still be the dream!

Suddenly, Rosario felt a drop of water fall on her arm; in amazement, she ran her fingers along the cold, wet trail it left on her skin, and rubbed the moisture between her fingers. Another drop struck the back of her head and slid through the strands of her hair to roll down her neck where it was absorbed by the collar of her gown.

Rosario, you are a fool, she thought. Naturally there aren't any stars when the sky is covered with thick, heavy rain clouds. She nearly laughed out loud, and for a moment even considered shouting out the news, letting her voice echo throughout the valley below. It's raining! At the very least she should run inside and wake Aníbal, but she decided to let him rest. Rosario went inside and listening to the tata-tat-tat of rain on the roof, she fell asleep.

Aníbal left early the next morning when two of Don Rafael's men came to get him—some problem at the hacienda. The sound of rain growing increasingly stronger made Rosario uneasy. Although the two field hands were standing there, listening, she asked Aníbal not to go, but he shook his head giving her such a hard look that she swallowed her words and her fears. The stern look of reprimand never left his face, not even when he kissed her and left the shelter of the veranda.

Rosario watched him leave; the hiss of the rainfall grew louder and the raindrops shattered into white, foamy spray that bounced back toward the sky. Tiny drops of water slid down her forehead, and hung onto the tips of her eyelashes until she brushed them away with her hand. Suddenly, aware of their passage across her skin, and feeling the tingle of their cold trails, her teeth started to chatter; she went inside. When Rosario took her shawl from its hook on the wall and put it on, it was already damp.

By noon, thin streams of water worked their way in through

the joints in the jalousies. Rosario was glad that the window was metal and strong, but the noise of the water pounding against the slats reverberated inside the tiny house until she thought everything would shatter with the sound. Outside, puddles formed into rivulets that trickled into streams that rushed down the mountainside with a roar. The creek filled and overflowed.

The rain never let up that day. By nightfall Rosario spent most of the time pacing from window to window to see if she could see Aníbal's Jeep. When it was dark, she crept into bed alone, the woolen blanket scratching the side of her cheek; she listened to the pulse of the rain strike the house and the ground around it.

It rained just as hard the following day too, and Rosario knew that if Aníbal had not returned it was because either problems at the hacienda were extremely serious, or because the road had become too dangerous. During the afternoon it suddenly got even darker, dark enough that she had to light the lamp to see her work.

"It's lucky, there's lots of fuel, isn't it, Mishu? No matter how dark it gets, I can still work."

Lost in a feline dream, Mishu never heard her. His paws twitched as if he ran.

Rosario laughed aloud. "You've never run a day in your life, Mishu, not even in a dream."

When the cat did not respond to her voice a second time, Rosario went back to work. In two more days, she estimated, the cloth would be finished, beating the deadline by three days. She sat back and dreamed of what she would do with the bonus. This time next month she could be sitting on the bus coming home from a long day at school.

She took the sewing box from the shelf over the work table. The letters from her teacher were hidden inside. She ran her fingers over the envelopes; it had been six months since she received the first one telling her of the school's decision to allow her to attend. The second letter sympathized with Rosario's problems, and contained offers of help. The third letter asked why Rosario had not answered. Rosario hid the letters again; she had been waiting until she had good news to share with her teacher. Rosario started to compose her reply in her mind as she worked. With renewed energy, she pierced the fine linen with the sharp needle and pulled the colored threads through the weave.

The sounds of the storm outside interrupted her concentration, however, and several times Rosario left her work to peep through the jalousie slats. It was no use, the minute she opened them, even if slightly, water poured in. She couldn't remember a time when it had rained like that, and wondered when it would stop.

Late that afternoon she heard a low rumbling sound. At first she thought it was thunder, but when she heard it again, she recognized the sound of earth moving. She had heard it only once before as a child, and it was not something easily forgotten. In panic she put down her work, and jumped to her feet. Even though the rain slapped her face, she opened a window near the bed. For the few seconds that she had it open, her clothes were drenched. Through the blur of falling water, she saw a raw, ragged mark in the side of the hill which was all that remained of the cliff. Rosario covered her mouth in horror; that site had been Aníbal's choice to build their home, and the cause of their first argument.

They would have built it there, near the house of her mother-in-law if Don Gustavo had not warned them about the cliff.

"Don't build near it," her grandfather had insisted. "Don't even let the goats up there."

"But its such a pretty view—"

"Pretty view! Is that all you can say? I did not think I had raised a fool for a granddaughter," he shouted. "Build there if you must, but learn how to fly first!"

No one else in the village had agreed with don Gustavo's opinion on the stability of the cliff, but to please him, Rosario told Aníbal there would be no wedding unless he build their home elsewhere.

Now staring at the red gashes in the side of the hill, Rosario crossed herself and gave a prayer of thanks. When the rain stopped, she would go to her grandparents' house and thank don Gustavo for being stubborn.

The rain never stopped that day; at dusk she heard another roar. The earth moved again.

Rosario grabbed the crucifix. Where was Aníbal? The wind grew louder and the rain fell harder. It was even too dark to see from where the land had been torn that time. Mishu meowed loudly for attention, but she ignored him. He jumped on the bed and watched her until the house shook, and another roar sent him back to her side; Rosario picked him up and held him while she prayed that the land beneath her house remain firm.

The house was strong, as strong as Aníbal could make it. Her grandfather had picked the plot of ground himself, yet the house shook in the wind, and each time, Rosario screamed. Another roar, her sewing shears fell to the floor.

Trembling she got up from her knees, and thinking only of escape, ran to the door. When she unlatched it, the wind shot the rain inside with the force of a high-pressure hose. The cat pulled free from her arms, digging his claws deep into her flesh, and leaving behind thin, jagged scratches, dove beneath the bed.

Rosario covered her face to protect herself from the rain. Water seeped into the wounds; she felt her arm burning. The wind pulled at her; it sucked at her feet and tore at her clothes, as if it would drag her outside. The floor was slippery and she fell, hitting her head against the door frame. Dazed, she tried to get back on her feet. When the door swung and slammed into her side, pain scorched her shoulder and her arm. Rosario took hold of the swinging door and held on, struggling to close it until suddenly, the door slammed shut. She latched it.

Panting and exhausted, Rosario stood in the middle of the room.

"Thank God!" she shouted. "Thank God!"

Everything inside the house was wet: the floor, the furniture, her clothes. With her heart still pounding, Rosario changed her clothes, but couldn't light a fire; the kindling too was wet. When she stopped shivering, she went to the worktable. Fortunately, she had covered her work with a heavy blanket and it had been spared.

The bright colors of the embroidery glowed in the dim light; the profusion of blossoms made her smile. She picked up the needle, and sat down. The sounds of the storm faded as one by one, new flowers took shape beneath her fingers. Rosario imagined the perfume they would give in a real garden, and slowly the whole house was filled with that scent. It became real, more real than the storm outside.

The following morning when Rosario woke, she blinked her eyes in surprise; she did not remember going to sleep. Fully clothed, she lay shivering on top of the bed covers. The house was quiet except for an occasional loud plop that divided each second as it passed. She got up, unlatched the door and went outside to stand on the veranda. The rain had stopped, but huge drops of water hung suspended in the still air. There was no way of telling what time it was; the world was wrapped in gray mist. Rosario stretched her hand toward the fog and watched it curl around her fingers. The heavy vapor rising from the earth carried a strange odor: sweet and tart, heavy, elusive. Mishu followed her outside, meowed loudly and sniffed the air with an expression of disgust on his face. Rosario laughed.

"It doesn't smell that bad, Mishu."

The cat flicked the excess moisture off his tail and returned to the comfort of the bed.

By noon the sun had burned through most of the fog, and the clear blue of the sky was revealed; white, fluffy clouds sailed by. Fog still curled around the base of the mountain below, and the town in the valley looked as if it had been packed in gauze. It was not until well after noon that Rosario could see the basins carved out of the earth by the rain, placid, miniature ponds reflecting the face of the sun like mirrors. Remembering the terrible sounds of the night before, she looked at the mountain. There were red gashes in its side where vegetation had been washed away and great chunks of earth had disappeared. Rosario saw little streams of water pouring from those wounds. Except for the sound of water dripping, all was silent. The beginning of the world must have been like this, she thought.

Where was Aníbal? Rosario walked from one end of the tiny veranda to the other searching for signs of his Jeep. As more of the fog lifted from the valley below, she saw that part of the road outside the village had disappeared beneath the side of the mountain. Rosario squinted into the clear, white light reflected from the remaining fog; had the mud slide taken any houses? Amparo lived near there, and she had five small children. When more of the fog lifted, Rosario clearly saw that huge chunks of red clay spilled over the asphalt, but they had stopped before taking her friend's house.

Rosario crossed herself, Alabado sea El Senor; there was much to be thankful for. With hard work the road would be cleared, and vegetation would heal all the mountain's open wounds; her garden had been washed away, but she would plant another. They had food and money to last them until then. God was good. And there was still her work. Now more than ever the tablecloth was important; they were going to need every penny to get the farm back on its feet. Rosario went to the worktable and picked up the needle, but unable to concentrate, she dressed and put on her boots to walk to the village. Just as she left the last step of the veranda stairs, however, she sank into the mud as far as her knee. Holding onto the wooden rail she tried to pull herself back onto the stairs, but the rain seemed to have quickened the earth and it sucked at her foot. Red clay oozed into the boot; Rosario held onto the wooden steps and pulled. Finally free! She scrambled up the steps leaving a trail of mud.

Late that afternoon Aníbal returned; Rosario heard the familiar screech of the Jeep's brakes, and she ran to the veranda. She watched him abandon the vehicle on harder ground and proceed through the mud on foot. Twice he almost lost his balance, the third time he fell with his arms outstretched.

"No," he shouted, "don't leave the veranda! One of us has to stay clean."

Kneeling in the mud and trying to find a clean spot on his shirt with which to wipe his face, Aníbal laughed. Hearing him, Rosario laughed too, and the sounds of their laughter tingled like breaking glass in the sharp, clear air of the mountain.

"Are you all right," he shouted as he struggled to his feet.

"Yes, I'm fine. You built a strong house."

"I'm sorry, Rosario, sorry that I was not here during the storm." Aníbal stood. "All during the night I prayed."

Rosario looked at him in surprise.

"I prayed too," she said. "For you. And me. But we're safe now."

"I see that Mishu kept dry."

The cat had walked down to the last step of the veranda. He stretched out his paw, touched the mud and retreated up the stairs.

Rosario laughed. "Yes, he spent most of the time under the bed. Here let me help you up."

"No, don't touch me! I'm not staying. I only came to make sure that you were safe. I have to go help clear the road. Did you see what happened?"

"You're leaving? But you just got here!"

"I'm sorry, Rosario, but they need me."

"And I need you too. Look at this place."

"The road is our only link with the rest of the world, Rosario. Clearing it must come first."

"Sometimes I think that everything else comes first. You left when the storm started to help Don Rafael; now you leave to clear the road. What about me?"

Aníbal sighed. "Don't be like that, little Rosario," he said. "It's unfair. I would have been here during the storm, but when I tried to cross the river to get back, the bridge had washed away. I'm going to make it up to you, you'll see."

"Well, I'm not staying here alone! I'll go with you and help with the road."

Aníbal started with a low chuckle and progressed to laughter accented with hiccups. With bronze colored mud smeared on his face, and wet hair hanging straight and dark, he looked like the picture of a wild, Indian spirit in one of her school books.

"I can't imagine a shovel in those tiny hands. But come if you want."

Aníbal climbed up out of the mud and sat down on the bottom step. "I'll wait here, but hurry or the sun will bake me hard as a brick."

"Then at least you would sit still long enough for me to see you!"

Aníbal threw his hands up into the air and shook his head. "Hurry up, woman! Please!"

When Rosario ran inside to pack a few things, she saw the worktable glowing in the gold-orange light. There was just one corner of flowers to finish—one day's work. She ran her fingers over the uniform stitches; each twist of colored thread represented a particular memory, some pleasant, some terrifying: the sounds during the storm, happy visits by her grandmother and friends ... She couldn't take the tablecloth with her through the mud, and she couldn't leave it behind. So close to finishing it, each stitch brought her closer to the bonus that Doña Gertrudis had promised.

"Rosario, what are you doing in there!"

"In a minute, Aníbal, in a minute."

That bonus! It would have paid for her transportation to the school in Santa Elena. Now after the storm, the money would go for food. Rosario ran her fingers over the embroidery and sighed.

Rosario returned to the veranda empty-handed.

"Well, where are your bundles? Aren't you ready to leave yet? The men are waiting for me, you know. And I'm baking!"

"Aníbal, I think it's best that I stay."

"I knew it! I did not think you would want to go through the mud."

"No, it isn't the mud. It's the tablecloth."

Aníbal stared at her as if he couldn't believe what he heard.

"What are you talking about?"

"The tablecloth must be finished on time for Doña Gertrudis. You know that she wants it for her saint's day celebration."

"Do you really think she'll still have that party?"

Rosario shrugged her shoulders. "That's not for me to say. My job was to finish the tablecloth by the time I promised."

"I hope that woman appreciates the time and work that you've put into that thing. For the past three weeks, it's the only thing you've done. You'll grow blind, Rosario!"

"I'm sorry. I did want to be with you."

"Well, maybe it's best that you stay here. You have food and water for the next two days in case I can't get back?"

"Yes."

Aníbal slapped at flies attracted by the drying mud on his arm.

"I'll try to come back tomorrow. Meanwhile I'll go wash off some of this mud; the bugs are driving me crazy. Watch our progress on the road when you work, and where you see the mud disappear the fastest, that's where I'll be. Everyone will say that Aníbal works like a madman because Rosario waits for him in a bed too long empty."

"Aníbal, don't tease me!"

"Why not? I love to see your face get red like that." He reached out with a mud covered hand to pinch his wife's cheek.

Rosario pulled back and nearly lost her balance. "Aníbal!"

He laughed, threw her a kiss and turned to leave.

"Aníbal, wait! Have you seen my grandparents?"

"Yes, they're fine, everyone in the village is safe."

"Thank God!"

"It was a miracle. There is a lot of damage, but everyone's house was spared. The fields are really bad, and some of the goats drowned, but it could have been worse."

"God has watched over us!"

"To tell the truth, Rosario, He could have done a better job!"

"Aníbal! Don't say such things!"

"Don't worry, Rosario. God forgives me!"

"Aníbal!"

"I have to go. I'll be back when I can walk to the house without sinking to my knees."

"Only to your ankles?"

"Only to my ankles! And to think that they say rich women take mud baths on purpose."

Rosario giggled. "They think it makes them beautiful."

"For some not even prayers would do that! Look at Doña Gertrudis. And even worse, her daughter-in-law."

"What daughter-in-law?"

"You would know about the daughter-in-law if you had gone into the village once in a while. Hasn't Doña Providencia come here with that news?"

"No. And I can't imagine what kept her away with that kind of news to share. So tell me. What daughter-in-law? Is it anyone we know?"

"Well, listen to this," Aníbal chuckled. "It's the first time I've been able to tell you something first."

"Aníbal, tell me!"

"Francisco came back with an American wife last week!"

"Oh, no!"

"Yes! Everyone's talking about it. Uph! You should see her, red hair, red face. Ugly!"

"Ugly?"

"Ugly!"

"Maybe she'll take a mud bath."

Aníbal made his way back to the Jeep; he kicked the tire to loosen some of the mud off his boot.

"There's enough mud here to make even that one beautiful!" he shouted.

He put his hat on and climbed into the driver's seat. With his hands on the steering wheel, he raised his head and looked at her from under the wide brim of his hat. The hat's shadow ran over the high bridge of his nose and down his cheekbone

He took off his hat and waved. "Am I beautiful now, Rosario?"

Without waiting for her answer, Aníbal started the Jeep's engine.

"Yes! Aníbal, yes! You are always beautiful!"

Although Rosario shouted, the unmuffled roar of the engine erased her words. She returned his wave and listened to the progress of his Jeep long after he turned the curve in the road, and she could no longer see him.

Rosario went inside. "Well, Mishu, one thing is certain. Aníbal is his old self again. I don't know what did it, but I'm glad."

She threw open her arms and danced around the room.

"When he comes home," she sang, "when he comes home, it will be wonderful!"

Mishu stared at her as she set up the work area; his front paws flexed and he unsheathed his claws. Stretching slowly he stood, whipped his tail side to side and meowed loudly as he pulled up threads on the bed cover.

Rosario stopped what she was doing and chased him from the bed. When he jumped to the floor, he circled the empty food bowl.

"Mishy! What a bad boy! Did you think that by clawing the bed cover I would feed you again?"

Ignoring his cries of protest, she picked him up and put him outside on the damp and muddy, wooden floor of the veranda.

Six

"Be careful when you play with Mishu; his claws are sharp!"

Twice Enrique tried to pick up the cat, and both times Mishu left thin, wavy, red scratches on the boy's hands.

"Ouch!"

"I told you to be careful! Mishu hates strangers. Go put mud on the scratches."

The boy laughed. "I've been in mud for days, Rosario! No more mud, please!"

"Don't tell me that they have you working on the road too?"

"Yes, and even some of the women. That's why Aníbal sent me—so you wouldn't worry. He said to tell you that he's not sure when he'll get home."

Rosario shook her head and smiled at the boy; he told her nothing she did not already know.

"Anyhow, you won't be too lonely today, Rosario. Your grandmother said to tell you that she's coming at lunchtime. And that she's bringing a huge pot of stew with her because you must be low on provisions."

"Well, that's good news! You deserve some candied papaya for bringing it."

"Thanks!" Enrique stuffed his mouth with the candy. "Are you really low on provisions, Rosario?"

Rosario sat in Aníbal's rocking chair. "No, Enrique, but my grandmother always worries about me."

"My mother is the same," he said and reached for more candy.

"Isn't it good that we have people who worry about us?"

The boy did not answer; his mouth was too full.

The breeze that came from the mountain was cool and dry; the sun was warm and bright, shrinking the puddles until all that was

92

left were dark stains on the earth's surface. Rosario closed her eyes and leaned back in the rocker. It was so quiet; she imagined hearing millions of tiny seeds swell and split open—tiny, hairy roots squirming in the soil.

"Look at those birds, Rosario! I wish I had my shotgun!"

"What a thing to say! Those little birds aren't good for eating."

"Who said anything about eating them? Pow! Pow! I could practice my aim with so many birds!"

Rosario shook her head and frowned. "What a terrible thing to say, Enrique. It's a sin to kill for fun! Especially birds."

The boy ignored her and walked to the other end of the veranda where a chameleon was sunning itself. Just as Enrique tried to grab it, the lizard jumped to the safety of the bushes at the side of the house.

Rosario watched the birds glide in formation, up and down in widening spirals until the leaders dove to earth; their flocks followed. No sooner were they down to feast on grubs then when a snapped twig—betraying the approach of a predator—frightened them. Wave after wave, the birds hopped into the air, rode the breeze, and went home to the sky.

Suddenly, Enrique reappeared waving his hands in the air and jumping up and down on the veranda.

"Good heavens, Enrique. What's the matter?"

"Rosario, I forgot to tell you the most important thing!" He picked at his teeth with his fingers. "I know something important that nobody told me."

"And what's that?"

"Just as I was leaving I saw some trucks come up the road."

Rosario stopped the rocker's movement. "Trucks? You mean Don Benito's trucks?"

"No, big trucks." He held his arms out to his sides then stretched even more. "Big!"

"Show me!" She jumped to her feet and grabbed the boy by the hand.

"There, Rosario, just on the other side of the slide."

"They look like military trucks."

"Yes, Rosario, they are! Look at those men getting out. The whole army must be in Soledad!"

"Don't you learn anything in school? The army is a lot bigger than that."

"How much bigger?"

"I'm not sure, Enrique, but surely much bigger than three truck loads."

"But those are big trucks, Rosario."

"I can't believe the government sent trucks just to help us!"

"And look down below, I think I see two more. Soledad must be more important than anyone thinks."

"I don't know, Enrique. I don't remember a time when anyone from the outside came just to help us."

Cupping her hands above her eyes, she squinted into the sunlight. The trucks lined up along the road; suddenly, more appeared, creeping up the curve of the mountain. She counted them.

"At least with this many extra men the road will be clear soon, and Aníbal will be home"

Enrique did not pay attention to her; he was busy trying to grab the cat again.

"Enrique, look! I think even more trucks are coming."

"I'm going back, Rosario. I've never seen an army truck up close."

"Maybe you should stay here."

"And miss the fun? All my friends will get to ride the trucks and see the guns."

"What guns?"

"Well, everyone knows that soldiers carry rifles and guns."

"Enrique, stay here! You've seen rifles before."

"Not army ones. Besides, they may even have cannons."

"That's ridiculous!"

The boy held out his hand as if he held a revolver in it. "Pow! Pow! You're dead, Mishu!"

Rosario slapped his hand. "Don't do that. Don't ever do that!"

"He scratched me."

"That's your own fault."

Enrique ran down the veranda steps.

"I'm going back to shovel mud. It's no fun here." He spit out the candied papaya and sped down the road.

* * *

At noon, Doña Providencia arrived with her pot of stew. She had so much news to tell that she hopped about the small house.

"I've never seen so many soldiers, Rosario!"

"How many?"

"I don't know, but surely there are hundreds, maybe thousands."

Rosario laughed. "I don't think so, Abuela."

"You know, Rosario, there is only one thing that troubles me."

"What?"

"That there are more soldiers carrying rifles than shovels."

Rosario's hands shook as she set the table. "What a thing to say, Grandmother! You know soldiers always carry weapons!"

Doña Providencia grabbed her granddaughter's shoulder and squeezed it. "To clear a road?"

Rosario took her hand and patted it. "Men always tell us women don't understand these things. Maybe this one time they're right. Come on let's eat lunch; I'm hungry."

Although she tried, Rosario was unable to concentrate on her grandmother's lunchtime gossip. She kept a smile on her face, but her eyes were focused on some indefinite point outside the window. When she failed to respond to one of Doña Providencia's anecdotes, the old woman rapped her knuckles on the table to get Rosario's attention.

"Rosario, is something wrong?"

"No, Abuela? Why?"

"Your head is bobbing up and down like a ripe fruit in a strong wind. And you're not eating. Is something wrong with my stew?"

Rosario shoved food into her mouth, smiled and chewed.

"Well, Rosario?"

"No, Abuela. It's delicious!"

"Well, listen to what I'm going to tell you."

For the next twenty minutes, Rosario listened. For once all of her grandmother's stories were new to her. Only one thing bothered her, however, and that was that Jorge Vicente's name was mentioned more times than she could count. It was that Jorge Vicente said this, or Jorge Vicente did that. Exasperated, Rosario groaned.

"Really, grandmother, can't you talk about anything or anyone else?"

"We don't get too much that's new happening in this place."

"How can you say that, Abuela? We've had drought, storms, mud slides, and now the soldiers ... "

"Yes, yes, and I'll get to all that, but up till now nothing has been as interesting as that man. Except maybe. ... "

"Except maybe what?"

"You know that I can't believe that I forgot to tell you before. Gustavo says that I'm getting forgetful and he must be right."

"Tell me, Abuela?"

"Well, the day that Francisco came home to Doña Gertrudis ... did I tell you that he came home with an American wife with red hair down to her waist and a child?"

"A child? Aníbal did not tell me that!"

"Aníbal told you? Oh, and I wanted to be the one!"

"Well, he did not say anything about a child, so your news is even better, Grandmother."

"Of course. Men don't tell stories right. They forget all the important details. The child is pretty even though she favors her mother. Doña Gertrudis can be thankful that at least the little girl's hair is not as bright red as her mother's. In fact it's almost pretty to look at, like dark mahogany. But that's not what I started to tell you, Rosario. Now what was it that I was going to say before I told you about the child?"

"It can't be too important, Abuela, if you forgot."

"But it was something I really wanted to tell you. Oh dear! That's what happens when so many new things happen at once. For years nothing new and then Jorge Vicente comes, and Francisco with his wife and child, and the two soldiers ... "

"What two soldiers?"

"But I just told you ... "

"When?"

"Just now. Weren't you listening?"

"Well, just tell me again, Abuela."

"Last week two soldiers came into the town—"

"Last week? Before the storm?"

"Yes, before the storm. Don't interrupt. You should have seen them; they were so uppity, walking around the town with their noses in the air, and clicking their heels everywhere they went—"

"What did they want?"

"They said they were looking for a fugitive who escaped from La Oriente prison four months ago."

"From Oriente? I don't believe that; Oriente is too far. And why would a fugitive come to Soledad, anyhow?"

"God knows. No one ever comes here."

"That's not true anymore, Abuela. Francisco came with his family."

"Well, the son of Doña Gertrudis is not a criminal and he belongs here."

"And how about Jorge Vicente?"

"He's not a criminal either."

"How can you be so sure, Abuela? He's a stranger."

"Not to me! Jorge Vicente is a wonderful person, Rosario. Why don't you like him? You don't even know him."

"And I don't want to know him." Rosario frowned.

"Well, as for me it's just as if I've known him all my life." The old woman put down her spoon. "What's the matter? Don't you feel well? All you're doing is pushing the food around the plate."

"I'm not hungry, Abuela." Rosario pushed her plate away.

"You've been working too hard, that's what it is. Why do you do it? You have a good farm, and your husband puts in long working hours."

"Yes, and every time we take four steps forward, something pushes us back five." Rosario pounded the table with her fist.

The old woman looked up in surprise, and opened her mouth as if to speak, but shaking her head, she remained silent and continued eating. Above the curve of the spoon, her small dark eyes glittered.

Rosario knew she was being watched; she rubbed the side of her head and sighed.

"I'm sorry, Abuela. It's just that I'm upset. There was so much damage ... "

"I know, dear. Just have faith that everything will be all right, and you'll see."

Rosario leaned back in her chair and sighed again.

"Tell me, what happened to the two soldiers? Where did they go next? And what did they say about the fugitive? What was his crime?"

"What two soldiers?"

Rosario shook her head and hid her smile with her hand.

"The ones you were telling me about. The ones asking questions about some fugitive?"

"Oh, yes, yes! The two soldiers. I don't know."

"What?"

"They disappeared."

"Disappeared? You mean they left without saying where they were going?"

"No, it's just what I said; they disappeared. One minute they were all over the town asking questions and the next minute, pouf! Gone! I heard them tell Tomás they were coming back to have lunch in the cantina, but they never returned. No one saw them leave. They just disappeared."

"Abuela, people just don't disappear. They probably smelled the bad odors coming from the cantina kitchen, and they ran to wherever it was that they came from. After all, you've tasted the food that Tomas prepares. Do you blame anyone for disappearing?"

Doña Providencia nodded her head, smiled knowingly, and took a huge spoonful of stew.

"Nothing that any man says or does makes any sense to me sometimes. You're probably right, Rosario. Oh, this stew is wonderful! Eat something, child! I want to tell you what Jorge Vicente said about the soldiers."

Shaking her head, Rosario got up, walked around the small room and stopped in front of the worktable. After wiping her hands on her skirt, she fingered the fine fabric covered with her embroidery. It had the most beautiful weave, and it felt so smooth.

"Rosario, for heaven's sake! Leave that alone and come finish your food."

The material had been imported especially for Doña Gertrudis; Rosario did not even remember the name of the country from where it came, but it had to be a wonderful place to produce something as fine as this.

"Rosario!"

Her granddaughter did not hear her. She was remembering how Doña Gertrudis had smiled when she first spoke to her about the job.

"I could have had the work done in the capital," Doña Gertrudis had said holding the linen up to the light. "Isn't it beautiful?"

Rosario nodded her head; she heard Doña Gertrudis as clearly as if she were in the room at that moment.

"Yes, it's true, there were many women in the capital interested in the job," Doña Gertrudis had told her. "But I insisted that only our own Rosario Alvarez could do justice to this material. Do well, and I know other ladies who will give you work, too."

Rosario had shivered with excitement, and she shivered now. Steady work and money coming in regularly, it was a dream come true. Of all people, her grandmother should be the one to understand!

"Rosario! You're acting so strange. Are you sure that you are well?"

"I don't always get this much work, Abuela. I've got to take advantage of it. The money will help carry us over these bad times. And if Doña Gertrudis is pleased with this job, and she recommends me to her rich friends, I'll have plenty more work."

The old woman put down her spoon and looked up. There was a sad, thoughtful expression in her eyes.

"Yes, steady money is always a good thing, child! I wish your parents had not died so young, and that your grandfather and I had more to give you, but ... "

Doña Providencia got up, went to the stove and served herself again. She sniffed loudly, squared her shoulders and held herself erect. "This is good, Rosario, and you'll have enough for dinner."

The old woman's voice quivered, and Rosario knew that it was just a matter of minutes before tears filled her grandmother's eyes. It was always like that.

Rosario walked over to her, squeezed her shoulder gently, and sat down at the table again.

"Without your help, I couldn't have come even this far, Abuela. You are the best grandmother in the world!"

"You and the old man are all I have left. That's why I worry about you working so hard. You must take better care of yourself. You are too skinny; you don't eat well; you don't rest. I get sad when I see circles forming beneath your eyes. And for heaven's sake, Rosario, you are seventeen years old already—"

"Yes, yes, I know!"

Suddenly, the quiver in Doña Providencia's voice, and the shadows of forming tears disappeared. "You know what? What? You don't even let me speak."

"I know what you're going to say."

"Well?"

"That I don't have a baby."

"Right! So tell me, how long are you going to wait?"

Rosario sighed. "It's God's will, Abuela, not my choosing."

"I'll tell you one thing, God isn't going to put a baby in a scrawny thing like you. Neither will your husband. Gain some weight and wear one of the beautiful blouses you make for other women. Then you'll see."

"You make it sound so easy."

"It is, child, it is." The old woman crossed her arms across her sagging breasts and nodded her head to accent her words.

Rosario looked down to avoid Doña Providencia's gaze.

"If you say so, Abuela, then it must be so."

"What you need is time to rest."

"Maybe you're right. Look, I'm almost finished with the table-cloth; why don't I spend the afternoon with the two of you tomorrow after I deliver it."

"Good! That's just what I wanted to hear! Every morning Gustavo complains how you have abandoned us."

"That's not fair. I couldn't leave here during the storm."

"Of course not, child, I know that."

"I don't know why he complains so much. I visited just eight or nine days ago."

"But he is old, Rosario. Eight or nine days is like a year to him. Besides it's been longer than that since your last visit. Jorge Vicente has been here exactly three weeks, and you haven't come since the day he arrived."

"For heaven's sake! Now you even tell time by his comings and goings. Soon the name of Soledad will change to Jorge Vicente's Place!"

"You don't have to be sarcastic, Rosario." Once again Doña Providencia's voice quivered.

"I'm sorry."

The last thing Rosario wanted was to upset her again. After all, what should it matter if her grandmother were taken in by that man?

"When you get to know him, you'll understand. He is the perfect gentleman; he's even charmed that harpy, Doña Gertrudis."

Rosario looked up in surprise and smiled. "Then he must be a magician, not just a gentleman!"

"That's true!"

The old woman laughed until tiny tears squeezed past her eyelids. She pulled out her handkerchief to wipe her face, took a deep breath, and dissolved into laughter again; the folds of skin beneath her jaw rippled, the flattened tears glittering each time they were exposed.

Doña Providencia swallowed another spoonful of food, smiling even as she ate. Remembering something else she had to say, Rosario's grandmother waved her crooked finger in the air. "And do you know what else I think? I think he's not a bad looking man. With a little more meat on his bones, he might even be called handsome."

"Abuela!" Rosario clutched at her breast and rolled her large, brown eyes in mock horror. "You're not supposed to notice such things!"

"Humph! I may be old, but I'm not dead. On the other hand, Teresa Victoria is the one to watch. Her heart has been turned upside down since that man came, and she's dreaming about getting married again!"

"Oh no!"

"That's right! She says her children need a father. Even if you don't like him, Jorge Vicente should be spared such a fate!"

Their laughter disturbed Mishu who had been sleeping in the sunlight by the open door. He got up and went outside.

*   *   *

The next morning, when Rosario felt the warm touch of the sun on her cheek, she opened her eyes, yawned and ducked under the covers. Out of habit, she had left the east window open, but this morning she did not have to get up at dawn; there was plenty of time to sleep until after the valley mist rose and stretched across the wide, blue sky.

She closed her eyes and tried to fall asleep, but sleep eluded her. With a groan of disgust, she kicked off the covers. It's just as well, she thought. The house showed the neglect it had suffered for all those weeks that she had worked on the tablecloth. It was time to set things straight. She dusted, removed the bed linen and dragged the mattress out to the veranda for an airing. All the embroidery threads were sorted by color and put away for the next project. When Rosario hung the broom on its nail by the stove, it was already late morning. She rushed to wash herself and dress.

Singing out loud, she brushed her hair and braided it with blue and white ribbons to match the embroidered flowers on her blouse. It was her favorite blouse, the one she usually wore to church or on special holidays. Rosario knew that her outfit would please her grandmother, and Aníbal always liked to see her in blue. She hoped to convince him to abandon the work on the road and come home with her that evening.

When Rosario locked the door, and walked out on the veranda, she noticed what a beautiful morning it was. Up to that moment, she had been busy with her work, and she had not stopped to notice how blue the sky was, or how clear the air. The sun was warm on her skin, and the breeze was cool. Everywhere dots of pale yellow-green outlined the dark branches, and the ragged side of the mountain was already obscured by whispy veils of green. Like wounds being bandaged, soon the storm's damage would be healed. Higher up, the white caps appeared to have grown larger; someday she would know why the tips of those mountains were covered in snow. It seemed logical that the closer to the sun, the warmer it would be, and yet high up in the mountains it got colder. Rosario clutched the bundled tablecloth to her breast and thought about how wonderful it must be to know things.

*   *   *

When she approached the large, white house belonging to Doña Gertrudis, she heard a soft tapping sound. It mingled with the songs of caged canaries kept inside the walled patio. There was a small, mahogany door leading from the patio to the side street. Normally it was kept closed, that morning it stood ajar. Rosario pushed it open all the way and entered.

The small water fountain in the center, which had stood dry during the long drought, had been refilled and its blue and white tiles cleaned. The waterlillies and the goldfish that used to swim among the white and purple petals had not been replaced as yet.

She saw Jorge Vicente working on a broken rocking chair. He wore the same black clothing as on the day he first appeared out of the shadow of the great forest, but it looked freshly laundered, and his boots had a mirror finish. Because the trees had not yet grown a new set of wide leaves to shade the patio, Jorge Vicente worked beneath a wide yellow and white striped awning that snapped in the breeze.

He looked up and saw her. "Buenos días, señora. It's a beautiful day, isn't it?"

Rosario had hoped that he would not notice her.

"Buenos días, señor. I did not know you were a carpenter."

He put down the hammer, spit out the tiny nails he held in his mouth, and wiped his lips with the back of his hand. "It's one of the many things I do well." The sound of his voice filled the patio; it drowned out the chirping of the canaries.

"Modesty is not one of your faults."

Jorge Vicente took off his hat and laid it on the table in front of him covering the handle of his machete. He ran his knobby fingers through his straight, black hair and laughed. "I've never believed in it," he said. "It's something invented by old women for secret reasons of their own! Now don't you agree with me?"

Rosario was surprised to feel her lips stretch into a wide smile.

"I don't know. I've never thought about such things."

"Of course not. They don't give you a chance to think with all their rules and chatter. In any case, I was hoping to see you again, señora. I want to apologize. I realized later that I might have frightened or offended you the first time we met."

"There's no need to apologize, señor."

"You are a gracious lady." He held his hand over his heart and bowed.

Rosario stopped herself from smiling again. "Why aren't you working on the road? I thought everybody was working on it, or is the work finished?"

"We were all working, but since the military arrived there are more men than they need. I decided to work here, out of everyone's way."

The wind rustled the paper wrapping of the package that Rosario held to her chest.

"Aha! That must be the tablecloth. Doña Providencia has told everyone about it. Congratulations on finishing it."

"Thank you, señor."

Jorge Vicente laughed and rubbed the side of his face with the back of his hand.

"We need not be so formal; this is not a formal time and place. My friends just call me by my given name."

"I don't know you that well, señor. And I like formalities."

The wide smile disappeared from Jorge Vicente's face. "From the first time we met I thought you were a clever woman. Yes, there is security in the rituals of formality, señora."

"I must go; I've taken enough of your time."

Rosario turned to leave; the sound of his voice stopped her.

"I would never say that you take up my time, señora." Jorge Vicente put down his hammer. "I should thank you for rescuing me from tedious work."

Rosario did not answer. She felt herself sway in the breeze like the branches of the avocado, and she dug her toes into the soles of her boots to anchor herself into the ground.

He looked around the patio and spoke almost too softly to hear. "You know, it's funny how both of us have been working to make sure that Doña Gertrudis has a perfect party next week. Even now the military is working for her because without the road, how will her guests arrive?"

"The rich lead enchanted lives, señor, everyone knows that. It must be wonderful to have no problems; just a few coins and pouf! Problems gone!"

He dropped his voice even lower. "Ah! So you think as I do!"

"I don't know how you think."

Suddenly, Rosario realized that Jorge Vicente stood so close to her that their bodies almost touched. She frowned because she did not remember moving toward him.

"Come," he said. "Sit down for a minute."

She felt his breath on her cheek. "I can't, I ... "

"Only for a minute."

Rosario looked up at him; her cheek brushed his shoulder. She had not intended to stare into his eyes, but she could not look away. It was as if his unblinking eyes held her immobile. His eyes were not dark in color as she had first thought, but green with yellow specks radiating from the iris with a dark, dark fringe of thick lashes—too dark and too thick to be real.

I've got to look away, she thought. Tilting her head slightly, she concentrated on the weave of his shirt.

"Here, sit under the awning where it's cool."

He spoke only in a whisper, but the sound of his voice hushed the twittering of the canaries and the steady hiss of the wind.

"No! I'll stay here by the fountain." She held the package tightly.

"Wherever you like, Rosario Alvarez."

From somewhere as if from a great distance she thought she heard the canaries sing, but she could not be certain. All she could listen to was the sound of his voice.

"I believe that it's evil to have so much when others do without. The rich should be forced to share their wealth. All of us should toil together and reap its benefits equally."

Again she felt his breath on her cheek, and feeling a sudden twinge in her stomach, Rosario panicked.

He's too close, too close, she thought. Thinking only of escape, she pushed away, but the heel of her boot got caught in a broken piece of floor tile and she stumbled. Jorge Vicente reached out to steady her; his long fingers easily encircled her arm. When she tried to pull her arm away, he held her.

Rosario stared at his hand; did it grow larger and more powerful while her arm seemed to shrink? She heard her voice echo inside her. "You're a fool, Rosario," it said. "There is no magic to this man. He's only flesh and blood." She shook her head and swallowed hard.

"Tell me what you think, Rosario Alvarez!"

There was authority in his voice; her impulse was to obey.

"Speak, Rosario!"

No one had ever used such a tone of voice on her, not her grandparents, not even Aníbal dared speak to her like that. Clenching her jaw, she looked him straight in his eyes and pulled her arm free.

"I think that not all of us toil equally, señor. If we did, Aníbal would not be working on the road, and you would not be standing beneath the shade that this beautiful awning provides. You do not stink of drying mud when you work! And I don't like being held!"

Jorge Vicente stepped back. "So," he said, "the little, brown bird has a sharp beak!"

"I'm not a little, brown bird. Save your poetry for someone else!"

Rosario felt as if his fingers had burned her skin where he touched her. She looked at her arm almost expecting to see red marks appear just below her sleeve. When she saw no blemish, she shook her head. "I'm so stupid!" she thought.

Suddenly the breeze gusted, and the awning snapped sharply, startling the canaries that flapped their wings against the golden bars of their cages.

"Yes, it's true," Jorge Vicente said as he looked down at his freshly laundered clothing. "There is no mud on my clothes now."

He returned to the shade beneath the awning and picked up the hammer and the tiny nails. "Buenas tardes, señora. Although I don't stand in the mud, I still must work. Like you."

Jorge Vicente no longer smiled; he put on his hat and picked up his hammer.

A large cloud forced its shade into the patio; without the sun, it felt unnaturally chilly. Rosario shivered and rubbed her arm. Somewhere in the house a door slammed; its sound, echoing through the house and patio was loud and sharp.

Rosario backed away from the center of the patio and only turned her back on him when she stumbled against the large ceramic urn waiting to be filled with flowers. Still tacking the elegant fabric onto the rocker, Jorge Vicente seemed absorbed by his work. The sound of his hammer softly tapping followed her as far as the kitchen door of the large house. Rosario wondered if he watched her from beneath the broad brim of his hat. She held her back straight and her head high in case he did watch.

*   *   *

Teresa Victoria was working in the kitchen when Rosario entered. She looked up, smiled and waved her soapy hands.

"Hola, Rosario, I did not know you were coming today. Is Doña Gertrudis expecting you?"

"I don't think so, but she'll be happy to see that I've finished the work." Rosario put the package on the table.

Wiping her hands, Teresa Victoria rushed to open it.

"How wonderful! Show me!"

"No, you know how Doña Gertrudis is; she'll want to be the first to see it. Call her for me, won't you?"

Teresa Victoria's smile faded. "I don't know if I should disturb her, Rosario. She hasn't been feeling well. Don Francisco has been taking care of everything lately."

"Don Francisco?"

"Things change, Rosario. We're no longer children playing in the plaza."

"Don Francisco. It feels strange to say it, but I guess you're right. When I think of him, all I remember is a skinny, blond boy with a bloody nose. So, he's grown up, and now we call him Don!" Rosario scratched the side of her nose and smiled. "He's come home for good?"

"Yes, I think so."

"That should make his mother happy. I didn't know that Doña Gertrudis has been ill; my grandmother did not tell me that."

"Did Doña Providencia tell you that he came back with a wife?"

"¿La Americana?"

"That's her. You should see her hair. Everyone stares when she goes out, and they say things about it, too. I think it's the most beautiful thing I've ever seen. When the sun hits it, it almost crackles like a cooking fire."

Rosario laughed. "You've been reading too many romance novels, Teresa. Besides, I heard she was ugly."

"Ugly? People around here talk too much. Anyhow, what do they know?"

"Then she's not ugly?"

"She's not ugly, but not beautiful either. She's just different, that's all."

"Well, as long as her husband is happy, what we think doesn't matter, I guess."

"That's what I say. And in the dark, the color of her hair won't keep away her husband."

"Is she nice?"

"I don't know for sure; she doesn't speak Spanish well. Every time she wants something, Don Francisco has to translate. But she smiles a lot."

"Well, that's good."

Fingering the brown wrapping paper, Rosario looked about the kitchen; it was almost as large as her house.

Teresa twisted the dishcloth in her hand.

"Rosario, why don't you wait here, and I'll get Don Francisco to see what he wants done about this tablecloth."

"But my agreement was with his mother."

"I know, but ... "

"How sick is she, Teresa? Is it serious?"

"I don't know how to tell you, Rosario. You know I don't like to gossip." The kitchen maid wiped the sink although it was spotless.

Rosario took the washcloth from her. "This is important to me, Teresa. You know that you can tell me anything."

"Rosario, you must not repeat this to anyone. Promise?"

"I won't say a word."

"Especially not your grandmother."

"For heaven's sake, Teresa! I've already promised. What more do you want?"

"The truth is that Doña Gertrudis spends the whole day locked in her room, even the shutters on the windows are closed. It's like a tomb in there; it's so dark. She says she hears voices."

"Voices? You mean that she's ... " Rosario tapped the side of her forehead with the tip of her finger.

Teresa Victoria sucked in the sides of her cheeks and nodded her head.

"No one is supposed to know. You must keep your promise not to tell anyone or Don Francisco will throw me out of the house."

Rosario took the maid's hands and patted them. "Francisco would never do that, Teresa, even if he is rich and a gentleman now. We all used to play around the fountain in the plaza when we were little. A person could not change so much."

"Yes, they can. Circumstances change, and people change, too; I've seen it happen."

"In any case, you can be sure I won't say a word."

"Not even to Aníbal?"

"Not even to him. After all, no one wants you out on the street with your five children."

"Four! You know I only have four, Rosario!"

"Yes, I know! I'm only teasing, Teresa."

Teresa Victoria smiled then rubbed her forehead with the back of her hand.

"If only I had a husband to care for me like you do, Rosario. It's not natural for a woman to live and work alone. Ever since Humberto died it has been hard."

"Yes, Teresa, I know. I know. And for heaven's sake, don't start to cry. Here, dry your eyes and don't worry. I won't say anything to anyone about Doña Gertrudis. Now, what am I going to do about this tablecloth? I need the money."

Teresa Victoria's eyebrows shot up into her bangs, and her mouth took on the form of a question about to be asked.

"The rains did damage the farm, you know."

"Yes, I heard. In the village we tend to forget about the land. But don't worry, Rosario, I'm sure that Don Francisco will take care of everything."

Rosario pulled out a chair and sat down. "I hope so!"

"Well, you wait here and I'll get him. Would you like a cup of coffee? I had prepared it for Don Francisco and his wife, but they didn't want any."

"Yes, coffee would be wonderful."

"Maybe I should pour a cup for Jorge Vicente, too. The poor man has been working all morning."

Rosario made a face. "Please, Teresa, call Francisco first."

"Rosario! You had better get used to being more respectful. What do you think he'll say if you forget and call him Francisco to his face, as if you were a member of his family or something?"

Remembering how Francisco used to chase her around the fountain in the plaza with a mud pie in each hand, Rosario smiled. The children in the plaza used to call him Paco then; he used to hate the name Francisco.

"It's not funny, Rosario."

"You're right. I'll remember to call him Don Francisco."

"Good. Now, I'll get him." Teresa Victoria looked out the window at the patio. "Jorge Vicente works so hard." Her voice trailed off wistfully.

"Teresa Victoria! For heaven's sake!"

"I'm going! I'm going!"

Rosario made herself comfortable in the chair and poured herself a quarter cup of the dark coffee from the fancy, silver pot on the equally ornate, silver tray. The milk pitcher held warm milk and Rosario filled the remainder of the coffee cup with it until the color was the right shade of beige. She scooped three spoons full of sugar into her cup, stirred it gently and sipped the hot liquid; it was delicious. Rosario leaned back in the chair and waited. The coffee in her cup grew cold.

"Rosario! How good to see you again!"

He was not as tall as she remembered him, and his blond hair, which had grown darker, had already started to retreat from his temples. Everything about him was different except for his eyes; they were still as blue as a clear, midday sky.

"Don Francisco, it's been a long time."

"Every time I hear an old friend call me 'don' I feel old." He crossed the huge kitchen in four strides, and took her into his arms. "I've been away too long. My God! You're as small as when I left— a woman in miniature. Are you married? Do you have children?"

"Yes, I married Aníbal, and no, we have no children."

"Aníbal? Well, well. You made a good catch. I'm married, too, and we have a little girl. Wait till you see her. Here, I want to introduce you to my wife. She doesn't speak much Spanish yet. Her name is Jennifer. Jenny, this is Rosario. We've known each other since we were little."

Rosario noticed that Francisco's wife was as tall as her husband. She was just as Aníbal said; tall and very thin.

"Mucho gusto, señora!" Rosario stammered. The bright red color of her hair startled her, and she had never seen anyone whose skin was speckled like Agustín's hens.

"I'm pleased to meet you, Rosario." Jenny extended her hand.

Rosario wasn't sure what to do; she extended her own hand and pulled it back, then extended it again. When their hands did meet, Rosario was surprised to find that Jenny's skin was soft and cool. Feeling that her own hand would scratch it, Rosario pulled away.

"She's shy, isn't she, Frank?"

"Women here don't shake hands."

"Oh, I'm sorry."

"Don't worry about it. You're the mistress of this house; you can't do anything wrong."

Jenny smiled, circled the room as if she looked for something and abruptly sat down at the kitchen table.

"Jenny, get up!"

"Why?"

"This is a table for servants, and you can't sit here in the kitchen."

"But you said—"

"Never mind what I said. Get up."

Rosario shifted her weight uneasily and for the moment was glad that she could not understand what they said. She turned her back on their argument and untied the package.

"What's she doing, Frank?"

"How should I know? She's got her back to us. Rosario, what's that?"

Rosario unfolded the fine linen and held it open for him to inspect.

"It's too big to unfold completely here, I made it for your dining table, Don Francisco. Doña Gertrudis wanted it in time for the party. She offered me a bonus if I finished early."

"Frank, it's a tablecloth! And it's gorgeous!"

Jenny fingered the linen and admired the tiny, even stitches of the embroidery. "Oh, look at the colors!"

Rosario smiled. Although she did not understand the words, she knew her work was appreciated.

"This is indeed good work, Rosario. I had no idea you had such talent."

"Thank you, Don Francisco. I did my best."

"My mother will be pleased."

Francisco dug into his pants pocket and pulled out a wallet. "Here, I don't know how much she promised to pay you, but I know that such work is worth at least this much."

Rosario looked at the bills that Francisco spread out on the table; it was twice the amount Doña Gertrudis had promised.

"Oh! Don Francisco, this is too much!"

Jenny stared at the money.

"Frank, is that all you're giving her?"

"It's more money than she's seen in a month."

"But in the States a tablecloth of this quality is worth a couple of hundred dollars! At least that much!"

"Jenny, I've told you a hundred times! We're not in the States."

"But—"

Francisco put his hands on Jenny's shoulders and pushed her towards the door.

"Please, Jenny, be quiet for once! We'll discuss it later when we're alone. Go check Sally."

Rosario knew that they were arguing; she pretended to be busy folding the tablecloth. Out of the corner of her eye, she watched the American woman stomp out of the room.

That one will keep Francisco walking the straight and narrow, she thought.

When Jenny was out of the room, Francisco rubbed his temples where his light brown hair seemed to back away from his touch. He soothed the frown lines on his forehead.

"Your wife is angry because you gave me too much money?"

"No, Rosario, that wasn't it. I ... "

Teresa Victoria appeared at the kitchen door. Her eyes and her mouth were both round and open as wide as they could go.

"Don Francisco! Don Francisco! Come quickly!" She leaned against the doorway, shaking her head. "You must hurry!"

"What's wrong? Is it the baby?"

"No, it's the soldiers!"

"Soldiers? What soldiers?"

"I thought that they wanted something to eat or to drink, but they're pounding on the door with their rifles and demanding to enter. Oh, please hurry, Don Francisco!"

Francisco's face drained of color. "Soldiers? Here at my door? What? Look, stay here!" He headed out of the kitchen. "No, on second thought, Teresa, go to my mother, and, Rosario, please find my wife and stay with her."

The two women moved closer together; Rosario put her arm over Teresa's shoulders to calm her.

"But—"

"Do as I say! Until I find out what's going on, you'll be safe here."

Following his orders, the two women ran into the interior patio to cross over to the bedroom wing. Jorge Vicente was gone. The rocking chair that he had been working on swayed gently in the breeze; part of the new seat covering was still unrepaired. The small patio door creaked as the wind pushed it open. Teresa ran to slam it shut and Rosario locked it with the crossbar.

"Maybe I should go to my grandparents instead, Teresa."

"No, don't be foolish. You heard what Don Francisco said."

"But if something's wrong, I should be with them."

"They're probably doing what we're doing, locking themselves in. Thank God the children are with their godparents in Alvida, far from here. Come on, Rosario!"

Rosario did not move; her hand still rested on the crossbar.

"Don't be a fool, Rosario. What could a woman do with a village full of soldiers? Stay here. No one would dare enter this house. They'll pound on the door, but just wait till they find out whose house this is."

Suddenly, they heard pounding on the small patio door; the two women jumped.

"Those barbarians! Just wait till they find out that the people who live here are rich and have powerful friends. Then you'll see them grovel!"

The pounding on the door continued.

"Come on, Rosario. Hurry! Until they discover the error they're committing, we shouldn't be where they are."

Teresa took Rosario to the room where Jenny sat with her crying child on her lap. Without another word, the kitchen maid disappeared in the direction of Doña Gertrudis' room.

"Rosario, what's going on?" Jenny asked.

The woman's freckled face was paler than before; Rosario shook her head and walked to the window. With the child trailing after her, Jenny followed.

"¿Rosario, qué pasa?"

Rosario looked at her in surprise; Teresa Victoria had said that she did not speak Spanish, and yet Jenny's accent was good.

"¡No sé, Doña Jennifer. No sé!"

The American smiled nervously and shook her head. Rosario cranked open the metal jalousies to allow them a view of the street below.

Soldiers swarmed through the village like an ant's nest that had been disturbed. Suddenly, they heard the crackle of a loudspeaker. The static was so bad that Rosario could not hear the entire message—just words, "Chalo Montez ... criminal ... terrorists ... surrender ... !"

Rosario crossed herself. "Madre de Dios! Are we at war?"

Suddenly, the door flew open. Francisco, accompanied by an officer, came into the room. Past them, through the open door, the two women could see soldiers.

"Frank, what's going on here?"

"They asked to search the house."

"Our house? What in heaven's name for?"

"They're looking for an escaped criminal, someone they call Chalo Montez, a terrorist sentenced to death for bombing government buildings and responsible for many deaths."

"Oh, my God! What makes them think such a person is here?"

"Soldiers working on the road found the bodies of two military men sent here last week to investigate rumors about some stranger staying in town. According to the captain, the stranger in Soledad fits the description of the terrorist. It looks bad."

"But why search our house? Look, Sally is frightened, and I'm terrified!"

"They're searching everywhere in town. Come on, Sally. Come to Daddy!"

He held open his arms, but the little girl shook her head and clung to her mother's knees. Jenny picked her up.

"There's a big reward for the man's capture, Jen. They're turning the town upside down."

"They can do that? Do they have a search warrant?"

Francisco hesitated before answering. "No, but we have nothing to hide."

"Frank, I don't like it."

"Neither do I, but how would it look if I refused? Don't worry, Jenny, nothing's going to happen to us. Come on, let me introduce you to the captain who has been waiting patiently. He's honored us by coming here himself, and I want you to be nice to him."

Jenny walked across the room to where the captain stood, but when she approached him, the child in her arms started to cry and would not be comforted. The smile on the captain's face disappeared; Francisco was embarrassed.

"It's the sound of the loudspeakers," he said spreading his hands out in front of him. "You know how children are."

The captain frowned, then smiled, his gold tooth shone brightly. "Of course. Everyone knows that children and animals don't like strangers or loud noises."

"Jenny, quiet the child!"

"I'm trying, Frank!"

Seeing the distress on Jenny's face, Rosario walked up to the mother and child, clapped her hands playfully and urged Sally to come to her. Rosario smiled when the child pushed away from her mother and jumped into Rosario's arms. The sudden movement took Rosario by surprise and she nearly lost her balance. Open-mouthed, Sally's parents watched their daughter cling to Rosario as if she had always known her. Rosario took the child into the small adjoining room that served as a nursery. She sat in the huge rocking chair with Sally on her lap, and sang to the little girl who played with the ribbons in Rosario's hair. Just when Rosario managed to quiet the child, however, the captain came into the room to look around. Immediately, Sally started screaming, and he withdrew. Through the open door, Rosario heard him question Francisco.

"Have you known the child's nurse for a long time?"

"Yes."

"Is there a chance that she knows anything about this Jorge Vicente or any of his friends?"

"Jorge Vicente?"

"Yes, that's the name that we believe Chalo Montez used during the time he hid here. To tell the truth, I don't even know if that's his real name. This man has used many aliases; he is an extremely dangerous man."

"I doubt that any one of us knows anything, Captain. You see my wife and I have just arrived from the United States. We were gone a long time."

"But this man Jorge Vicente did some work for your family."

"An act of charity, Captain. The man insisted on working for the food given to him. In this house we never refuse food to anyone. My mother just felt sorry for him. Had I been here, maybe things would have been different, but as I said before, my wife and I have just returned."

"Then you haven't heard of the problems we face in the capital with these terrorist criminals?"

"No. I heard nothing. We spent no time in the capital; I wanted to get home to Soledad quickly."

"Well, then let me warn you to be careful because the countryside isn't safe either. Many of these small towns hide and aid the terrorist criminals. Why they do it, I'll never understand. When we find out where these animals hide, we have to go in and clean out the nest."

"Dangerous work, Captain."

"Yes. And difficult. I will have to talk to your mother since she is the one who hired him."

"My mother is ill."

"I'm sorry to hear that, but there are the bodies of two men out there crying for justice. Were you in my position, you would do the same. I will speak with your mother."

"Follow me, Captain, and I'll explain."

Their voices faded as they left the room. Rosario rocked the child and comforted her until her mother came into the room.

"This is crazy, crazy," Jenny said waving her hands in the air. "I'll never get used to this place."

Rosario smiled and shook her head as she handed the child to her mother.

"I'm sorry, Rosario, I keep forgetting you don't understand. Gracias, Rosario, for taking care of la niña."

"No fue nada, señora."

The two women waited in the small room; they paced back and forth stopping only to look through the barely open slats in the jalouslie window whenever the Jeep with the loudspeaker drove by. "Stay in your homes ... surrender Chalo Montez ... " Rosario and Jenny smiled nervously at each other.

"It's all right now, Jenny," Francisco said when he entered the room. "The soldiers are leaving."

"He went into your mother's room?"

"Yes."

"Did you tell him that she wasn't well?"

"He insisted on seeing her."

"My God, Frank! How can you put up with this?"

Francisco shrugged his shoulders. "Things are different here; you'll get used to it."

"I don't think so, Frank. You never said anything about soldiers searching a person's house whenever they feel like it. The nerve of him going into a sick, old lady's room to bother her!"

"For heaven's sake, Jenny! Things like this don't happen every day. This is just an unfortunate episode."

"But they searched our house!"

"Jenny, please! We have no choice. Besides, there's no harm done."

"No harm done! Soldiers come into our house, into my bedroom, into Sally's nursery, and you say no harm done? This would never happen in Connecticut!"

Francisco shook his head and sighed. "How many times do I have to tell you? This is not Connecticut! So they came in? So what? We have friends, important friends; no one would harm us."

"And what if you did not have your friends?"

Francisco shrugged his shoulders. "Why worry about what isn't true, Jenny?"

"But what if?"

"What if doesn't count. And I'm tired of this conversation."

Rosario listened and wondered if they always spent their time arguing; she started to leave the room. Francisco stopped her.

"Rosario, I want you to stay with Sally."

"I have to go to my grandparents, Don Francisco. I'm worried about them."

"No, don't leave. You've heard the loudspeakers; everyone must remain indoors until the soldiers finish the search."

"But I have to go to my grandparents. They're old, and they need me."

"Don't you understand? You can't go! Now listen to me, Rosario, don't you give me a hard time, too." Francisco lowered his voice. "Besides, that Captain also mentioned Aníbal's name. If he knew that you were his wife, things might go bad for you. He said that your husband is reported to be a friend of Jorge Vicente, and that Jorge Vicente is Chalo Montez himself. Is that true?"

"What would I know about terrorists, Francisco? As for Aníbal, this is a small place. Here everyone knows everyone else, but I would not say they were friends exactly."

"For your sake, I hope they aren't. Those soldiers smell blood. They know that Chalo Montez was in this house and they're not leaving here. At least I've convinced the Captain that we are innocent, and that this terrorist took advantage of my mother's charity when I was away. If they were to believe anything else, they would burn the house down."

"I don't know anything, Francisco! I spend all my time working in my house outside the village. I know nothing!"

"For your sake I hope that's the truth and that they believe you. When they find Jorge Vicente, even if he isn't Chalo Montez, they'll tear him into pieces, and any friend they find with him."

Rosario shook her head and shuddered. "Don Francisco, you remember Aníbal, don't you? He's not a criminal, a terrorist."

"I knew him a long time ago, and even then I did not know him well."

"But you did! You did!"

"Don't contradict me, Rosario! I said I did not know him well."

"Aníbal would never hurt anyone! Never!"

Francisco took her by her shoulders and shook her. "Control yourself, Rosario, lower your voice! The Captain is still in the house; I offered him food and drink for his consideration to our family."

She covered her mouth with both her hands. "I'm sorry, Don Francisco. I don't want to cause you any trouble; I should leave."

"Frank, did you just tell her that the Captain is still here? Did I understand you right?"

"Yes, dear. Don't worry. He's sampling some of Teresa Victoria's cooking and the best wine from the cellar. He'll be here for a long time yet, and God willing, in a good mood."

"I've never heard of such a thing! Listen to that racket outside. The loudspeaker is still blaring the same threats about not hiding the criminal. I can see soldiers roughing up some of the people at rifle point, right outside our door, and the Captain responsible for everything is eating and drinking in our home! How can this be possible?"

"Jenny, please! I'll explain things later."

"I don't see what there is to explain. This is not what I thought it would be like here. Nothing at all."

"Jenny, please. Not in front of Rosario."

Hearing her name, Rosario smiled and extended her hand in front of her. "I know that you're busy, Don Francisco. You have your own family to take care of. I'll leave now. My grandparents are old and they're all alone."

"I see that you are as stubborn now as you were as a child. If you insist on leaving, the least I can do is to ask the Captain for one of his men to escort you to your grandparent's house."

"That's kind of you, but I prefer to go alone. If my grandparents see me in the company of a soldier, they'll think something is wrong. Don Gustavo might even have a heart attack!"

"Don Gustavo is still having his attacks?" Francisco smiled faintly and shook his head. "Some things never change. Look, I'll ask the captain for a pass so that the soldiers won't bother you on the street. Luckily, your grandparent's house isn't far from here. Listen! The loudspeaker is still warning everyone to stay inside, but with a pass, you should be able to get through. I wish you would stay."

"Thank you, Francisco. It's kind of you, but it's best that I leave."

"I told them you were my maid. When I heard Aníbal might be involved, I was afraid for you. At least this way the Captain thinks you were out of the country all this time. Now if no one tells him any different, you'll be safe."

Rosario's eyes opened wide. "No one in Soledad will say anything to the soldiers, would they, Francisco?"

"I've been gone a long time, Rosario. That is something you would know better than I. I hope for both our sakes that, like Don Gustavo, things haven't changed."

"You haven't changed, Paco. Thank you."

He squeezed her hand. "No one has called me by that name in a long, long time, Rosario. It's good to hear it again."

Seven

The sun hung lower than the highest mountain peak, and in a short while its glowering face would be hidden by the wall of mountains that ringed the town. It was the in-between time when the day breezes die and the evening breezes are not yet born, and shadows grow long and thin, reaching out across the narrow streets—a quiet time.

It had taken Francisco over an hour and a half to get the pass for Rosario because the captain refused to talk about it until he had finished his meal. Clutching the pass in her hand, she left the protection of the high-walled patio and went into the street.

Rosario had never seen the village look so empty; all the doors were locked and the windows shuttered. She shivered; it was the same feeling she got whenever she walked through the cemetery to visit her parent's graves. The streets of the village were so quiet that Rosario could hear the sounds of her footsteps rise from the hard ground, strike the cement houses lining the street, and ricochet into the deepening twilight. Suddenly, the crackle and static of the loudspeaker sizzled down the empty street, and when she heard it, her body flinched as if she had been struck. The first time she was stopped, Rosario held the paper with the captain's signature on it in front of her, and they allowed her to pass without comment. At the second checkpoint, however, just as she had folded the pass and put it in her pocket, the Jeep with the loudspeaker screeched to a halt in front of her, blocking her way.

"Who is this?"

"Just a woman with the pass from the captain."

"He doesn't waste any time, does he?"

"He's a big man with big appetites, sergeant."

"And so am I! Hey you, woman! Look at me. I'm prettier than

the captain. How much for me?"

Rosario could not look up at the soldier because tears filled her eyes and spilled over her face. She heard the soldiers laugh as she squeezed past the Jeep that blocked her way.

"I don't think she likes you, sergeant!"

The men laughed even harder, but no one tried to stop her. Rosario ran all the way to her grandparent's house. When she got there, she found the door bolted. She pounded the door with her fists and kicked it, but it wasn't until she screamed the names of her grandparents that the door flew open and she fell inside.

"Ay, Rosario! Rosario you're safe! Thank God!" Her grandfather's voice cracked with emotion.

Doña Providencia rushed past Rosario to lock the door.

"Old woman, leave the door alone and help her to her feet!"

"Shut up, you fool. What if they come back?"

"The soldiers were here, Abuelo?"

"They've been everywhere, child. Everywhere. What's happened? You've been crying!"

"Nothing happened, Grandfather. I was just so scared!"

"You should not have been out on the street, child!" Doña Providencia shook her finger at her. "How did you get through?"

"Don Francisco talked the captain into giving me a pass."

"What captain?"

"The one who searched his house."

"They searched even there!"

"I heard that they're searching everywhere. That's why no one's allowed outside, and Francisco had to convince the captain to give me this pass."

"God bless that boy! He was always a good boy,"

"He's not a boy any longer, Providencia."

"He'll always be a boy to me. We will go to his house when the soldiers leave and give him our thanks for helping Rosario."

The old man nodded his head in agreement. "Yes, it's important to show our respect to someone as rich and as powerful as he. As much as I wanted to see you, child, I'm afraid that this was not the day to come. But since you're here, and safe, come now, give me a kiss."

In spite of the churning in the pit of her stomach, Rosario smiled. Don Gustavo never failed to make her smile. With her fingers, she smoothed his wrinkled forehead before kissing him.

"Do I have your blessing, Grandfather?"

"You always have my blessing, child."

Rosario ran her fingers through his hair; the silver strands slipped through her fingers like the silk she used in her needlework. She had not inherited the gentle curls that framed his face, nor the bright green eyes. Those eyes, according to her grandmother, had driven the young women of Soledad to distraction—Soledad, and all the surrounding villages as well. When she turned to embrace her grandmother, Rosario was calm; it was as if the incident in the street had happened a long, long time ago.

"Rosario, when you were at the house with Don Francisco and his family, did you find out why these soldiers are here? They wouldn't tell us."

"They're looking for someone they call Chalo Montez, but that's just an alias. I've never heard of him. Have you?"

"No. And what could he have done?"

"He's a terrorist. He's bombed buildings and killed many people."

"Ohh ... " The old woman sat down. "So that's what they've been saying on the loudspeaker!"

"You know they didn't fool me for an instant. I knew they didn't come just to clear the road."

"That's right, Abuelo. The man that they're looking for is wanted dead or alive!"

"So many men to capture just one criminal?" Doña Providencia shook her head. "He must be extremely dangerous! But there's no one like that in Soledad!"

Rosario swallowed hard and looked down at the floor. "No one from our village, that's for sure. But there is an outsider here, Abuela."

"Who?"

"Jorge Vicente!"

"No! That's not possible!" The old woman covered her mouth with her hands and gasped. "Rosario, do you think they're looking for him? I can't believe that."

Don Gustavo slammed his fist into the palm of his hand; beneath his white, bushy eyebrows, his green eyes glittered. "Lower your voice, woman! Think! What other man here could be the object of such a search, Providencia? From the day he got here, all he's talked about are the sins of the government. That man is trouble; I knew it! He's got almost everyone in Soledad agreeing with him too, and now we're all in trouble."

"It's true. I know for sure that they are looking for Jorge Vicente; I heard them."

"I thought you just said that the terrorist's name was Chalo Montez."

"I heard the captain explain to Don Francisco that Jorge Vicente and Chalo Montez are one in the same."

"I don't believe it."

"The whole village was taken in by that man except us, Grandfather."

"How could he fool me when I don't believe in anything!"

"Gustavo, that's not true!"

"Don't tell me what's true. I don't believe in much, and least of all in governments. Governments serve only the people in charge, not men like me, who sweat and stink after an honest day's work. You can go crazy listening to them. They offer you heaven and earth, but they take your money and call it taxes; they take your sons for the army, returning only broken or lifeless bodies; they take your soul in the name of loyalty and obedience; they let you use only dead land, dust, and from this dust you either feed your babies or bury them in it. And everything is for the good of the people! In the city, in their buildings, professors and students argue about which type of government is good for the people. But they never asked me what I think. Fools! Only a man like me knows the secret to a good life: a plot of fertile land beneath your feet, and a fertile woman in your bed!"

"Gustavo, it's indecent to talk like that in front of Rosario."

"But Abuelo, we need order and laws ... "

"Lies! All we need is to believe in God!"

"Please, don't get so excited! It's not good for you."

Don Gustavo ignored his wife's objection. "Politicians!" He spit into the cuspidor. "What they do is put their heel on a man's neck. Chalo Monez, or Jorge Vicente, if that's his real name, is no different. He talks about fine ideals; he uses fine words, and people listen to him. Fools, I tell you that they're all fools! Even Aníbal listens to him and believes. Doesn't your husband understand that Jorge Vicente would replace a bad government with another bad government? There would be a different heel mark on our necks that's all."

"I didn't know that Aníbal was that taken in by him."

"Taken in by him? They're almost inseparable, or so people say. It's a bad friendship. I feel it. I'm afraid of it."

"Gustavo, that's enough! You'll frighten the child."

"Child? She's not a child; she's a woman. You're the child, allowing sweet words and fancy manners to cloud your judgment!"

Rosario got up and pretended to fetch something from the cupboard. Why didn't she know this? Why hadn't Aníbal told her?

Doña Providencia came up behind her and patted her on the shoulder. "Don't worry, Rosario. I'm sure that Aníbal is safe."

"Are they together now, Abuela?"

"I don't know, but don't worry. Aníbal can take care of himself."

"I can't help worrying, Abuela. I haven't seen him for three days; he said he would be working on the clearing of the road. I thought he was sleeping here. He has been here, hasn't he?"

"We haven't seen him, Rosario."

"Now I am frightened!"

"What are you two whispering about? Did you hear me, Rosario, what I said about that man?"

"Yes, but I think you exaggerate; a man can't be so evil ... "

Doña Providencia stepped in front of her husband and signaled him not to speak.

"And he isn't," she said. "Not really, Rosario, don't worry—"

"Woman, get out my way! And will you stop feeding her lies? Now listen to me, Rosario. When, as a young man, I came to Soledad, I didn't come just to work my land and raise my family in peace. Peace. The only peace we find is in the grave."

"You shouldn't say such things, Gustavo."

"Stop telling me what I should and should not say! And stop interrupting me. Am I the only one who can still see? Rosario! Stop fussing with those dishes and sit down. I have to tell you something."

Rosario took a deep breath, put down the dishes and turned to face the old man in the wheelchair. Don Gustavo focused his eyes on his granddaughter's face.

"You're like your grandmother, did you know that? You believe what you want to believe."

Doña Providencia jumped to her feet, her hands on her hips, ready to defend herself.

"Sit down! No one's talking to you, just about you."

Rosario saw the expression on her face, and spoke up to avert an argument. "She says I'm like you, Grandfather."

"Well, if you are, then you know that the land is everything, the only thing. You work it and it feeds you. No one from the outside helps unless they plan to take more than a fair share. I know, Rosario, because when I was young I believed I was going to change the world. I left my parents and my friends and I never looked back. The world was going to be a better, brighter place. But in just ten months, I buried my dreams in an unmarked, shallow grave. I learned that causes are fought only for the sake of leaders, sitting safe behind an army.

"When I came to Soledad I was looking to start over again with a new name in a new place. Everyone thought I was dead, and so I was free. Jorge Vicente had the same look that I had so many years ago. But while I became part of this place, he would destroy it!"

"Abuelo, I never knew! Tell me ... "

Don Gustavo started to cough; Doña Providencia and Rosario both ran to help him.

"I knew it," his wife said, "I knew you would have an attack."

"It's not an attack; I'll be fine," he said between cough spasms.

"Please, Abuelo, just be quiet and relax."

Don Gustavo took a deep breath then shot out his sentence as if it were one long complicated word.

"That's what people say to old men. Am I supposed to sit here and watch the flowers bloom? Is that a life?"

"Quiet! What's that?"

"Someone's screaming!"

Rosario ran to look out the window. "Oh my God!"

"What is it, Rosario?"

"The soldiers have shot someone, but I can't tell who. I'd better go find out!"

"No! Don't go out!" Don Gustavo coughed and shouted.

"Shot someone? That's not possible ... "

"Look for yourself. Now they're pointing their weapons at Enrique."

"But, Rosario, he's only a boy ... "

"Rosario, get back from the window. Close it! Provi, lock the door!"

"It is locked, but do you think that'll do any good if they really want to come in?"

"We have to do something! My God! I can't tell who's stretched out on the ground. They're animals! What's going on here?"

"I don't understand!" Doña Providencia shook her head. "They were so polite when they searched the house."

"They probably didn't find Jorge Vicente and they're taking out their anger on the people." Don Gustavo's hands trembled.

"I don't believe it, Gustavo. I don't."

"I told you, Providencia. From the beginning I told you that they were after that Jorge Vicente, but you wouldn't believe me."

"I still don't believe it—he's too decent a man, he—"

"He didn't come here to visit any dead cousin. He's been hiding here, and we were all too stupid to realize it."

"Old man, I won't believe it."

"I don't care what you believe because you're a fool, Providencia! All these years I've lived with a fool! Rosario, get away from that window!"

"They have a group of men. What does it mean?"

"It means that they're taking his friends instead."

"Aníbal!"

"Do you see him, child?"

"No, but maybe they already have him. They're putting the men into a truck! Abuela, look! Were they all friends of Jorge Vicente?"

The old woman nodded her head and turned away. She walked over to the crucifix on the wall and crossed herself.

"Oh, God! I don't see Aníbal. Where is he? Some of them are only children. Look, there's Enrique. They're taking him, too!"

"Aníbal's too smart to get herded like a goat, but I hope he's not with Jorge Vicente when they find him!"

Doña Providencia stopped praying long enough to shake her head and glare at her husband.

"Abuela, why didn't you tell me that Aníbal and Jorge Vicente were such close friends?"

"I didn't want to upset you, Rosario. I knew you didn't like the man, and anyhow, I don't like to be accused of carrying tales!"

"You talk about everyone and everything in town, yet you didn't tell me that?"

"I'm sorry, Rosario, I didn't think it was important at the time."

Rosario turned away from her. The military trucks started their engines. Even the pottery on the shelves trembled as the vehicles started to roll past their house on their way out of the village.

"It's no good, Abuela. I can't see well enough through the window!"

In spite of her grandparent's objections, Rosario lifted the crossbar from the door and ran outside.

She made her way to the lead truck and tried to look inside the spaces of the slats that made up the sides, but she could not see inside.

Other women ran along the side of the trucks calling out the names of husbands, brothers or lovers. She wanted to call out her husband's name, too, but she was afraid that hearing his name, the soldiers might ask, "Who is Aníbal?"

And someone might answer, "He's the friend of Jorge Vicente!"

The trucks filled the narrow street with noxious fumes; Rosario's eyes burned and she found it hard to breathe. Gasping for air, she followed the trucks as they crept through the town, trying to see through the spaces in the slats, wanting to find Aníbal, yet praying that he was not there. Suddenly, Rosario lost her balance, and she scraped her hand on the cement wall, but she did not fall; instead Rosario stepped into something sticky and slippery. Even without looking down, she knew what it was; the salty smell of it filled her nostrils. Rosario froze; her breathing grew difficult. Out of the corner of her eye the puddle of blood glowed red-orange as the rays of the setting sun skimmed its surface. Little by little, Rosario forced her muscles to respond and she backed away from it, but wherever she stepped, she left behind the red outline of her foot. At last the remaining trucks rumbled by. When they were gone, Soledad was quiet.

*   *   *

Long after the trucks were gone, the village remained silent: no one gathered in the plaza at night; the cantina was closed; few of the faithful heeded the call to Mass, and people spoke in whispers behind shuttered windows and locked doors.

Doña Providencia and her husband insisted that their granddaughter not go to her own house until Aníbal returned. Reluctantly she agreed, but by the fourth day Rosario once again insisted on going home.

"Poor Mishy. He'll starve if I don't go home to feed him."

Don Gustavo threw his hands up into the air. "This is the worst excuse you've given us, Rosario. If that cat doesn't grow fat on field mice and lizards, then he deserves to starve. How can you forsake us for a cat?"

"It's not that, Grandfather. It's just that I keep thinking that Aníbal's there, or that he left me a message."

"Your husband is not a fool, child. He knows to come here looking for you."

"What if he's hurt? What if he needs me? It's been four days since the soldiers came; we can't hide forever, fearing that they'll come back."

Don Gustavo's eyes closed and he sighed deeply, leaning his head against the high back of the wheelchair.

"Grandfather, are you all right?" Rosario smoothed his forehead with the tips of her fingers.

The old man sighed again. "I wish I were not stuck in this thing."

Doña Providencia dropped the blanket she was folding and sat down opposite her husband.

"Remember that it's the will of God, Gustavo. The will of God!"

"Don't lecture me, woman. I know all about God's will, but I can still wish it weren't so. If I were a whole man, I could protect you and Rosario. Now that they've found us, there is no hiding from the soldiers. Like hungry wolves returning to the goat pen, they'll be back."

"Don't frighten the child with such nonsense, Gustavo. There's no reason for the soldiers to return. Everything will be just like it was, Rosario, you'll see. Aníbal will be here any day with a wonderful story to tell, and we'll go back to worrying about drought and floods."

Don Gustavo coughed and aimed a wad of saliva into the spittoon.

"It must be wonderful to have such faith, Provi, but surely, not even you could believe such foolishness."

"For you, everything I say is foolishness and nonsense. For all these years, my words are foolish. What makes you so wise, old man?"

"For heaven's sake, woman, don't shout!"

"What shall we do, Grandfather?"

"Not we, Rosario, you. There's not much that your grandmother and I can do, but you, Rosario, you should go."

"Go?"

"Yes, leave Soledad. Perhaps even leave this country."

"Gustavo! No!"

Rosario laughed and shook her head. "Don't joke like that, Grandfather. I can't leave Soledad."

"I wouldn't joke about such a thing, child. And why can't you leave?"

"I can't leave you and Abuela."

"Soon this old woman and I will leave you; our separation will have to come a little sooner, that's all."

"Grandfather! I won't listen to this!"

"Don't think that because you have two good legs you can talk to me like that. Now, sit down."

Rosario slid into the chair next to Don Gustavo.

"How would Aníbal find me?" she asked in a soft voice.

"He'll find you. You'll let us know where you are and we'll send him to you."

"This is a terrible idea, Gustavo. Rosario would be just as safe here as anyplace else."

"We can't take that chance, Provi. Things have become ugly and her husband is not here to protect her. She could go north. I've always regretted not having gone north."

"No! Rosario alone? That's impossible! Where would she go? Who would care for her? People die trying to get there." Suddenly her eyes glittered with tears. "Old man, you are babbling. Don't listen to him, Rosario. He's lost his mind!"

"Old woman! Be quiet! People die everyday. What does dying have to do with anything?"

"It's impossible to talk to you."

"For God's sake, Provi, go make us something to eat."

Doña Providencia jumped out of her chair and faced him with her hands on her hips and the vein above her eye throbbing. She opened her mouth wide, as if she were a volcano about to erupt, but no sound emerged. Silence hung between them as the fine veils of dust that drifted through the sun's rays, sparkling for a moment, faded in the shadow. The old woman's hands fell to her side; she looked older than Rosario had ever seen her.

"Yes, I think I will make something for us to eat; later we can talk about what should be done."

Squaring her shoulders, Doña Providencia walked to the cupboard where the vegetables were stored. She picked out what she needed for the stew and reached for her sharpest knife to peel the tough vegetable skins.

"Rosario can go with the American," she said suddenly.

"What's that, Provi? For heaven's sake, stop muttering! What did you say?"

"There is a rumor that Don Francisco's American wife is leaving. Maybe Rosario can go with her. At least she would not be alone, and she would have the protection of someone rich and powerful."

"How have you managed to hear a rumor? You haven't been out since the soldiers came, except for church."

"I heard it in church."

"In church? When do you have time to gossip in church? Doesn't the priest keep you busy enough with prayers?"

"What would you know about prayer?"

"Is Doña Jennifer leaving Soledad for good, Abuela?"

The old woman shrugged her shoulders. "I don't know. All I know is that she is leaving."

"Bad business. Good women do not abandon their husbands."

"The rich aren't always bound by rules, Gustavo. Besides it's none of our business."

"Tomorrow I'll go ask Teresa Victoria if it's true."

"Oh, it's true, Rosario. Consuelo even told me that poor Francisco has to sleep alone."

Don Gustavo aimed at the spittoon and missed. "Provi, you were discussing such things in church?"

Doña Providencia glared at her husband.

"Abuela! How could Consuelo know such things?"

Doña Providencia chopped the tubers. "I don't know," she said, "we had little time to talk."

"Remember, Abuela, I told you how Doña Jennifer liked me. Maybe she would take me with her to care for the little girl. I would be earning some money as well, and when Aníbal comes home I'll surprise him."

Doña Providencia and her husband looked at each other and remained silent.

"What do you think, Abuelo?"

"I don't like it. Don Francisco might think you disloyal— traveling with his faithless wife."

"But at least he would know that his daughter was in good hands, Abuelo."

"Yes, that's true. Then I think you should go talk to Doña Jennifer right now, Rosario."

"But, Gustavo, why the rush? And look how ugly the sky is. What if Rosario goes out and it rains? She could get sick!"

"I have a bad feeling, Providencia. Bad. We have to let her go!"

Doña Providencia put down the knife, walked to the door and removed the crossbar.

"Your grandfather is right. I'm being foolish." She stood tall and straight with the crossbar at her side like a staff. "Hurry, Rosario, go! And take your shawl in case it rains. Ask Teresa Victoria to intercede for you, and for God's sake, be careful!"

* * *

When she arrived at Doña Gerntrudis's house, Rosario found the small back door locked. She rang the bell several times; the delicate melodies of the chimes sounded unusually harsh and strident, echoing against the stillness of the afternoon.

"Who's there?" Rosario heard the voice of the gardener through the heavy wood of the door.

"It's Rosario. Let me in!"

The door remained closed. Thinking that the old gardener had not heard her, Rosario called out again, "Let me in, Pepe. It's beginning to rain!"

The cover of a small opening used to verify the identity of a caller slid open.

"I'm sorry, Rosario. It's best that you go home!"

"What do you mean, go home? Let me in! I want to talk to Teresa."

"Teresa's not here; she left for Almeda to see her children."

"Then let me talk to Don Francisco. And hurry, Pepe, I'm getting wet!"

"I'm sorry, Rosario, I can't let you in."

"What?" Rosario threw her body against the door.

"Please be reasonable. Everyone knows that the soldiers are looking for Aníbal, too. How can I allow the wife of a fugitive enter this house? People would say it's because we were sympathizers! Then what would happen when the soldiers returned?"

"Pepe Torres! I'm not the wife of a fugitive, I'm Rosario! You know me!"

"Rosario is the wife of a fugitive!"

"How can you say such a thing?"

"I'm only repeating what I've heard."

"Who would say that? Who?"

The old man looked down at the tips of his sandals and shook his head side to side.

"Please, Pepe. I must talk to Don Francisco."

"I'm sorry, Rosario." The gardener closed the cover of the small window in the door.

"Pepe!"

Her voice echoed down the empty street; its shrill sound startled her. For a long time, Rosario stared at the locked door; twice she pushed against the thick mahogany before leaving.

She had not gone far when she heard loud voices in the direction of the plaza. Knowing that it would be wiser to return to her grandparent's house, Rosario decided to ignore the growing commotion. She turned the corner and started to climb the little hill when the door to Enrique's house opened and members of the boy's family filed out of the house, filling the narrow street. Rosario turned to investigate, but before she could get close enough to hear what was being said, Consuelo, Enrique's sister, screamed and ran in the direction of the plaza. Without hesitation, Rosario followed. A small group gathered in front of Don Rafael's elegant home that faced the plaza.

"What is it? What's the matter?" Rosario asked a young man standing at the edge of the growing crowd.

"One of Don Rafael's field hands found the bodies in a shallow grave by the side of the road."

"Bodies! Whose bodies?"

"I don't know. Don Rafael's grandson is missing and he's calling for workers to go see."

"Don Rafael's grandson? How did that happen?"

"You know how wild he is. When the soldiers came, he was with Rosalita, and he probably had to prove how much of a man he was. I heard that the soldiers just hit him over the head and threw him into a truck. They never asked who he was. Don Rafael will go crazy if one of the bodies in that grave is his grandson."

"Yes, I know, that boy is the man's whole life. What's wrong with Consuelo?"

"Someone called Enrique's family ... you know ... just in case. Did you know that he's also missing?"

"How about me? I haven't had word from Aníbal, and no one came to get me ... "

"Aníbal! What do we care about Aníbal?" Consuelo pushed her way through the crowd. "He's the reason my little brother's missing!"

"Consuelo! Please! How can you say such a thing?"

"Look at how we've suffered! Can you deny that it's all the fault of Aníbal and that man Jorge Vicente, his friend?"

"That's a lie! Tell her," Rosario yelled at the growing crowd, "tell her that she's wrong!"

People looked away.

"What's the matter with you people? It's me. Rosario!"

The field hand who had been talking to her, tapped her on the shoulder. "Señora," he said, "please, maybe it's best that you go home."

"If you knew who her husband was, you wouldn't talk to her!" Consuelo's voice was shrill.

Rosario crossed herself. "Tell me," she asked the field hand, "tell me where is this unholy place? I'll go and look for myself."

"You can't go there alone."

Rosario took his hand. "Tell me where it is!"

The drizzle in the air grew into a light, steady rain.

"In the south field, by the road. But it's too far for you to walk."

"And you can't ride with us, Rosario!" Consuelo spread open her arms in front of the truck that was to carry the workers and villagers to the south field. "We don't want you!"

"Leave her alone!"

"Look at that! Aníbal's not even cold in his grave and already she has another protector!"

"Don't listen to her," he said. "Come on there's room here."

Rosario shook her head. "No, thank you. You've been kind, but I don't—"

"Do you want to go, or not?"

"Yes, but—"

"Then come on." He pulled her up onto the truck. None of the other passengers complained.

It was a short distance, but the truck had to move slowly because of the road's muddy condition. Squeezed between the side of the truck and the field hand who had helped her, Rosario bowed her head to join the other women reciting prayers in rhythm to the truck's slipping and swaying in the mud, but the words stayed inside like a tiny bone lodged in her throat.

The rain stopped falling just as the truck pulled off the road; thin streaks of sunlight barely penetrated the mist——droplets captured the light, reflecting tiny rainbows.

Don Rafael's workers followed the field hand with shovels in their hands to the site of his discovery; the women were told to keep away, but all of them ignored that order. Rosario stood by the side of the truck; she had started to enter the field, but after approaching the site about halfway, she found she could go no further. Without realizing it, she had inched backwards until she pressed against the muddy fender of the truck. She saw hope in the eyes of those who pushed past her, but Rosario knew better. There was no doubt in her mind that this was the place; the odor of decomposing flesh seemed to bubble up through the puddles on the ground. Rosario felt a bitter, vile taste rise and burn her throat. She gagged and spit out the fluids filling her mouth, but the taste remained. Suddenly, she heard a scream; Rosario straightened up, took a deep breath and ran towards it. Even at that distance, she could see that Manolo and Carmen Rosa claimed the first body. Fixing her gaze on the retreating clouds, Rosario covered her mouth with her hands so that no one would hear the litany she chanted: "Thank God it's not Aníbal!"

She heard another scream, then another and another until none of them was separate from the other. All the sounds merged until it was like the howling of the wind through the forest, or the roar of the earth moving. Peering through the folds of the mist, she saw Don Rafael kneeling on the ground, his arms around the body of his grandson, Tito. It grew quiet; the boy's mother pushed through the crowd.

"Let me through!" she cried.

Rosario inched closer and could see and hear everything clearly.

The boy's mother pulled at the old man, but he would not release the body. "Give me my son!"

The woman beat the old man with her fists; he held on tighter. She turned to a group of Don Rafael's field hands. "Help me!"

The field hands looked at each other and shook their heads.

"Don't turn away!"

A man stepped forward; he was the field foreman. Diego took off his hat and bowed his head.

"I'll try, señora. Don Rafael might listen to me."

"Yes, you're right. He might listen to you. Hurry, Diego, please!"

The foreman knelt alongside Don Rafael and poked his shoulder, "Patrón? Patrón? It's me, Diego."

Don Rafael buried his face deeper in the boy's chest.

"Patrón, please listen to me! You must give the boy to his mother."

Several times the foreman repeated his plea, but Don Rafael ignored him, rocking back and forth on his knees, smoothing back his grandson's hair away from his bloated face. Before rising to his feet, Diego crossed himself. The small crowd watching him did the same, then dispersed as other discoveries were made, and new cries filled the field.

"Rosario!"

Through the noise and confusion, she thought she heard her name. Rosario held her breath and listened.

"Aníbal? Is that you?"

Rosario squinted through the mist and concentrated on shutting out all other sounds.

There! Across the road on the other side of the steep bend, a man waved his arms, but he was too short and too slender to be Aníbal. He waved his hat, "Rosario!"

"Eugenio!"

"Wait there!"

Rosario wiped away the tears from her cheeks with the back of her hand.

"Eugenio! Thank God! Thank God you're here!"

He was out of breath when he reached her.

"Rosario, I've been looking everywhere for you. Your grand-parents are frantic with worry. All they could tell me was that you had gone to see Don Francisco and that you never came back."

He stepped back from her, looked closely at her face noticing that her eyes were red from weeping.

"Are you all right?"

Rosario nodded.

"And what the hell are you doing here, Rosario? This is no place for you. No! Don't look over there! You don't want to see that!" Eugenio put his arm around her shoulder. "Come on, let's get out of here."

She pushed away. "No! I have to see if Aníbal—"

"You thought that he was there? Oh God, Rosario! Don't you know where he is? Didn't he tell you?"

Rosario shook her head.

"That's bad. But you know how much he's had on his mind lately."

"No I don't know."

Eugenio laughed nervously as if she had just told a joke. "Then you'll have to scold him when you see him, little sister. Chase him with rocks like you used to chase me!"

"I don't see anything funny, Eugenio. For God's sake, have respect for the dead!"

"I'm sorry." Eugenio coughed loudly into his hand. "I just wanted you to smile."

"There's nothing here to smile about."

"Aníbal's safe."

Rosario grabbed his arm and squeezed it tightly. "Are you sure?"

"Sure. You really didn't expect to find him there, did you?"

"I don't know what I expected to find, Eugenio, but I had to come. I haven't seen him for days; I didn't know if he was safe or rotting in the ground!"

"Rosario, don't talk like that"

"And why not? It's the truth! What'll I do, Eugenio? There are still some men missing. And Aníbal doesn't come home—"

Eugenio sighed, pulled her close to him as if to kiss her cheek and whispered in her ear. "Aníbal's alive; he's well!"

"You keep on saying that. How do you know?"

"Rosario, please, don't shout! Just take my word. I know." Eugenio looked around to make sure no one was near. "Come on. I get nervous standing here."

"And where should I be? At home? Do you think I would be less nervous there, waiting and praying? Take me to him, Eugenio."

"I would if I knew where he was now. All I can tell you is that he is safe away from here." Eugenio coughed again.

"Are you sick, Eugenio?"

"It's nothing, just this foul weather, that's all. What's important is that you should not stay in Soledad. Let me help you, Rosario, you must leave right away!"

"Leave Soledad!" Rosario whispered the words slowly as if afraid to part with them, and when at last they were spoken aloud, her eyes opened wide and her brow wrinkled in pain. "My grandfather said as much, but ... "

"Don Gustavo is a wise man. You must do as he says."

"I'm not going anywhere until you tell me what you know, Eugenio!"

"Hush! Lower your voice!" he took her by the arm.

"Too much is happening that I don't understand."

"I know, little sister, but there's no time to talk. We have to go. Now!"

Rosario pulled away from Eugenio's grip, and wrapped her shawl around her tightly, even though the sun's heat was dissolving the clouds.

"Am I the only one who doesn't understand?"

"There's no need for you to understand; I'm here. Now trust me. Until you find your husband, I'll make sure you're safe." He reached out to take her shoulder again.

"I can take care of myself!" she pushed him away.

"Don't be like that. I know that you can take care of yourself," he took her hand in his and held onto it tightly, "but against these soldiers you'll need help. Luckily, they don't know you're Aníbal's wife yet ... "

His voice faded, and his shoulders drooped; in seconds he seemed to age, and for a moment she thought that he had been changed into someone else. Rosario had to remind herself that this was Eugenio: the one who always had a bottle of something special hidden away, the one who dragged his guitar to the fields, and kept the neighbors awake with his bawdy songs. Rosario blinked her eyes several times; this did not even look like Eugenio, the one who collected jokes that made you wince and frown and laugh all at the same time.

"Eugenio?" She smoothed away the unfamiliar expression on his face with her fingers. "Eugenio, I'm afraid."

"I know, Rosarito. So am I."

"Some of the people have been saying terrible things about Aníbal and Jorge Vicente."

"I know."

"Yet I can't leave my grandparents."

"You must. They'll understand."

"But ... "

"I'll come back to Soledad after you're safe, and I promise to look after them."

Rosario cupped his face in her hands and stared deep into his eyes.

"Listen carefully to me, Eugenio. I'm tired of not knowing things, and, most of all, I'm tired of being told what I must do!"

"I thought you were going to kiss me, Rosario; instead you scold me! It's not my fault that you don't know things. I can't change the way things are."

Rosario sighed, dropped her hands to her side and turned her back to him.

"I don't like the way things are!"

At that moment the sun broke through the clouds; the vague outline of each mountain emerged sharp and distinct. Rosario watched as the snowy, jagged mountaintops seemed to ignite and glow with a white fire. Within seconds, each peak hurled shards of light into the dim valley below.

Without moving, Rosario watched the progress of the sunlight as it unfurled, snaking its way around the curves of the mountainside. She felt a rush of warm air advance toward her; frightened, she stepped back, following the retreat of the shadow. She turned to face Eugenio, and suddenly, sunlight streaked across her cheek;

she felt its sting. Her eyes filled with tears; sharp lines blurred, and bright colors ran into each other. She wiped her eyes; everything shifted into focus. The air was so clear that it hurt to look through it.

"It's for your own good! You must leave!"

"How do I know what's for my own good? How do you know?"

Rosario stroked her cheek; she felt her skin tingle beneath her fingers. The colors around her were so bright that she wondered why she never noticed them before.

Eugenio cleared his throat. "Men always know these things, Rosario. You know that. Anyhow, it's simple. The soldiers will do anything to get to Jorge Vicente; they'll use Aníbal to get to him, and they'll use you to get to Aníbal. See? Simple!"

"Are you sure?"

"Yes! Why are you so difficult?"

The last of the clouds gave way, and shards of fire pierced the muddy earth; Rosario felt its heat burn through her clothes. Streamers of mist rose from the wet ground, thin and arched, stretching toward the sun.

"I have to say goodbye to my grandparents; I won't go if I can't."

Eugenio cleared his throat once again and patted her shoulder. She stiffened slightly when he touched her.

"You know, Eugenio, just a little while ago, grandfather said something important."

"Rosario! We don't have time!"

"He said that he could see the way things were, but that he also had the right to wish they were different."

"Rosario!"

She ignored him. "Sometimes we have to do more than just wish, Eugenio ."

"I don't understand a word you're saying."

"And I can see the way things are, but I never even wished."

Eugenio sighed with impatience.

"And I've just realized something else, Eugenio."

"What now, Rosario?"

"Wishing is not enough; it's never enough."

"You know, Rosarito, I should just leave you here! Lucky for you my conscience won't let me. Go and say goodbye to your family. And you might as well pack a few things, but don't take long. We only have a couple of hours; I want to leave before nightfall."

"I hate the thought of nighttime coming so soon; the sun just came out."

"Nighttime comes every night; why should this night be different? What's the matter with you, Rosario?"

"I don't know."

"Well, you better get yourself straightened out. We have to travel tonight."

"Shouldn't we wait till morning? After all, how far can we travel before it gets dark?"

Eugenio nodded his head in the direction of the bodies on the ground, then stared at the narrow clouds disappearing at the horizon.

"No," he whispered, "we can't wait, and we won't stop once the sun sets."

"But we can't see in the dark."

"Neither can anyone else."

Eight

Zayas heard wonderful music, music that curled its way into his chest and expanded there, pushing against his heart and lungs until he shattered like a crystal goblet hurled against a stone wall. Pieces of him spun, twinkling against the darkness; it was the birth of a million stars. Darkness melted at his touch. Suddenly he was whole again, yet with radiant stars nested inside him; his flesh was transparent. Unafraid, he saw his blood rush through his veins, and flood his heart—so wonderful to watch—his heart yawned and filled the spaces of his chest with each breath. The light grew brighter and whiter with flecks of warm violet ...

Caught between his fingers, the light grew heavy and split into strips of color that streamed from him and arched through a colorless place. Suddenly, a giant hand appeared; it gathered the strands of colored lights and braided them into a multi-colored ball. Only for a moment did the ball of lights rest within the circle of giant fingers. With the flick of a wrist that spanned the Milky Way, the ball was hurled through space toward Zayas. It lit the distant darkness; the closer it got to him the smaller it grew as if it had left part of itself behind. It was the size of a baseball when it came to rest in the palm of his own hand. He stared at it in surprise, and when he looked up, the giant hand was gone. Falling to his knees, Zayas crossed himself; it had been a long time since he had felt that need.

Even as he prayed, the ball of lights and colors warmed his skin, releasing their varied perfume, one color at a time. Zayas closed his eyes and smeared the colors across his cheeks in thin, wavy streaks; he sighed with pleasure. The best color was the bright, clear blue that matched the color of his eyes ...

Zayas sat upright in his bed unsure of what it was that had

awakened him. He rubbed his eyes, yawned and peered into the semi-darkness, trying to see past the fuzzy outline of his bed. Shaking his head, he thought about the dream; it was so real. His knees shook when he got up and walked to the window, kicking clothing and newspapers out of his way. There where the light was brightest, he looked closely at his fingertips for signs of color.

It's a good thing, he thought, that dreams are the only thing in this world guaranteed private. The boys in the casino would never let him live it down if they knew that he had dreamed of painting his face like a woman. Like a woman! Zayas snorted. People could say many things about him—and he had no doubt that they probably did, but never, never could anyone say that he behaved like a woman!

Zayas ran his fingers over his face as he had done in the dream, and he felt his flesh quiver as if he had received an electric shock. Holding onto his stomach, he blamed the dream on something he had eaten the night before. Zayas rubbed his eyes and licked his lips; he was thirsty and hungry, and he wanted a smoke.

Moving first one pile of clothes, then another, he staggered around the room looking for cigarettes. There had to be, he decided, ten or fifteen opened packs of cigarettes lost somewhere in the apartment—probably beneath the dirty clothes. His friends were right; as much as he hated to admit it, for once they were right. He had to hire a maid.

Zayas kicked a pair of shoes out of his way. For the past six months since he had moved into the apartment, he had bragged about having enough money to hire a maid to wait on him hand and foot, but each time a woman came for the job, he found fault with her. After each interview, his friends poked each other in the ribs and laughed. They said that he was too much of a miser to hire a woman even now that he was rich and soon to be the casino manager. Zayas did not like being teased, but on this one issue he had remained silent and let them think what they wanted. The truth was that he did not like the idea of a woman in the apartment—not all the time—touching his clothes, looking through his mail, and most of all, listening to his private conversations.

The one thing he hated most about this new apartment was that no one in the building kept any secrets; the maids were fond of gathering by the service entrance to gossip about their employers. Every time he saw a group of them gather, he went out of his way to break them up. The maids all hated him, and although it was odd, Zayas felt good about that. How they would love to pull a maid of his into their group! Zayas did not want to think about it, but things in the apartment had gotten out of hand, and he would have to hire someone, anyone. After all, he thought, there was no law that said he had to keep her. The first peep out of her slanderous mouth, he would bounce her out the door and on to the street. Zayas grunted with satisfaction; he had made up his mind to hire the next woman to come for the job. It was as good as done.

Meanwhile, he stood wide-awake in the midst of the biggest mess he had ever seen, unable to find his cigarettes. He looked at his watch; it was too early to be up. He needed his rest more than his grumbling stomach needed food. Deciding that if the room were darker it would help him sleep, Zayas pulled at the drapes to close them completely. The heavy drapes kept parting, no matter what he did, and a thin streak of sunlight poked past the center opening. It looked like an arc of lightning at rest, stretching out across the king-sized bed, dividing it in half.

From the tangled sheets, he heard a soft moan. Zayas arched his eyebrow in surprise when the girl stirred and rolled onto her back, her arm falling against the empty pillow that still held the shape of his head; he had forgotten she was there. He grinned and headed for the bed.

Sunlight fell across her face; her mascara had shifted to the highest part of her cheekbone, staining the satin pillowcase. Bright like the flame of an acetylene torch, sunlight inched down the length of her nose and open mouth. The night before, he had been drawn to this woman because of the way her silver-blond hair shimmered in the low lights of the casino. With a twinge of disappointment, he noted that in the sunlight her hair had the luster of dirty aluminum. Shaking his head, he noticed her dark roots.

Zayas frowned; the sleeping girl also frowned and covered her face with her arm. On her wrist she wore a bracelet engraved with a fancy 'L' outlined in tiny diamonds. Lucy? Lydia? Lilly? He rubbed his moustache with the tip of his little finger. Linda? No, that was too common; her name was something classy.

Once again the girl moaned in her sleep, her lips formed the shapes of words hurled at some antagonist in her dream. Suddenly, she arched her back and stretched several times before rolling over onto her side. Her face dove into the shadow, and now the arc of sunlight outlined the large exposed breast, its dark nipple erect, quivering with each breath. Zayas reached for it, but just as he was about to cup the breast in his hand, someone started pounding at the back door. With a start, Zayas pulled his hand away and looked around the dim room.

"What the hell!"

He thought of ignoring the interruption, but the pounding at the door grew louder. With a sigh, Zayas pulled free a corner of the sheet and covered the woman.

"Later, baby," he said, patting her satin-covered buttocks. He grabbed his trousers from the floor and went to answer the door.

Even before he got.there, Zayas knew that it had to be a building employee. Building security was too strict for outsiders to enter unannounced. The only employee insolent enough to be so indiscreet was old Cheo, the security guard at the service entrance. Zayas made a fist, one of these days ...

His new life in this apartment would have been perfect without Cheo, who took too many liberties because they were both from the same hometown. Cheo was constantly giving him news about the old neighborhood. No matter what Zayas said or did, the man did not seem to understand that he had no interest in the old town, the old people, or the old times. At first Cheo had proven himself useful in many ways, and Zayas was polite to him; that, however, only seemed to encourage Cheo. Zayas felt obligated to complain to the building manager.

Nothing changed. The concierge had merely shrugged his shoulders and asked Zayas to be patient with the old man; good help was hard to find. Zayas insisted that something be done; the concierge nodded his head and flipped through the papers on his desk. Nothing enraged Zayas more than being ignored; he slammed his hand on the desk. One thing led to another; words simmered, then boiled over until the conversation ended in a shouting match with Zayas insisting that he would move. Neither the concierge, nor anyone else who heard about it, took the threat seriously; there was a two year wait for vacancies in all the desirable buildings.

In a lengthy, carefully worded letter, Zayas complained to the building owners, but they were obviously fond of the old man, calling him harmless and honest to a fault. Harmless! Harmless! Zayas crumpled their reply in his hand, rolled it into a ball and threw it across the room. Cheo was as harmless as a tarantula; sweet, little old men like him usually were. And who was really honest these days? Everyone had an angle; it was the first lesson that Zayas had ever learned, and he had learned it young.

Zayas yanked open the back door to his apartment. Bright sunlight reached into the dark interior and stung his eyes.

"What the hell is going on here, Cheo? Do you know what time it is?"

Cheo looked up at Zayas from beneath the shadow of his cap's brim and grinned.

"Sí, señor," he said, "it's almost one."

"And when are you going to learn to use the intercom and the doorbell?"

"So sorry, señor! I forgot."

Zayas did not like the way that the man said señor, as if the word were an insult. Damn the man, he thought, damn him and everyone else trying to put him down.

"So, what the hell do you want, Cheo? You know what I told you in the past about waking me before four in the afternoon!"

"Sí, señor, but this is an emergency!"

The man stared straight into his eyes; there was no humility in that stare, nor in the way that he stood with his hands on his hips, his chin held straight out. The man dared too much; Zayas controlled his temper.

"Emergency? What emergency? I see nothing wrong except for that bright sunlight shining in my eyes and the hot tiles burning my feet."

"It's your cousin, señor, Eugenio, the one from Soledad ... "

"I don't have a cousin."

"This is why I came myself, señor, because I remember him well."

"This is nonsense. I have no cousin! And I know nothing about Soledad."

"Oh, sí, señor, I remember him. Your aunt Naomi's second husband's child by his first wife, the one that died with the influenza when the boy was only six. And you must remember that Soledad was where your mother was born—"

"Don't bring my mother into this—"

Cheo crossed himself. "May she rest in peace along with all the angels in heaven, señor. I said only that she came from Soledad and her sister's name was Naomi. Your mother left Soledad very young; Naomi stayed, but she visited often. I remember how Naomi—she was such a saint—took in the boy and raised him like her own son. You can't have forgotten the time when they visited your father's house at the western edge of Don Emilio's sugar cane plantation. She was so beautiful with long, light brown hair and bright blue eyes—like your's!"

"Will you be quiet? You're giving me a headache! I said I don't have a cousin."

"Be careful, señor! It's a sin to deny one's own. Maybe Eugenio was not blood, but he is family, just the same!"

"Then you have a better memory than me."

"You were so young, but I remember, just like it was yesterday ... two little boys playing in the rows of cane, even after they were told not to. It was terrible: little Eugenio got bitten by a bad spider. I remember the beating you got because you were older and should have known better."

"Cheo, I'm sick of your stories."

"Forgive me for bringing up bad memories, but you can't deny your cousin, and especially not now."

"Why not now?"

"Because, señor, I'm sorry to tell you that he's dead!"

Zayas felt his body quiver. He shook his head; the news should mean nothing to him, not after all these years.

"Señor? Did you hear what I said?"

Zayas dug his fingertips into the smooth mahogany door frame and looked past Cheo at the twenty-three stories of cement balconies circling the west wing of the building like bracelets on a woman's arm. Even those areas used solely by the maids and workmen were decorated by potted palm trees and red hibiscus blossoms that nodded only slightly in the heavy, still air.

After so many years, each time the winds died, Zayas remembered standing at the edge of the cane plantation, where the air was always this heavy and this still, and mosquitoes rose from the ground, droning until the fields were full of their sound.

He remembered the time that he had led Eugenio into the sugar cane field hoping to lose an unwanted playmate. It had been so easy; Eugenio was so trusting. Zayas, however, enjoyed his freedom for only the brief minutes that it took him to run through ten rows of cane. The younger boy's scream had crackled through the heavy stillness, yet Zayas had been convinced that Eugenio cried only to get attention. Zayas ignored Eugenio's cry for help. He was already out of the field when Zayas heard the words "araña, araña" and he realized what had happened. Just the memory of it made him shiver; he hated spiders.

No, he had never forgotten, although he tried. With his fist, Zayas punched the door jamb.

"Damn," he shouted. "Damn!"

Could it be true? Had death now caught up with Eugenio, twenty years later? Cheo's voice droned at the perimeter of his memories. Once again Zayas felt the sharp jolts of fear and guilt that had spurred him on that August afternoon as he ran for help. Sweat running down his face, mosquitoes drawn to those trails dripping from his face and arms, he ran to get his father. Never had Zayas prayed as he did that day, "Please, God, don't let him die!"

Suddenly, the memory faded completely; Zayas blinked his eyes and looked at the old man as if he had just that moment appeared out of the sunlight and out of the heat.

"Señor? You remember now?"

"For God's sake, man! What do you want? You've delivered your message, now leave me alone!"

"What shall I tell her? She's been waiting for a long time."

"Who?"

"But I just told you! The woman waiting to see you downstairs."

"What woman? What are you talking about?"

"The one who brought you the news of your cousin's death."

"I don't want to see any woman! Send her away"

Cheo shuffled his feet and took off his cap. "She's been waiting a long time, señor."

"That's not my problem. Who told her to come here?"

Cheo shrugged his shoulders.

"Is she his wife?"

"I don't know."

"Probably looking for a handout. Send her away; I'm too sleepy to see anyone."

Cheo did not move. Jaw clenched and eyes glittering, he looked up at Zayas, but he did not speak.

Zayas enjoyed slamming the door in the man's face, but no sooner had the door settled into its frame than Zayas yanked it open again. He stared at the empty space above the old man's head.

"Cheo, she'll have to wait until I bathe and dress. I'll call down when I'm ready to see her. She's not in the lobby, is she?"

"No, she's waiting in the security office."

"Good."

Cheo turned to leave; Zayas stopped him. "Wait, I'll get some money so that you can buy her something to eat, in case she's hungry."

"That's not necessary, señor."

"What do you mean by 'That's not necessary, señor?' Eh?" Zayas mimicked the old man's speech.

Cheo put his cap on his head again; he squared his shoulders and thrust his jaw forward.

"We have already provided food for her. It was the least we could do."

"Who is we?"

"Those of us downstairs."

"So I suppose that every employee in the building knows she's here?"

"Not everyone, señor."

"What are you standing there for? Go on, get out."

Without a word, Cheo pivoted on his heel and marched away toward the service elevators.

The wide, cement balconies full of flowering plants in fancy containers were like highways leading into the clear open sky. Cheo walked through those corridors with such an easy familiarity that watching him, Zayas ground his back teeth until his jaw hurt.

Look at him! Damn it!, Zayas thought to himself. How insolent! The man acts as if he belonged here!"

* * *

With her eyes closed and her head leaning against the filing cabinets, the woman sat in a corner of the main security office.

"Thank goodness, you've come!" Cheo said when Zayas entered. "We just don't know what else to do for her. She keeps throwing up and she has terrible fever. Maybe the food didn't agree with her."

Zayas groaned. "The woman is sick?"

"Yes, señor, and we think you should call a doctor."

Zayas looked around at the people crowding into the office: two guards and three maids, all nodding solemnly in agreement.

"But why should I call a doctor?"

A maid gasped. "¡Ave María purísima!"

With a wave of his hand, Cheo silenced her.

"Señor, she is family! Your family."

"Cheo, I don't need you to tell me what my duties and responsibilities are. Since my mother died I have no family. I have no one, and I owe nothing to anyone. Is that clear?"

"Sí, señor. I meant no offense."

The maids inched out of the room; Zayas could hear one say to the other, "See, I told you so!"

For the first time, Zayas looked directly at the woman in the chair. Although it was hot in the room, her hands trembled, holding the shawl tightly beneath her chin, and her teeth chattered. He looked away quickly.

"I think it's dengue fever," Cheo whispered, and the two other guards in the room nodded in unison.

Zayas knew they were watching him; he walked over to where the woman was sitting. With her shawl over her head, he could see little of her face, only the point of her chin and the sharp curve of her cheek. She was extremely thin. The clothes she wore were dirty and torn in several places, and there was a stain on her shoulder that looked like dry blood. Zayas stepped away from her; she smelled of goats and rotting straw.

"Surely she has someplace to go," he whispered to Cheo.

"There are many places a country girl like her can go, señor. They would welcome her in the streets; pimps are always looking for new flesh to peddle."

"One of these days, Cheo ... "

"I didn't mean it, señor. Sometimes I say things without thinking. Forget that I said it, and we'll think only of her. Poor little thing! She needs help, señor."

"She needs a bath!"

Cheo nodded his head, "Yes, that's also true." He walked over to her and patted her on the shoulder. "Señora, this is Jose Zayas Torres, the man you are looking for."

When the woman looked up at him, her shawl fell away from her head. Her skin was pale; beads of perspiration outlined her eyes which were large and round and dark. There was no expression in those eyes, nor any quiver in her mouth. He had expected tears, hysteria, pleading, all those tricks that women used so well. Zayas shook his head; this was not normal. He shifted his weight, swaying side to side.

"She looks all right to me, Cheo."

The old man sighed.

"My wife and I would care for her, but there's no room at our place, and we have no money for a doctor."

"And I do, right? Every single time one of you needs a handout, you come to me. Do I look like a bank? And I have no guest room in my apartment for good reason."

"Please, señor, don't shout at this old man. He's been kind to me." Her voice was soft and low, yet it parted the waves of heat in the security office to reach him, clear as church bells ringing at noon.

Zayas whirled around to face her.

"I shout at whomever I please, señora. I don't take orders from beggars!"

As soon as he had spoken, he regretted his words; there was a gold light glowing in her eyes that suddenly reminded him of his dream earlier. He rolled his hands into fists. Ridiculous! All of it was simply ridiculous. Only country people believe in revelations.

"I look like a beggar, but I'm not. I came only because I promised Eugenio. He made me swear I would come. Now I will go, señor."

Rosario stood and held onto the back of the chair; Zayas noticed that she breathed heavily, as if her words had taken all her energy.

"Señora, please, you'll fall. Sit. Sit." Cheo rushed to help her.

"Look, Cheo, this is your problem. I have things to do." Careful not to look directly into her eyes, Zayas turned and started to go out the door.

Cheo rushed after him. "What about the maid's room in your apartment, señor? You wouldn't even know she was there."

"The maid's room? For heaven's sake, Cheo, you expect me to—"

"I heard that you were going to hire a maid. Anyone you hire would be a stranger, señor. This woman is family, señor Zayas, family."

"Maybe. Anyhow, that's what she says."

"It probably would only be a few days, señor. Just a few days. She told me she's looking for an American woman, her employer I think."

"Employer? She has an employer?" Zayas turned around and faced her. "Tell me, woman, what do you do for this employer?"

"I am the maid of a rich American."

"Speak up. I can't hear you!"

"Come back into the office, señor Zayas, she's too weak to shout."

Zayas reentered the office. "Now what was that you said about a rich American?"

"I am the maid of a rich American. I take care of her child too. They can't get along without me."

"Sure, and you work in the mansion looking like that!"

Rosario looked down at her clothes and covered a large rip in her skirt with her hand. "No, not looking like this."

"Well, what happened?" Zayas ignored Cheo's furious head shaking.

Rosario spread out her hands in front of her as if she would push away something awful, and looked up at Zayas. Her thick, black eyelashes were clumped together with huge tears. His mother had eyes like that, he thought, so large, so round, so innocent— alive with a light of their own. Zayas shivered. People used to say that it was the grace of God. When he was a child, he used to believe it, too.

Her mouth opened and closed; her lips shaped the words, but no sound emerged. With hands still shaking, she pulled her tattered shawl tightly across her chest.

Cheo helped her into the chair.

"Señor," he said, shaking his head and looking at the floor.

The security office grew quiet. The two other guards, the one seated at his desk and the one standing by the door, looked at each other then hurriedly looked away. The guard by the door turned abruptly on his heels and left; the remaining guard picked up a stack of papers and sorted them. The rustling of the papers falling into neat piles grew increasingly louder.

Zayas felt tired. "What's your name, woman?"

"Rosario. Rosario Alvarez Maldoñado."

"I've never heard that name before, but then Eugenio and I weren't close. And where do you come from?"

"From Soledad."

"Oh, yes, Soledad. I've never been there."

"Forgive me, señor, but you were there once. It was long, long ago when you were a small child and you must have forgotten."

"How do you know this? I don't know you!"

"Eugenio told me. At the time of your visit I was just an infant."

Zayas rubbed his forehead with the back of his hand; he perspired heavily. Somewhere a telephone rang; its persistent ring caused his eyelid to twitch.

"Doesn't anyone answer the telephone around here?"

The guard nodded at the quiet phone on his desk and shrugged.

Zayas covered his twitching eye with the palm of his hand. "How will you find your employer?"

"She said she was coming to the capital. I was to meet her here."

"This is a big place, not like Soledad. Where did she say she would be?"

"Eugenio knew where; he was going to take me to her. Then, so many things happened."

"What happened?"

"Please, señor, I can't talk about it; it was terrible, terrible."

"There, there, señora. Terrible things are best forgotten. Isn't that so, señor Zayas?"

The twitch in his eye grew stronger; Zayas reached for his cigarettes. "But Eugenio told you to come here, why didn't he just send you to your employer?"

He breathed the smoke in deeply and exhaled it slowly; smoke rushed into the still air at the center of the room and hung low in the room until a guard turned on the ceiling fan.

"I don't know. He said he would take care of everything ... Oh, poor Eugenio!" Rosario dabbed at the corners of her eyes with her torn and dirty shawl. "Just before he died, he gave me this to give to you. He said it once belonged to your mother and he wanted you to have it."

She reached into her skirt pocket and pulled out a tiny bundle. "Here, señor, this belongs to you. This is why I came. Eugenio said this was more important than anything else."

Zayas reached over, took the bundle and opened it. Inside was a a large, silver medal. It was his mother's patron saint, the Lady of the Miracles. The cigarette fell from his fingers and rolled across the floor; his hand shook. It had been twenty years since he had last seen the holy image. His mother had given it to Eugenio that awful August afternoon when the spider's poison still burned inside his body because she had believed in its power to protect the wearer from death. When Zayas saw his mother place the medal in Eugenio's hands, he tried to take it away. He cried and screamed and kicked. "It's mine!" His father dragged him out of the house and slapped him in front of everyone. "You nearly caused his death, Pepito; we owe him this. It's a debt we must pay."

"But Mamá promised it to me! It's the old witch's medal; she can't give it to him!"

"If Eugenio ever returns it to you, Pepito, then you will owe him whatever he asks. For now, the Lady of the Miracles is his!"

Twenty years later, his mother's medal was his at last; Zayas closed his fist over the tarnished medal. His eye stopped twitching and his hand grew steady as he caressed the graven image with his fingertips. Blessed by the famous rainmaker of Soledad just before

she disappeared into the great forest for the last time, it was the
only thing he owned that had belonged to his mother.

"Thank you for bringing this to me, señora," he said, trying to
control the quiver in his voice. Zayas slipped the medal into his
breast pocket. "Now, tell me, were you my cousin's wife?"

She looked up at him; her gaze was steady.

"No, señor, he was my brother."

For the first time he could look into her eyes without flinching.
The strange light on her face was gone; Zayas relaxed and patted
the bulk of the medal in his pocket. He thought he could feel
warmth radiate from it and spread over his chest.

"Eugenio had no younger sister."

"I was adopted."

"I see. Yes, that's possible; my aunt Naomi could never resist
an orphan."

"Do you have a husband?"

"No."

Zayas raised his eyebrows in surprise. "All country girls marry
young. What's wrong with you?"

Rosario looked at the floor and shook her head. "I don't know,
señor."

"Well, I just don't want any problems with some jealous husband or boyfriend."

"I have no one."

Cheo, who had been silent up till that moment, clucked his
tongue. "You are a virgin then?"

Rosario looked up at the old man in surprise. "What did you
ask?"

"For once Cheo is right in asking such a thing. It wouldn't be
proper for you to stay in my apartment, you know, unchaperoned.
I want no problems."

Even the security guard dropped his pretense of working; the
shuffling papers stopped.

Rosario covered her face with her hands; her voice was muffled.
"There will be no problem for you, señor. I am not a virgin."

"And I want no male visitors in my apartment."

"I understand," she whispered.

Cheo heaved a sigh of relief and smiled. "Then it's settled ...
"

"Quiet, Cheo. Nothing is settled until I say it is."

"Of course, señor Zayas. I talk too much, but it's my only
fault."

"Will you please be quiet!"

Rosario stood and walked over to where the two men stood near the door.

"Please, señor. I need little and all I ask is that you help me find Doña Jennifer. There cannot be too many rich Americans here. And she has bright red hair."

Zayas laughed. "All Americans are rich. And the women change their hair color so often, they themselves forget the real color. If that's all you know, how will you find her?"

"I don't know, but I will."

"And until then?"

"I'll work for someone else. I won't be a burden to you. I'll pay rent. I'll work for you."

Zayas scratched his moustache. "You're too sick to work."

"I'll be well soon. I'm strong."

"How soon is soon?"

"I don't know, I—"

"You don't know much, do you?"

Rosario bowed her head and whispered, "Sí, señor. That's true."

"And you'll need decent clothing. We can't have people see you like that."

"I'm a seamstress. All I need is a needle and thread, señor. Needle and thread, that's all."

"I thought you were a maid."

Rosario wiped her face with the edge of her shawl, smearing the dirt on her cheek; perspiration continued to pour. She held her breath for a few seconds and looked up at him.

For a moment, he thought he saw the light reappear in her eyes. He moved away from her.

"A person can learn to do many things, señor Zayas."

Zayas scratched his moustache again and thought of the condition of his apartment. "No doubt you've heard that I have an empty maid's room. You may stay in that room until you're well. I may even have work for you until you find your American with the red hair."

With the tip of her finger, Rosario wiped perspiration from her upper lip. "Thank you," she whispered. "Thank you! You are so kind."

Zayas ignored the faint snicker from the security guard at the desk. "Cheo, I have things to do. Here are the keys to the ser-

vice entrance to my apartment. Ask your wife if she will take this
woman to the maid's room and care for her until she's well."

"I will ask her, but she already has a job."

"It won't take up much of her time, and I'll pay her a little
something for her efforts."

Cheo's eyes opened wide. "Did you say that you'll pay?"

"Well, of course! I don't expect favors; besides, I'm sure that
the girl will pay me back when she is well."

The old man sighed. "Of course, señor. I'll ask my wife; I know
that she'll be happy to help."

"Well then, now it's settled." Zayas marched out of the office.

The guard at the desk got up, adjusted his belt, walked to the
doorway and watched until he saw Zayas disappear into the elevator. "He has a heart of gold, that one!" He spoke loudly so that
his voice would carry into the hallway where everyone could hear
him. "I'll find your wife, Cheo, you stay here with her."

Rosario heard everything, but it was as if their voices had retreated into a deep cave and she could not understand what was
being said. As the pain in her arms and legs grew stronger, even
focusing her eyes became difficult. The light in the room seemed
to fade and she was not sure, but she thought that someone had
helped her to her feet ... did she walk, or was she carried? She
felt dizzy and when she put out her hand to steady herself, Rosario
discovered that she was in a bed! It was not her own bed, and she
frowned. Why was she not in her own bed? Then she remembered
and wondered why she had forgotten the journey from Soledad
to the city. How could she have forgotten that long trip on foot,
the hiding by day, the cold at night, the sounds of guns firing—
their echoes carried by the mountains until they were swallowed
by the forest—the thirst, the fear of being recognized even when
they were far from home?

Rosario closed her eyes and tried to sleep, but although the bed
was comfortable, and although it was the first night in two weeks
that she did not have to fight the mosquitoes or the damp night
air, sleep was impossible. The pain in her elbows and in her knees
grew stronger and at the base of her skull, her muscles tightened so
violently that she felt as if she were being bludgeoned. She tried
to get out of bed to turn on the light and found that she could not
move; each effort brought only more pain. Have I been poisoned?
Was the whiskey bad? Or am I really sick? Dengue? Rosario knew
about dengue, but she had always been spared before ...

Rosario could not decide which was worse, lying in bed with her eyes open, or with her eyes closed. With her eyes open, shadows danced around the unfamiliar bed. Unable to focus her eyes, the shadows expanded and whirled about the room. Like ribbons tangled by the wind, Rosario watched the shadows weave themselves into massive knots, tight with no light escaping, yet pulsating as if they breathed. She flattened her body against the mattress of the hard bed. It's not real, she told herself, but the shadows still reached out for her. Rosario closed her eyes.

The moment her eyes closed, however, the bed seemed to rock violently from side to side, and up and down, spinning in one direction and then the other. Just when she thought she would lose the insides of her stomach, Rosario opened her eyes, and immediately closed them when she saw shadows hovering above her. They were so close, too close; if only there were more light in the room, more light.

"Turn on the light!" she screamed. "I need the light!"

Something cool and damp touched her face.

"Take it easy, Rosario. It's all right. You're safe."

"Who's there!" Rosario opened her eyes, but saw only indistinct shades of gray. "What if I'm dead!" she thought.

She heard a woman's voice as if from a great distance.

"It's just bad dreams from the fever, Rosario. You'll be all right."

"You'll be all right." Those had been Eugenio's words! The same, exact words he had used to convince her to follow his plan. All during their two week trip to the capital, he had repeated the story for her over and over again until she half-believed it herself. The lies he wanted her to tell left an awful taste in her mouth each time he had her rehearse them. Whenever he was not looking, however, Rosario would cross herself and whisper a silent prayer for forgiveness, but the bad taste in her mouth wouldn't go away. The night before, entering the city, he caught her crossing herself and they had argued.

"Who's going to believe you, if after every word you cross yourself? Don't be stupid, Rosario!"

"I just can't lie to people like that, Eugenio. I can't!"

"Yes, you can. Anyone can do it; it's easy."

"But it's a sin ... "

"If you talk to anyone, the soldiers might come for you! If you tell anyone the truth, you may cause Aníbal to die. Is that what you want? Do you want Aníbal dead?"

"No, Eugenio!" Rosario covered her ears. "No! How can you say such things to me? I won't listen!"

"I'm telling you the truth! You can't avoid hearing the truth by plugging your ears! Take your hands away."

Rosario looked down at the ground and remained silent; Eugenio shook her.

"You're not stupid, are you? You'll lie, won't you!"

"Yes, I'll lie. There, I said it. I shall lie! Just like you want!"

"Good!" Eugenio said and ripped her sleeve.

"No, Eugenio, that's my good blouse. Stop it!"

"I've explained it all to you a hundred times, Rosario! You have to look awful. People in the city aren't like us; they don't open their doors to strangers easily. You're going to have to make them feel sorry for you."

He ripped the fringe of her shawl and the edge of her skirt.

"There! That should be enough. We shouldn't overdo it. They're not stupid in the city."

"Isn't it enough that this man Zayas owes you a favor?"

"You are such an innocent, Rosario. I know what I'm doing, and you must do what I tell you. You've never been away from Soledad; you don't know how mean everyone is outside. Now drink this."

"That's whiskey; I've never had whiskey before, Eugenio. It'll make me sick!"

"That's the idea. You must be sick for the people in the city to feel sorry for you, but not so sick that they'll be afraid of you. Whiskey is just the thing."

"But so many lies, Eugenio!"

"All necessary, Rosario. Now drink!"

"Lying is a sin!"

Eugenio sighed an exaggerated sigh and took a long swallow from the bottle.

"Dying on purpose is also a sin. Have you forgotten the things we've seen? Rosario, please! I've explained it all so many times. Troops kill people who help the rebels, and the rebels kill the people who don't want to help them. Soon they'll be no one left to kill and I guess they'll have to kill each other. Someone has to be left alive when it's all over. I want it to be us."

"Don't talk so much about killing, Eugenio; I don't like it."

She took the bottle and drank. The whiskey tingled her mouth and throat like hot peppers. Rosario suppressed the urge to spit.

"And to think that Aníbal is mixed up in this mess. I thought he was smarter than that, Rosario."

Rosario shook her head. "It was the stranger; Jorge Vicente bewitched Aníbal."

"No, Rosario. There's no such thing as witches and spells; I want you to forget such nonsense—although if there were witches I'm sure Jorge Vicente would be one. Oh, it's true that he has power; I've felt it myself. Every time he opened his mouth, all of us stopped what we were doing to listen; and everything that he said seemed to be God's truth. Even stealing from Don Rafael and Doña Gertrudis did not bother me; they have so much that they wouldn't miss what we took anyway . . . but killing the two soldiers . . ."

Rosario crossed herself.

"You killed the two soldiers?"

Eugenio took another long drink from the bottle. "No, I had no part in that. I wouldn't do it."

"Who did it then?"

"I don't know. Someone else."

"Tell me who?"

"No, I can't. I told you, I don't know."

"I know that Jorge Vicente must have had a hand in it, but who else?"

"Rosario, please!"

Rosario pushed away the bottle of whiskey that Eugenio held out to her. "Not Aníbal! Aníbal wouldn't kill!"

Eugenio remained silent. He looked down and avoided her eyes. "I never said Aníbal's name."

"Tell me who then!"

"No!"

In a rage Rosario struck him with her fists. "Tell me," she screamed. "I want to know! I have to know!"

From deep within her fever's shadows, Rosario thought she heard echoes of her own voice. Suddenly Eugenio was gone, and in his place Rosario saw only shadows once again. City noises reached her from the street below; the alternating brightness of day and the shadows of night merged. Rosario felt lost. There were times when she thought that she was well, but whenever she tried to move, the pain in all her joints bound her to her bed. Just when Rosario thought that she could no longer endure the fever and the pain, she awoke one night to find that both were gone. Rosario felt vacant. It was strange not to feel pain, or the heat that pushed against her skin and forced its way outside her in streams of sweat. She rubbed her elbows from where the pain had seemed to radiate; all that she felt was the touch of her own fingers. Rosario sighed; she felt more alone than ever without the pain for company.

Her thoughts were interrupted by a loud door slam; Rosario clutched the bedcovers and pulled them up to her neck. There were a few minutes of silence followed by the sounds of shattering glass. Laughter, high pitched and unrestrained, like the call of a wild hawk, made Rosario shiver. She moved her head first one way, then the other, listening until it was impossible to stay awake, and she allowed her head to fall back against the thin pillow. She was not alone. Here there was a world past the shadows where people still laughed. When there was nothing left to listen to in the darkness; her eyelids closed and she slept.

For the first time in a long time, Rosario dreamed, and in that dream it was warm and a faint breeze licked at her cheeks. She was in her garden. Having been cleared of all its weeds, the ground was ready to receive seed. With one hand, she used a stick to poke a small hole, not too deep, and with the other, she placed the seed carefully in its bed. By rubbing a pinch of earth between her finger and letting the fine grains drift down, she covered each one. The sun's light grew hot; she felt its heat on her back as she knelt in the field. It was late afternoon; the sun had reached the crest of La Gata mountain. Breathless, she stared at the sky; the sharp peak had pierced the sun and held it up like an arm holding forth a torch, or perhaps it was a candle on a distant altar. Rosario held out her arms to the sun's light that reached beneath her sleeve to caress her arm. She smiled and knew that it was good. At that moment the corn sprouted, its leaves a virginal green, spread open like arms also eager for the sun's embrace. All around her the corn wriggled its way through the soil and grew, ankle high, knee high, to the height of her shoulders and beyond. Rosario crossed herself and clasped her hands to her breasts. God was great! The field was filled with corn for as far as she could see, even to the edge of the blazing altar in the sky. She had to tell Aníbal about the miracle, but when she opened her eyes, it was a woman's face that she saw and she realized that she was not home. Immediately, Rosario remembered what Eugenio had told her, and most important of all, what Eugenio had refused to tell her.

She looked at the two women who had entered the room. The taller one with her gray hair pulled back into a bun at the base of her neck was Tita. The other one whose hair was brown with only a few strands of gray and whose face was round and red, Rosario knew, was Moncha. Rosario did not know how she knew this, but she did, and she also knew that these were the women who had cared for her.

"Good morning," Tita said as she cranked open the windows to let in the morning light. "I see that you've slept well; there is still a smile on your face. It must have been a wonderful dream."

"What did you dream? Did you dream about numbers?" asked Moncha.

"Numbers?"

"Yes, numbers to play in the lottery," Moncha explained. "My sister's son had a dream in which he saw the numbers 466. Well, my sister played it for two weeks and would you believe that she won enough to pay her rent for two months!"

"That was lucky." Rosario agreed.

"So, did you dream about numbers?"

"No, not about numbers."

"Moncha, for heaven's sake! All you talk about is winning the lottery. Life is never that easy. Only hard work pays the rent."

Moncha ignored Tita. "Then you must have been dreaming about love. Why else would you wake up smiling—a young girl like you?"

"No, not about love, either. I don't remember what the dream was about; it was just a good dream. And I feel good, too."

Tita smiled; she had one gold tooth. "Maybe you'll eat breakfast today."

"Yes, I think I will; I feel hungry."

"Moncha, go downstairs and get the tray."

Moncha shook her head and stood up. Free of Moncha's weight, the bed swayed slightly and Rosario thought for a moment that the fever and its companion nausea were returning; she held tightly onto the sides of the mattress.

"I'm sorry, but I can't. I start work at eight-thirty today."

"Go ahead, Moncha. I'll do it then."

"I'll come back at lunchtime instead, Tita. And since you're feeling so much better, Rosario, I'll come with a huge lunch tray."

Moncha smiled again, her almond shaped brown eyes almost lost in folds of flesh.

"Thank you," Rosario said. "But I don't want to be a burden to you. Now that I'm better ... "

"Listen to the child, Tita. Burden! This should be the least of my burdens! Isn't that so, Tita?" Moncha laughed.

Moncha's laughter was a pretty sound, like high pitched church bells whose notes were clear, yet rich. Rosario returned her smile; there was something about Moncha's laughter that made her feel at home.

When her companion left, Tita shook her head. "That laugh of her's drives us all crazy! But Moncha has a heart of pure gold. Come now, can you get up? We should put fresh sheets on this bed and you must bathe."

Rosario was not sure she could stand, but with Tita's help, she did. "How far do I have to go to bathe?" she asked.

"Right here in your bathroom."

"My bathroom? Where are we?"

"In the maid's room of señor Zayas's apartment. Sit down in that chair until I finish stripping the bed."

"Does he have to come in here to use the bathroom?"

"No, silly. He has his own bathroom. This is for your use."

"Just me?"

Tita laughed. It was a loud, sharp sound, like a dog barking. "Yes! Just you! Don't you have bathrooms in Soledad?"

"Of course. But only the rich have so many."

"Well, señor Zayas is a rich man, but he was not always so fortunate. My husband knew his family when Zayas was just a boy. They were just as poor as we are; don't let all his fancy airs fool you. He's just like us. But then you must have known him from before. Aren't you a relative?"

Rosario did not answer. Eugenio had warned her. "Don't talk about Aníbal, or me, and especially not about Jorge Vicente. Act stupid; city people expect us to be stupid. Most important of all, avoid gossip; it could get you in trouble. All you have to do is wait for me to find Aníbal and bring him back. You must keep your mouth shut tight until then. Understand?"

Remembering Eugenio's words, Rosario looked at the floor. She knew that Tita waited for her reply. "Can I lie down, Tita?" It was all that she could think of to say.

"No! No! The bed has fresh linen now. Take a shower first. It'll make you feel better. Come on, I'll help you."

"That's kind of you, but ... "

"Don't argue. And don't tell me that you're shy; this isn't the first time I've helped someone wash. Come on, we don't have time for modesty. Take off your underclothes, they're filthy. Moncha has already washed and mended your other things. They're in the closet."

Rosario had never taken a warm shower before; the forceful jets of water startled her. "It's like a hard rain," she said. "Only this water is warm."

Tita laughed. "Now I know you're really from the country."

Rosario frowned. What did she mean by that? She had to be careful. As quickly as she could, she lathered her body and hair and rinsed herself clean. When she stepped out of the shower, the cool air struck her wet body and she shivered.

Tita handed her a towel; it was thick and soft.

When Rosario finished drying herself, she looked around the small bathroom. "Tita?"

"What's the matter, Rosario?" the older woman asked. She had gone into the bedroom to dust the furniture.

Rosario looked at her clothes on the floor. "I have nothing to wear."

"In the closet there is a robe. It belongs to Zayas, but he has so many that he won't miss it. Wear it until we can find you something else. You can get back into bed now. Are you feeling better?"

"Yes, thank you."

"Good. Now tell me, who's Aníbal?"

Wide-eyed, Rosario gasped and held onto the edge of the night table for support. "How do you know that name?"

"You screamed it in your sleep almost every day. He must be important, if you dreamed about him."

"I dream about many things and many people." Rosario looked down at the starched and ironed sheets.

"Do you have the gift of prophecy?"

"No, they are just dreams. Nothing more."

"Many country people have the gift, that's why Moncha asked about the numbers."

"I don't know anything about that."

"So, who is Aníbal?"

Rosario sighed; the woman was persistent. "He was someone I knew."

"From your hometown?"

Accented by the beating of her heart, she remembered Eugenio's warning. "Don't tell anyone anything, Rosario!" Rosario pretended to swoon; she made herself fall on the floor.

Tita dropped what she was doing to help Rosario onto the bed. Through half-closed eyes Rosario watched the woman straighten up the bathroom and tip-toe out of the small bedroom with the bundle of laundry in her hand.

"Don't tell anyone anything, Rosario!"

Engraved on the back of her eyelids, she could almost see Eugenio's worried face. Waiting for him to return with Aníbal was going to be difficult. Very difficult.

Rosario had only intended to keep her eyes closed in case Tita should decide to return, but in just minutes she drifted into a deep sleep. When she awakened, sunlight filled the room. It was a small room, able to hold only a bed, a bureau and a small chair, but it had three doors: one led to the tiny bathroom, one was the entrance and one was a closet door. Rosario giggled, three doors for just one bedroom! In the house that Aníbal had built for her, there was only one door, for the entire house only one door—two if you counted the one at the outhouse, but that was only half a door. Unlike the bare wooden floors of her own house, this floor was covered with a light blue tile that had tiny white flowers at its edges. There were also two large windows, one at the head of the bed and one on the wall near the foot of the bed. Through the opened, metal slats of the window, Rosario saw that the sky was a deep shade of turquoise unaccented by clouds, and suddenly she had a need to know if she could see the mountains that ringed Soledad.

The door opened just as she had swung her legs over the side of the bed.

"Wait, let me help you out of bed!"

Moncha rushed to help Rosario. "You must be careful not to do too much too soon. You're so weak that the dengue might come back, and it's always worse when it comes back. Do you want to spend another two weeks in bed?"

"Two weeks! Have I been here two full weeks?"

Rosario pushed away from Moncha's grasp and fell against the bed. "Two weeks ... "

"Why are you surprised? When my Elena came down with dengue, she was in bed for at least three."

Rosario looked past the metal jalousies at an oblong cloud that drifted by. Two weeks! Eugenio had promised her that in about a week or ten days at the latest, he and Aníbal would come for her. She knew that she should not ask, but the words filled her mouth and dropped from her lips before she could stop them. "Has anyone called or asked about me?"

Moncha's voice was sharp. "I would have to ask Cheo or Tita to be sure, but I think not. Anyhow, why should anyone ask about you? They told me that you said that you had no family."

Rosario stammered. "I thought maybe ... I thought that my employer ... Doña Jennifer ... ."

"Oh. Well, no, no one has come to inquire about you. That's true, they said you were looking for your American employer. But how would she know you were here?"

"I don't know, Moncha. I was just hoping ... I've been such a burden to you."

"You have been no such thing. And don't worry about finding that American; stay here. This is a good place to work, although it needs a strong, healthy woman to put it into order."

Rosario tilted her head. "Put it into order?"

"Yes," Moncha laughed. "You were too sick to notice it when you arrived. Had you been well, you might have run away, but it's lucky for you that it is the way it is. If it weren't, señor Zayas wouldn't need you, and jobs are hard to get. There is plenty of work here—that's for sure—and if you'll take my advice, you'll take your time doing it so he'll need you for a long time." Moncha threw back her head and laughed again.

Rosario found Moncha's laugh contagious. Although she did not know why, she laughed, too.

"Eat your lunch and I'll show you, but only if you promise that you won't let it scare you! And don't tell Tita! She wants to show you herself."

"If it's that bad, maybe you should show me now."

"Lunch first. You must build up your strength. You are going to need it."

"Moncha, how can I eat thinking about what you've said. Let me see it now. Anyhow, the coffee is too hot."

With a big grin on her face, Moncha threw open the bedroom door and held out a hand to help Rosario up from the bed. After satisfying herself that Rosario was steady on her feet, she led her into a hallway that also served as a laundry room. There were piles of dirty clothes everywhere. Rosario gasped.

"This is nothing, Rosario. Wait till you see the kitchen and the living room, but be quiet because Zayas is sleeping now."

Rosario whispered. "But it's noon; doesn't he work?"

"Of course, but he works at night. He's the manager of the biggest casino in the capital. Rich people go there and throw away fortunes in minutes. Oh! How I wish I could be around those crazy, rich people just to catch a little of what they throw away!"

Rosario did not want to insult Moncha by saying she did not believe what she heard, but her look of disbelief said it all.

"It's the truth, I swear! Huge plantations have been lost with the turn of a card! And diamonds as big as your fist have been used to buy chips that disappear faster than the ice cubes in their drinks. You should know how the rich are; after all, your employer is an American."

Rosario nodded her head. "It's just that I've never gotten used to such wealth."

Moncha sighed and nodded her head, too. "I wish I could get the chance to get used to having so much money. Señor Zayas did not seem to find it too hard; I wouldn't either."

"He must be rich. Look at all these things!"

Moncha kicked at a pile of shirts blocking their way. "Yes! Imagine having so much money that you don't have to worry about washing clothes. When they get dirty, you just throw them out!"

Rosario's eyes opened even wider. "Is that what he does?"

"That's what it looks like, doesn't it? Come on. The kitchen is straight ahead."

"What's this place?"

"This is where you will wash all these dirty things in that machine. I doubt that it's ever been used."

"Oh! But where do you hang them to dry?"

"That machine there dries them."

"A machine dries clothes?"

"Yes, yes. Come on. I'll show you later, or Tita will. Don't worry!"

The kitchen was just past the laundry. It was a large square room ringed with white cabinets. The counter tops were made of the same quarry tile that covered the floor. All the cabinet doors were open and their contents—pots, pans, dishes and glasses— either filled the sink, were stacked on the counter tops, or weighed down the small table in the corner. Rosario wrinkled her nose. A large, full and uncovered garbage can in the middle of the room filled the air with a stench that described its contents.

"Oh, my God! There is no place to walk!"

"Yes, and be careful where you step. There's broken glass right near where you're standing, and you're not wearing anything on your feet!"

Rosario held onto Moncha's arm as she stepped over the glass. The dining area and the living room were both covered with newspapers, beer cans, empty bottles of gin and glasses either half-full or smeared with the remains of their drained contents.

"Is it always like this?" Rosario asked.

Moncha shrugged her shoulders. "I had never been in here before you came. He only gave Tita the key to the service entrance to be able to look after you. Already he's complaining that she's held onto the key for too long, and he would be angry if he knew I had it. It's a good thing that you're feeling better." Moncha giggled. "We all suspected it was like this. In spite of all his fancy airs, we knew."

In the midst of the debris there were narrow paths where the pale green carpet was visible. The paths led from the front door to the kitchen and a wider fork led to a door that was closed.

"That's the bedroom," Moncha whispered. "I'd love to peek inside, but come on, let's go back. He's probably sleeping, and he's usually never alone."

"His wife sleeps late, too?"

"Not his wife, silly. The man isn't married. Do you think a wife would put up with this?"

"Oh!"

The two women retreated to the maid's room.

"Now you know why I bring you a tray from downstairs," Moncha said. "I don't think that even the rats will feed in that mess."

"Rats!"

"Don't worry! It's only a figure of speech; there aren't any rats. The building is constantly fumigated, and no one has complained of rats yet. I know for sure that there are roaches, though, because Sarita, the maid next door, told me. Her employers have already complained to the building manager, and he's told Zayas that he must clean up and allow the exterminator in here. He acted so insulted, and told the manager that he would use a private exterminator to get rid of the roaches that come to him from next door! The master of the house, Don Miguel, Sarita's employer, was so angry that his face turned red and he had trouble breathing. Sarita says that every night she must put down poison along the walls that separate the two apartments, and she swears that the fumes are killing her. So you see? Not only does he need you, but you would be doing all of us a service if you stayed to work."

"But this will take forever."

"That's good. Believe me, that's good. Now listen, he sleeps all day, so you must be quiet, but then he's gone all night. You can even have friends over, and he'll never know. It's a perfect situation!"

The minute that she reached her room, Rosario sank down on the bed. "It's too much for one woman, even an army of women!"

"Don't be foolish. You'll do it a little at a time. When you get your strength, back it won't seem so bad. I would start by eating my lunch; it's good. I made it myself, but by now the coffee is cold."

"It's fine, Moncha. I like my coffee cold."

"I'll ask Cheo to send in one of the building porters to remove that garbage before its odor suffocates you in your bed, or seeps into the next apartment. The rest of the work you must do yourself because señor Zayas doesn't want anyone in his apartment. He probably thinks that someone will steal his garbage. In any case, no one likes him enough to offer any help. And that's good for you, too. Think of it, he'll be dependent totally on you!"

"Why doesn't anyone like him, Moncha?"

"We have our own reasons; they don't have to be your reasons. Anyhow, except for the times you need money for food, or supplies, or your salary, you'll probably never see him. Just keep out of his way."

Moncha got up from the small chair and put it back into its corner. "That's all for now, Rosario, because now I have to go back to my own job downstairs. Don't forget, I'm sending up a porter, maybe two, to take out the garbage. They'll come to the service door in the laundry room. If they come to the front door, don't let them in. Those pirates have to be taught manners."

Moncha chuckled, then seeing the look on Rosario's face, she hastened to add, "Oh, they're not real pirates! That's just what I call them. You're so serious, Rosario. Why are you so serious?"

She picked up the empty tray. "Remember, I'll return tomorrow; Tita will bring you your dinner. And try to stay in bed for at least one more day. Tomorrow, I'll show you the rest of the building, and maybe, if you feel like taking a walk, I'll show you the market on Wednesday. OK?"

"Yes, Moncha. Until tomorrow."

Rosario tried to stay in bed, but she was restless, and she got up and walked to the window. In the distance she saw mountains that were so straight, and whose peaks were so sharp, like the fangs of a wild cat, that they had to be her mountains. She would never be lost as long as she could see the peaks that surround Soledad.

Two weeks. She had been away two weeks. Where in those mountains was Aníbal? And why hadn't he come to her? Her head started to ache; what if Eugenio had not found him? What if something had happened to Eugenio? To Aníbal? She wondered how long she would have to stay away from Soledad, before the people forgot the soldiers and stopped blaming her? It was unfair. Never, never in her life had she done something bad, yet people she had known her whole life had turned away from her, had slammed their doors in her face. Her hands started to shake. What if she could never return? What if she had to stay in this place for the rest of her life? If only Aníbal came back and told them it was a lie, then everything would be as before: tending her garden in the morning, lunch with her grandmother, evenings in the plaza listening to the music, and gossiping with her friends. Rosario crossed herself and said a prayer for Aníbal's return, and another prayer for the safety of her grandparents. She watched the sun's progress across the sky and decided that she would do as Moncha said: make señor Zayas dependent on her so that he would not send her away. This was where she had to be when Aníbal came for her, otherwise, he would never find her in the city. No matter how much work it took, no matter how difficult he became, señor Zayas would have no reason to complain about her work.

The sun was ready to slide into the sea behind the mountains. Like the torch in her dream, its light was gold. Rosario held her arms open. In a moment of magic, the sun's rays—now cool and gentle—reached out for her, and she was enveloped in a balloon of golden light that floated above the city and took her home. Rosario knew that if she were to open her eyes, she would find herself still in the maid's room, so she kept her eyes closed until the air grew chilly and she could no longer feel the caress of golden light.

Nine

With a sharp snap of her thumb on the lighter's wheel, Jennifer lit her fourth cigarette in two hours; Robert's plane was late. The man with the long moustache at the information counter gave her a blank stare when she returned to demand a reason for the delay.

"Nothing is ever on time in this country!" Jennifer hit the counter with her hand.

He raised one eyebrow slightly and shrugged his shoulders. "Sometimes we have to be patient, señora."

The man smiled, but it was not a smile as Jennifer understood smiles; it was simply a spreading of excess skin over yellowing teeth and nothing more.

His homily on patience was the last thing she wanted to hear. Jennifer shook her head; hair pins fell to the ground, and the red hair she had forced into a sophisticated French twist was free to curl at odd angles around her face. All that remained of that morning's efforts at the dressing table was a tangled knot at the base of her neck. Catching a reflection of herself in an airport shop window, Jennifer threw the half-smoked cigarette to the ground, crushed it with the ball of her sandaled foot, and yanked out the remaining hair pins. After a long search in her purse, she remembered having left her comb on the dressing table. The only remedy was to use her long, red fingernails to control her hair, which did not help at all. Locks of hair kept falling down over her forehead and sticking to her damp skin; puckering her lips, she aimed a long breath of air at the curls, but it was hopeless.

"Do what you want!" she said and shook her head. In seconds her entire head was covered in tight curls.

"I look like a maniac," she thought. "What'll Robert think when he sees me?"

166

Ever since childhood, Jennifer had always worried about what her brother, Robert, thought, until she met Francisco Ramírez Hernández at school, and married him in spite of her family's objections.

"Bobby already thinks I'm nuts; now I look the part."

Lighting another cigarette, Jennifer resumed pacing in front of the arrivals gate along with others who waited for Flight 967 from New York. The crowd grew restless; more people surrounded the information desk. The volume of their voices grew until even the static message of the loudspeaker was drowned out. The few who had heard the message rushed to the arrivals gate; others, seeing the sudden movement, followed. Flight 967 had landed.

Arriving passengers found an almost solid wall of people waiting at the gate; no one could get through without shoving and pushing. Airline employees arrived, yelling louder than everyone else and waving their arms in an attempt to move people away from the exit. Their efforts were useless.

Jennifer stood at the edge of the crowd. A year ago it had been the same when she arrived with Frank and Sally. Up until that day, she had never thought of herself as a woman easily frightened, yet the noise and the confusion had rattled her. All those people pressing in against her, the loud voices, the sudden tears followed by laughter, women kissing, babies crying, men kissing each other (Jennifer had been shocked by that), made her feel like a little girl on her first visit downtown. She remembered how tightly she had held onto Frank's arm until he asked her what was the matter. It was only a year ago; it seemed like ten.

Jennifer smiled when Robert appeared at the gate; even from a distance, there was no mistaking his long, thick and curly hair. Inherited from their father, red hair was one of four things they had in common, along with being tall and having the same greenish-brown eyes. In high school, where Robert had played basketball, his nickname was Stop Light. In all her twenty-seven years, Jennifer had never played sports, but that did not stop friends from calling her Stop Light Two. Jennifer chuckled; she hadn't thought of that nickname in years.

The effect of Robert's appearance on the waiting crowd was just what Jennifer expected, but Robert did not seem to notice that most of the people moved out of his way and looked up at him with their mouths wide open. Two men, one of them a photographer, jumped in Robert's path. Jennifer pushed people aside to get to her brother.

"Mr. Alexander, Mr. Alexander!" One man spoke English well, although heavily accented. "Welcome to our country. Is it true that you've come to look for a place for a new factory?"

Robert shook his head. "I'm flattered by all this attention," he said, "but I'm not here to open a new factory. I'm here on personal business ... nothing else."

The reporter repeated the question. Robert squared his shoulders and adjusted his tie, and was about to say something rude when he spotted Jenny trying to get to him.

"Sir, personal business means just that, personal!" He turned abruptly and pushed his way through the crowd. Unwilling to give up the interview, the two journalists followed him. The photographer quickly took a picture when Robert went to Jennifer and gave her a quick hug.

"Mr. Alexander! Mr. Alexander?"

With an exaggerated sigh, Robert turned and faced the reporter who issued a question with each breath that he took.

"Gentlemen, this is my sister (you'll note the family resemblance) and the reason for my trip is only family business. If I decide to build a factory here, you'll be the first to know. Now if you'll excuse us ... "

Robert arched his thick and bushy eyebrows until they resembled the letter 'm' on his forehead. When the men failed to withdraw, another change of expression flattened the 'm' until an almost straight line ran across his forehead; his green eyes glittered, and the muscle at the corner of his eye started to throb.

The reporter backed away nervously. "Of course, Mr. Alexander," he said.

"Hello, Jennifer," Robert said. His voice had a hoarse, thick quality that gave people the impression he had just been awakened from a deep sleep. "It's been a long time."

"Yes," she agreed. "I haven't seen you since graduation. You did not come to the wedding." As soon as she heard herself say those words, Jennifer bit her lip. She hadn't meant to get started on that sore point, not after all this time.

Robert frowned. "I thought you had stopped smoking, Jennifer."

"I did ... for a while."

"Well, you smell like an ashtray."

Jennifer shrugged. "I've been nervous lately."

"So I've heard. Do you have a car or do we look for a taxi?"

"Taxi. Don't you have to pick up your luggage first?"

"This is all I brought with me, Jenny." He held up a small suitcase. "I don't intend to stay here any longer than I have to, you know."

She led him to the waiting line of taxies. "I did not ask you to come, Bobby."

"Mom did. She's been on the phone day and night, crying and carrying on about you. I knew I'd never get any peace until I dropped everything I was doing and came down here."

"You know how overly dramatic Mom is."

They got into a cab, and Jenny gave the driver her address.

"Your Spanish is getting good, Jenny."

"I've had a lot of practice."

He smiled and covered her small, blue-white hand with his large freckled one. "I really came because I wanted to, Jenny."

She smiled up at him. "I know, Bobby. Thanks."

Robert cleared his throat and adjusted his tie. "I don't know how much I can help, though."

"Let's talk about it later, Bobby. For now, let me catch up on news from home. How's Susan?"

"Pregnant."

"Again? When did you have time to do that? From what I've heard, you never leave the office. Your work has become your leisure, your mistress."

Robert shrugged his shoulders, yanked off his tie and opened the top three buttons of his shirt. "Who told you a dirty lie like that?"

"Who else? Mom says that you're too busy to even visit her, but she's so proud of you. She sent me a clipping of an article in Fortune Magazine where your name appeared at least six times! Mom underlined each one."

It was hard to tell when Robert blushed; his face was always so ruddy. "Yeah. Things have gone well for me. How's the baby?"

"Sally's not a baby anymore. She's almost four, and, thank heaven, not as tall as I was at that age. Mom calls her an undeveloped peanut. Sally must take after her father's side of the family." Jennifer chuckled. "But she's smart. I think our side will take credit for that. Wait till you hear her speak Spanish!"

"Does she speak any English at all?"

"Of course she does, Robert. Don't be such a dope."

"You're the dope, coming down here."

"Don't fight with me, Bobby. Not now."

"You're right; it's just that the whole family is worried. There have been some reports in the papers, no extensive coverage, just a paragraph here and there, and you know how nervous Mom gets."

Jennifer sat straighter in her seat. "What have you heard? The papers here don't report much."

"I bet they don't. Look, how much further to your place? Why did you get a cab with no air conditioning?"

"Just a few more streets, Bobby."

"Have you been in touch with your husband?"

"He'll be here Tuesday."

"Tuesday! I did not want to have to wait that long. Why don't you call him and ask him to come in this weekend?"

"Can't call him."

"Why the hell not? I'll talk to him, if you want."

Jennifer sighed. "You don't understand, Robert. There aren't any phones there."

"What do you mean, no phones? In the whole town there isn't one phone?"

"That's right!"

"The man's a businessman, isn't he? How can he carry on business without a phone?"

Jennifer smiled. "You wouldn't last a day down here."

"You better believe it, Jenn. Even at the house we have two lines now."

"Business is that good?"

"Couldn't be better. The new Jenny Doll is going to be sold on the west coast this Christmas."

"A Jenny Doll? You named one for me?"

"Yeah."

"I can't wait to see one."

"When you and Sally come home, she can have a room full of them. For God's sake, how many more turns? Aren't we there yet?"

"In a few minutes, just around this corner."

"Thank God! I don't see how you take this heat!"

"Like everything else, grouch. You get used to it."

"Is that your building?"

"Yes. You sound surprised."

"It's not what I expected."

"You think that everyone lives in huts here?"

"How do I know? You tell me there's no phones ... "

"In Soledad there are no phones. This is the capital, plenty of phones here, although, they might not always work."

"Well, excuse me. I've never had to come here before, you know. And you keep hearing about all the poverty ... "

"Oh, there's poverty here, for sure. You'll see."

"Not me, I don't want to see any of that stuff; I'm not the curious type. I hope you have air conditioning!"

When the cab pulled up to the curb, Robert pulled open the door and jumped out, not waiting for the doorman to open the taxi door for him. Jennifer paid the driver and joined her brother in the lobby where everyone stared at him. Once again he appeared oblivious to the scrutiny he received. Francisco was like that too, she thought. He could walk stark naked down a crowded street with the dignity of a crown prince on the way to his coronation. Funny how she had never noticed that similarity between Frank and Bobby before. She had always thought of the two men as being completely opposite, worlds apart; it was what attracted her to her husband in the first place.

When Jennifer introduced Sally to her uncle, Sally shied away from him; Robert glared at Jennifer.

"What's the matter with her?"

"You're a stranger."

"I'm her uncle."

"You never came to visit us, Robert."

"Yeah, well ... after you walked out on Jimmy Kent ... "

"Not now, Robert." She rolled her eyes in Sally's direction. "Someone's listening."

Robert sighed. "Yeah, I guess you're right. I should've brought her a doll or something to break the ice."

With a little urging from Jennifer, Sally went to her uncle and held out her hand.

"What's this?" he asked. "You want to shake hands?"

Sally nodded solemnly.

"You making up for your own lack of formality with your daughter? I've never seen such a serious four year old."

"She takes after her father."

"She looks more like Dad; she has such pale green eyes. Pretty. And she has our hair."

Jennifer laughed. "I don't know if I'd call that a blessing. Anyhow, thank God it's darker than ours; it looks almost normal."

Robert scratched his beard and grinned. "I resent that, Jenn."

"Me, too. Just a minute, Bobby. I want you to meet her nanny."

"Her nanny? You certainly are living well!"

Jennifer laughed. "Yeah! Don't you love it?"

"You know how to live, Jenn. No one can take that away from you."

Jennifer called the nanny into the living room.

The young woman was smiling when she came into the room. But when she saw Robert, however, she stopped dead in her tracks and looked down at the floor.

"It's all right, Carmen Ada. This is my brother, Robert Alexander."

"Robert, this is Sally's nanny, Carmen Ada. She's wonderful with her."

"Hello, Carmen."

The baby-sitter bobbed her head and took Sally by the hand. "Mucho gusto, Don Robert. Bienvenido."

"What did she say, Jenn?"

"She's welcoming you, Robert."

"You let the help use your first name? My goodness how you've changed, Jenn. In Connecticut ... "

"This isn't Connecticut, Robert. They use first names here because it's friendly, but they use the word "Don" in front of it as a title of respect. I like it."

"You're going native, Jenn. Tell her whatever it is you're supposed to say that's friendly, polite and all that garbage. I don't want to be outdone in the social graces." Robert wiped his forehead with his handkerchief. "And for God's sake, Jenn, turn up the air conditioner."

Jennifer laughed out loud. "My brother thanks you for your welcome, Carmen Ada."

Carmen Ada looked up at the tall American, smiled and quickly lowered her gaze once again.

"She's shy, isn't she, Jenn?"

"Most of the women here are like that."

"Well, at last something I like!"

"You would."

"Where do I put this bag?"

Noticing the small suitcase that Robert held out, Carmen Ada asked if she should take it to the guest room.

"No, Carmen. My brother will carry his own bag."

Carmen Ada arched her thin eyebrow in surprise.

Jennifer pointed Robert in the direction of the guest room.

"Second door to the right, Bobby. You can go freshen up before dinner."

"Thanks, Jenny. I'll be right back."

"And hurry it up. I'm starved."

When Robert went into the guest room, Jennifer sat down on the sofa and took Sally on her lap.

"Now, little girl, tell Mommy what you've been doing all day."

Sally held out her hand and started counting on her fingers. "First I colored," she said, "but the yellow broke. Then we went to the park; I rode the swing."

"That's wonderful, Sally."

"Yes, I had ice cream, too."

Jennifer frowned. "Carmen Ada, I've asked you not to give her sweets."

"It was just a little, Doña Jennifer. It was so hot in the park and the ice cream was so good!"

"Well, just a little is all right, I suppose. Today is a special day. Sally, honey, you met your uncle today."

"He's got hair like us, Mommy." Sally patted her head.

Jennifer laughed. "Yes, honey. Just like ours. Are you hungry?"

The little girl shook her head.

"Has Sally had dinner, Carmen Ada?"

"No, Doña Jennifer. She hasn't been hungry. It must be the heat."

"It was probably the ice cream."

"I will give her a bath now. Maybe she'll eat later."

"I hope so. And no more sweets!"

"Sí, señora."

"My brother Robert and I will eat out."

Carmen Ada nodded her head, smiled and held out her hand to Sally. "Come on, princess. You can play with the bubbles in the tub."

Sally pushed away from her mother and ran into the bedroom; Jennifer laughed and shook her head.

"She really loves her bubble bath!"

"Sally is a good little girl, señora. So loving."

Jennifer walked up to the nanny and put her arm around her shoulders. "You're a sweetheart too, Carmen Ada."

The young girl blushed and looked down at the floor.

Jennifer patted her on the shoulder and went into her bathroom. She showered quickly, put on fresh clothing and combed her hair.

When she finished, she went into Sally's bathroom. The little girl was chin deep in a bubble bath.

"Don't let her stay in the bath too long, Carmen Ada."

"Sí, Doña Jennifer. Just a little while longer, she's having so much fun."

"Between the two of us, we spoil her, Carmen Ada."

"No, we can't spoil her; she's too good."

Watching her daughter play with the bubbles, Jennifer smiled. "She is an angel, isn't she?"

"Sí, señora, un angelito de Dios!"

"Don Robert and I will not be out late; he must be tired after his long trip. Did Isabel fix the guest room as I asked?"

"Yes, Doña Jennifer."

"Good. I can always depend on the two of you."

"Of course, Doña Jennifer."

"Goodnight, Carmen Ada. And Sally, honey, be a good girl while I'm out."

"Okay, Mommy."

Jennifer turned to leave; Carmen Ada dried her hands quickly and ran after her.

"Señora, wait!"

"What is it?"

"Please, Doña Jennifer, be careful tonight."

"Careful?"

"There was another bombing this morning," she whispered.

Jennifer glanced over to the tub where her daughter was still playing with bubbles, and she dragged Carmen Ada out of the bathroom.

"Another one? I did not hear anything, Carmen Ada."

"Yes, I heard. It was an American restaurant where tourists usually go."

"Oh my God! Was anyone hurt?"

"I don't know, Doña Jennifer, but I'll find out."

"Which restaurant, Carmen Ada, which? One near here?"

"No, señora, not one near here. But, please, be careful."

"Thank you for telling me about it. We'll be at the Golden Rooster."

"I hear that's a good place, Doña Jennifer. My friend Linda has a brother who used to work there."

The two women heard a knock at the bedroom door; wide eyed, they stared at each other until with a sigh of relief, Jennifer whispered, "My brother."

Robert opened the door. "Hello? So this is where you are. Are you ready, Jenn?"

"You look human now, Bobby. Yes, I'm ready. Why don't you wait for me in the living room?"

"Sure."

"Have a good time, Doña Jennifer. And please," she lowered her voice, "be careful."

"I will. Thank you. Goodnight."

"I'll follow you to the door and make sure it's locked."

"No, that's not necessary. I'll be sure to lock it. Stay here with Sally." Carmen Ada nodded her head and returned to the bathroom.

Robert was waiting for her on the terrace. The sun had set and the city's lights were coming on, twinkling through the waves of heat that rose from the cement streets.

"It's a pretty view, isn't it, Bobby?"

"Yes, it is. What did the baby-sitter look so worried about, Jenn? Is it my being here?"

"Don't be silly! It's ... " Jennifer started to tell him about the latest bombing, then changed her mind. Carmen Ada's favorite pastime was gossip. As far as Jennifer knew, this was just another rumor. Rumors about bombings were common. Both Carmen Ada and the cleaning girl, Isabel, told her about a new bombing or a threat of a bombing daily, yet rarely was there anything confirmed in the newspaper. The lack of official confirmation did not seem to matter to Carmen Ada; she trusted the reports of her friends. As far as Jennifer herself knew, only two bombings had been reported, and they had been minor incidents attributed to malcontents, labor problems. Why disturb his first night here with what could be nothing more than a rumor? Robert looked at her, waiting.

"It's nothing, Bobby. It was just some building gossip. Let's go to dinner. I've picked out a special restaurant for you to try. It's even air-conditioned."

"Some tourist trap?"

"Of course not! This is a local place catering to upper crust natives. You'll love it."

"As long as they have steak!"

"For heaven's sake, Robert! Steak?"

"Steak!"

When they left the apartment, Jennifer locked the door and listened for the reassuring sound of the bolt sliding into place; she pushed against it once more to make sure the safety lock held. She turned to leave and saw Robert also trying the door lock.

"Better safe than sorry," he said and took her arm.

At the restaurant, they ate in silence, and when the coffee was served, Robert stretched out his long legs, tilted back his head and yawned.

"It's been a long day, Robert, maybe we should go back to the apartment instead of having coffee."

"No. It's best that we talk, Jenny. Let's get it all out in the open."

Jennifer took a deep breath and held it.

"We have to talk sooner or later, Jenn." He leaned forward in his chair. "What's been going on between you and your husband? What's wrong?"

"Nothing. Really, Bobby, nothing's wrong between us, except . . . "

"Except what? Mom said you wrote her that you were leaving him."

"Well, yes and no."

"Jenn, don't talk in circles. This is me, remember; you can tell me anything. Has he abused you? Your daughter?"

Jennifer held out her hands in front of her and waved them in the air.

"Oh, no, Robert, nothing like that. Nothing like that, believe me!"

Robert rubbed his temples; he looked relieved. "Then what?"

"It's that place. Soledad."

"But you must have known that living in the middle of the country was going to be primitive. You should have stayed in Connecticut where you belong."

"No, Bobby. You have it all wrong; it was nothing like that. The place was beautiful, and the people were friendly enough."

"So, what's the problem."

Jennifer reached for a cigarette; Robert frowned.

"Do you have to?"

Jennifer sucked in the sides of her cheeks and squared her jaw. "Yes."

She fumbled with the pack of cigarettes, and her hands shook so badly she couldn't light a match. Robert took the matches from her and lit her cigarette; Jennifer inhaled the smoke deeply.

"Thanks," she said. "The problem did not start with Francisco, he's a good husband and a wonderful father. The problem did not even start when I met his mother, and, let me tell you, Robert, that woman has all kinds of problems. She definitely needs a shrink! I think that even Dr. Rivers would have his hands full with her. I could have handled it though, in time, but everything went wrong when the soldiers came."

"What soldiers? When?"

"Don't interrupt, Bobby. Let me tell it my way."

"Go right ahead; we have all night." Robert sat back in his chair, raised his glass to his lips and found it empty. "Waiter!"

Jennifer crushed the cigarette. "Okay," she said, "this is what happened."

Robert did not interrupt her once; with his hands folded in front of him, he listened to her story about the trucks full of soldiers, the search for the terrorists, the finding of the mass grave. At the end he drained his drink, rubbed his forehead, and shook his head.

"That's a horror story, Jenn," he said. "No wonder you're a nervous wreck; you've been through a lot."

"Frank, keeps telling me not to worry, that the soldiers would never bother us because we're rich, and he has powerful friends who protect us, but ... "

"But?"

"How can I live in a place like that. You did not hear those women crying, you did not see the bodies, and that smell, Robert! The smell! I'll never forget that!" Jennifer brushed away the tears that started to roll down her face.

"Several of the dead boys couldn't have been more than fourteen. Fourteen! At home they chew gum, hang out and chase girls. Here soldiers pull them out of their houses and shoot them!" Jennifer shuddered. "I don't want my child growing up in a place like that, a place where you die because you don't have rich and powerful friends to protect you. And ... "

"Yes?"

"I feel guilty that my family is safe and those others died. I want to go home, Robert."

"Your home is with your husband now, Jenn. You say he's a good man ... "

"But it's a terrible place. After it happened, I couldn't sleep nights and during the day, I was alone all the time. There was no one I could talk to, not even Francisco, who spent all his time in the fields doing—God knows what he was doing—and I don't care. All I could think of was that I was going to end up like Doña

Gertrudis, his mother, locked up in some dark room afraid to come out. I just couldn't stay."

"That's rough!"

"Yeah. I have to go home."

"That's no problem, Jenn, if that's what you really want." Robert covered her trembling hand with his own. "Pack your things, and we'll take the first flight out that we can get."

"It's not that easy. Frank won't leave, and I understand his feelings. His mother is here, and she's not well. She needs him to care for her. I even told him to bring her with us, but she won't leave her bedroom, much less the country. Frank is just like her, stubborn. He says that he was born in that house, that he loves it and wants Sally to grow up there. The land is his inheritance; he won't give it up. All he talks about is what he can do to make improvements, the new houses for the workers, the new roads, but it's nothing to me. I keep seeing those bodies. I can't sleep; everything I eat gives me heartburn, and I cry all the time."

"Leave without him."

"I can't! You don't understand ... he says I can't take Sally."

"What?"

"Frank says that he won't give up his daughter. If I want to leave I can, but he won't let me take Sally. He knows damn well I won't leave her!"

"He can't do that! You're her mother; children always go with their mother. In any case, she's an American citizen, Jenn."

"She's also his child, and laws are different here. Especially if you're rich and have powerful friends. He even sent his lawyers to the apartment to talk to me, and they advised me not to try to leave."

"Let them try to stop us. We'll fight them from Connecticut. We'll see how far they get then!" Robert's fist struck the table; the glasses rattled, and one overturned. Waiters rushed to their table, but with a wave of his arm, Robert shooed them away.

"I don't even have a passport ... '

"Of course you do—"

"Listen to me, Bobby! He must have taken it from my bag. And he has people watching me!"

"Watching you! Isn't this getting a little out of hand, or is it just that you're becoming a little paranoid, Jenn?"

"No! They don't even try to hide it. They come to the apartment to make sure all is well, so they say. And I see them in the lobby."

"If all that is true, then how about your nanny and the maid?"

"I never thought about them like that, but I guess so; after all, he hired them, and he pays them."

"It's a good thing I came down then. When he gets here on Tuesday, we'll settle this. We'll discuss it like civilized people and we'll settle this once and for all. Don't worry, we'll do whatever it takes, no matter how ugly it gets. Don't forget that you have family too, and that he's not the only one with powerful friends. Frank'll know he's been in a fight!"

Jennifer reached for a cigarette from the half-empty pack on the table. "The worse part is that I still love him, Bobby." She pulled the unlit cigarette out of her mouth and threw it on the table. "I never thought that it would be like this!"

Robert scratched his beard and sighed.

"It's never easy, is it, Jenny? But on Tuesday we'll straighten everything out. Just another few days, Jenn. Just hang on for another few days."

Francisco never came to visit his wife and daughter on the Tuesday that he was expected, nor the following day either. On Thursday of that week, Jennifer noticed that the two men who took turns keeping an eye on her were no longer in the lobby of the building, the maid failed to come in as usual, and Carmen Ada did not return to the apartment following her day off.

The next morning, when Jennifer got up, she found Robert already up and dressed. He had prepared a pot of coffee; it smelled strong.

"This isn't like Carmen Ada not to come, not to call. Robert, I'm worried. What are you doing up so early, anyhow?"

"I couldn't sleep, and since I had run out of clean laundry, I got up to take care of it. I made some coffee. Here, have a cup."

Jennifer frowned as she poured the coffee. "Ugh! This is mud!"

"Put in a lot of milk, and forget about the coffee. Listen, Jenn, I'm really beginning to worry."

"Maybe Carmen Ada will come in today."

"Has she ever just not come in?"

"No."

"Well, there has to be a reason. And it's not just Carmen Ada either. Those men you pointed out in the lobby are no longer around, and how about the maid?"

"It's probably nothing, Robert. Don't worry. Maybe it's some holiday I don't know anything about."

"No. Something's wrong, Jennifer. People just don't take off like that. If it were a holiday, someone would've said something. Don't you have a phone number where you can call the two women?"

"They don't have phones, Bobby."

"Addresses?"

Jennifer shrugged her shoulders. "Francisco took care of hiring them. I never bothered with addresses and references."

"For heaven's sake, Jenn! That's damn irresponsible!"

"What's the difference, Robert? I can cook and take care of Sally by myself for a few days."

"That's not the point. Those women are staying away for a reason, and I'd like to know what that reason is."

"Of course, you're right. If only Francisco would come."

Jennifer walked over to the pantry, opened the door and busied herself rearranging the groceries.

"I can't help thinking that there's some connection there, Jenn. Something's going on, and I think we should find out what it is!"

"Lower your voice, Bobby. Don't wake Sally!"

"For heaven's sake, Jenn! Why aren't you worried?"

"Frank will come in a day or two, and he'll take care of whatever it is."

"What if he doesn't?"

"That's ridiculous, Bobby. Nothing's going to keep him away from his daughter. He probably just forgot to pay them or something."

"No! You're the one who is ridiculous, Jennifer. If they had not been paid, for sure they would've been up here demanding their money. What if something's happened to him? What if he can't come?"

Jennifer stopped searching through the cupboard and turned to face him.

"What are you saying?"

"I don't know what the hell I'm saying. It's just that I have an uneasy feeling in the pit of my guts, Jenn. I did not get to where I am today by ignoring my instincts. Something is terribly wrong here, and you're too busy looking through that closet to realize it."

"Well, we have to eat, don't we? I have to see what we have."

Robert pulled her away from the cupboard. "For God's sake, get away from that pantry! I can't believe that you're this stupid! Shit, Jennifer!"

Jennifer put down a box of cereal on the kitchen counter and reached for the pack of cigarettes near the ashtray. With one quick motion Robert hit the ashtray with the palm of his hand and sent it hurling across the room.

"Will you forget the damn cigarettes, Jennifer? Talk to me!"

Jennifer sucked in the sides of her cheeks, and pushed back her hair from her eyes. "That was a good ashtray," she said.

With his fists clenched at his sides, Robert stared at her. "No one gets me as mad as you do, Jenn."

She blinked her eyes slowly, smiled and walked past him into the living room.

"Come on," she said, the angle of her lips, the tilt of her head suddenly frozen into position, like a photograph. "The view from the terrace is so beautiful, especially in the morning."

She opened the sliding glass door and stepped outside. There was a slight breeze; the drops of mist on the terrace railing shimmied as it passed.

With his mouth hanging open, Robert stared at his sister, looking at the familiar lines of her face, yet finding an expression that was alien. He hesitated, following her onto the terrace where she faced the sunrise.

"Jennifer?"

She threw back her head and sighed deeply. "I haven't snapped, Bobby, and I'm not stupid. I know you're right, but I don't know what to do. So I keep busy doing mindless things like rearranging the pantry, because it's all I know how to do." She covered her face with her hands.

Robert put his arm around her shoulder. "That's not true, Jenn. You're a sharp woman; Mom and Dad did not spend all that tuition money for nothing. Stop putting yourself down." He pulled her hands away from her face and found her smiling.

"Bobby! That's the nicest thing you've said to me in years!"

"For crying out loud, Jenn! You never change. It's just like when we were kids. You soften me up, then you laugh at me. I fell for it again. I don't believe it, but I'm glad you're okay now."

Jennifer leaned on the terrace railing. The sun's rays were just reaching over the horizon and shining through the tallest buildings of the city. The morning mist would burn away soon and the mountains in the distance, once unveiled, would resume their position as the dominant focal point, but even as she stared at them, they seemed to retreat into the horizon. She took his hand.

"You're right, Bobby. Something must've happened, but I don't know how to find out what it is. Francisco always took care of everything ... and before him, Daddy did, or you. You always took care of things."

"I have reservations for tomorrow ... "

"Oh, Bobby, please! Cancel your reservation!"

"If I don't get back soon, I won't have a business to go home to."

"I guess you're right. I'm being selfish, and it's time I did for myself, Bobby. Leave if you have to; do what you have to. I'll be fine." Jennifer sighed deeply and clenched her jaw so that the tiny, blue veins in her throat grew.

"For heaven's sake! Cut it out. Stop playing the role of the martyr, Jenn; you're no good at it."

Jennifer smiled. "I mean it. It's time I grew up."

"Now you're being noble." Robert grinned. "I don't know which is worse."

With a sigh of exasperation, Jennifer stamped her foot. "What do you want from me, Bobby?"

"I want you to stop playing games, Jenny. I can't stay here and just wait. We have to start taking some action of our own!"

"What do you suggest?"

"First, we should go to the American Embassy and tell them that you lost the two passports. With luck they will replace them right away, and we can get the hell out of here."

"What about Frank? If something is wrong and he needs me—"

"First you want to leave him, then you want to know if he needs you. Make up your mind, Jenn."

"I can't, not until I find out what is going on here. Since no one has a telephone, we'll go in person."

"Where?"

"To the horse's mouth!"

"What?"

"We'll go to Soledad, stupid."

"But, Jenn, that's a four hour trip into the mountains."

"And worth every minute if we find out what's going on. If we leave now, we'll make it in time for a late lunch."

"We don't even have a car."

"We'll rent one."

"Great! I'll get dressed."

"I'll wake up Sally."

* * *

It was nine-thirty in the morning when they left, and by eleven the rented car was having problems with the steep incline of the road.

"Don't try to force it, Bobby. Just slow down."

"Slow down! Shit! We're almost standing still. I swear that we're going to have to get out and push."

Jennifer laughed. "It's all right; we'll just take longer to get there."

"At this rate, it'll be next month. Look at that! Even that truck just flew by. Maybe we are standing still!"

"Don't worry, Robert. Now you have more time to enjoy the scenery. It's beautiful here, you know. Do you want me to drive so that you can see it better?"

"No way! If I'm going to slide down hill backwards all the way to the capital, I want to be at the wheel."

Jennifer tried to cover her smile with her hand. "Wait till we make the return trip. We'll make up for any lost time."

"Oh, yeah? Why?"

"Well, look at the other lane."

"Oh my God! They really are sliding down to the capital. I hope they all have good brakes!"

"I hope that we do, too."

"Shit, Jenn! Where do you get that strange sense of humor?"

"Look, Robert. We can see the coast from here. There's an observation deck up ahead. Pull over."

There were no other cars on the observation deck. Jennifer took Sally by the hand. "I want you to hold my hand real tight. Understand?"

Sally nodded and pulled her mother to the edge of the deck, where a railing, badly rusting, held a faded sign.

"What's it say, Jenn?"

"It gives the name of this deck and it's elevation."

With both his hands on the railing, Robert looked down the steep drop.

"Careful, Bobby! The railing isn't secure."

Robert stepped back. "You think they would be more safety-conscious. Someone could get killed by going over the side."

"Someone already has."

"You're kidding!"

"No, I'm not." Jennifer stood as close to the railing as she dared. "Look, see those crosses?"

Robert nodded.

"They mark each death."

Robert counted them. "Eight! You mean that eight people have died here?"

Jennifer smiled. "People say that some jumped for the sake of a lost love."

"That's a crock of shit!"

"Oh, Mommy! I feel like a bird!" Sally flapped her free arm. "I think I can fly!"

Robert grabbed her arm and dragged her away from the viewing platform. Sally opened her mouth to cry, saw the look on her uncle's face and remained quiet.

"You're not a bird," he said, "and you can't fly! Come on. Let's get back to the car. You too, Jenny."

"In a minute, Bobby."

Jennifer stared at the horizon where the sky and the sea met in swirls of blue. The wind drew out the white clouds into thin ribbon that arched across the sky; streaks of white foam snaked across the sea.

"I've been away just five months, and I had already forgotten how beautiful it is," she whispered.

"We're wasting time, Jenn."

Slowly she allowed her gaze to travel inland over the many shades of green.

"This must be what people mean when they say that the world is at your feet. I feel the way the gods must've felt when they looked down from Mt. Olympus."

"Well Sally isn't a bird, and you're not a Greek goddess, so let's get moving."

"Don't you feel it, Bobby? How beautiful it is, how ... "

"Yeah, it would be a great place for a country villa or a resort, but we have business to take care of, Jenn. We'll admire the view some other time."

Jennifer sighed. "I guess you're right, as usual. Let's go."

"How much further?"

"Over that next mountain." Jennifer turned and walked to the car.

Robert whistled. "I hope this car can take it. And it looks like it's foggy up there."

"Those are clouds. It's the only place I can think of where I can reach out and touch a cloud."

"When it touches ground it's fog, plain, ordinary fog."

"No, Robert. It's a cloud, and when we get there, Sally and I are going to reach out and grab it. Right, Sally?"

Jennifer's daughter giggled and stretched her arm up over her head.

"No, honey, not now. When we reach La Gata."

Robert shook his head and got into the car. "It's fog," he told the little girl. "Just fog."

Sally giggled again.

Just fifteen miles from the observation deck, their car was stopped by a roadblock.

Firmly, yet politely, the soldiers told Jennifer and Robert to turn back. No one was allowed past that point. It was for their own safety, the soldiers explained; civilians could not enter. Over and over, Jennifer explained that they were merely trying to reach Soledad. The men at the roadblock shook their heads.

"Soledad has been evacuated for the protection of its inhabitants."

"The entire town?"

"Sí, señora. There are no civilians left in the area. Please turn around and go home."

Because Jennifer continued to protest, four soldiers ran to stand in front of the car, feet wide apart, their rifles ready. They were young. Had it not been for their military gear and the weapons they held, they might have been any group of high school boys out on a hike, but they did have weapons that were pointed at the three of them.

Sally pulled at her mother's sleeve. "Mommy?"

Jennifer heard the sound of a rifle bolt sliding into place.

"Bobby, let's go!"

Without another word, Robert put the car in reverse, made a U-turn and headed back to the city.

Three hours later, tired and hungry, they entered the lobby of Jennifer's building. The concierge handed them a large box that had been delivered in their absence. Jennifer recognized her husband's handwriting. Noticing how pale his sister looked, Robert took the box.

"Don't say a word," he said, "not a word until we're upstairs."

Jennifer held Sally's hand so tightly that the little girl complained. Lost in her thoughts, Jennifer never heard her.

The box contained several bankbooks, Jennifer's and Sally's passports, a large amount of cash, some jewelry, Francisco's will and a letter. Jennifer's hands shook as she tore open the envelope. She read it silently, over and over again, until Robert objected, and then she read it aloud for him. It had no date.

Dear Jennifer,

I was wrong for trying to keep you here. It was only because I love you and Sally so much that I behaved the way that I did. Forgive me. Something terrible has happened here in Soledad. Two days ago army troops arrived, hundreds of them. They forced the people from their homes, loaded them onto trucks at gunpoint and took them away. People did not have time to pack. Even now I can't believe that it happened. They took everyone, men and women, the children and the old people too. The soldiers told some of the people that it was for their own safety, that armed rebels were in the area, but I was told by the captain who ate at our house that it was because the people in Soledad provided aid to rebels and terrorists. The evacuation of the town was designed to ensure the end of that aid. I don't know what aid they were talking about. I certainly did not help any terrorist, and I don't know anyone who did. Maybe Don Rafael did—to get even for the death of his grandson. I don't know for sure. It seems like a terrible price for the whole town to pay for the crime of one old man. From the terrace in our bedroom, I could see dark smoke everywhere. I thought that there was fighting going on, but I found out later that the soldiers had burned the fields. I don't know what they've done with the livestock. The people of this town have lost everything. This morning I heard a dog barking somewhere in the town; it was so quiet without the people that I heard it clearly. Then I heard a shot, and everything was quiet again. Up until then, I had not shed one tear, but the silence was too great. I wonder which dog it was? When the soldiers came to our house, I told them that my mother could not get up from her bed. Last month she took to her bed, and I thought nothing of her complaints until her face took on the look of a skull. I knew even before the doctor said anything that it was only a matter of days. She has always wanted to die in this house, in her own bed. Out of respect for our family, the captain said that we could stay, but only for a short while—until she dies. I am sending you everything that you need to leave the country. Go back to Connecticut where you and Sally will be safe. I can't bear the thought of leaving this place. Every day the captain comes to inquire after my mother's health, and to remind me that

I have to evacuate as soon as she is buried. Other houses in the area have been blown up so that they will not provide shelter to anyone. If she knew what fate awaited this house, she would spit in the face of the angel of death. I've written to every important person I know in the capital, but no one has answered my letters. I will stay here as long as I can, Jennifer. Please understand. There are things that I must do. When my mother dies, and the house is destroyed, there will be nothing left for me here. I'll travel to Connecticut so that we can start over again. We can be a family again—if you'll have me. Please take care of yourself; you and Sally are all that I have left. With love, Francisco P.S. Kiss Sally for me.

Robert got up from the living room floor where they sat with the contents of the box scattered about them.

"I normally wouldn't say this, but I need a drink. I really do."

"Me too, Robert. Oh, God! I can't believe it. The whole town!"

"Here."

Jennifer held the glass with both hands and sipped the gin and tonic that sparkled in the low light of the apartment.

"That's some government they have here, Jennifer. My God! Those poor people!"

"I hadn't heard anything about it in the news reports."

"Did you expect them to publicize a thing like this?"

"No, but it seems that news of it got out anyhow: the baby-sitter, the maid and the men downstairs."

"The letter says that it happened only two days ago."

"Yes, but there's no date. It could've happened two weeks ago, for all we know."

Robert let the cold drink slide down his throat. "Yeah, that's true."

"Mommy, I'm finished with my bath! I'm hungry."

"Take care of her, Jennifer. I'll make plane reservations for the three of us."

"I don't know, Bobby ... "

"You don't know what? How to make a snack for the kid?"

"No, stupid. I don't know if I should leave."

"Have you taken leave of your senses? Of course you have to go!"

"But I can't just run away like a scared kid."

"I'm going to run like a scared kid. That's the smart thing to do. Besides, you were going to leave before."

"That was different ... "

"You bet your ass it's different. Before you had a choice and now you don't!"

"I can't leave him. Not now when he's in trouble and he needs me."

Robert ran over to where she stood in the doorway and grabbed her by the shoulders.

"He needs you to get the hell out of here so that he can take care of whatever it is that keeps him here."

"I can help him—"

"Like hell! You'll be in the way, Jenn, believe me. There's nothing that you can do. I think—"

"Mommy, I'm hungry!"

"And that's another reason. He needs to know that your daughter is safe. For once in your life, Jenn, do what's right."

"Mommy!"

"Just a minute, Sally!"

"I want milk!"

"Remember the sound of that army rifle being loaded, Jenn? Do you ever want to hear it again? Do you want to see it pointed at you, or at Sally?"

"No!" Jennifer turned to go into the kitchen. "You're right, Bobby. We'll pack right after we eat."

"And I'll go to the airline office. I want to do this in person."

"Why not use the phone?"

"I want us out of here as soon as possible, and I can be more convincing in person. They'll take good care of us, all right!"

"Convincing? But you don't even speak the language and their English usually is awful."

"Don't underestimate my linguistic abilities, Jenn. Besides, I have a powerful amount of vocabulary right here in my wallet." He patted his breast pocket and grinned broadly. "It's an international language."

Jennifer smiled faintly and shook her head. Frank and her brother were so much alike!

"I still say that you should use the phone, so that I can talk to them."

"I don't need you. Make me a sandwich; I'll eat it when I get back. This shouldn't take too long."

Robert never ate that sandwich. It stayed on the kitchen counter long after mold spilled out from between the stale pieces of bread.

Ten

Just one week after receiving the miraculous medal, Zayas was appointed permanent casino manager. Everyone had expected that the manager would be someone brought in from the outside. In fact, several of the dealers had made it clear that anyone from the outside was preferable to Zayas being in charge. Even before the new manager left the conference room, the news had spread through the sixteen floors of the hotel. After the initial shock, employees clustered around Zayas to congratulate him. Later they retired into small groups to comment on the news; tongues clicked, heads shook and shoulders shrugged. Who could explain such luck? Only Zayas, whose face never lost its smile, seemed to accept the turn of events with aplomb. He even knew exactly what the employees said about him when they stood in small groups, whispering, but Zayas didn't care. Their words were like ripples in an ocean. He was the manager.

Whenever he was alone, he reached for the medal, rubbed it and whispered his thanks, because he knew that this unexpected good fortune was due entirely to its magic. He knew this because whenever he held it in the palm of his hand, it glowed. Convinced that the forces guiding his destiny were great, and that nothing was beyond his reach, he dreamed of vast wealth and great power—perhaps public office. For the time being, however, he was happy with his own small office and a big raise in pay. After celebrating, he polished the medal and bought a heavy, gold chain so that he could wear his amulet always.

He paid off all his old debts and immediately took on new ones; a man in his position had to dress well. When he walked into the casino wearing his new diamond tie clip and matching cuff links, there was no mistaking those open-mouth stares and the long, admiring glances. Zayas pretended that he did not notice the stares, nor hear the whispers, but, in fact, he kept a mental tally.

Daily, he flaunted the cut of his new clothes and the flash of his gems; only the miraculous medal was kept hidden beneath the ruffles of his blue, silk shirt and tie. He never removed the medal except when he made love, and then he would place it in its pouch and hide it. He told himself this was because he did not want anyone to see it, that he was protecting it from the sudden assault of someone's evil eye. The truth was that he felt uneasy parting soft and fleshy thighs while the image of the Miraculous Virgin gleamed at the end of the chain around his neck. And so he hid it in its pouch, then buried the pouch under his clothes in the dresser, where it would not see all the things he did in bed.

During the weeks that followed his appointment, Zayas put in even longer hours at work; no detail was too small, no transaction unimportant. To the annoyance of the head housekeeper, Zayas decided to supervise the work done by the cleaning staff in the casino: the slot machines had to gleam, no speck of dust distorted the images reflected by the floor-to-ceiling mirrors in the entrance hallway, and the woodwork at the tables had to feel like silk to the touch. When the dealers reported for work, he inspected their attire and grooming with the same care that he inspected casino furnishings. Dealers complained, but never to his face. Zayas could tell by the expressions on their faces that they were a little frightened of him, and that pleased him. It was the way it should be; if the workers did not fear the boss, there was no respect. Once he called in the hotel manicurist for three of the dealers; he took her fee from their wages and no one failed inspection again.

His duties were many, but when his work was done, there was always a woman waiting for him. Everyone knew his type, and whenever a blond with large breasts came near the casino, dealers took bets on how long it took before Zayas rested between her thighs. Part of the wagering also included the exact length of time that his infatuation would last before he found another. "We always play with fresh decks, don't we?" It was his favorite joke; whenever it surfaced, everyone knew that his current companion was on her way out, and even heavier wagering took place in the employee lounge.

Zayas was so busy with his new duties that he spent little time at his apartment, often sleeping in the hotel to better supervise the maintenance staff. One early morning, however, he came into the apartment and Elsie, his current favorite, asked why the place was empty. Zayas yawned and took a good look; except for the large sofa, one chair, and two tables, the living room was indeed empty. Thinking for a moment that he had been robbed, he turned on all the lights and rushed to the telephone before realizing that the only thing missing was the litter. Zayas replaced the receiver on its cradle; what a joke it would have been had he called the police to report missing garbage! With a sheepish smile on his face, he ran his fingers over the ornate moulding that outlined the entrance to the dining room; it was not only clean, but polished as well. He could smell the lemon scent, and there were traces of oil still clinging to the mahogany.

"I hired a maid."

"A maid? You never mentioned a maid. What does she look like?" Elsie threw her purse on the sofa and crossed the living room to where he stood.

"I don't know. She's just a country girl, nothing like you."

Zayas took her hand and pulled her toward him. Elsie pushed him away, and with a toss of her head, walked to the center of the living room where she stood with her hands on her hips.

"I should meet this new maid and instruct her on how to do things. If you don't supervise these women, they get lazy, you know."

She ran her fingers across the surface of the coffee table; her fingernails clattered like castanets.

"I know," Zayas replied. He took off his tie and threw it over a lamp, tilting its loose shade.

"Why don't you buy some furniture? I always thought that a rich man like you would have many beautiful things. You need new end tables and lamps. And look at that ugly dining table!"

"I'm too busy looking at you!" Zayas came up behind Elsie, cupped her huge breasts in his hands and kissed her neck. "I do have beautiful things—right here in my hands."

Through the soft, clinging fabric of her dress, he felt the nipples of her breasts grow hard, and he kissed her again.

She made a sound that Zayas would never have been able to describe; it was a cross between a groan and a growl. It excited him more than the weight of her breasts in his hands. Suddenly, she was wriggling out of his grasp again.

"But this place ... "

"I don't want to talk about furniture now, Elsie. Let's go to bed!"

She looked over her shoulder at him, her hair falling over her face; he could see only part of her grin.

"You're driving me crazy!"

Elsie rubbed her buttocks against him. "I can do a lot for you, José." She turned to face him. Her mouth was open and her tongue, pointed and curved, flickered at the edge of her small, gold tooth at the side of her mouth. "If I could stay here with you, I would supervise your maid for you, and you wouldn't have to worry about anything. I know everything about fixing up a place. You'll see." Her voice was husky and low like a cat's warning.

"Sure," he said and dragged her into the bedroom.

The next day he got rid of Elsie as soon as he could; whenever any of his girls wanted to help him, he ended the affair. When she was gone, Zayas pulled on his robe to protect him from the chill produced by the new, more powerful air conditioner. He went out and stood in the middle of the living room where Elsie had stood the night before. Pivoting on his heels, he examined every inch of the room. Elsie had been right; he needed new furniture. He squinted his eyes and tried to imagine the living room redecorated in many different ways; the effort excited him almost as much as Elsie had the night before. This would be his next project; the next time he entertained, his guests would know that he was a man of means and good taste. He even had a maid!

For the first time since her arrival, Zayas went looking for his new maid. He found her in the laundry room surrounded by a large pile of wrinkled shirts and another of folded, ironed ones.

"Good morning," he said. "What is your name? I've forgotten."

Rosario answered without looking up from the cuff she ironed.

"I'm happy to see you recovered."

"Thank you."

"You've done a good job of cleaning up. I'm pleased with your work so far, Rosario."

She put down the iron and smiled. "Thank you, señor."

"Can you cook?"

Rosario nodded.

"Well then, make me a cup of coffee."

"We have no coffee, Don José."

Zayas raised an eyebrow. "Well, a glass of juice then."

"There is nothing."

"What are you talking about? I'm not a poor man, you know; we always have plenty of food." Zayas stalked into the kitchen and opened the refrigerator; it was empty. He yanked open the pantry door; not even dust rested on its shelves.

"For God's sake! What is this? Why is there nothing here? What have you been eating?"

"Moncha and Tita have been kind enough to bring me something to eat and I have a little money ... "

"No! No!" He waved his arms above his head. "You should have asked me for food money. I've been so busy that I've forgotten, that's all. Moncha and Tita should have reminded me. What will everyone say when they find out that my maid has to go begging throughout the building? Do you want me to be a laughingstock?"

With each sentence his voice grew louder and higher pitched, so that the final word rang out like a shot in the apartment.

Rosario's eyes opened wide and she stepped back into the laundry room. "I'm so sorry, Don José. I did not know—"

"Get out of there! How can I talk to you if you hide? Stop whatever you're doing right now. I'm going to give you money so that you can go to the market and fill these empty shelves. And I want to see this refrigerator bulging with food. Then you're going to pay back those two harpies for every bite of food that they have put in your mouth! Do you understand?"

"Yes, Don José. Right away."

"And be quick. I also want to you to prepare my lunch."

"Yes, yes!"

"And I take no starch in my shirts."

"No, no starch. I'll take care of everything, Don José."

"Good."

Zayas returned to his room, found his wallet and pulled out several large bills.

"Rosario!"

"Sí, Don José. I'm coming!"

"Here. Money for the market and payment to the two hags that took care of you. Make sure that you pay them when they are in a large group so that everyone knows I pay my obligations."

"As you say, Don José."

"And don't let them cheat you in the market!"

"No, Don José! I'll be careful."

"Money doesn't grow on trees, you know."

"No, of course not, Don José. I'll bring back plenty of change."

"See that you do!"

*   *   *

Believing that refrigerated leftovers would poison him, Zayas insisted that all his meals be prepared with fresh produce. To comply with his demands, every morning at seven Rosario left the apartment with her shopping basket on her arm to go to the central market. Moncha had taught her how to get through the tangle of traffic and streets, and Rosario quickly discovered that the city was not as big or as confusing as it appeared. When she was no longer afraid of getting lost, she began to experiment, taking a turn here and a crossing an unfamiliar street there, until she was as confident in the city's streets as she had been in Soledad.

The most indirect way to the market took her through streets paved with blue stone, and lined by trees clipped perfectly round on the sides and flat on top. Many of the houses were protected from the eyes of passing strangers by high, cement walls covered with bougainvillaea. At times, from behind those walls, Rosario heard the sounds of women busy with household chores, and through the tall, ornate wrought-iron gates, she often caught glimpses of children playing on walks paved with red tiles and lined with flowers. Whenever she approached the big house past the main intersection—the one that was painted pale pink—she always stopped to listen to canaries whose songs spilled over the cement walls and sparkled in the glare of the street. During the silent moments when the canaries rested, she heard the soft rush of water spilling from the upper tiers of the patio fountain into the lilly pool below. Although she could not see over the protective cement wall, Rosario imagined how it must look. Each time she walked by, she added to the mental picture by standing still and listening for as long as she could. There was always a guard standing in front of the huge, wrought-iron gate; his bulk could have easily filled half the space of the wide gate, and he always had a machete in his hand. Every time he saw her linger by the patio wall, he frowned. At first, his frown was enough to scare her away. In time, she learned to wait until he actually started to move toward her before she ran.

The quickest way to the market was the route that she liked the least. It led directly to the coast; following the curves of the shoreline, it shimmied past the wooden, unpainted shacks of the poorest part of the city, past the piers where half-dressed men loaded and unloaded the great ships, and ended at the central market. She took that route only when she was in a hurry. The stares of the workmen on the docks, the smell of rotting seaweed and fish, and the unfriendly glares of the women, who pulled their naked children out of her path, made Rosario shiver.

The most exciting route was through the commercial district. There was so much to see that Rosario made it a point to walk up the side of one street when she approached the market and back on the other. The next day, she chose another bustling street, up one side and then down the other, walking slowly and peering into the windows at the unlimited variety of merchandise. Not bold enough to enter the stores, she always stopped to watch the elegant women who did. Wearing dresses of fine linen and high-heeled shoes, the ladies left trails of perfume from their chauffeured cars to the entrances of the stores. Through the glass of the storefront window, Rosario could see shopkeepers drop everything, and with a wide smile and eyes glittering with anticipation, rush to their customers.

The central market, itself, however, was like nothing she had ever seen. Each merchant stood in front of his stall calling out his inventory, insisting that his was the freshest, the most varied, and the lowest priced. Some aggressive vendors habitually grabbed the arms of passing shoppers and tried to drag them inside. Frightened by the sudden yank on her arm the first time it happened to her, Rosario soon learned to put the shopkeeper in his place by the following the example of other women: a shout, a shove or a low-level curse, depending on her daring. The next step was to inspect the merchandise with a frown on her face (the frown was important so as not to look eager) and, if interested, begin haggling. Because she looked like a poor, country girl, the merchants only paid attention to her if the market was not busy. When maids and cooks known to be in the employ of the rich, the powerful and the famous came to shop, however, Rosario was always ignored. If she was in the process of haggling when they came in to shop, the merchant, eager to get rid of her and be able to wait on the more desirable customers, stopped haggling and settled for a lower price. Rosario would then grab her purchases and skip out of the vendor's stall with a broad smile.

With her food shopping finished, Rosario always walked past the largest fabric store in the city. Although her bundles were many and heavy, she would stand in the hot sun admiring the linens, the laces and the silks placed just outside the shop to lure customers inside. Whenever the store clerks approached to ask what she wanted, Rosario always shook her head and ran. One day, Rosario was admiring the weave and color of a bolt of linen, and the storekeeper himself sent word that he wished to speak with her.

Rosario followed the store clerk into the dimly lit shop cooled by
three huge ceiling fans. The owner introduced himself and asked
where she had bought her blouse. Fingering the tiny embroidered
flowers that circled the neck and ran down the front, she told him
that she had done the work herself. Whistling with admiration, the
shopkeeper called his wife to admire Rosario's work.

"Buy some material and make a blouse for me to sell," he said.
"If your work is always this good, there'll be a good profit for both
of us."

Suddenly, her bundles were not heavy and her arms no longer
ached. She stood up very straight, and in a loud, clear voice, asked
him how much she would make.

"First, let's see how good your work is, and how quickly it sells.
If it's as good as the one you're wearing ... " The man shrugged
his shoulders and smiled.

The next day Rosario went to the market with her own purse in
her pocket. She had earned extra money by sewing for the ladies
in the building, and she also had the money that Zayas paid her
the week before. She worried about spending it because she was
saving everything to help get started on the farm once Aníbal came
for her. Twice the night before, she had convinced herself not to do
it, but when she told Tita about the shopkeeper's offer, she urged
Rosario to go ahead.

"Everyone in the city knows Don Clemente's shop, and everyone knows that he is an honest man. He won't cheat you, Rosario!
Do it!"

Just one week after she bought the fabric, the needles, the thread
and a sharp pair of scissors, the blouse was finished. It hung in the
shop window only one day before it was sold, and Don Clemente
begged her to make another. With her share of the profits, she
was able to buy fabric for three more blouses, but she only bought
enough for one.

When the second blouse was sold just as quickly as the first,
Don Clemente urged her to quit her maid's job. The offer was
tempting: she would live and work in a room above the shop (she
could pay rent out of the profits) and he would give her a helper
to sew the blouses; all she had to do was embroider. She would
be a fool not to accept the offer, he told her, and deep inside,
Rosario knew that he was right. One thing stopped her; if she
left Don José's employ, how would Aníbal find her? Nothing Don
Clemente said could change her mind. Finally, they agreed that
he would supply her with the cut blouses; she would embroider,

leaving the construction of the garment to the women in the shop.

Everyday when she walked to the market, Rosario looked for Aníbal among the faces of the men she saw, hoping that he had come to the city looking for her. She thought about what it would be like seeing him and running into his arms, and she imagined the look on his face when she showed him her earnings. More than once, when she saw a man whose shoulders were broad, or whose hair curled around the light of the sun, or whose laughter, loud and deep, exploded from his soul, she stopped in mid-stride, and with her heart pounding, she would run after him, calling Aníbal's name. She was always disappointed.

As the months passed, Rosario grew restless inside the apartment. She found dozens of reasons to go out on the terraces: to dry the floor tiles when it rained, to water the plants, to wipe the city's dust from the sliding glass door. Each time she looked down at the crowds on the streets, she searched for Aníbal; she would know him even at that distance. During the day, whenever the doorman called on the intercom to say that there was someone to see her, Rosario ran to the door, patting her hair into place and smoothing her skirt. Always, it was a delivery man, or one of the decorators with a new fabric sample, or sketches for Zayas to approve. Nights that Zayas worked, the intercom never buzzed and the telephone never rang, but if by chance it did, the sound of it hurled her heart into the pit of her stomach, her hand trembled almost too much to hold the receiver, and her voice was barely able to squeak out, "Diga". Each time it was a stranger's voice asking for a stranger's name, and each time her disappointment and despair grew. It had been seven months since Eugenio had left her. Seven months! In her room, all her things were packed and ready, and she never tired of untying the bundle whenever she needed the combs or the ribbons that she bought for her hair.

Waiting for Aníbal, she watched the seasons change; spring had fled at the first blast of summer's heat and now it was past early autumn. Days grew short and cooler, although heat and humidity still forced their way into the folds of the city at midday and lingered until dusk. Afternoons, when there was no more room for heat, the skies darkened and cracked; rain, thunder and lightning spilled out.

During the day when the skies were overcast, many women wore shawls to keep the cold air away from their bones, and at night everyone wore something warm. Rosario smiled when she saw them bundled against the cold. Life in the mountains had

made her immune to the chilly air, but as winter approached, she
shivered. When the winds grew stronger, Rosario unpacked her
bundle to pull out her shawl. This time, however, she did not
repack her things.

*   *   *

With the help of professional, interior decorators, Zayas filled
his apartment with beautiful things: brass lamps, porcelain vases,
sets of leather bound books to fill an antique case and an imported,
crystal chandelier for the dining room. He occupied his days with
tradesmen who brought him samples of this and swatches of that,
who told him what wonderful taste he had, and who insisted that
his apartment would become a palace. Zayas spent more money
than he planned, but when the work was completed, and he dug
his toes into the deep, velvet pile of the cream-colored carpeting,
and watched the sunlight break up into rainbows as it struck the
brass and crystal dining room chandelier, he knew that his great
expense was worth it.

He wanted to show off the elegance of his home, but because
he had been so busy with his job, and with redecorating his home,
he had not had the time to get involved with any woman after
Elsie. He wanted to point out the glitter of the fine crystal, the
patina of the mahogany credenza, and the weave of the imported
fabric that covered the new sofa, but there was no one except for
Rosario, who said that everything was "nice" and "lovely," and
who moved through the apartment like a shadow, appearing out of
one obscure corner and vanishing into another. Her silent comings
and goings annoyed him; he joked about putting a bell around her
neck to warn him when she was near. To make matters worse,
Rosario never smiled when he made one of his jokes; that annoyed
him most of all. After several months, he grew accustomed to her
presence, and when she no longer startled him by popping out from
behind the drapes that she was cleaning, or by jumping up from
behind the sofa, he ignored her.

Zayas decided to throw a party for his friends: he invited everyone, even the head housekeeper at the hotel, who surprised him
by accepting the invitation. When she arrived, he noticed with
satisfaction that she could find no fault with the condition of his
apartment. More than once, he spotted her checking for dust along
the molding; when she found none, she left, visibly annoyed. The
party was a success, but Zayas was disappointed when he realized

that his guests were more interested in the size of the bar, and the skill of the bartender, than in appreciating the beauty of his home. These were his friends, though, and he was willing to forgive them until, he saw cigarette ashes on the imported fabric of the newly covered sofa, spilled drinks on the cream-colored rug and some- one's jacket tossed over a silk pleated lamp shade. Panic stricken, Zayas pretended to become ill and put an end to the party imme- diately. No one wanted to leave; there was so much food and drink still untouched. Desperate, Zayas filled their eager arms with bot- tles and packages of food, pretended to swoon and ordered Rosario to show them the door. From his bedroom, through a tiny crack in the door, Zayas watched them leave and heaved a sigh of relief when, at last, the apartment was empty.

Although he was not tired, he went to bed early. Lying in the center of the huge bed, he stretched out his arms and legs, trying to reach the sides with the tips of his fingers and toes. The bed was too big and too empty. He gathered the pillows that he had thrown on the floor and piled them on the bed around him. With some of the empty space filled by pillows, Zayas relaxed a little and thought. This was supposed to have been his finest hour, yet he felt sad. He was surprised at what he felt; he should feel anger. Anger was strength, rage was power, and sadness only led to weakness. Nevertheless, there was no mistaking the emotion; he cursed him- self for allowing it to sneak up on him. Zayas kicked the pillows away and realized what the answer was. It was simple, so simple that it had eluded him at first. He needed new friends. New and better friends, refined friends, cultured friends who knew how to appreciate fine things. Yes, that was his next project. Immediately his ill mood disappeared; he started planning and fell asleep.

The next morning, he got up early and yelled to Rosario to prepare his breakfast. When she did not answer, he went looking for her. He found her in the laundry room pulling out tablecloths from the washing machine, where he had put them the night before. He was horrified that she pulled them out of the machine, even as it agitated, to scrub them by hand in the huge sink.

"Rosario! What are you doing?"

She dropped the scrubboard. "Washing the tablecloths, Don José. These food and wine stains ... "

"The machine does that for you."

"It can't. Look, it just moves the water around. How can it clean this?" She held up a corner of the damask cloth stained with the colors of many fancy sauces.

"Give it a chance. The machine will clean everything."

"Yes," she said with a smile. It was the first time that Zayas had ever seen her smile. "It will clean, but not clean enough."

Zayas laughed out loud. "My mother used to say that! But then she did not have this wonderful machine. Just let it do its work, and you'll see. For all these months, you have been using the machine, haven't you?"

"Sometimes, when things aren't too dirty. You aren't pleased with my work?"

"Of course, I am. It's just that I don't want to see you working so hard. My mother's knuckle were always red and rough from scrubbing." Zayas took her hands in his. "See? Your hands are just like hers used to be. Here, let me show you how it works."

"Yes. Thank you." She pulled her hands free and hid them behind her back.

When he finished showing her the functions of all the dials, and how to separate the clothes and how much laundry powder to use, he closed the lid and started the new cycle.

"There, now you can do something else until it finishes. It's the efficient, modern way to do things."

"How do you know so much, Don José? I feel so stupid!"

"You're not stupid, Rosario. It's just that no one ever taught you. If you need to know anything else, just ask me."

"Yes," she smiled again, "I will. Thank you."

"Now make me a cup of coffee. And one for yourself too. We'll wait and see how well the machine works."

"Excuse me?"

"Sit down and have a cup with me."

"Maids don't sit down for coffee with their employers."

"That's true, but we'll have coffee anyhow. After all, you are more than my maid; you are family. Come on. Tell me about my cousin Eugenio."

Rosario paled.

Noticing her discomfort, Zayas remembered the circumstances of her arrival months before. "I mean, tell me about when you were children—things like that."

Rosario looked down at the floor. "Yes," she stammered. "I can tell you that."

Zayas sipped his coffee and listened. At first her sentences were short and clipped. He could tell that she was uncomfortable, but by the time they pulled the first load out of the machine—and it was spotless—Rosario told him funny stories about the people she knew. Despite them being strangers to him, Zayas felt as if he could go to Soledad and recognize them, strolling through the plaza. Rosario continued to talk, even as she folded and ironed the laundry. There was a lilt in her voice, and a peculiar warble to the sound of her laughter that Zayas had never heard before. She was really pretty, he decided.

*   *   *

Rosario took care of everything; the apartment was consistently immaculate. She had his meals ready when he wanted them—she was a wonderful cook—and she took such care of his wardrobe that he always looked as if he wore new clothes. Word of her expertise with needle and thread had spread beyond the building, even beyond the neighboring streets. From the beginning, Zayas had noticed little bundles of clothes that were not his on Rosario's worktable in the laundry room, and more than once Zayas saw her sitting at the table surrounded by fabrics and colored threads, her head bent over her work, so absorbed that she did not hear him.

At first, he had considered prohibiting her from sewing for others—people might think that he paid her too little. He thought about it and decided to allow her to continue; she would not ask him for a raise in pay if she had plenty of money of her own, and in any case, he admired her ambition. Zayas also admired her energy, until one day it struck him that too much ambition might not be in his interest.

The night before, he had overheard the wife of a hotel owner complain to her husband that her trusted maid had disappeared with several of her most valuable pieces of jewelry. Suddenly, everywhere he turned there were terrible stories of servants stealing from their employers. He had never considered suspecting Rosario, and although he liked and admired her, what did he know about this woman aside from what she chose to tell him over coffee? What if she deceived him? Zayas panicked. How could he have been such a fool as to trust someone he did not know? After a week of sleepless nights, he decided to test her by leaving large sums of money and valuable jewels out of the safe where she could take them—if that was her inclination. Zayas hid nearby, ready to pounce on her the minute that greed overcame her. When nothing was touched, he left them out for a week, until Rosario called his attention to it, and asked him to please put his valuables in the safe. Instead of feeling relieved, Zayas grew more concerned.

Rosario seemed too good to be true, and Zayas knew that no one was ever that good. He watched her more closely. He got in the habit of rising earlier than usual to monitor her: she was always cleaning, or cooking, or sewing at the kitchen table, or standing on one of the terraces looking west toward the mountains, her hands clasped at her breasts and lips moving slightly. Zayas was sure that she prayed, but what did she pray for? His wealth?

He doubled his efforts and timed her trips to the market; they were brief, her accounts accurate. When he purposely made errors in his sums, she always returned the extra money. Running out of ways to trap her in some indiscretion, he returned to the apartment at odd hours during the day and night. She was always there either dusting, sweeping, washing or caring for the many beautiful plants that he had bought—at great expense—to fill the terrace in the style of the great penthouses in the city. When not at the market, Rosario was always there, and she was always alone. Other maids invited friends, from time to time, to keep them company, or to lunch when they thought their employers would be away for the day, but there was never any sign that Rosario indulged in the practice. Zayas frowned and then he smiled. At last he had something to work on! It was unnatural to spend so much time alone. Only people who wanted to hide something avoided company.

He waited until she went to the market the next morning and searched her room. It was an easy room to search, being practically empty. When he found her savings, he thought that he had finally found her out, but with the money there was also a piece of paper with her sums—so much from her job with him, so much from sewing for the neighborhood ladies, and so much from the embroidery of blouses for a shop in the business district. Red-faced, Zayas put everything back in its place and left her room.

*   *   *

Everyday when the newspapers were delivered to the building, Rosario was the first of the maids to ride the elevator down to pick up a copy. When the vendor handed it to her, she did not look at the front page, pretending that what was written there held no interest for her. Often, the headlines spoke of atrocities committed by the many bands of rebels in the mountains. One morning, photographs on the front page of people dead, or dying, made even the men gasp. Crowding around the piles of newspapers, many of the building's employees took turns staring at those terrible pictures;

they all shook their heads, trembled with rage and turned away. It was not often that they paid much attention to Rosario, but knowing that she was from the mountains, they asked why people living outside the city were such savages.

Rosario thought of Soledad where people barely spoke above whispers so as not to frighten sheep or scare away songbirds, and she shook her head.

"We are not savages!" she said and surprised everyone, including herself, by her angry tone. "We believe in Christ and the Blessed Mother, just like everyone else!"

Oscar, the porter, held up the front page of the newspaper and waved it in front of her face, "How do you explain this?"

Rosario looked down at the floor; she wanted to say many things, but she bit the tip of her tongue to keep from speaking. This is exactly what Eugenio had warned about; she told the group that she knew nothing of politics or terrorists. It did not interest her.

"Oh, come on! You must know something," Oscar insisted. "If this madman, Jorge Vicente, were holding a knife to your throat, you would be interested!"

Jorge Vicente! The sound of his name peeled away her composure, and she trembled.

"You should not say such things," she said.

The men laughed. "It's too bad that the rebels aren't like Rosario," one said. "The fighting would've been over the first day!"

Rosario backed away from the group. "I'm not a rebel," she whispered, "just a maid! I clean, I cook and I sew; that's all I know."

"Women! They never know anything!" said the newspaper vendor.

Cheo joined in saying, "Thank God! Keep them stupid; it's better for us!"

The men guffawed; the women objected loudly. No one noticed that Rosario had walked away from the group and taken the elevator. She was in a hurry to get back to her room to read the newspaper before Zayas woke up; her eyes twitched with anticipation.

Back in the apartment, she read each page carefully, searching, yet not wanting to find the names of the people that she loved among the lists of the dead. At the end of each search, Rosario was not sure whether to feel relieved that no one she knew was reported killed or missing, or feel disappointed because she still knew nothing. After the first six weeks, she had decided that if it were not reported in the newspaper, then those she worried about were safe, at least for that day. Her grandmother had told her that bad news and death were the two things sure to find everyone. So after reading the news section, she sat back, always a bit more relaxed, and read the society pages.

During the past seven months she came to know the names of the debutantes; she followed their escapades, and was sometimes shocked, but mostly delighted by them. The more she read, the more she became fascinated by the antics and the scandals that touched their lives, their engagements, and their upcoming marriages. Lastly, she read the obituary pages, saying a quick prayer for the dead, although she did not know them. When she finished reading, she folded up the papers, carefully smoothing out the wrinkles so that Zayas would never know she had read them first. Each time she read the newspapers, Rosario felt as if she had just been visited by her grandmother. Often she pretended that it was Doña Providencia who told the stories to her, and as she was filled by the stories that she read, her need to go outside on one of the terraces was not as great. But when the cleaning, dusting and waxing were done, when the laundry was folded neatly and put away, and as soon as the dinner was prepared and the table set, she could not force herself to stay inside. When Zayas was home, she pretended that she had to clean the terrace.

She knew that he watched her. His increasingly strange behavior puzzled her. She worried that he might think she was being lazy on the job, and she worked even harder to prove to him that it was not so, but Zayas watched her even more. He no longer hid his actions and stood in the open, staring at her as she scrubbed the floors or peeled the vegetables, and if she went outside, he followed her to the terrace to watch her every movement. Rosario became afraid. At night she locked her bedroom door and pushed the large dresser in front of it, but Zayas made no attempt to approach her. He stopped coming to the kitchen for his morning coffee. To make things worse, he was home more often than before, coming in at odd hours. Once, thinking that she was alone in the apartment, she heard footsteps behind her and turned around to find Zayas, his skin pale and his eyes dark and burning, staring at her. She tuned her ear to his footsteps.

The day before, Rosario was polishing the silver when she felt that Zayas was in the room. Forcing herself to appear calm, she looked up and asked if he wanted something.

"How did you know?" he asked. "How did you know I was here?"

Rosario shrugged her shoulders. "I heard you come in, Don José."

"No, I was very quiet. How did you know?"

"I just knew," she said never raising her eyes from the small, silver spoon that she polished.

Zayas took two steps backwards. "I was quiet," he insisted, and without another word, turned and left the apartment.

That week there was an article in the newspaper about people who suddenly go mad. Rosario thought of the machete that she had found under Zayas's mattress, and although he was not as tall or as strong as Aníbal, with a machete as sharp as that one, he did not need much strength. She read and reread the column on madness, but it did not tell her enough. The next day at lunchtime, Rosario took the elevator down to the main floor where Tita was working. When Tita saw her, trembling and on the verge of tears, she made Rosario sit down and share a cup of coffee with her.

"Now, tell me, Rosario, what's wrong?"

When she confided her fears to Tita, the older woman merely laughed.

"That Zayas is strange, but I don't think he's crazy. I bet he's just trying to figure out if you're stealing from him. Many of these rich people get the idea in their heads, and they start creeping around, hoping to catch you."

"Stealing? I don't steal!" Rosario jumped up from her chair, spilling the coffee.

"Calm down, Rosario! I did not say that you're a thief. Now, come, sit down, and I'll pour you another cup!"

"I'm so sorry, Tita! Look what I've done. Here, let me clean it."

"Rosario! Now, you listen to me. Sit down! I'll take care of everything. You're getting too excited over nothing, and that's not good for your health. Good, just sit down and listen."

Rosario sat with her hands in her lap; Tita cleaned the table and repoured the coffee.

"I know Zayas," she said. "And I know that he's always afraid that people are stealing from him. I say that such a suspicious mind was created out of great guilt. Don't you agree? After all, an innocent person doesn't suspect other people like that. Don't worry about it; he'll get tired of sneaking in and out of the apartment soon enough."

"But he stares at me!"

Tita sat back down in her chair, studied Rosario's face and smiled. "Well, you should be used to having men stare at you, now that you've put on some weight and have color in your cheeks. You are pretty, but you're not a blond, and your tits don't stick out to here!" Tita held out her hands at arm's length in front of her own chest. "After all these months, you must know that's what he likes. Don't you?"

"Yes, but—"

"No buts, Rosario. You have nothing to worry about ... unless you find him attractive? Men can sense things."

"Tita! How can you say something like that!"

"Ah! Rosario! I've never seen you blush. It would not be the first time that a maid falls in love with her employer. Zayas has his strange ways, but he is handsome and rich. Do you find him attractive, then?"

"No! Truthfully. I've never thought of him in that way."

Tita tilted her head and looked at Rosario from the corner of her eye. "Are you sure? You're a young woman, Rosario. Don't you need a man?"

"No!" Rosario slapped the table and was about to jump from her chair again; the look on Tita's face stopped her. "Yes," she whispered. "I feel the need for a man, but not him!"

"Sit still, then. You remind me of a yo-yo jumping up and down."

Tita blew across the surface of the coffee to cool it, but when she tasted it, it was still too hot. She put down her cup.

"What man interests you, if not Zayas? Do you have a lover?" Tita clapped her hands like a child; her eyes sparkled. "You've never said anything about a lover, Rosario. Tell me; I can keep a secret. I won't even tell Cheo."

Rosario sighed. "There's no one, Tita."

"But there was someone, someone from your hometown. You called for him when you were sick with fever."

Rosario pressed her lips together.

Tita shook her head and patted Rosario's hand. "You don't have to talk about it, if you don't want to. Forgive me for asking."

Rosario was surprised to hear herself reply. "Yes. There was someone from my hometown."

"A man you loved?"

Rosario felt tears fill her eyes, and Tita's image blurred. "Yes," she whispered, "a man I loved."

"What happened?"

It was a simple question, but Rosario did not know how to answer it. So much had happened that she could not tell her friend. She wiped her eyes and sighed. "He left."

Tita's eyes opened wide. "He abandoned you?"

"Yes."

That was the truth; for the first time in seven months, she realized that was the truth. Rosario felt as if she were choking.

"For another woman?"

Rosario looked at Tita; life was simple for her. She had her husband, her children were grown and married and had provided her with grandchildren; her home was secure. Tita was gentle and kind; the only pain she had ever felt was the pain of childbearing. Rosario shook her head; she would fill in the rest of the story with lies. Eugenio had been right; lying was getting easier all the time.

"Yes. For another woman."

"All men are beasts! Now, I know why you left your home, but it's not your shame. You are young and pretty, and a good worker. He did not appreciate you; he was not a good man!"

"No! He was a good man!"

"Hush! Don't defend him; he's not worth it, Rosario. When you find another man, you'll realize that he was not good enough for you. He probably did you a favor by leaving."

Rosario shook her head so hard that her braid hit her across the cheek. "I don't want another man."

"Maybe you don't think so now, but you're too young to be without a man to warm you in bed. Listen, Rosario, you must stop hiding yourself away in this place. There are many men in this city who would readily take his place."

"I don't think so, Tita."

"Don't interrupt me. I'm older than you, and I know what I'm saying." Tita grinned and lowered her voice. "Jacinto, the doorman, follows you with his eyes every time you go in and out. Haven't you noticed?"

"I don't use the main entrance, Tita. You know that."

"Well, maybe you should start using it once in a while. And you could give him a little smile, and maybe he could give you a little something, eh?" Tita's eyes shone. She puckered her lips and rolled her eyes.

"Tita! He's only a boy!" In spite of the tight feeling in her chest, Rosario smiled.

"He's just your age. You only feel old because you've been crying over someone who doesn't even care for you. Seven months you've been without a man. Seven months! Soon you'll forget what it's like to be a woman. Forget that worthless man; warm your bed with Jacinto."

"Tita! For heaven's sake!"

"Leave heaven out of this. Look, admit it. Your lover is never coming back."

"No!"

"So, you still think he's coming back? Why do you waste your time? If you haven't heard from him in all these months, forget him. Jacinto would appreciate you; he's not bad looking, you know. If I were younger and free, I would—"

"Tita! How can you say such things? He's not even a full grown man!"

"Well, then teach him what he needs to be a man. He'll be grateful. Look at me and Cheo. I'm older than him by ten years! He was just a boy, but I taught him what gives me pleasure, and we have been happy for a long time. Very happy. Do as I say. Do you want me to talk to Jacinto for you? By the time I finish whispering in his ear, his craving for you will be unbearable!"

"No! Tita, please don't!"

Tita reached across the table and caressed Rosario's cheek. "As you say, but don't wait too long! Oh! Look at the time! You'll have to leave, Rosario. I should go back to work now."

"I'll help you clean up before I go."

"Thank you, Rosario." Tita started to get to her feet and then sank back into her chair. "It's still early in the day, and yet I feel so tired."

"You work hard, Tita."

"Yes. And I'm not young anymore, Rosario. That's what it is! It must be old age; I feel so tired all the time. Except when I'm in bed with Cheo, then I feel like a young girl again."

Rosario patted her hand. "You're not old. You're much younger than my grandmother, and she still climbs the hills to my house."

"You had your own house?"

Rosario bit her lip; she had to be careful! "Yes."

"No wonder you mourn. A worthless man is easy to forget, but even I would mourn the loss of a house. Was it far from a town?"

"Not so far that my grandmother could not visit."

"I should go into the hills too," she laughed. "It must be the pure air that keeps her strong. Next time you'll tell me all about your house, and the mountains. I've never been to the mountains, you know. I was born in the city."

Rosario smiled as she picked up the cups and wiped the table.

"Next time I come, I'll tell you all about the mountains."

But Tita died that weekend, and Rosario spent all the money she had made that week for a wreath of white and pink flowers for her grave. All the building employees went to the funeral where Cheo sat, slumped in a chair, surrounded by his grandchildren. Every time someone approached to offer condolences, he repeated his story.

"It was so sudden! One moment she was cooking and the next she was gone!"

"It is better that way, Cheo," a young woman replied. "She did not suffer."

"Now, she is with God," said the priest who had just come in.

"I want her with me."

"You will be together again, Cheo. Soon, you will be with her in heaven."

Cheo looked up at the priest and shuddered. "I don't want to die!"

"We all die, Cheo. But we are happy because we will all be together in heaven."

The priest made the sign of the cross over Cheo's head.

Cheo shuddered again. "I want her alive and with me. I don't want to have to die to find her."

The priest patted Cheo's shoulder and walked away.

Knowing how close Tita and Rosario had become, the other maids in the building tried to console Rosario by drawing her into conversation, and inviting her to eat lunch with them. Rosario refused each invitation with a faint smile and a quick shake of her head. At first, they commented on how sweet it was of Rosario to mourn someone she had not known long, but after three weeks they started to show their impatience.

"You have to go on living," they said. "Not even Cheo is carrying on like you!"

One day, disappointed that Rosario would not talk to them about Zayas and his women, (nor would she allow them into the apartment to look at the wonderful things they heard were there) they joked that she and Zayas deserved each other.

Before Rosario could say anything in her own defense, Moncha chided them. "That's cruel and unfair. She's just a country girl and doesn't know any better."

Rosario was not sure that she liked Moncha's defense, but she kept quiet. It was best that they thought whatever they wanted.

"You're just interested in her because you think she'll give you a number to play." Rosa stuck her tongue through the missing spaces in her teeth. "Tell me, Moncha, how many winning numbers has she given you?"

"I've told you, and I've told Moncha that I don't have those kind of dreams!"

"Shut up, Rosario. No one is talking to you! So, Moncha, tell us. How many numbers?"

Moncha stammered. "You heard her. Rosario says that she doesn't dream about numbers."

"Of course she does, Moncha. Country people and children always dream about numbers; everyone knows that. She just doesn't want to share them with you. So, has she given you any numbers?"

Moncha looked at the floor.

When they were alone that afternoon, Moncha once again asked Rosario for a number to play. When Rosario refused, she went looking for the other maids and told them that they were right. "She really thinks that she's better than we are!"

And from then on, Moncha's expression darkened whenever Rosario walked by.

With Tita gone, Rosario spent more and more time standing on the one apartment terrace that looked west toward the mountains; looking at them, she felt closer to home.

She wanted to write a letter to Doña Providencia, but she was afraid. Eugenio had warned her not to get in touch with anyone from Soledad. She was worried for her grandparent's safety, and could only trust that Eugenio had kept his word to look after them, even if he had not kept his word to return with Aníbal.

The day before, the newspaper had carried a story stating that the police were investigating Jorge Vicente's stay in Soledad, and Rosario overheard some of the porters whispering about people disappearing. The rumor was that anyone connected to Soledad was being picked up for questioning. And everyone knew that if you were taken into the blue and white police building, you never came out again. Rosario could not believe that all the stories she heard were true; they were too awful. She told herself that no one would bother two old people, but she prayed for them.

She felt helpless to protect herself. No one except for Cheo and Zayas knew the name of her hometown, at least, she hoped that no one did. And she began to fear the harsh looks that the other maids cast in her direction. She should have given Moncha a number or two.

All she could do was whisper to the wind, and imagine that it carried her thoughts back home, and listen, in case the winds carried back a reply. The wind brought her many sounds: the roar and the rush of traffic on the street, music from one of the apartments below, and even whispers not meant for her ears, but these were not the sounds she wanted to hear. Rosario continued to pretend.

Each time she went out onto the terrace, she looked down at the streets and searched for a familiar walk, a glimpse of clothes that she had washed and mended, the sight of curly, brown hair with golden lights trapped in its waves. At night she slept lightly, listening to the sounds of cars on the city's street, trying to sort out which might belong to Aníbal.

One night she awoke from a dream, drenched with sweat and shaking. She was sure that she had heard Aníbal's voice calling her from the other side of the door. Calling his name, she moved aside the barricade that she habitually piled against the door. When she threw open the door, Rosario found just the dark quiet of the apartment. Her heart beat louder than the chimes of the clock in the hall; it was three in the morning. It was a perfect time for Aníbal to come. She ran into the living room and when she did not find him there, she opened the terrace door and went outside. Hanging over the terrace railing, she searched the shadows of the street below. Nothing. The moon hid behind some clouds. No shadow moved. When the moon, free of its cloud cover, lit the terrace in shades of gray, Rosario turned to go back inside the apartment. With her hand on the handle of the door, she saw the reflection of the moon in the glass. Rosario turned to look at it; the moon was too close to her, so big, so bright. She raised her hand, and for a moment almost believed that she could poke a hole in the shimmering fabric of its face.

Suddenly, she knew that Tita had been right. The truth of it was clear; it stared back at her defiantly. She took it into herself, and feeling no pain, or sadness, Rosario marveled at her acceptance of it.

Aníbal was never coming back. She spoke the words aloud; her voice, thin as the breeze, slid past the corner wall of the terrace.

"Aníbal is never coming back!"

*   *   *

That morning after a difficult night's work, Zayas tip-toed into the apartment and found Rosario on the terrace, staring at the mountains, dark and jagged shadows leaning against the horizon. Something had to be done about her behavior. He watched her from behind the folds of the drapery.

The huge orange disk rose in the sky; it peeked through the city's few tall buildings, lighting up obscure corners with a cool, gentle orange that ignited city dust into streams of holiday glitter, curling skyward from the gray streets. Outlined by light, Rosario's body was an onyx silhouette set in gold. She stood so still, her fists clenched, her eyes closed so tightly that imitating her for only seconds caused a cramp in his leg. He shook his leg and twisted his ankle, first one way then another, until the knot that had formed, disappeared. What was she doing? Watching her, he felt his body stiffen again, and he thought he could hear the short distance between them crackle with energy streaming from her. For a moment, he felt it touch him; he rubbed his face with tingling fingertips, but the feeling that dozens of mosquitoes crawled on his skin would not go away. Zayas backed away from the terrace before she could see him; he returned to the hotel. She was, he was convinced, either a saint, or a witch. The revelation left him shaken.

Although he tried, he could not erase the image of Rosario on the terrace, nor could he forget the surge of energy that had snaked through him, leaving behind an invisible trail. For hours, he could follow that trail with the tips of his fingers and his memory recreated the tingling that he had felt. Everywhere he looked he saw her: on the streets, in the casino. Just when he thought he could not stand it anymore, a crisis in the casino surged out of control, demanding all his time and energy. For a full week, there were bomb threats and police and hysterical patrons to deal with; the memory of Rosario standing on the terrace faded.

For two more weeks, Zayas dealt with crisis after crisis. There was no time to go home; he stayed at the hotel and sent for his clothes. Bombs had been found at two other hotels; the threat was real. An American businessman had been kidnapped. Employees of the building where the man had been staying were arrested for questioning. Zayas shuddered. What bad luck, to be working in a building where some stupid, rich man got himself kidnapped! But bad luck seemed to be everywhere, because when the man's body was found, many of the city's tourists checked out of their hotels. They crowded the airport, fighting for seats on outbound planes. The lobby was chaotic for two full days; when it was over, quiet settled in like dusk over a cemetery. The casino was empty; dealers stood like soldiers at their stations waiting for players who never showed. After waiting four nights for the players to come back, Zayas decided to go home; there was nothing more to be done.

He brought home a woman to spend the night. At the height of their lovemaking, Zayas looked at her face (he loved to watch his bed partners, and had placed lamps around the bed to spotlight their expressions.) This girl was particularly responsive, and she excited him more than most. Suddenly, he watched in horror as the girl's curly, light blond hair darkened and straightened into a long, heavy braid woven with ribbon of many colors. It was Rosario's face that he saw! Zayas froze, then cried out and jumped from the bed.

"What is it? What's wrong?"

With her makeup smeared, and her hair in disarray, the woman looked grotesque. Zayas closed his eyes. He could not speak, and when Paula tried to pull him back into the bed with her, he avoided her touch. After just a short while, her words of concern changed to insults; Zayas merely shook his head and turned his face to the wall. Paula dressed. Minutes later, he winced at the sound of the door slamming, but there was nothing that he could do. Every time he opened his eyes, he saw Rosario's face, and that image would not go away until he pulled the miraculous medal from its pouch and slipped the chain over his head.

What he needed was a drink to clear his head, and a smoke. When he crossed the living room on his way to the liquor cabinet, he saw that the doors to the terrace were open; the drapes fluttered slightly in the morning's waning breeze. The air felt unnaturally cool and Zayas pulled his robe tighter around him. Just as he was going to close the doors, he saw Rosario standing by the terrace railing as he had seen her many times before. Again! When did the woman sleep?

The sun had not yet appeared on the horizon and in the faint light, he could see her only as a dark gray shadow, but he imagined that the expression on her face was the same as when he last saw her. He shivered and watched; as dawn grew brighter, he saw that he was right. Eyes slightly closed, mouth partly open, hands clasped at her breasts, and this time, the rising sun created a halo for her head that ran the length of the thick, dark braid resting between her shoulder blades. The wind tugged at the shorter strands of hair around her face; the halo extended there too, creating a golden fringe around her face, a crown of light. He shook his head and reminded himself that she was only a woman, his servant. She was not a saint, not a witch, just a woman. Zayas shook his head and rubbed his eyes. What was the matter with him? Rosario was merely a good woman who went out mornings to the terrace to pray; he felt ashamed of his suspicions and his spying, and vowed never to allow his imagination to get the better of him again.

Remembering Paula's insults before she left his bed, however, Zayas grew angry. Of course, he could not perform in bed with this shadow praying on his terrace day and night; he had to get rid of her. He stepped out onto the terrace.

The breeze was strong; he had to hold his robe together. Already the sun's rays had strengthened, heating up the cement of the city below, burning off the dampness that rose skyward in thin, curling streams. Zayas had expected to find profound silence on the terrace, like the silence of an empty church. Instead, the noise from the street traveled up the sides of the buildings to join the plaintive hiss of the breeze slicing past the edges of the stone facade.

"Rosario!"

She did not answer. He knew that she had heard him because her body stiffened at the sound of his voice.

"Rosario! What the hell are you doing out here at this hour of the morning?"

Even before she replied, he knew that she had been crying. He considered retreating into the living room; the last thing he wanted was to listen to a woman's voice full of tears.

"I'm sorry if I disturbed you, Don José, I'll leave right away."

"Just keep that in mind for the future. If you want to look at the sunrise, or anything like that, use the terrace by the servant's entrance, not this one. Is that clear?"

"Yes, Don José, I'm so sorry." She looked down at the ceramic tiles painted in a Moorish motif. "May I leave now?"

"Yes." He watched her walk past him, her shoulders bowed down, her feet dragging.

She was just a woman; he reminded himself—a good woman.

"Rosario!" He was surprised at how gentle his voice sounded. "Now that I'm wide awake, you might as well make me some coffee, and we can talk. We haven't had coffee together for a long time; you can tell me why you've been crying."

Rosario avoided looking at him. "I haven't been crying."

"Well, it was not the morning mist that left those wet streaks on your cheeks. Was it?" He hesitated and looked out at the horizon.

"Is it something that I've done?"

"Oh, no, señor!"

Zayas took a deep breath, and put his guilt feelings to rest. "Then maybe I can help. Go make us some coffee. We'll have it here; I don't enjoy this terrace as often as I would like."

"But the wind ... "

"It will die down by the time the coffee is ready. Go on!"

A short while later when Rosario returned with a tray, the wind had indeed disappeared, and the mist had burned away. It was pleasantly cool. He watched her pour the coffee; her hand was steady and there were no more tears in her eyes. Good, he thought. Perhaps it was just that time of the month; whatever had happened, it was not any of his business. Smiling, Zayas took the coffee cup from her and tasted the coffee; it was perfect, light and sweet just the way he liked it. She was a good cook, a perfect maid.

The temperature on the terrace was warming up quickly; soon he would have to move into the shade. Zayas pulled over an empty chair and put up his feet. Everything was perfect; he yawned and sighed.

"I'm hungry, Rosario. Why don't you make me something to eat before you sit down?"

"Sí, Don José. Right away."

"And has the paper come yet?"

"It's too early."

"Give me yesterday's then; I haven't read it."

He saw her hesitate, and unmistakably, her hands trembled. "Rosario?"

"Right away, Don José!"

He read the paper from the back to the front; everything that interested him was in the back: the results of the horse races and the winning numbers, the results of the sporting events on which he had wagered, the comic section. A year before, he would have tossed the newspaper to the floor when he was done, without ever looking at the front page, but now he folded the pages neatly and in order. With the last fold, he decided to read the news; there might be something new on the bombings. He needed to read good news; but when he read the headlines and saw the pictures on the front page, Zayas frowned and lit a cigarette. Another bombing. When will they ever stop? But it was not a tourist hotel this time. This time a school bus lay on its side like a huge, ripe banana with its center part peeled away. Seeing the young victims, Zayas shook his head. They should cut your balls off, he thought, looking at the pictures of the suspected terrorists.

There was nothing distinctive about the pictures—they were blurred and of poor quality—except for one photograph of the suspected leader, Jorge Vicente. There were hollows beneath the man's cheeks that were filled with shadows, and his eyes were dark and deeply set, and there was a glittering sharpness in his gaze that reminded Zayas of the machete he kept beneath his bed. Zayas had known men like this when he lived on the plantation with his mother. These were men to be avoided, men who were so evil that even the touch of their shadow was poison.

The news story was graphic in its descriptions of blood, gore and suffering, and he almost put it down before reading the paragraph that stated the terrorists' motives for this latest attack: " . . . in retribution for the death of the town of Soledad . . . "

The death of Soledad!

Zayas yanked his feet down from the second chair, jumped to his feet and looked around the terrace.

"Rosario! Rosario, come here!"

She did not answer, but Zayas didn't notice. He was busy reading and rereading the story of the bombing and all the secondary stories relating to it. Never far from his mind was the image of Rosario, passing through the rooms of his apartment, rushing from shadow to shadow, and drifting like the breeze across the terraces, staring past the horizon.

Eleven

Of all the children in Soledad's one-room elementary school, none had ever waited as impatiently as Rosario for the daily reading lesson. The reader, a children's edition of Bible stories, had pictures of young girls, whose long, golden locks curled about their shoulders and cascaded down their backs to brush against the pink and blue blossoms scattered on the ground. Rosario dreamed of having hair like that, and more than anything, she wanted a circle of light to surround her head, just like the girls in the book. Although her classmates groaned and complained about the reading lesson each day, Rosario reached eagerly for the reader, after carefully washing her hands—a child's hands had to be clean before fingering the book's pages, swollen thick with humidity.

Rosario never lost that feeling of awe for printed pages, easily extending her reverence to newspapers. Until the day that she read the story of school children murdered by a terrorist bomb—illustrated by so many pictures there was barely room for words—she had believed everything she read.

There, for the world to see, was a picture of the men accused of the crime. Although the photograph was of poor quality, she recognized Aníbal standing next to Jorge Vicente, both of them dressed in revolutionary uniform, pointing rifles at an unseen target. Squinting hard through her eyelashes (as if she could erase everything she saw, except Aníbal), she stared at the photograph for a long time. It didn't work; neither the image of Jorge Vicente, nor that of the rifles, would go away. Rosario reread the story, every detail, and when she came to the evacuation and razing of Soledad, she shouted, "No!"

The sound of her voice startled her; she looked up to see if someone had entered the kitchen.

217

"It's a lie!" she said, realizing only then that the sounds came from her own throat.

Her fingertips trembled; touching her lips and throat, she discovered that they still vibrated from the passage of her words. Tiny drops of perspiration trickled down her face. Rosario could not wipe her face fast enough to feel dry, and when she folded the newspaper and smoothed it flat with her hand, the newsprint smudged, staining her fingers. She wiped them on her apron.

To escape the heat, she went out to the terrace to stand in the shade, where the air felt almost cold. The minute she saw the mountains—they looked the same as ever, untouched and serene— her fever disappeared. Rosario closed her eyes and tried to imagine what the town would be like without its houses, without people in the fields, or children running around the fountain in the plaza. In her mind, she walked the familiar streets to her grandmother's house and stood before its polished, mahogany door, remembering how solid it felt, built to last. Rosario shook her head. Like the mountains and the river that flowed through it, cold and clear, a town was forever. Everyone knew that a town could not die. Even when buildings crumbled, there were always people to clear away the rubble and rebuild. The newspaper story had to be a lie, and Rosario knew then that she would never trust printed words again.

Since everything printed in the newspaper was false, Rosario decided to return to her duties and ignore what she had read. It was getting late. From the kitchen window, she saw that the sun was past its mid-point in the sky. Few people went outside at this time of day. Rising in steady waves from the pavement, the heat forced even mosquitoes to hide—droning in the shade. Nevertheless, the marketing had to be done, or there would be no food for her employer's dinner. Rosario rushed to get ready; although she despised midday heat, she left the apartment gladly. In spite of the heat lurking in the streets below, going out was preferable to the fluff of the carpeting, the deep folds of the drapery and the stale air-conditioned air. Zayas did not like it when Rosario tried to ventilate the apartment. He preferred hearing the hum of the air-conditioner to the hiss of the wind.

When she got to the market, Rosario found it even more crowded than usual. Everyone talked about the bombing; everyone claimed to know at least one person who knew a victim, and everywhere loud voices demanded vengeance. Angry people denounced the troops that had allowed hillbilly terrorists to slip through their fingers. Only a few spoke in whispers about the pitiful town that

had paid too high a price for helping terrorists. Some said the
bombing had triggered the evacuation; others insisted it was the
other way around. Nothing was certain except confusion. Rosario pushed into one crowd, and then into another, listening, but
not believing what she heard. Only once did she falter; the man
speaking claimed that he personally had witnessed dozens of trucks
being driven away from that area.

"Those trucks," he said as he raised his calloused finger in the
air, "were filled with people!"

The listening crowd responded with a long, "Ooooh!"

The man is either lying or crazy, Rosario thought. If Soledad
had been destroyed, she would have felt it; she would have had
a special dream. There would have been some kind of sign—
something. A sign.

She could no longer tolerate the crowds, the heat and the smells
of the market; Rosario walked back to the apartment, her empty
basket swinging on her arm. As she approached the building, she
saw Luis, the porter, about to remove a dead cat from the alley
near the service entrance.

"Why do they always come here to die?" he asked. Luis always complained in a loud voice—even when there was no one
around to listen. "And why does it always happen when I'm on
the job?" He scooped up the body of the cat with two pieces of
scrap plywood.

"I had no time to make a coffin," he laughed.

Rosario watched him toss the orange-striped cat into the huge
trash bin. And Rosario thought Mishu! But Mishu was safe in
Soledad. But Soledad was gone! Rosario held onto her basket
tightly, the split reeds in the handle pierced her skin and tiny drops
of blood ran down.

The soft plop of the cat's body landing in the bin was as loud
as a bomb's blast. Rosario recoiled from the sound and looked
around her, ready to run. No one in the area seemed concerned;
she started to ask Luis about the sound, but it was obvious that
like everyone else, he had heard nothing. She closed her eyes and
held her hands in front of her face.

Was this the sign that she had asked for? No! She shook her
head. If it were the sign, she would know it at once. Rosario
crossed herself.

"What's the matter with you, Rosario? It's only a dead cat. It's
a sin to pray for animals. Didn't you know?"

When Rosario did not answer him, he shrugged his shoulders

and walked away. In his loud, raspy voice, he told everyone he met that it was only a dead cat. As usual, other workers ignored him.

Rosario crossed herself once more. So much had happened since that morning. It was as if each minute lasted for a year—the trip to the market was a lifetime long, and the flight of the dead cat's body into the trash had stretched out as long as ten lifetimes. She needed to be on the terrace where she could be alone; there the breeze was cool and she could think. She sat on the terrace all night.

The next morning, Zayas found her there. He found her too soon. There had not been enough time to think; talk was impossible. Fortunately, Zayas was more interested in coffee than talk; Rosario rushed into the kitchen to prepare it. Keeping her hands busy calmed her, and only then was she able to think; but just as Rosario was about to make sense out of the jumble of her thoughts, she heard Zayas call. How was it possible to hear him so clearly from the terrace?

He called again.

"Coming!" She knew that he could not hear her; it was pointless to answer.

Rosario rushed the preparation of his breakfast, but in those quiet moments, she kept hearing the sound of the dead cat fall into the trash bin. Finally, Rosario pushed away the dishes, slammed the pantry door shut, covered her ears and ran into her room.

It made no difference. Sitting on the edge of her bed with her face in her hands, Rosario continued to hear that terrible sound, over and over again; and when it stopped, she saw the faces of people she had known in Soledad. They passed before her as if they strolled on the plaza after the evening meal. And she heard their voices, and the soft strumming of a guitar out of tune, and she smelled the aroma of dinner and coffee ... suddenly they were gone.

It was the sign!

She had been foolish enough to ask for a sign and it had been granted. Doña Providencia had always told her to beware of making wishes. Now she knew what her grandmother had meant.

It was truly a sign.

Rosario crossed herself.

Zayas called her again; there was a tone in his voice she had never heard him use. Rosario rubbed her forehead.

It seemed so long ago that she believed in forever. Now she

knew that nothing was forever, not love, not a town ... and rivers go dry and mountains are washed away by rain.

Tears filled her eyes and rolled over her cheeks, splashing on the tiny, embroidered flowers of her blouse, darkening the bright colors. When her tears saturated the fabric, Rosario felt cold. The tears stopped.

There was no time to mourn, or to wipe her face.

No time.

Everything she owned, she threw onto the bed. Out of habit, she started to fold them neatly, but upon hearing Zayas call—she had lost count of how many times he called—she finished quickly, tossing everything into a bundle and tying it securely. Rosario pulled out her money from its hiding place. She counted and divided the money into three smaller amounts and hid it on her person. It was all she had earned since leaving Soledad, except for the money spent on the wreath for Tita's funeral.

How many flowered wreaths would it take for Soledad? How many flowers to cover the grave?

"Rosario!" Zayas knocked at her door.

Rosario smoothed her skirt, making sure that the small purse in her pocket was not noticeable. She wiped her face with her sleeve and opened the door.

Zayas waved the newspaper in her face. "Why didn't you tell me?"

Rosario looked down at the hem of her skirt and shook her head.

"I don't know why," she whispered. "Maybe it's because I did not believe it."

"And you believe it now?"

"Would they print lies just to scare us?"

"This is terrible, terrible! Look at these pictures! The school bus ... the face of the dead American—"

"What dead American?"

"This one! A rich and famous industrialist who comes here to build a huge factory, and to give jobs to everyone. Instead, he's butchered."

There was a picture of the body of the American whose throat was slit, and next to it a picture of him taken at the airport when he arrived. There was a broad, confident smile on his face, and he had his arm around a woman who also smiled. Rosario thought that there was something familiar about her.

"May I see the picture again?"

She reached for the newspaper, but Zayas ignored her. Holding the newspaper out of her reach, he continued to wave the crumpled pages in front of him as if they were a sword.

"The man's family is leaving today. You can bet that they'll never come back here! Do you have any idea what this will do to the tourist business?"

"No, I ... "

"They'll stop coming for sure."

"Who?"

"The tourists, that's who. The hotels will be empty and the shops will close. This is bad. It will hurt the casino. And to make matters worse, what is this I read—about Soledad helping terrorists?"

Rosario held her hand in front of her. "I don't know anything, only what I read, just like you."

"No, Rosario, not like me. You're from Soledad. You know for sure."

"I know nothing for sure, Don José." She shook her head. "I could not believe it when I read it. How could they have done such a thing?"

"These terrorists are animals, that's how."

"No! No, I mean the troops."

"What troops?"

"The ones in Soledad."

"Well, what do you expect? They were forced to do what they did. They could not allow those people to go on helping madmen. It had to stop; the town had it coming!"

"Don't say such a thing! There were many children, and women, and old people in that town. How were they guilty?"

"There were children on the school bus. Were they any less innocent?"

"No! No!"

"Look at these pictures, Rosario. Can you make excuses for the criminals? It's horrible!"

"Take them away, Don José. I don't want to see them anymore." Rosario rubbed her forehead with her fingers; her forehead felt hot, her fingers cold. "They shouldn't be allowed to take pictures like that; no one should ever look at pictures with so much blood!"

"Rosario, listen to me now. Forget the pictures. This is even more important. Do you know these terrorists from Soledad?"

"The men I knew at home were not terrorists, Don José. They were good men, men who went to church on Sundays."

"And planted bombs on Thursdays?"

Rosario took a deep breath and held it; Zayas was impossible. She saw him look past her to her bundle on the bed.

"You're packing? Where are you going? You never told me anything about leaving."

"My grandparents were in Soledad."

"What grandparents? You told me that you had no family. Why, Rosario?"

"I thought it was best."

"Best for what?"

"I don't know! It's not important now. I have to find them, Don José. They're old; they need me."

Zayas scratched his moustache. "I'm discovering too many things at one time. I don't like it; I don't like surprises."

"Don José, my grandparents ... "

"Do you know where they are?"

"No, but—"

"So where are you going to go to find them? Do you think you can just go to the nearest street corner and look around? Are you planning to go to the police and ask? They might throw you in jail just for being from that damn town."

"I have to do something."

"Why? They're in no danger. They'll probably come here when they can, and then I'll be stuck with two old people."

"No."

"It's good that you realize that there's no room for them, and that they can't stay here, Rosario."

Zayas paced the room, stopping once to look at her. He sighed and shook his head.

"Well, they can stay for one or two days until you find a place for them, but that's all."

"But—"

"Sure, they'll come; they always do. All you have to do is wait."

Rosario shook her head.

"Why are you shaking your head?"

She remained silent.

"Rosario, I'm talking to you! Don't they have this address?"

Silence.

"Rosario, answer me!"

"No! They don't know where I am. No one knows where I am!"

The moment that she heard the echo of her words in the small room, she regretted having spoken.

Zayas stepped back from her as if her words had singed him. "No one?"

Rosario squared her shoulders. "No one."

"I knew it. It's true then!"

"What's true?"

Without answering, he turned abruptly and left her room. Rosario followed.

With a sudden sweep of his arm, Zayas threw a laundry basket to the floor and kicked it with his foot. In the kitchen, the silver coffee service clattered to the floor; he threw the newspaper over the spreading, brown puddle of coffee.

"Clean up this mess," he said and stalked into the living room.

Rosario ignored his order, stepped over the spilled coffee and followed him. "Señor—"

"Did you clean it up?"

"Not yet. I—"

"Get out of here. Go do your job; it's what I pay you for! Go on, get out! I don't want to see your face! I have to think."

"But, Don José, I don't understand. What's the matter? What have I done?"

"How dare you ask what you've done? As if you did not know!"

Zayas took a few steps toward her; instinctively, Rosario stepped back. His face had lost almost all its color, matching the pale ivory of his teeth; the vein in his neck swelled.

"For a long time I've wondered why you were so alone, no calls, no guests. The thought that you were hiding occurred to me, but, no, I could not believe that."

Zayas grabbed her arm. "You looked so sweet and innocent! Who are you hiding from, Rosario?"

"No one!" She wriggled free of his grasp.

"I'm not a stupid man, Rosario. No one comes as far as I have unless he has brains." He tapped his forehead with his finger.

Rosario held her hands up to her mouth and when she spoke, her words were lost in them.

"What did you say? Don't try to tell me that you're praying." Zayas snorted and smoothed his moustache.

She let her hands drop to her sides. "I don't know anything."

"That ignorant, country girl act doesn't fool me anymore, Rosario! You might as well tell me the truth. What do you know about the Soledad terrorists?"

"Please, believe me. I know nothing about terrorists!"

"You do know! I can see it on your face. You know everything. Maybe you even work for them?"

"No! That's not true."

"They sent you here to spy on me, did not they?"

"No!"

"My God!" Zayas seemed not to be able to stand; he held onto the back of the sofa. "Are they planning to kidnap me like they did that poor, miserable American?"

"No! No!"

Slowly, Zayas straightened his body, folded his arms in front of his chest and smiled as if he had just thought of something. It was not a pleasant smile. "I should call the police. What do you think of that, Rosario?"

"But why? Why call the police?"

"Maybe you'll tell them what you won't tell me."

"I've told you everything there is."

"You've told me nothing. For all I know, it might not be safe for me on the street, or even here. God knows what you've told the terrorists about my wealth and my position."

"I haven't talked to anyone about you."

"Liar!"

"I'm not a liar," she shouted.

It was the first time since leaving Soledad that she had raised her voice, and the vibrations of the sounds coming from her throat surprised her for the second time that day.

Eugenio had told her to be careful: that meant never getting angry, never drawing attention to herself, and it especially meant thinking twice about each word before it left her mouth.

"So? You are not a liar? Even that's a lie, isn't it?" Zayas sat down on the sofa and wrung his hands. "How can you do this to me after I took you in when you were sick and had no place to go? Is this how you repay my kindness?"

"I've done nothing to hurt you."

"Tell me about the men in the newspaper article. They're wanted terrorists from your hometown. Everyone knows everyone else's business in those small towns. I know you know them."

Rosario clenched her jaw and stared at the space between his head and the ceiling. Lying had become an easy thing to do, but not this time; she felt dizzy, and heard a roar in her ears. There wasn't enough oxygen in the room to fill her lungs. Rosario reached out to steady herself, but there was nothing within reach and she grabbed a fistful of air.

Zayas jumped to his feet. "Oh, this is a waste of time! I'm going to call the police; you'll talk to them."

"No, Don José, please, don't call!"

"So! I was right, wasn't I?"

"No. It was never like that, Don José. Never!" Rosario felt tired.

"Tell me, then."

"I've never spied on you and I've never planned to harm you ... you gave me a place to live, and a job ... but it's true that I've been hiding."

"I knew it! All the time I knew it!" Color returned to his face, too much color, Rosario thought. If the color were a measure of the anger that he felt, he might try to harm her. She considered running to her room, but she held her ground.

"My husband—"

"You're married?"

"Yes. My husband, Aníbal, he—"

"He beats you? Is that why you're hiding? Is that all it is?"

For a moment, Rosario hesitated. It was clear that a story about an abusive husband was what he wanted to hear. It would be easy to create such a story for him, but not this time. This time she would tell the truth.

"No, he never beat me. He was a good man, a good provider—"

"Why did you leave him—if he was so good?"

"He follows Jorge Vicente."

"What? Say it again!"

"I did not leave him; I would never have left him! He left me. I've waited for him to come back, but now I know he never will! He left me to follow Jorge Vicente!"

Zayas grabbed Rosario by the arm and dragged her to the kitchen where he had thrown the newspaper. Saturated by the coffee, the picture of mangled school bus was barely visible. He pointed to it.

"This same Jorge Vicente? The man responsible for that atrocity?"

Rosario nodded her head.

"That Jorge Vicente, the one in the picture? That one?"

"Yes, and that's my husband with him." Rosario heard the tones of pride and love in her voice; she had not meant to sound that way, but it did.

Zayas gulped and stared at her. He released her arm. She rubbed the indentations that his fingers had left.

"I did not mean to do that. You won't tell your husband that I hurt you?"

"No. I won't tell him because I know he wouldn't like it." For a moment Rosario felt protected, as if Aníbal were with her, and she smiled.

Seeing her smile, Zayas groaned. "Oh, my God!" His legs seemed to fold under him and he slid into a chair. "If I had known who you were ... "

In Soledad, many of the young men used to pay her mock homage—to keep Aníbal happy, they said. But that had happened in fun, in a town that no longer existed—and the young men? Who knew where they were?

"I'm no one, Don José," she said. "I'm nothing, just a country girl."

"But your husband is a wanted man, a criminal, a murderer!"

Rosario flinched. His words hurt.

"What'll I tell him if he comes looking for you?"

"Tell him I died."

"What? How can I tell him such a thing?"

"In a way, it will be the truth."

"Will he believe me?"

"No, but he'll be satisfied. Don't worry; he'll never come."

"I suppose he's too busy killing innocent people."

Rosario flinched again. "It's not his fault; it's Jorge Vicente. He came out of the forest like an evil spirit; I saw him—even then I knew ... "

"What are you talking about?"

"When Jorge Vicente came to Soledad no one knew he was a terrorist. No one saw him like I did, and they listened to him. He talked about a new world where everyone would have everything to make life worthwhile. People believed. It was a wonderful, new world ... a world worth believing in."

Zayas held onto the sides of his head. She saw him reach inside his robe and pull out the medal she had brought from Soledad for him. It was the first time she had seen it since the day she arrived. Free of its tarnish, it reflected all the colors of the room. Zayas rubbed the face of the Miraculous Medal.

"All this time I've been hiding a terrorist!"

"No, Don José! Listen to me! I am not a terrorist! Only Jorge Vicente is responsible. He came to Soledad and worked magic on Aníbal with his words. It had to be magic; my husband would never do such a thing unless the spell was strong. That's the truth! I swear that's the truth!"

"That's garbage, Rosario. There is no such thing as magic! Your husband is with Jorge Vicente because he wants to be. That's the truth. And you are his follower's wife. How can you be any different?"

Rosario felt her hands knot up into fists. The image of his face, twisted and ugly, filled her line of vision; she shook with the effort of controlling a sudden and violent urge to strike him. Her hands curled into fists and rose, as if with a life of their own.

The glint of metallic light caught her eye; it was the Miraculous Medal. Zayas stroked it between his fingers; it was a caress.

Rosario crossed herself. To think of hurting a human being was a terrible sin. What's happening to me? she thought, and quickly whispered a prayer begging for forgiveness.

"What is it? What are you muttering?"

Rosario took a deep breath. Again she felt dizzy, but it would pass. She took another breath to cleanse herself of the anger.

"Don José, listen to me, please. If Aníbal committed these crimes, they are his sins, not mine. No one has to pay for another's sins. I could never harm anyone. You have to believe me."

"Believe you? You've lied to me from the first!"

"Believe then that I would never bring harm to you."

"Don't be stupid! You've already harmed me! When the police find out that I've been sheltering you, they'll assume that we're in it together and arrest me, too. I've heard all the stories about what happens to people in those jails." Zayas shuddered. "That such a thing would happen to me!"

"I would tell them that you're innocent."

"And you think anyone would believe you, the wife of a butcher? I might lose everything, even if they did. My home, my job ... I was even going to buy a car next month ... "

"They would believe me; it's the truth ... "

"I don't think you know what the truth is, Rosario. And as for the police, the truth is anything they want to hear. What am I going to do?"

Rosario shook her head and covered her ears. She turned to leave the room.

"Where are you going? We're not finished talking."

"There's nothing left to say. I'm going to my room to get my things."

"Your things?"

"Yes. There will be fewer problems for you if I leave now. I know how to keep my mouth shut. Don't worry."

"Better for me?" Zayas laughed, but there was no mirth in that sound. "Don't worry? It would have been better if you had never come, then I wouldn't have to worry. Go on, hurry up, get your things and get out!"

Rosario ran to her room and grabbed her bundle, but when she went to the servant's entrance she found Zayas blocking the exit. With the silver medal in his hand—the chain had broken and dangled and shimmied in the light—he stared past her as if he could see through the walls.

"Put down your bundle, Rosario," he said.

His voice was cold; she had never heard it so cold, and she shivered.

"I've changed my mind, Rosario; I can't let you go."

"What do you mean?"

"It's for your own good, Rosario. You just can't go into the street. Where would you stay; who would protect you? Besides, no matter where you go, if they find you, they find me. I can't risk that."

Rosario shook her head and tried to push past him. "I don't need to be protected."

With his free hand, he held her at arm's length, and looked at her as if for the first time. "Maybe you're right, but put your things down anyhow."

Rosario put down her things and backed away from Zayas. She did not like the strange light in his eyes, or the way that he continued to rub the Miraculous Medal.

"Don't you understand? The police will think I'm involved; they'll hold me responsible." Zayas opened and closed his fists. "You'll have to leave the country, you know. I can't think of any place here that you'll be safe. No one would be sympathetic toward the wife of a child killer."

"I can't believe that ... "

"Maybe you are really a country girl, to be so naive. Do you think that I'm making up the danger? There have been many rumors of people disappearing; I'm going to make sure it never happens to me!"

Rosario sucked on the inside of her cheek and remained silent.
"You'll go north."

"I can't do that."

"We'll get you papers—a passport, a visa and an airline ticket—
"

"I have to find my grandparents—"

"Forget that! Don't you see? The worse thing you can do is
attract attention to them. They are safe as long as no one turns
them in."

"Turn them in? For what?"

"God knows for what! For being related to you, to your husband ... right now, knowing you is like holding a loaded pistol to
my head. It would be the same for them. You'll go north where
they can't find you, and we'll all be safe."

"All that takes money, Don José. I don't have so much. Perhaps, I shouldn't leave; there must be a place here where I can
hide. That way I could be near by if they need me. This madness
can't go on forever."

"And if it all ends tomorrow? So what? Who will ever forget
what Jorge Vicente and his men have done? Do you want to be
the one to pay for their crime? Or maybe you'll sacrifice your
grandparents?"

"But I haven't done anything; neither have they."

"It doesn't matter. Someone will have to pay. They'll arrest you
for questioning, and once inside the jail ... you'll say anything.
They'll think you're trying to protect your husband."

"But I keep telling you that I don't know anything."

"Even if I was to believe you, the police won't." His voice
dropped to a whisper. "And women have it harder than men,
Rosario. You know what I mean."

"Even in Soledad, we aren't that innocent. I understand perfectly what you're trying to say, Don José. I'm afraid, but—"

"No. No more arguments. This is the right thing to do; it's the
only way that we can both be safe."

"But to go north! I don't know anyone and I don't speak their
language. How will I get along?"

"So what? Many people go north. They get along just fine."

"And I've heard that many people die along the way."

"Those are the ones who try to crawl over the border, and they
get speared like iguanas. You're going to go like a lady, on an
airplane. Everyone will think you're a tourist."

"I've never flown on a plane, and I don't look like a tourist."

"Leave that to me. I'll buy you clothes, we'll fix your hair ... "

"I don't know—"

"You never know anything! Aren't you sick of not knowing anything? For someone as stupid as you, it would be best to keep your mouth shut and do as you are told."

For the second time, Rosario felt her hands close into tight fists. "I don't like being called stupid. I am not stupid!"

"Oh? So now it's not convenient to be stupid. Well, maybe you should try feeling gratitude. I've been good to you; don't forget that. You owe me something."

"You never gave me anything; I worked for everything, and I never cheated you. In fact I gave you more than you paid for."

Zayas raised his hand as if he would strike her; Rosario held her breath until he lowered it again.

"Don't ever talk to me like that again," he said, underlining his words by jabbing her on the shoulder with his finger.

She pushed his hand away and stared into his eyes. "Don't touch me!"

"It's a good thing that you're leaving, Rosario." Zayas cut off the ends of his words with a sharp snap of his teeth.

"I wanted to leave earlier, Don José; you wouldn't allow it. Remember?"

"That's right. I wouldn't allow it because I had my reasons. Don't be impudent; you're only my maid."

"Not anymore." There was a hint of a smile on her lips.

"Yes. And as soon as I can arrange things, you can get the hell out of here!"

*   *   *

On the terrace, Zayas watched the night sky through a haze of city vapors and reflected lights. As a boy, he used to stay up to watch the stars. In the country, the stars were so bright that it hurt to look at them. With his mother's gentle snoring always in the background, he used to listen to the night sounds—some soft, some strident—and dream of swimming among those stars. Sometimes he stood on his toes and pretended to dive into the night sky, where he swam with the same ease as in the lagoon, among the long arms of coral ... but watching the stars was a habit he had left behind, along with his childhood.

Eight hours before, he had watched Rosario board the plane; everything went well, better than he expected. The man that he hired to do the work was the best, and worth the huge sum that he charged for creating the papers Rosario carried. No official at the airport questioned either the passport or the visa identifying her as a student on her way to an American university.

Rosario had played her part well, too, although he felt her arm tremble when he dragged her through the corridors of the airport. Rosario worried only when she first saw the metal wings of the airplane, and clutched her new leather handbag to her chest.

"It's so big!" she whispered. "I feel like a mouse being fed to an eagle!"

"Don't talk nonsense, Rosario! It's only an airplane. And you are not a mouse, just a woman."

For a moment he had thought that she would change her mind and refuse to go. "Go on, Rosario! Before it's too late, go on!"

When she did not move, he pushed her; Rosario stumbled. People turned to stare at them. Zayas put his lips close to her ear.

"Damn it, Rosario! People are looking at us. That's the last thing we want!"

When she did not move, he pushed her again; this time she resisted. Zayas felt desperate. He would do anything, give anything if she would get on the plane and leave.

"Look, Rosario, take this; it'll protect you."

He removed the Miraculous Medal from his pocket, the ends of the broken chain twirling around each other. Zayas placed it in the palm of her hand. "Now, hurry up before the plane leaves without you!"

He looked at his watch and tapped its crystal.

Her fingers curled around the medal; it felt warm and comfortable in her hand.

"Don José ... "

"What is it now, Rosario?"

"I want to thank you," she said. "You really are a good man."

She looked as if she were going to cry ... Zayas took a deep breath ... Rosario was too fragile; she would never make it, even with the medal to help her.

Zayas looked down at the ground.

"Thank you," he said. "But you have to get on the plane, Rosario. Hurry!"

"Yes. I'm going. Goodbye, Don José," she said. But she did not move; she seemed incapable of it.

"Goodbye. For God's sake! Goodbye. Get on that plane and stop wasting time, Rosario! I don't need gratitude. What I need

is for you to get out of my life so that things can get back to normal. You're like poison to me. Did you hear what I said? You're
poison!"

She opened her mouth twice; her words were drowned out by
the crackling loudspeaker calling the last of the passengers to board
the plane.

"I'll drag you onto that plane if I have to," he said, and grabbed
her arm.

Rosario slapped at his hand. "No one will ever drag me anywhere that I don't want to go, Zayas. No one!"

Her eyes glittered and with her hands on her hips and her mouth
pressed into a straight line, her rage was evident.

"Please, Rosario!"

"Thank you," she said. "And here, here is your medal. You
told me that there is no such thing as magic. Now I believe it.
Take it back; it's useless."

Without further hesitation, Rosario boarded the plane as if she
were a seasoned traveller.

With his mouth hanging open and holding his amulet tightly in
his hand, Zayas realized that she was stronger than he had thought.
He watched the plane roll down the runway, take off, climb, bank,
turn, and rise, disappearing into the clouds. But she was a fool for
not taking the medal; he put it back into the safety of his pocket.

Zayas took the bus home because his funds were dangerously
low; everything had cost much more than he had expected. As
usual, the bus was crowded and lacked air conditioning; every
window was open, and still, it was too hot. With the scent of
his cologne washed away by streams of perspiration, Zayas felt
his clothes stick to his skin. People squeezed together to allow
even more riders to get on. Reluctantly giving up the space he
had staked out for himself, Zayas cursed and held onto a metal
bar above his head to steady himself. He fixed his gaze straight
ahead; it was best not to catch anyone's eye. Each time he looked
at his hands, he saw the white bands of untanned skin across two
of his fingers. Up until the day before, they had been covered by
diamond rings. At least he still had his watch, but if he weren't
careful, someone on the stinking bus might rob him of that as well.

Not wanting anyone from his building to know that he had
ridden the bus, Zayas got off two stops before his own and walked
home slowly, allowing time for his skin and clothes to dry. Once
in his apartment, he called in sick to work—his absence from the
casino for the third night in a row. It was time off he could not

afford, but the past two and a half days had been hectic and he needed rest. Zayas showered, poured himself a drink, grabbed a fresh pack of cigarettes and went out onto the terrace.

He waited.

For the past eight hours, every shadow that moved in the breeze startled him, and he had to remind himself not to turn around, expecting Rosario to be there. She was gone for good and he did not have to worry about her any more. He could go naked in the apartment, if he wanted, and smoke his cigarettes without having Rosario rush to the windows to let out the smoke—and the expensive, air-conditioned air as well.

Sitting on the chaise lounge, he stared at the stars through half-closed eyes and wondered where Rosario was now. Over and over again he counted the hours on his fingers, marking the progress of her journey: Rosario must be above the ocean, or Rosario must be having lunch, or Rosario must feel the cold of the northern sky by now. Zayas told himself that he should not care, but he did, and he sighed and looked at his watch; eight hours had passed. If something had gone wrong, he would have heard about it.

The sun was about to rise and still he had not slept. Zayas leaned back on his chaise and yawned. Twice during the night he had gone into his room and stretched out on the bed, and twice he returned to the terrace. He stayed to watch the sunrise, but clouds suddenly rushed in and blocked the sun. It was as if dawn would never come and twilight was extended indefinitely.

After fighting this unusual bout of insomnia for another two hours, Zayas decided to go to work; it made no sense to stay at home if he could not rest. While dressing, he heard the door bell. It rang several times before he remembered that Rosario was not there to answer it.

It was Cheo. Annoyed, Zayas leaned against the door.

"What are you doing here at this hour of the morning? Don't you ever sleep? And how many times have I told you to use the service entrance? What do you want anyhow?"

The old man held his hat in his hand. "I heard that Rosario left here for good. Luis says he saw her leave with a suitcase. Is that true?"

"Yes, that ungrateful bitch took off. I think she had another job offer. In any case, she is gone for good."

"I would have liked to say goodbye. Where did she go?"

"I don't know and I don't care."

Cheo shook his head. "I thought that Rosario was different, more responsible."

"They're all alike."

"At least she did a good job while she was here." Cheo looked past Zayas's shoulder. "The apartment is beautiful!"

"Yes, she did a good job."

"Now you'll need another maid to keep up the apartment. Let me know when you want her."

Zayas blinked his eyes and shook his head. "Who?"

"The new maid. My cousin's youngest daughter is looking for employment. You'll need someone to polish the furniture, clean the rugs and water the plants. And to cook—my cousin's youngest is a wonderful cook! Besides, a man of your position needs a maid. She is a good worker, a good girl."

"I'm sure she is, Cheo." Zayas patted the old man gently on the shoulder. "But I don't need another maid."

Cheo rubbed his shoulder where Zayas had touched him. "Are you feeling well, señor?"

"Everything is fine, Cheo. Thank you."

"I guess I'll go now."

"No! Don't leave!" Zayas pulled the old man into the apartment. "Come in, Cheo," he said, "I'll make us some coffee and you can tell me about everything that's new at home."

Cheo's mouth fell open, and he stumbled backwards. "Thank you, señor, thank you!"

He twisted his hat and held it to his chest. "But I can't right now; I have to work. Maybe some other time?"

"It's all right then, Cheo. I understand. Some other time for sure."

Zayas closed the door.

*   *   *

They had given her a seat by the window and the first thing she did was to pull down the shade. The children in the seats next to hers complained to their parents that they could not look out of the window. Rosario ignored them and refused their parent's request to pull open the shade. She strapped herself in tightly, closed her eyes and held onto the sides of the seat the whole time the plane taxied on the runway. She held her breath when she heard the engines' roar. The plane rushed into the wind for its take-off, and when she felt the wheels leave the ground, Rosario cried out.

"Mamá!" the little boy's shrill voice cut through the mechanical sounds. "I think this lady is sick!"

Rosario opened her eyes. "No, no! I'm not sick," she said. "Don't bother your parents."

"I think she's just afraid, Tomasito. Are you afraid?" asked his sister.

"Aren't you?"

"Oh, no!" the children said in unison.

"We fly a lot," the boy explained. "Our father works for the airline. Isn't that true, Linda?"

Linda had long curls that bounced up and down. "Flying is fun! It won't be so noisy soon."

"Here," Tomasito held out a stick of chewing gum. "Chew this and your ears won't hurt."

Rosario smiled. "Who told you that?"

"My father."

"Chewing gum will protect my ears from the noise?"

"No!" The children laughed when Rosario held the stick of chewing gum up to her ears. "Not from the noise," the boy explained, "from the pressure."

"Pressure?"

"Just chew it; it works. Ask my father if you don't believe me."

"No, don't bother him. I believe you." She unwrapped the stick and put the gum in her mouth.

"Can we look out of the window now before the plane goes above the clouds?"

The last thing that Rosario wanted was to open the shade, but the children stared at her wide-eyed with just a hint of tears shimmering at the corners, ready to drop and slide over their pink cheeks. There was no way that she could say no. Rosario nodded her head and allowed the boy to reach over and lift the window-shade up. So that she would not have to see, she turned her head, but all around her, the other cabin windows were also uncovered.

The only thing to do was to close her eyes, but afraid that the children would notice, she decided not to. Gripping the armrest, Rosario pressed her forehead against the glass. It felt cold.

"Look," Tomasito pointed out. "It's the clouds already!"

Rosario saw the clouds brush against the window, leaving behind little streams that streaked across the glass. Being in the clouds was nothing more than being covered by fog. Rosario smiled and relaxed; it was the work of Providence, protecting her from the sight of the land below.

"Oh, we missed everything!" Linda complained. "Now we won't see anything but stupid clouds."

Without warning, the plane emerged from the clouds and the sun's light pierced the tiny windows of the cabin. Everyone rushed to lower the shades. Shielding her eyes with her hand, Rosario looked at the mounds of white beneath them. Out of the corner of her eye, she saw a shadow to the side of the plane and strained to see what kind of giant bird could follow them this high and this far. Rosario wondered if the eagle's eyes could see through the clouds to scan the land below, searching for prey.

Suddenly, the airplane banked to the left and Rosario realized that it was the plane's shadow sliding over the sparkling, white peaks and curling in the dull, blue-gray valleys of the clouds. Rosario giggled nervously; the fear that had begun to stir in the pit of her stomach vanished. Eagles are never afraid.

Rosario looked down, but clouds continued to obstruct the view. From this height, above the clouds and close to heaven, soaring above mountain peaks—higher than even the eagles can fly—she would know everything, if she could see.

With every muscle in her body tightly clenched, she wished for the power to see through clouds. Rosario held her breath and crossed herself. A small circle opened, like an eye waking up; the clouds parted, unveiling the coastline and the sea.

It was magic!

The colors of the land flowed into each other—soft streaks of greens and browns. The sea glowed like starched, polished cotton—blues and grays—while the sky like sheer, dotted silk held the clouds.

"Look, children," she said. "Look! It's beautiful!"

They crowded around the tiny window.

Rosario stared at the horizon, clapped her hands and laughed aloud. The children looked at each other; the boy tapped his temple with his finger, and his sister made a funny face, but Rosario paid no attention to them. For the first time in her life, she was able to see the land and the sea and the sky all at once. Rosario pointed out the place where all three met. Seeing it was as wonderful as she had always dreamed it would be.

Too soon the clouds rushed in and sealed the opening; the view was lost. The children complained, then ran to tell their parents what they had seen. Rosario leaned back in her seat and closed her eyes. There, on the backs of her eyelids, captured as if by a camera, the clear image of the horizon continued to astonish and delight her. Rosario smiled. It was hers forever.